TRUTH WILL OUT

A. D. Garrett

corsair

CORSAIR

First published in Great Britain in 2016 by Corsair
This paperback edition published in 2017 by Corsair

1 3 5 7 9 10 8 6 4 2

Material from Laurence Cranberg, 'Plea for Recognition of Scientific Character
of Journalism', from *Journalism Educator*, December 1988, reproduced courtesy of
SAGE Publishing.

ISBN: 978-1-4721-5099-8

Typeset in ITC Garamond by SX Composing DTP, Rayleigh, Essex
Printed and bound in Great Britain by CPI Group (UK) Ltd, Croydon, CR0 4YY

Papers used by Corsair are from well-managed forests
and other responsible sources.

MIX
Paper from
responsible sources
FSC® C104740
www.fsc.org

Corsair
An imprint of
Little, Brown Book Group
Carmelite House
50 Victoria Embankment
London EC4Y 0DZ

An Hachette UK Company
www.hachette.co.uk

www.littlebrown.co.uk

For Brenda, always calm as a cucumber.
1927–2015

1

Bad Timing

Gail Hammond was having a hellish day. Her mother had called at lunchtime: Dad was poorly – he'd had a fall in the garden, banged his hip. The hospital said there was nothing broken, but could she come and take a look? Gail was about to begin a stint on nights; she needed her rest. Mum played the guilt card – she hadn't been to see them in over a month; it was only half an hour by train from Chelmsford to London – and what good was it, being a nurse, if she couldn't even help out her old dad?

So Gail had cancelled her plans for an afternoon snooze and caught the 13:09 from Chelmsford. If she got the seven o'clock train back, she'd be home around seven-thirty – plenty of time to shower, change, grab a bite to eat, maybe even put her feet up for an hour before heading out to work. But Mum was fretful, in need of reassurance, and Dad did seem to be in a lot of pain, so Gail comforted and soothed, went out to pick up Dad's prescription, then cooked a light supper and tucked them both up in front of the TV before leaving, reluctantly, an hour later than planned.

The trip home was stop-start all the way, held up by 'an incident' on the line. As they trundled through green fields and small towns at a crawl, the summer sun lowering in the sky, Gail checked her watch and shifted in her seat, astonished and perversely irritated by the quiet acceptance of those around her. She called her supervisor in A&E twice to let him know her progress; he was understanding, but they were short-staffed – he was struggling to cope.

'I'll be there just as fast as I can,' she promised.

Six short minutes from journey's end the train's intercom crackled; the conductor announced that there had been a points failure at Chelmsford – they were backed up behind two other trains. The twenty or so people in her carriage groaned as one. They would make an unscheduled stop at Ingatestone, the conductor said. A bus would carry them the rest of the way. Gail felt a pang of dismay – her shift started in fifteen minutes – a detour by bus would add another fifty minutes on to her journey.

As the train drew to a halt at the platform, she dialled her boss. The strain in his voice made her wince. 'Don't worry,' she said, 'I'll grab a taxi.' She raced from the platform to the exit, thinking she'd be lucky to see even a single cab waiting: Ingatestone was a small commuter town, a minor station stop; it didn't even have an official cab rank. She dodged past someone wheeling a document case and hurried out on to the service roadway that ran past the red-brick Victorian station frontage. Four minicabs were lined up at the edge of the car park; word must have got out to the local cabbies. For a second, her heart lifted, but half a dozen passengers were ahead of her. A single-decker bus idled on the main car park; maybe she should head for that. Two people in the queue got into the first cab, leaving three more, with just four people to cater for – maybe she had a chance, after all. She watched eagerly; the queue for the bus dwindled, the last of the passengers climbing on board as two more people got into the third cab – the last one was hers! She strode to it, relief flooding through her, but as she reached for the door a man jostled past, throwing her off-balance, knocking her phone out of her hand. 'Hey!' she said, bending to pick it up.

He ignored her, sliding into the passenger seat and slamming the door after him.

Gail straightened up, phone in hand. 'What the hell are you doing?' she shouted, but the man turned away, and the cab swung out from the kerb and was off.

'Hey!' she called again. She glanced over her shoulder, but there was no one to share her outrage: the bus was already turning into the lane. 'No – wait!' She ran a few steps, but it picked up speed, accelerating away.

Gail turned full circle. The car park was almost empty – she was stranded. Listening to the roar of the bus retreating down the lane, she swore softly, just about ready to weep with frustration. She took a breath. *For heaven's sake.* 'So you'll be late for work,' she told herself. 'It's a pain in the neck – but at least no one died.' Her inner balance restored, she wiped the grit off her smartphone and began scrolling through her contacts for a cab firm. The phone buzzed in her hand. Her boss.

She hesitated, then hit 'Answer'. 'Paul, I'm so sorry, I—'

She broke off, seeing a grey Mondeo sweep down the lane towards her. A sticker on the driver's door bore the logo

3

of A2B Cabs – her favourite taxi service. The driver wound down his window. 'You all right, love?'

'I am now,' she said, climbing in next to him. Then, to her boss: 'I'm in a cab. Should be with you in half an hour, tops.'

She grinned at the driver as she closed the phone. 'I think you just saved my life.'

2

Believe no one, doubt everything, and remember
– everyone lies.

NICK FENNIMORE

Aberdeen, Monday

'Gail Hammond's partially clothed body was found two days after she disappeared. She had been sexually assaulted, strangled with a ligature and left in a ditch on a country lane near Willingdale, eight miles west of Chelmsford.'

Professor Nick Fennimore was giving a public lecture in one of the shiny new riverside buildings at Robert Gordon University, Aberdeen. He was tanned, having spent a few weeks advising on a murder investigation in the United States' Midwest with DCI Kate Simms, and although he had a healing scar on his forehead – a souvenir of his visit – he felt fit. It was mid-June, exams were over and most of the students had gone home for the vacation, yet he had an audience of three hundred. This presentation was part of the 'Science Matters' festival – a 'summer pops'-style series of free public lectures and seminars for techies, science geeks, the mildly interested and the morbidly curious.

On the projector screen behind him, a grainy CCTV image, date-stamped eight years ago: a grey Mondeo on a railway station car park; a small, fair-haired woman slipping into the front seat of a car. 'CCTV at Ingatestone Station, Essex,' Fennimore said. 'That is Gail Hammond. Several passengers noticed her hurrying off the train – those who boarded the bus saw a man muscling ahead of her in the queue for taxis – she was rather slight, as you can see. The cab driver who picked her up was identified as Tom Killbride.'

He clicked through a series of traffic-cam images, creating a time-lapse sequence of Killbride's Mondeo progressing through traffic lights and junctions en route to Chelmsford. The final image on the screen: Killbride in the driver's seat looking surly, with an anxious-faced Gail Hammond beside him.

'Oddly, they never made it into the city centre. Killbride dropped out of sight until ten hours later, when he was seen heading west on the A414.' Fennimore called up a map of Chelmsford and the surrounding area. 'But he vanished again between these two traffic cams.' Fennimore used a laser pointer to highlight the two locations, about half a mile apart. 'The next time Killbride showed up was in Chelmsford the following night, picking up a fare in the city centre.'

He got a rumble of response: the audience shifted in their seats, exchanging glances and murmured comments. Fennimore gazed around the tiered seats, enjoying the sound of crime enthusiasts leaping to conclusions. Tracking left to right, his eye snagged on a still, silent figure in an aisle seat, second row from the back.

Josh Brown, Fennimore's doctoral student. Josh was in his mid-twenties; he was dressed urban style in T-shirt, combats and hoodie. Camouflage – and it worked; he merged well with the younger students. But this was not a student lecture, and the student's sludgy colour palette stood out among the summer pastels of the general public. Fennimore himself wore a shirt and tie under a lightweight grey suit: delivering lectures or visiting crime scenes, he never felt properly dressed in casual clothes. Josh met his gaze but glanced quickly away.

'What happened during those missing hours?' Fennimore asked. 'Killbride told police he'd dropped Ms Hammond on Parkway, a busy arterial road into Chelmsford town centre. But why would she ask to be dropped at the side of a busy road ten minutes' walk from the city centre? Broomfield Hospital was another *four miles* on from there, and she was already late – surely she would head straight to the hospital?'

He saw the answer to his questions in their faces.

'Killbride said he didn't know why Gail asked him to drop her at that point. Nor could he account for his journey along the A414, ten hours later.'

The next slide showed the same map, but with a location marked in red. 'This is where Gail Hammond's body was found on a country lane, a half-mile from the A414. Coincidentally, this was between the last two traffic cameras to sight Mr Killbride's car.' He added the locations of the two traffic cams and sketched a shallow-sided triangle between the three points on the map; an arrowhead, pointing irresistibly towards Killbride's guilt.

He clicked on to a photograph of police cars on a country lane, a white 'incitent' over the ditch, CSIs kitted out in white Tyvek suits. 'Killbride was picked up soon after police gained access to Ingatestone Station's CCTV recordings.'

Fennimore pulled up an image of a microscope slide; on it were three bright green fibres. 'These are fibres from a rope – possibly a tow line. Twenty-three distinct strands of this stuff were embedded in the skin of Gail's neck and caught in her hair. And although none of these particular fibres was discovered in Killbride's car, fibres from her clothing were.' The audience stirred, and he added, 'Of course, you would expect that – after all, she was a passenger – but these fibres were found in the *boot* of his car. Now, Gail Hammond had no luggage – all she was carrying was her shoulder bag and her phone. So how did those fibres get from the front seat into the boot of the car? And why were fibres from her trousers and blouse found on his jacket, shirt and trousers?'

He left these questions unanswered, for now.

'Killbride was recently divorced; he lived alone in a flat on the edge of the city. His credit card and a search of his computer revealed that he regularly accessed online porn. A year earlier, Killbride had been arrested for the false imprisonment of an eighteen-year-old girl.'

Another murmur from the audience; he would come back to that wee red herring later.

'He was considered a loner and "a bit weird" among the other cabbies. He claimed that he hadn't left his flat between dropping Gail off and heading to Chelmsford railway station the next evening. Witnesses confirm that they *did* see him cleaning his car during the afternoon, but his Mondeo was missing from its usual parking space all morning. He later admitted meeting with a man in a lay-by on the A414 to buy drugs – Mr Killbride had a little cocaine habit – but he denied driving into the country lanes. He was off the grid for thirty minutes somewhere between those two traffic cameras.

8

Killbride said his supplier was late, that he'd waited "a while" – he couldn't be more specific. Unsurprisingly, the phantom dealer couldn't be traced, and the police decided it was yet another lie.

'But the most damning evidence of all . . .' The audience leaned forward as one. 'Killbride's blood was found on Gail Hammond's shoes.' Fennimore called up an image of Gail's black lace-ups. He repositioned and magnified the image; five tiny drops of blood had been marked on the photograph: two on the stitching of the left shoe; one on the edge of one of the eyelets, and two more on the toe cap of the right shoe. 'Blood spatter,' he said. 'Point-five of a millimetre across. DNA analysis proved beyond a shadow of a doubt that it was Mr Killbride's blood. And it revealed that he has a relatively rare genetic condition – he is 47,XYY karyotype. In plain English, he has an extra Y chromosome, which is unusual and interesting.' Fennimore paused. 'But is it relevant?'

A few people nodded, eager.

'Well,' he said, 'all right, yes, it is . . . The Y chromosome is what makes an egg develop into a male infant. Common sense would tell you that having an extra Y chromosome would make you more male, yes?' A few more nods in the audience. 'And XYY males *do* tend to be tall.' The next slide was of Tom Killbride, photographed at his wedding, with the bride and her parents. He towered over the group. 'As you can see, Killbride is no exception. The prosecution argued that his genetic quirk made him prone to aggression, criminality and social abnormality – they quoted a 1960s study to support their case, and the press helpfully came up with all *kinds* of entertaining stories about "super-males" and violent criminals.' Fennimore clicked through slide

9

after slide: killers and madmen – all cursed with the XYY abnormality.

'Killbride was prone to severe nosebleeds – he'd had a doozie two days before Gail disappeared, and required a nasal cautery at Broomfield Hospital to stop the bleeding.' Fennimore gave the younger members of the audience a meaningful look: 'One of the grosser side-effects of cocaine addiction, kids.' A few tittered.

'Gail Hammond was an A&E nurse; Killbride's defence claimed that she must have been splashed with his blood during his hospital visit. Police checked the story – he was, indeed, at Broomfield Hospital two days before the murder, just as he'd said. Unfortunately, Gail wasn't. Her work records showed she wasn't on duty the day he came in. He'd lied – just as he'd lied about dropping her off on Parkway, miles from her destination. Just as he'd lied about not being on the country lane where her body was found. Tom Killbride was charged with Gail Hammond's abduction and murder. And he was found guilty.'

There was an audible outrush of breath from the audience, murmurs of approval. *Interesting*, Fennimore thought – they didn't know the rest of the story. But Killbride had been tried at Chelmsford Crown Court, five hundred miles and a country-and-a-half away from where they were sitting. It wasn't so surprising that his Scottish audience hadn't paid too much attention to an eight-year-old case, tried in the English courts. Fennimore smiled.

'But Tom Killbride was innocent,' he said.

In the audience, unnoticed by the professor, a man, better camouflaged than Fennimore's student, watched with bitter contempt. *Oh, he's quite the grandstander. A real showman. Performance like that, they should be charging admission.* The man huffed air out through his nostrils, resisting the urge to start a slow handclap, and instead forced a smile. *Let him talk — it's what he's good at.*

Fennimore waited for the rustle of consternation to settle to a murmur of dissent. He explained that a pressure group had taken an interest in Killbride's case and began a campaign to have the cab driver's conviction overturned. They called Fennimore in to review the forensic evidence.

'There are lots of reasons why miscarriages of justice happen,' he said. 'Trial by media, the prosecution over-estimates the value of the evidence, the defence is weak or even incompetent, police fail to disclose evidence which could help the defence.' He paused.

'All of these were true in the prosecution of Tom Killbride. As for the "weird-therefore-bad" culpability argument?' He winced. 'Do me a favour — I mean, *I'm* weird — but no one ever charged me with murder.'

That got a laugh, loosened the tension a little.

He pulled up the image of Gail Hammond easing into the passenger seat of Killbride's car. 'Killbride did indeed pick Gail up at Ingatestone Station. He was a licensed minicab driver — that was his job — that was what he was *supposed* to do. Okay, technically, he should only have picked up passengers who'd booked through his firm — but that's not a hanging offence.'

'What about the false imprisonment charge?' someone called out.

'Good point,' Fennimore said. 'Why on earth was he still driving a minicab with that kind of record?' He lifted one shoulder. 'The fact is he *didn't have* a record. Killbride was never charged. The supposed "victim" was drunk, threw up on the back seat, refused to pay her fare, let alone the clean-up costs – and she tried to do a runner. Killbride locked the doors; she called the cops.' He spread his hands. 'She with-drew the accusation after she sobered up – even apologized. The question is, why did the police leave the false accusation uncorrected on file – worse still – why was it entered into evidence? Was defence counsel asleep or did he just not give a damn?'

Fennimore clicked to a photo of the roadway where Killbride claimed to have dropped off his passenger. 'Okay, so why did he drop Gail off at Parkway?' A grey railing ran alongside a roadway blurred by speeding traffic. Beyond the railing stood light industrial units and office blocks. 'Common sense tells you it's not a good place to leave a young woman at that time of night,' he said. 'Doesn't it?' He got a few nods of agreement. 'Well, Einstein said common sense was the collection of all the prejudices acquired by the age of eighteen. So let's ditch the common sense and do some actual fact-checking instead. Walk twenty yards north-west along Parkway, this is what you see.' He clicked to the next slide, a picture Fennimore had taken himself, barely a year ago.

A row of Edwardian red-brick houses stood at a right angle to the main road. Three concrete bollards blocked the street to traffic from Parkway. 'There's pedestrian access only at this point,' Fennimore said. 'So Killbride *couldn't* have turned into the street, even if he wanted to. But walk two minutes down that row, take a right, then a sharp left and you're in the street where Gail Hammond lived.'

A few people shifted in their seats.

'Did Ms Hammond go to her flat after all? Her car *was* parked there – perhaps she decided to drive the rest of the way. Gail was known to keep a "ready bag" in her car with a clean uniform in it – she'd come straight from London, so she wouldn't have had a uniform with her; maybe she realized she'd have to stop by her flat to pick one up, and took the short cut from the main road.'

The next slide bore the words:

'Locard's exchange principle: every contact leaves a trace.' Gill Grissom, *CSI*

The smiles in the audience said they recognized the oft-repeated phrase from the TV series.

'Let's look at the fibre and blood evidence.' Fennimore folded his arms and trotted down the steps from the stage into the audience. He offered his hand to a man in the front row and after an embarrassed hesitation, the man took it and they shook.

Fennimore held up his right hand. 'This gentleman now has, oh, about fifty shades of grey wool fibres from my jacket on his right hand.' He got a few smiles from the women at that. 'And I will probably have fibres from *his* clothing on *my* skin – along with sweat and skin cells, sloughed from his palm.'

A woman a little further along the row wrinkled her nose and Fennimore gave a theatrical shudder. 'I know ...' He made a feint for a young couple in the front row and they shrank back. Laughter broke out.

He stepped back, serious again. 'Every contact leaves a trace,' he said. 'It was a hot summer the year Gail Hammond disappeared. Tom Killbride often wore a jacket to work, but he'd take it off if he got too warm and leave it on the seat next to him until he found a moment to stow it in the boot of his car – so his jacket was bound to pick up fibres from the car seat, and carpet fibres from the boot. Picture this: Gail sits in the car. Her trousers and top pick up fibres from the car seat, from Killbride's jacket, a few fibres from the car boot carpet, too – and she leaves contact trace from her own clothing. Look at the details of the fibre evidence, and you'll find that trace from Gail's clothing was found only on the seat of Killbride's trousers and the *back* of his T-shirt.

'He was seen cleaning his car the following afternoon. Now, I don't know about you, but when I'm vacuuming my car, I often sit in the passenger seat to get a better angle on the hard-to-get-at corners on the driver's side.'

He saw recognition in some of the faces.

'*Every* contact leaves a trace,' he said again. 'Physical evidence is not proof of guilt. Not everything found at the scene of a crime is relevant to the crime: there are hammers that are not used as bludgeons, knives that are guilty of nothing more violent than slicing a lemon. Fingerprints, DNA, blood – can all prove that someone was present, but it's the *context* and *interpretation* of the evidence that make the case. Or prove innocence.

'The investigator's job was to look at the evidence from both sides – not to construct a case to prove Killbride was a killer. But the police wanted a result; the CPS wanted a clean, quick prosecution; the family wanted justice for Gail; the public wanted to feel safe on the streets again. So *nobody* looked for an innocent explanation.'

He brought them back to the image of green fibres on a microscope slide. 'Not a single fibre from the rope ligature used to strangle Gail Hammond was found on Killbride or in

14

his car. Why? The prosecution said that was irrelevant – the blood evidence on Gail's shoes more than made up for that. Gail had scratches on her neck, and a broken fingernail – her parents and her friends said she wouldn't have given up without a fight – she must have given him a bloody nose. But there wasn't a mark on Killbride, not a scratch or bruise – and the only DNA under Gail's fingernails was her own.'

Fennimore took a moment to look into the faces of the audience and was pleased to see that some were adjusting their earlier judgements.

'The local paper reported on the trial every day, and Gail Hammond's supervisor rang the police as soon as he saw the news about the blood on Gail's shoes. You see, Gail *was* on duty two nights earlier, when Killbride came in to A&E: she'd gone in on her off-duty to cover for a staff absence. Her supervisor gave a statement to the police; he'd been so upset after Gail's death that he completely forgot to update her work log with the extra hours. The work record provided by the hospital's human resources department was incomplete. It was possible – even likely – that Gail had come into contact with Killbride during the course of her shift. She wouldn't even have to get that close: Killbride's mouth and throat would be full of blood – he'd be coughing and choking. And a vigorous cough can travel at the speed of sound.'

He waited while they pictured this.

'Oddly enough, the police never got back to Gail's supervisor. He wasn't called to give evidence and his statement was never passed on to the defence. In fact, I only discovered this little gem when I interviewed staff personally.

'But the prosecution has to hand over any evidence that might undermine the prosecution or strengthen the defence's case, right?' Fennimore dipped his head. 'To a point. The full disclosure rule only applies to evidence they have in their possession at the time disclosure is made – and that would be *before* the start of the trial. This came out *during* the trial, so technically the police did nothing wrong. They didn't include the notes in the bundle they sent out to me either. Which is why a case reviewer should start the investigation over again, like it was day one. Believe no one, question everything – and remember – *everyone* lies.'

He clicked back to the slide of Killbride at his wedding.

'So we come to Killbride's "sinister genetic make-up". After all, the 1960s study found a high percentage of convicted criminals had XYY syndrome. Which was a steaming pile of—' He flashed up an image of *Crapshoots and Bad Stats*, his popular science text, and got a few smiles.

'The study was flawed by poor sampling and experimental bias. But journalists who couldn't count to twelve without taking their shoes and socks off started misinterpreting experimental results they didn't understand, and behold – a medical myth was born.

'XYY males are the same as the rest of us – they get married, raise kids and are no more prone to violence or criminality than you or me.' He paused before adding darkly, 'It *is* true, however, that they tend to be a bit on the tall side . . .'

A faint ripple of laughter ran around the auditorium.

'The investigators never checked Gail Hammond's car – she didn't use it on the day, so it was dismissed as irrelevant. But what if *her* car was the crime scene and not Killbride's?' He raised his eyebrows. 'I just had to know.'

The next slide showed a red, weather-faded VW Polo.

'Gail's car,' he said. 'Her parents sold it, but eight years on the buyer still owned it. Killbride's appeal team paid to have the car forensically examined. Trapped under the headrest, they found seven bright green fibres matching those embedded in the ligature marks on Gail's neck. And here's the clincher: a fragment of torn fingernail was discovered in the groove of the seat rail runner. The new owner had adjusted it to his leg length the day he drove away in her car, and there it remained for eight years.'

Fennimore showed them images of the fragment side by side with post-mortem photographs of Gail's torn fingernail. It was a good match. 'The fingernail had viable DNA under it . . .'

The camouflaged man sat up straight.

'. . . Gail's DNA,' Fennimore concluded, and the man settled back in his seat, mirroring the posture of the man next to him: one leg bent at the knee, the other stretched out.

'It now looks like Gail was abducted and murdered in her own car.'

The camouflaged man picked up a pen and began doodling on the notepad in front of him.

'If only police had checked Killbride's claim that he dropped Gail off at the roadside . . .' Fennimore said. 'But all that tosh about highly aggressive XYY "super-males" quite turned their heads. They stopped looking – stopped even *thinking*.'

He went to the final slide: a newsprint photograph of a pale but smiling Killbride standing next to his barrister on the steps of the Supreme Court. The headline: KILLBRIDE INNOCENT.

'You got Tom Killbride off, but Gail Hammond's killer is still out there.'

Fennimore located the questioner in the middle of the second row. A student, he guessed, but not one he recognized.

'You're right,' he said, ignoring the confrontational tone. 'There are no happy endings in such sad tales; all we can hope for is justice. Tom Killbride found justice because of the hard work of people who didn't even know him. Gail Hammond still waits for hers.'

'The murderer made fools of the police,' the student said.

'They made fools of themselves,' Fennimore corrected. 'They decided that Killbride was guilty and then systematically set out to make the facts fit.'

'The killer cleaned up after himself – he's smart – forensically aware,' the questioner said.

'What makes you think that?'

'Essex Police say they have no new leads in the case.'

'They're being modest,' Fennimore said. 'Justifiably so. But they now have the green cord fibres – which they didn't have before. The killer *thinks* he knows what the CSIs are looking for: DNA and fingerprints. So he cleans up before he leaves. But it isn't all about DNA – it's about having the determination to keep looking, even when it seems there's nothing to look for. The evidence doesn't go away. It will still be there, waiting for someone to come along who is lucky enough or smart enough to see the stupid mistakes he made.' He checked himself – this was sounding too personal; he could almost hear Kate Simms's voice, mocking, gently chiding: *Listen to the ego talking. This isn't about you, Fennimore, this is about Gail.* He began again.

'The murderer missed the rope fibres. He missed Gail's broken fingernail – beginner mistakes – *amateur* mistakes. He was lucky three times over – in the botched police investigation, in the dishonesty of the prosecution, and in Killbride, who made such a plausible stooge. But now we know the real killer is out there. People are looking for him, and he *will* foul up – even if he never attacks another woman in his sorry life. Even if he never so much as *wolf-whistles* after a woman in the street. Because these types are impulsive and narcissistic; he'll lash out at someone who injures his fragile ego, or he'll drive too fast on a bellyful of booze; he'll steal, or stalk, or swindle – and he *will* reveal himself.'

3

Salford Quays, Manchester, Wednesday

Julia Myers looked down at her daughter. Lauren was high
and happy as only a six-year-old can be, energized by the
music and romance in the film. They walked from the cinema, Lauren holding her hand, skipping, rising on her toes
and performing half-pirouettes as she recalled scenes and dia-
logue, extending her free arm in balletic gestures, re-enacting
the role of the heroine. Julia let her prattle, searching the rows
for her car, worrying vaguely about the rattle she'd heard
on the drive in; they had already paid a fortune replacing
the cam-belt – their finances couldn't stand another expensive repair. The retail park was jammed with hundreds of
cars reflecting shards of light and heat. Some had already
begun the rush hour journey home, pulling out of parking
bays, edging on to the access road. The air smelled of exhaust
fumes and ozone; the metallic rasp of bromide catching the
back of her throat.

'If I was a princess, I would make my horrible stepsisters clean the steps of the palace on their hands and knees, with a – with a . . .' Lauren struggled for an appropriately harsh punishment. 'A toothbrush!'

'That wouldn't be very kind,' Julia said.

'So what? *They* were cruel and now I would be getting my own back on them.'

'You know, *you* can be cruel sometimes, too,' Julia said, knowing her daughter was talking about her own grievances. 'When you—'

'I'm thirsty,' Lauren interrupted. 'I want an Oasis.'

This was deliberate – a challenge. 'When you eat the wrong things,' Julia said, trying to be reasonable, cursing her own weakness for having given in to Lauren's pleas for 'just one' Day-Glo treat while they watched the film. 'Foods with artificial colourings in them, for instance.'

'Where's my sweeties? I want them.'

This was how it always went: explanations met with challenges, firmness with resistance; belligerence too often turning to full-blown tantrums.

'Those sweeties are the reason you're acting up right now,' she said.

'I'm *not* acting up!'

Julia remained silent, and after a moment Lauren began again, her tone wheedling. 'You could take out the yellow ones.'

'The sweets are gone, Lauren. All of them. I've thrown them out.' Lauren stopped dead, jolting Julia's arm.

'They're mine – I *paid* for them out of my own pocket money!'

Julia sighed inwardly: telling Lauren was a mistake; allowing herself to be drawn into an argument was a mistake. Feeling control slipping away from her, she said, 'I'll get you some more,' adding before she could stop herself: 'The kind *without* the cranky colours.'

She offered her hand, but Lauren folded her arms, scowling. 'Don't WANT them. They taste like puke.'

'Lauren . . . now you know that's not a nice word to use.' If she could just get her to the car, get her home, she might retrieve the situation—

'Puke, puke, puke, puke, PUKE!' Lauren yelled, a telling spite in her voice. Her eyes glittered. A hard grey-black sheen in her irises told Julia that it was already too late. She grabbed Lauren's hand and began marching grimly to the car, aware of disapproving looks from onlookers queuing on the access road.

'Don't—' Lauren moaned, instantly tearful. 'Do-oh-oh-ooon't!' She leaned back, digging in her heels like a fell walker on a precipice, her hand clammy and cold in Julia's.

As they passed McDonald's, she snapped upright, clinging instead to Julia's arm. 'I'm hungry.' Ready to concede, pretending her show of temper had never happened. 'Mummy, I'm *fine* – I'm hungry, that's all. I just want a *Happy* Meal.'

'I think you're happy enough, don't you?' *Stop it, Julia. Stop baiting her and allowing her to bait you. You're the grown-up here. Get her home and detoxed – it's not her fault – it's yours for caving in.*

Lauren twisted her hand and pulled, her damp fingers slipping free of Julia's. She darted towards the golden archway, heedless of the cars. Julia lunged, her fingertips brushing the cotton fabric of her daughter's T-shirt. Lauren arched her back, evading her mother's grasp, her laughter high and hard; the crazy sound of additive-induced mania.

22

A gap in the line of cars. Lauren leaped into it as the next car accelerated forward. Julia screamed. Lauren turned, her eyes wide – saw the danger too late.

A squeal of brakes and the world seemed to stop.

The car bounced on its suspension, a centimetre from Lauren's midriff. Then Julia was moving again. She dragged Lauren on to the walkway and crouched in front of her, seizing her by her narrow shoulders. 'You stupid girl – you could have been killed!'

A tremor ran through her daughter's bony frame. Julia pushed back images of Lauren crippled, Lauren broken – pushed hard against the deep black nothingness of Lauren, gone. But Lauren must have seen the horror in her mother's face: her lip trembled and she began to wail. Julia wrapped her arms around her, scooping her up. 'All right,' she murmured. 'It's all right, baby . . .'

'I'm sorry, Mummy. S-s-orry, Mummy . . .'

This was also part of the pattern coming down from a high: tears and appalled sorrow. Julia carried Lauren, patting her back as the child continued to sob, soothing her with nonsense until she found the car. The boot was open a fraction and Julia released the catch and slammed it shut with a small rush of relief. No repair bills. Feeling doubly lucky, having got away with leaving the car wide open like that, she lowered Lauren into the child seat. Lauren had subsided into sighs and hiccupping sobs, but clung to her for a second before letting go. Julia helped her with the buckle and wiped the tears from her daughter's face. 'Okay?' she said with a smile, and Lauren gave a single nod, avoiding her eye.

'Sorry, Mummy,' she whispered again.

'Chin up, YP.' Julia stroked her daughter's cheek with

one finger. The nickname brought a wan smile to the little girl's face, and, satisfied, Julia went around to the driver's door.

The interior was hot and she caught a faint whiff of something animal, male, slightly acrid. She glanced in the mirror and saw that Lauren had wrinkled her nose, too. 'Daddy left his stinky gym clothes in the boot again,' Julia said.

'Pooh!' Lauren giggled, holding her nose. Her eyes still glistened with tears, but she was all right – back to her old self – her real self, as Julia saw it.

'Daddy's in Big Trouble, isn't he, Mummy?'

Julia held her gaze in the mirror, widening her eyes and nodding, deadpan.

Lauren snickered behind her hand; she was a daddy's girl, but once in a while she and Julia would share a moment of allegiance like this, and Julia's heart would swell with love for her child. She swung the car out and they trundled along the row.

At the first speed bump, the car jangled and Julia's stomach tightened. 'That damn rattle,' she muttered, peering into the mirror as if it would reveal the cause.

Instinctively, Lauren glanced over her shoulder. 'Is something broke?'

'Broken,' Julia corrected automatically. 'I hope not, sweetie,' she added with a sigh.

She turned left out of Salford Quays, cutting through the back-way to avoid traffic, heading northward to Prestwich, and home, maddened by the faint-but-constant jangle of metal on metal. The exhaust, maybe? But they had that replaced only two years ago. The suspension? God, they really couldn't afford that . . . As they approached the A56, passing a cluster of car dealerships on one side of the road and an abandoned furniture outlet on the other, they hit a pothole and Julia winced.

'It's getting worse,' Lauren said, sounding anxious.

'It's just the road – makes it sound worse than it is.' Julia forced a smile in the mirror. 'Don't worry, Daddy will look underneath when we get home.'

'But, Mummy,' Lauren said, and there was real fear in her voice now, 'it's not *underneath* . . . It's *inside*.'

A trickle of sweat turned to ice on Julia's backbone and she looked in the mirror just as the seat next to Lauren tipped forward. Something moved in the shadows – a black shape emerging from the boot of the car.

A dog? *Jesus! How did—?*

Julia gasped, twisting in her seat; the beast was crawling into the passenger compartment, its movements jerky, weird.

Lauren cringed, grappling with her seat-belt buckle. 'Mummy—'

Julia focused on the road; she needed to stop, but the car behind was too close. Pull off into one of the car parks? She looked for an opening.

Lauren screamed.

Julia stared horrified into the mirror. The dog–creature metamorphosed. A hand shot out. It was a man. A *man*. There was a man in the car – and he had Lauren!

Julia reached back to grapple with the intruder. The car bumped the kerb and she corrected the wheel. A horn blared and through the passenger window she saw a car loom close; she swerved to avoid a crash. Gripping the wheel with both hands, she faced forward again.

A lorry. Yards away. Julia jammed on the brakes and the car shuddered to a halt. More car horns, the squeal of tyres on hot asphalt, but the man didn't flinch. He kept a tight grip on Lauren's wrist with his right hand as his left snaked around her neck. He was clothed entirely in black and he wore a black ski-mask. Julia saw the flash of a knife blade and then the man spoke:

'You watch the road,' he whispered. 'I've got her.'

4

Informed betting is methodical. Guessing is merely desperate.

JON J. NORDBY, *DEAD RECKONING*

Aberdeen, Wednesday

'Is that you, Professor?'

Fennimore halted mid-step; Joan. He'd hoped to sneak up to his office, but not much got past the forensic science department's office manager unseen. Her office door stood open, and Joan's desk was positioned so that, like Hecate, guardian of the household, she could see all that passed in her kingdom.

'I wondered when you'd show your face.' Joan dressed as she spoke: with femininity and care, but no frills. As for the occasional flounce – Fennimore guessed that she saw it as a special prerogative for having to deal with all the clever dim-wits whose academic affairs she managed.

'I'm guessing it's been bad?' he said, trying for conciliatory.

In answer, she reached down beside her chair and heaved a grey mail sack on to her desk.

Fennimore groaned.

'Phone calls, too,' she said. '*Twenty* requests for interviews. Notoriety does seem to seek you out, doesn't it?' Her precise Aberdonian tones sounded particularly clipped today.

He couldn't argue. Instead, he peered into the sack; there was a disturbing number of black-edged cards and an even more disconcerting flowering of peach and lemon-yellow envelopes.

'You're all over the Internet.' Joan clicked through her computer screens to an online newspaper. Here's *The Scotsman*: '"Amateur Killer Still at Large," says Forensic Expert.' She clicked on another link. '"Police Stopped Thinking" – they're not the only ones, are they, Professor?' she asked tartly.

Fennimore sighed. The public lecture, intended to draw attention to the university and its work, had more than fulfilled its promise. The student who had asked about justice for Gail Hammond had video-recorded the exchange – every uncensored, disparaging word – and posted it on YouTube.

Joan's phone rang, but she pre-empted his escape, raising a finger, commanding him to wait. 'You again, Mr Lazko?' She arched an eyebrow at Fennimore and he shook his head. The manager's gaze didn't waver. 'As I told you earlier, the professor is not expected in today.' A pause, then: 'Very well.' She added a note to her memo pad. 'I'll be sure to let him know.'

She handed Fennimore the note as she hung up. 'He says you've to ring him urgently.'

Fennimore crumpled it without reading it and dropped it into her bin.

'That wasn't his first call,' Joan said.

'So I gathered. It won't be his last.'

'You know, it might be better to talk to him and be done with it.'

'No,' he said. 'It wouldn't.'

Joan frowned. Still watching him, she began typing, her fingers rustling over the keyboard. She shifted her gaze to the screen to read and seconds later, she said, 'Oh. I see.'

Fennimore doubted it, but he was grateful not to have to explain.

'I'll make sure he doesn't get through.'

'I'd appreciate it.' Fennimore grabbed the mail sack, but she rapped his knuckles lightly.

'I'll deal with the condolence cards and the pastel-coloured *billets*.' Fennimore began to thank her, and she sniffed. 'Aye, well, you can thank me by keeping your head down – and you will have to sort through the pile in your office yourself.'

'There's more?'

She answered him with a look.

They were stacked in date order on his desk – fifty or more letters, postcards and notelets in the few short days since the YouTube clip had gone viral. The university's spam filters had junked most of the crank emails, but he hadn't thought that people would go to the bother of handwriting their unwanted messages and actually paying for a postage stamp.

The moment he sat down, his phone rang.

'While you're sorting that lot, you might think about getting to work on the mess up there.' Joan again; she had timed his journey to his office perfectly. 'It needs to be cleared by the end of July.' The Andrew Street building was to become part of a luxury hotel chain and they wanted access by the beginning of August. 'You'll like it at Garthdee,' she went on, her tone uncharacteristically cajoling. 'It's on the riverfront, overlooking the park.'

'Joan, if I want a view, I'll go hiking in the Lakes – it's the *absence* of view that helps me think.'

'Well, that's a pity,' she said tartly, 'because this building is sold, and if *you* don't organize yourself, Estates and Property Services will.'

Fennimore glanced around at the clutter of bookcases, stacked two-deep with reference texts; the boxes housing case notes, coursework and periodicals; his comfy day-bed, buried under a pile of box files.

'Tell them they'll need a forklift.' He hung up and slumped in his chair. He *liked* this building, with its nicotine-yellow lecture room, scarred by his more flamboyant demonstrations; his office with its spectacular winter sunsets; he *liked* over-looking granite buildings, stone walls and grey streets.

He sighed, turning his attention to the task. Joan had stacked envelopes stamped with university logos in a smaller bundle. A Post-it note stuck to the topmost commanded: 'Read these first.'

He picked up his letter knife and obediently made a start.

There were two invitations to speak at conferences in the following year – and a call for papers for a third. These he set aside to read later. The next half-dozen were pastel *billets* the senders had smuggled through Joan's spam filter by slipping them inside plain brown envelopes. He placed them in a fresh pile for shredding – a precaution against any of the crazier missives falling into the hands of the media. Then came a request from one of the broadsheets for him to write an opinion piece on miscarriages of justice. He junked it, feeling a slight pang of guilt: the university's publicity department would kill for a full page in the 'quality' press. But press were press, and Fennimore had an ingrained suspicion of the lot of them. He continued for half an hour, until he came to a plain buff envelope. It began with an apology of sorts:

'I was wrong about you – I know that, and I'm sorry for it – but you and me have a lot in common—' Suspicious, Fennimore skipped to the signature. Carl Lazko. He tore the letter in two and tossed it. Sorry didn't *begin* to make amends for what Lazko had done to him. He lashed out with his foot, sending the bin skittering across the floor to a corner, where it rattled against a stack of plastic tote boxes and came to rest.

He gripped the desk, his mind lurching back five – almost six – years to the last time he saw his wife and daughter. If he had been home that weekend – been there to protect his wife and child . . . Rachel and Suzie had disappeared from their rented house near the police training centre in Hampshire, where Fennimore was working on case reviews at the National Crime Faculty. That weekend he had arranged to meet Simms at a hotel – a conference, he'd called it. A 'tryst', Lazko had called it. Nothing happened – not then – but when the truth came out it had almost destroyed Simms's marriage, and Fennimore had lived with the guilt in the years since.

Even after the national press moved on to other stories, Lazko always seemed to be on the periphery of Fennimore's vision, dogging his steps. When they found Rachel's body in the Essex marshes six months later, the reporter was at his door well ahead of the pack, in prime position to snap Fennimore being led to a police car. The detectives had been there to take him to identify his wife's body, but Lazko's newspaper ran a review of events and carefully positioned it under Fennimore's picture. The implication was clear: Fennimore was a suspect.

He paced to his office window, resisting the impulse to

hoof the bin and its contents on to the landing. The sun beat down on the grey pavement below, creating a shimmer of summer heat haze, rare in the cold stone streets of the Granite City, and he was transported for a moment to the United States' Midwest, to the case he had just worked on with Kate Simms. Her placement with St Louis Police must be finishing soon. He hoped they could become friends again. He took a few breaths and felt better.

Yes, he thought – even *thinking* about Kate did him good.

Fennimore rubbed a hand over his face and got back to work: the next item had been sent special delivery. A document to sign perhaps, or a request for help on a case review. He picked up his letter knife and slit it open, glad of the distraction. It was just a single slip of paper, printed on one side:

'Every contact leaves a trace – but what good is that, if you can't find him?'

Him? This had to be about his lecture on YouTube. So this was to do with Gail Hammond's killer – the real killer – the one who got away. Fennimore checked the postmark on the envelope: Manchester.

'If he made stupid mistakes, why hasn't he been caught? If you're such a genius, why can't you find your own daughter? What is it – five years? Are you stupid or did you just stop caring? Well, what goes around comes around. Everything – all of it – it's all on your head.'

Fennimore crushed the letter in his fist and flung it across the room. Every day for nearly six years he'd been tormented by what Suzie might be going through. But he rejected outright the possibility that she was already dead, refused to accept the odds were stacked against her ever coming home. He was no fool – he knew he was no more worthy of a happy ending than the next man – and he would call any other man a fool for holding on to such self-deluding hope. But this was Suzie, his daughter – his little girl – and he wouldn't let go of her until he had clear, cruel evidence that she was never coming back.

He logged on to his laptop and called up an image: a girl in her mid-teens walking down a sunny street, a high wall on one side, a cobbled roadway sloping down to her left. She was with an older man; she looked serious, perhaps even unhappy, striding out in heels and a knee-length dress. The image, attached to an anonymous email, had arrived in his university inbox only a month before. The message: 'Could this be your daughter?' He had waited for a follow-up that never came. There was no ransom demand, no 'psychic' medium claiming special knowledge of his daughter's whereabouts, no taunts from the Internet trolls whose mission in life was to add to the pain and suffering in the world. All he had was the picture and a question he still couldn't answer.

It *could* be Suzie – he had aged-up a photograph of his daughter, and there were several similarities – but, maddeningly, the subject's hair concealed her left temple – which might otherwise have revealed Suzie's one distinguishing feature: a small diamond-shaped scar from a skateboarding injury when she was ten.

He had turned once more to Kate Simms for help. Simms searched CEOP, ICMEC and Interpol's FASTID databases and got a big fat nothing. She had worked her contacts in Interpol, and Fennimore did now know that the girl had been photographed in the eighth arrondissement of Paris.

Fennimore scrutinized the photo for the millionth time. The worst of it was, the man in the picture looked familiar.

Fennimore was convinced they had met – had tortured himself with that possibility – but he would reach for a name and on the point of recognition, it was gone.

Fennimore had flown to Paris as soon as he got back from the States, had haunted the eighth arrondissement, pestering locals and tourists with the photograph, but it was hopeless.

He opened the Facebook page he had set up on Suzie's behalf, checking through scores of comments and posts, vetting their content, filtering out the sad cases and the trolls. Finally, he gave up and did what he'd been wanting to do all along: he checked the time – it would be mid-morning in St Louis, not too early – and he Skyped Kate Simms.

She looked lean and tanned, her dark brown hair tied in a ponytail, revealing a face free of make-up and glowing with good health. Kate's placement with St Louis PD had clearly paid off, adding another notch to her career belt.

'You just caught me,' she said, answering the question he didn't dare ask. 'I'm at the airport – my plane's due to leave in less than an hour. I'm guessing this is about your YouTube debut. You're quite the Internet sensation.' She smiled, her brown eyes dancing with mischief.

'Ah, you've heard . . .'

'Becky told me.'

'Well, it's brought out the media hacks,' he said. 'It beggars belief – I mean how the *hell* does a forensic lecture go viral, anyway?'

'I don't know,' she said, teasing. 'I guess you could piss off the police – and a load of journalists – call them incompetent for good measure, then upload your tirade on to the Net?'

'They are incompetent, and I didn't upload it – a student did. A media studies undergrad and blogger, keen to build a rep.'

'Well, he did a bang-up job.'

Fennimore winced. 'You watched it.'

'Becky sent me the link, too – daughters can be very helpful that way.'

He ran a hand over his face. 'I'm such an idiot – I had no idea he was recording me.'

'Digital age, Nick – everyone's being recorded – all the time.'

'About that,' Fennimore said. 'I rang to tell you that Carl Lazko has called several times.'

Her face froze. 'What does he want?'

'The usual, I suppose.'

She took a breath. 'What will you do?'

'I'm thinking of heading back to Paris.'

'The photo again.' She looked more sad than annoyed. 'You know, the Paris police checked it out—'

'Kate, listen – I think I've pinpointed the photographer's location.'

'Nick—'

'There's a bridge about sixty metres upriver on the Seine; he had to be standing on that bridge. He'd need a telephoto lens, but it's perfect – the angle, elevation, all of it.'

'I don't see how that helps,' she said.

'Neither do I, but it's *something*.'

'It's *crazy*.' Her eyes flashed, but she stopped for a moment and went on more calmly. 'Do you think they'll come back – is that it?'

He didn't answer.

'Come on, Nick,' she said, her tone softer now. 'You're the betting man. What are the odds?'

'Sometimes backing an outsider pays off,' he said, knowing he sounded truculent and irrational.

She stared out of the monitor at him. 'You taught me that there are good bets and bad bets—'

'And this one is lousy,' he said for her. 'I know. But what if they live in the area?'

'I've been living in Manchester for over a year – there are neighbours in my *street* I haven't seen yet.' She paused, and he saw a mixture of concern and frustration on her face. 'Even if you had that little corner of Paris under surveillance twenty-four/seven, the chances are they'll never go back.'

Fennimore's head started fizzing. He *couldn't* be there twenty-four/seven, but there was a way to improve the odds of catching them if they did return. Kate was speaking and he made an effort to listen.

'Stop torturing yourself, Nick. It's a bad bet.'

'You're right,' he said, trying to quell the excitement in his voice.

She sighed, moving closer to the webcam, and he had the feeling that if she could, she would reach out and touch him. 'But you'll go anyway, won't you?' she said.

5

Abduction, Day 1

Dark.

The ground feels damp under her; the air is thick and musty. Her tongue feels swollen and her throat hurts. Julia Myers coughs and she hears a slight echo – the room is empty, large. A basement maybe. A cellar?

She hears a whimper.

'Lauren?' Her voice cracks and she coughs again, the pain tearing at her throat. Instinctively, she tries to move her right hand to soothe it but her wrist is tethered; her left foot too, so that her arm is crossed in front of her and she can't stretch out. She tests the strength of her bonds – there's no give. She feels with her free hand – hard plastic. She is seated, her back resting against the same hard something – a metal frame? Yes, a frame – iron, judging by the rusty oxide smell coming from it.

Her feet are cold: she is wearing socks, but her shoes are

gone. She reaches down with her left hand and makes contact with cool, gritty stone – sandstone maybe. That and the echo make her think of a church. A church is better than a basement – isn't it? Entrances and exits – more hope of escape?

Faint scratching sounds to her right. *Rats.* She thinks she can smell them. A faint *tick-tick-tick* some distance away. A clock?

Lauren groans, stirring uneasily, and Julia slides her right foot out, making broad exploratory sweeps, and at last makes contact. Lauren must have her back turned to her; Julia strokes it clumsily with the sole of her foot.

Something rustles, moving furtively across the stone floor. Simultaneously, she feels a slight tug of her hair. A high squeak close to her ear – she jerks convulsively and her head cracks against the metal frame. She shouts in pain.

Lauren starts up, kicking her away.

'No! No! No!' she shrieks. 'Get away!'

'It's all right,' Julia calls. 'Lauren – darling – it's okay.'

'A spider! I felt it!'

'It was *Mummy* – just Mummy. I'm here.'

'Why's it so dark?'

Why *is* it so dark? Julia casts about, but the darkness clings fast to her and the imagined space seems to shrink, closing in, swathing her, so that she feels half-smothered. If she reaches out, she is certain she will touch something soft, yielding. Her breathing comes fast.

You have to stay calm. You HAVE to hold it together – for Lauren. For both of us.

She forces herself to extend her hand, finds only empty space. She calls, 'Hello?' and her voice comes back faintly: '*Oh?*' like an exclamation of mild surprise.

'Mummy?'

'It's night-time,' she says, because she can't think of a more reassuring explanation. Can't get the words *dungeon, cave, pit* out of her head.

'Where's the man?' Lauren's voice is high and strained. 'Why won't he let us go?'

'I don't know, sweetie. But Daddy will be looking for us. And the police. Anyway, we won't wait for them – we're going to find a way out of here – okay?' She stretches out her foot and feels the pressure of Lauren's small hand.

'Okay, sweetie? Lauren?'

'I'm nodding.'

'I can't see you,' Julia says, trying to make it sound conversational.

'I can see you a bit.'

'What else can you see?'

'There's something grey up there.'

'A window?' Julia turns her head, staring into the darkness, widening her eyes, but sees nothing.

'I can't tell,' Lauren says. 'Just grey.'

'Okay. What about on the floor? Can you see anything around you?'

'A bucket – what's *that* for?'

Julia nods to herself. Their abductor doesn't intend to needlessly humiliate them; he will allow them to retain some dignity, it seems.

'What else do you see, love? My handbag?' Her phone is in there, a nail file, maybe even nail scissors—

'Nnnn . . . *yes*! Not *your* bag, like a shopping bag.'

'Can you reach it?'

Lauren moves and she loses contact. It feels like her child

has been snatched away on a thread, into the void. Stilling the panic that threatens to overwhelm her, Julia holds her breath and listens hard. After a moment, she hears the rustle of a plastic carrier bag. *She's all right. Keep calm.* 'Can you see what's inside, Lauren?'

'Not see. Feel. Packets of crisps and biscuits, I think. And there's something by it. Heavy, got a lid on it.'

'A water container?'

'Don't know.'

'Can you push it over to me?'

'I'll try, but there's something on my leg.'

Julia feels a fresh spurt of alarm. '*On* it?'

'*Round* it – plasticky stuff, but hard, so you can't get it off.'
So Lauren is bound, too.

'Just do what you can,' Julia says, keeping her voice steady, though her heart weeps for her little girl.

Lauren strains and grunts. 'I *can't* – it's too *heavy*.'

'Try pushing with your foot – can you do that?'

Lauren doesn't answer, but then Julia hears the gritty hiss of something heavy inching across the sandstone towards her. 'Good girl!' she cries. 'Keep going – don't stop.' Reaching experimentally with her right foot, Julia is able to hook the container and bring it closer. It's large, plastic, cylindrical, and she can hear liquid sloshing inside – several gallons, she estimates – which is good, because leaving them that much water must mean he intends to keep them alive for some time.

Steadying the barrel with her right knee, she draws it close to her body and feels for the top with her left hand. It's a screw-top but it won't budge.

She tries again – keeps trying until her fingers, the palms of her hand, burn with the effort.

'Is it water, Mummy?'

'I don't know, darling. I can't—' She tries again. Her hand slips and she gives a small yelp.

'Mummy, I'm *thirsty*,' Lauren says.

'I know,' Julia answers, remembering Lauren asking for a drink as they left the cinema – that must have been hours ago. 'It's okay. Wait – I'm going to try something.' She struggles to get the bottle into a better position, then lifts the hem of her T-shirt and uses it to grip the lid. She wrenches and twists, straining to loosen the bottle top for ten minutes, until her back muscles ache and her hand cramps, but it's no good – the lid won't shift.

Julia begins to weep softly.

6

Manchester, Thursday

Kate Simms arrived into Manchester airport mid-morning, jet-lagged and exhausted after a journey of delays and re-routes, and missed flights. Nine hours she had waited – in Toronto airport, of all places – for a tornado outbreak to run its course. Finally she took a cab home on a grey summer day in the rain.

The hallway of her Victorian semi seemed narrow and dark after the spectacular blue skies and golden sunshine of St Louis. She lowered her bags to the polished boards and shivered. The English summer had been slow to come and it seemed equally reluctant to stay.

Simms called out, but her voice fell flat in the chilly hallway. Kieran would be at work – English school terms ran later into the summer than in the Midwest – so she listened intently for sounds of her five-year-old playing. The house was silent. She dumped her keys in the bowl on the hall stand and saw a note propped against the mirror.

It was from her mother: 'Timmy fretting. Couldn't wait any longer. Back for lunch.'

Clearly her mother still hadn't forgiven her for leaving the children and Kieran and travelling halfway around the globe. Simms's brother was a career soldier; she had pointed out that he regularly left his wife and two kids at home while he went on tours of duty. Her mother's answer was that her son was a war hero. Simms had no argument with that, but she resented the implication that she, on the other hand, was just playing at cops and robbers.

She longed for Becky, her sixteen-year-old, who had completed her GCSEs and was in London visiting some old school friends, a post-exam treat.

With a suppressed sigh, Simms moved through to the kitchen, but even this room – the heart of the house – seemed peculiarly cold and uninviting. She felt like a ghost, an unwelcome visitor in her own home.

'Welcome home, Kate,' she murmured.

She needed to sleep: her eyes were dry and scratchy and she felt disorientated, almost drunk with exhaustion, but she was determined to see Timmy first, so she put coffee on to brew while she showered and changed, then opened one of her suitcases and sorted some clothes for a wash. As the washing machine thrummed, she took out her laptop and sat at the breakfast bar, looking through the photographs she'd stored from her trip. Her email notification pinged and she scrolled down the list, smiling at messages of goodwill from the St Louis PD team.

An hour later, nodding over her laptop, she heard the scratch of a latch-key in the front door and flew into the hall.

Her mother came through the door, Timmy a few steps in

front of her. Simms could swear he had grown two inches in the months she was away.

'Timmy!' She opened her arms wide, crouching, ready for him to come racing down the hall.

He hung back, grabbing a handful of his nanna's skirt for security.

Simms looked up as her mother placed a reassuring hand on her grandson's damp cap of curls.

'Give him a minute – it's bound to feel a bit strange at first.' Her tone was conciliatory, but Simms caught a gleam of triumph in her eyes as she said it.

7

Abduction, Day 2

Julia wakes with a start. She feels feverish and her throat aches horribly. For a moment she is comforted by the warm, solid weight of Lauren's body against her lower leg. She adjusts her position slightly and Lauren stirs. Her daughter's fingernails scratch the fabric of her jeans. The weight shifts – it feels wrong. Julia struggles to rouse herself. It's not Lauren, it's something crawling over her shin. She feels the sickening warmth of the animal through the weave of her sock. Its hairless tail flicks around her ankle and she screams, kicking out. The rat squeals and scuttles out of range.

'Lauren? Lauren!'

'Mummy!' She sounds hoarse, drunk with sleep.

Julia stares into the gloom and thinks she can just make out Lauren's outline.

'Are you all right? It didn't touch you, did it?' She casts

about for something – *anything* – to use as a weapon. 'Come here, darling. Come as close as you can.'

Lauren edges closer, and Julia sees her daughter's face as a pale smudge. Her eyes are becoming dark-adapted and Lauren is now a vague, shifting shape in the uncertain light. She aches to hold her little girl, but the bindings prevent her reaching out. Lauren leans against her and the heat of her little body is searing. She *has* to get at that water.

Julia reaches for the bottle and tries to break the seal on the cap again – grinding it with her teeth, bruising her lips against the hard plastic. Lauren whimpers.

'*Shhtop it* . . . Mumumum . . .'

Lauren's limbs feel floppy and way too hot. Dehydration, high temperature – if Julia doesn't get her cooled down, Lauren might start fitting. It has happened once before when she was a baby – an ear infection – her temperature soared to 102; she suffered three fits before the hospital team could bring her fever down.

'Lauren. Wake up. Wake up *right* now, do you hear me?' Julia commands.

Lauren groans, lifting her head and Julia catches the dull gleam of something in her hair. A hair slide. Her heart lifts.

'Listen to me, Lauren,' she says. 'I know how to get the water open – I need your hair slide, but I can't reach it – you have to pass it to me. Do you hear me? Lauren?'

No reply, but Julia feels her daughter's hands on her shin as she pushes herself upright. Julia reaches under her right arm with her left, straining the overworked muscles.

Lauren starts grizzling. 'I can't – my hands won't work.'

'Don't cry, darling. It's all right. Keep trying.' Julia swallows, feeling delicate tissue at the back of her throat tear. She coughs, crying out with the new shock of pain.

'Mummy!'

'It's all right,' she croaks. 'Just keep trying – *please*, Lauren.'

Lauren snuffles and complains, but a moment later, Julia sees, faintly, her daughter's greyish form stretching out towards her. She reaches under her imprisoned right arm again, pulling against her bindings, extending her left arm until it feels like it will be wrenched from its socket.

'Down a bit, Mummy,' Lauren says. 'You're too high.'

She moves her hand down and her fingertips brush against something smooth. The hair clip.

'Don't let go!' She shifts a little and feels something pop in her back. Ignoring the pain, she extends her index and middle finger, trapping the clip.

'Good girl! It'll just take a minute, then you can have the biggest drink ever.'

But she can't see Lauren's face any more; only her outline, shifting, formless, as if she is already fading. *The dark – it's just the dark, that's all.* Julia wipes tears from her own face and tries again.

Her hands are sore from her previous attempts to open the bottle, but she works at the hair grip with her teeth and her fingernails until the metal clasp gives.

'It worked, Lauren – I'm going to get the bottle open.'

Lauren mumbles something.

'Sweetie, don't go to sleep.'

No answer.

Julia straightens the metal of the clip. Working one-handed, by touch only, she rasps the point against the plastic of the tamper-proof seal, not wanting to think how she will tilt the bottle sufficiently to let Lauren drink without losing half the water on the dirty floor.

Solve this problem, then we'll think about the next.

She carries on, her hands raw, sweat dripping into her eyes, but it won't give. Julia heaves a dry sob and rests her forehead in the crook of her arm for a second.

'Mummy . . .'

'I can't do it, Lauren — the plastic is too hard.' She stretches out her foot to find her daughter in the darkness, but the bottle is in the way and she bumps it with her knee. The water sloshes maddeningly and the side of the container gives a little. Which gives her an idea.

She takes the broken clasp of the hair grip and punches a hole in the side of the container, feeling for the first, blessed drop of water. It's dry.

No. No — this isn't right. She tries again; still nothing happens. Panic flutters in her chest. *Lauren is dying — you have to work this out. Think!*

It comes to her as a line drawing from a textbook — air pressure and vacuums — schoolgirl physics. She feels for the top of the bottle and tilts it with her knee, gauging the water level. Then she punches the clip into the air gap. One, two, three times. Is it her imagination or was that the whisper of expelled air on her cheek? She finds the first puncture hole. There is a tiny amount of seepage. Tentatively, she tastes it.

Pure, sweet water.

Sobbing now, she drives the point of the hair grip in again and again.

'Lauren.' She feels for her child with her foot. Lauren is still, a heavy, uncooperative weight under the sole of her foot.

'Lauren — you have to wake up. Look — it's water.'

Lauren whines, but does not move.

'Please, Lauren. *Please* . . . wake up.' She prods the child roughly with the point of her toe. 'Now you listen to me, Lauren Myers. You wake up. *Right now.*'

Lauren's fingers close around the ball of her foot and push her away.

'Stop it, Mummy. Leave me a*lone!*'

'Water,' Julia says. 'Look – Lauren, look – it's water.'

Lauren stirs and slowly, painfully slowly, she sits up.

Julia can definitely see her shape now, as through a brown fog. She shuffles the container forward. 'It's leaking out of the side. See? Can you reach it?'

'No. Mummy, I'm too *tired.*'

'No. No! Don't go back to sleep.' She gives the container another tentative shove.

Lauren says, 'Ow!' Then, 'It's wet.'

A moment later, Julia hears the happy sound of her daughter licking and sucking the precious water from the side of the container.

8

Once a newspaper touches a story, the facts are lost
forever, even to the protagonists.

NORMAN MAILER, *ESQUIRE* MAGAZINE

Aberdeen, Thursday Evening

The taxi dropped Fennimore at his Union Terrace apartment
building at 8 p.m. He climbed the wide, echoing staircase
feeling tired after his Paris trip, but with some small hope.
The sun hung low over Aberdeen, still a good hour away
from sunset at this time of year.

He made coffee and drank it black, standing at the window
of his sitting room, looking down on the dense canopy of trees
bordering the gardens. His apartment was on the second floor
of a converted bank. It had one bedroom, and a combined
sitting- and dining-room with kitchen and bathroom off.
Plain and compact, because all he needed was a place to
eat and sleep, and recently refurbished, because he wanted a
place he could leave unattended for weeks without worrying
about leaks or burst pipes. Most of his books and personal
correspondence were in tote boxes in his university office. He
appraised the room, wondering if he could make space for

the accumulated papers from twenty years of academic work, but the prospect was overwhelming, and he abandoned the task for the twentieth time that summer.

The red light was blinking on his answerphone; he was ex-directory, but that was no guarantee of privacy, even post-Leveson. He eyed the flashing light with dislike, thinking of Carl Lazko. Leave it? He sighed. It would only eat at him until he dealt with it, so he refilled his cup and stood close to the machine so that he could hit the delete key fast. The first five, as he'd expected, were from Lazko. He wiped them before the journalist got to the last syllable of his name. A few more from other journalists requesting interviews. The next was a message from the firm that managed his accounts and investments: they needed to clarify a few points – could he please ring Mr Vincent in—

Fennimore stopped the message but left it on the machine. He had no patience with accounts and tax returns: he sent his receipts, income and royalty statements direct to the firm, and they saw to it that his liabilities were fulfilled and investments were made in a tax-efficient way. The money came in, it went out, he wrote cheques from time to time, made transfers when asked – beyond that, he had no interest. He would have to respond at some point, and maybe he would feel better inclined in a day or two. He sipped the last of his coffee and stared at his shoulder bag, leaning where he had left it next to the front door, thinking about taking one quick look at his laptop. Kate would call that obsessive. He shrugged. *What the hell.*

He set down his cup, but before he reached the bag, his landline rang. With Kate still in his mind, he picked up.

'Professor Fennimore? It's Carl Lazko – please don't hang up.'

Fennimore cut him off, pulled the phone jack out of the wall socket, scooped his bag from the floor and headed out.

There was a short cut across Union Terrace Gardens, and he headed for one of the access points: the sunken gardens were bounded on his side by a stone balustrade. The air carried the sharp-sweet smell of new-mown grass and the sound of shouts and laughter – the warm spell had continued, and families and sightseers sat in brightly coloured clusters across the lawns. He paused at the top of the flight of steps, then changed direction, keeping to the road and skirting the edge of the park instead. He stopped on Rosemount Viaduct to admire the ruin of Triple Kirks; he planned to climb its spire before the developers moved in to turn it into yet another city centre bar. The echo of a lorry passing under the viaduct on Denburn Road sounded like the moan of a trapped bull, but a sharp right took him into the relative quiet of St Andrew Street and his destination.

Fennimore went straight to the tiny staff common room on the third floor to brew coffee.

Josh Brown was seated at the low table, a sheaf of papers next to his laptop, a stack of books on the floor beside him.

'Josh,' Fennimore said.

'Professor.'

The student closed his laptop and tapped his fingers nervously on the lid. It was new, Fennimore noticed – a replacement for the one he'd had stolen a couple of weeks before.

'I wanted to apologize for my screw-up on the American investigation,' Josh said. He had withheld vital information about a serial killer, which put two victims in grave peril.

'You already have,' Fennimore said. The student's actions were hubris, rather than malice, but Fennimore couldn't work with someone he couldn't trust, and he intended to hand Josh off to a new supervisor. Josh was bright, he would know that, and he must be waiting for the hammer to fall.

Fennimore took a mug down from the shelf and tossed a few coins into the donations tin. Technically, he was still Josh's doctoral supervisor, so he felt obliged to ask how the thesis was going.

'Good,' Josh said, and his hand went to the stack of papers on the table. Fennimore nodded, keeping his expression bland.

The spark of hope that flared in the student's eyes was quickly extinguished.

Fennimore splashed coffee from the jug into his cup and headed quickly to his office.

Josh Brown scowled miserably at the papers on the coffee table. He had meant to explain his actions, to try and make the professor understand that his intention had been to help – he'd screwed up, no question, but—

'Give it a rest, Josh,' he muttered, disgusted with himself. There were no 'buts' in the case. A man died who might otherwise have lived – a bad man, it was true, and Josh had few qualms about his death – but a boy was still missing in the Oklahoma backwoods, and maybe the bad man could have saved the boy's life. 'Idiot,' he muttered.

He opened his laptop. On the screen was an image stolen from Fennimore: a photograph of a girl in an orange sundress walking next to a man on a sunny street in Paris. That was the day everything turned to shit. He knew now that his actions that day might just have screwed up Fennimore's best chance of ever finding his daughter.

Josh groaned, pushed his fingers through his hair. 'You stupid bloody *idiot*,' he said again.

Cold sweat broke out on his face and neck; he felt sick. He stood, but stumbled over his books, almost launching headlong into the door. He kicked them out of the way, made it to the sink and dry-heaved, then splashed cold water on his face, leaning over the bowl until the nausea subsided.

He should go home, but his thoughts would only follow him there. So he yanked a few paper towels from the dispenser, dried his face and poured more coffee, the glass jug clattering against his mug.

For two hours he picked up books and put them down unread. He scanned his notes, but couldn't make sense of them; highlighted journal extracts without judgement or intelligence, and at last he threw them on the table in disgust. He was staring blankly at the mess of notes and books and extracts on the coffee table when he heard Fennimore's office door slam. He sighed; he wasn't going to get any more work done, anyway – might as well head for home. He closed the books and stacked them on the floor, giving Fennimore time to leave before making his way slowly down the stairs.

It was dark. Mist had rolled in off the North Sea, so Josh could barely make out the traffic lights at the crossroads. Grey mist against grey stone; he would have to find his way home by touch, the fog was so thick. He paused on the steps of the building to take out his mobile phone and turn on the GPS, but heard footsteps. The mist thinned and he saw Fennimore a little way ahead, walking alongside the curved wall towards Blackfriars Street.

He held still, hoping the professor wouldn't notice him,

and, as he watched, a second figure ghosted out of the mist, turning the corner into St Andrew Street from the opposite side.

The man called Fennimore's name. English accent, from the south-east, like Josh's own. Josh felt a stab of animal fear.

Fennimore spun to face the man and the figure crossed the street at a run.

No. No – this can't be happening. Josh stashed his phone and broke into a sprint. By now Fennimore was in close quarters with the shadowy figure. The man's right hand went to his pocket and Josh came at him from the side, slamming him against the wall. He gripped the stranger's right arm, holding it where it was, wrenching the left arm up his back.

'What d'you want, you fucker!' Josh snarled.

'Josh.' He could hear Fennimore's voice, but like he was in another room – in another *dimension*.

'Call him off, Fennimore.'

The man sounded panicky. He struggled, but Josh increased the pressure on this left arm.

'Bloody hell, Fennimore,' the man yelled. 'Call him *off*!'

'Josh. It's okay.' The professor tapped him on the shoulder. 'I know him – and much as I would like to see this obnoxious bastard squashed like a bug, you should let him go now.'

Josh released the man's arm, but spun him round, yanking his right hand out of his pocket. 'Let's see what you got,' he said.

'Business cards,' the man said, opening his hand. 'Just business cards. Jesus *wept*, Fennimore – will you *please* put your Rottweiler on a leash?'

Fennimore actually smiled.

'Josh, this is Carl Lazko. He's a regional hack with London

ambitions – and he doesn't know when to piss off and leave things alone.'

Josh knew the name. He appraised the man: he was barely average height, podgy, with thinning hair, a small, pinched nose, and large, dark eyes.

'You heard what the man said – piss off.' Josh twisted Lazko's wrist and gave him a shove as he let go, sending him a couple of steps back the way he'd come.

Lazko staggered, but righted himself and turned, standing his ground. 'Will you just hear me out?' he said, addressing Fennimore.

'After what you did?' Fennimore said. 'And now you're doorstepping me *again*?'

'Well, you don't answer your messages – what else was I supposed to do? Look, I trekked all the way up here – the least you can do is listen.'

'The *least*—' Fennimore took a step towards the journalist, and Lazko backed off.

'Okay, that didn't come out right. Look, I swear I'm not after an interview or a quote.'

'Bollocks,' Fennimore said.

The journalist looked hurt. 'It's all over the Net – you got Killbride off—'

'He was *innocent*.'

Josh heard the suppressed rage in Fennimore's voice and he went up on the balls of his feet, ready to act.

Lazko pointed a trembling finger at Josh. 'He needs to stay cool – 'cos if he goes for me again, I'll have him nicked.'

Josh took it down a notch, waiting on a signal from Fennimore.

'I'm not here to hassle you,' Lazko said. 'Just – I need help.'

Fennimore threw back his head and laughed, the echo bouncing between the wall and the university building opposite, like pebbles on rock. 'You think I'm going to help *you*? You're a funny man, Lazko.'

The journalist licked his lips. 'You're pissed off with me – I get that .' He stalled, started again. 'And I want to say right from the off, I know you had nothing to do with Rachel and Suzie's—'

'I don't give a *shit* what you think of me,' Fennimore said. 'Did it ever occur to you that while you put the focus on me, you kept police eyes off the guilty man?'

Lazko opened his mouth and closed it again. He nodded as though making a decision. 'Okay,' he said. 'You're not ready to let go of all that. I get it. But, seriously, this case is right up your street. Goes back to 2008. Graham Mitchell – convicted of the murder of a prostitute. I'm convinced it was a miscarriage of justice.'

Josh shifted his stance and Lazko's gaze fixed on him. Even softened by the swirling mist, that dark-eyed stare was off-putting and Josh had to resist the impulse to look away.

'Police decided they'd got their man, forced a confession out of him, stopped looking for anyone else,' Lazko said, keeping his eyes on Josh for a few seconds longer. 'Just like Killbride.'

The professor tilted his head. Josh saw it and so did Lazko.

'There's a case summary,' Lazko pushed on. 'Wouldn't take more than an hour to read through. If you want, I could—'

'You know where your can stick your case summary,' Fennimore said.

Perversely, Lazko seemed encouraged, and Josh knew why. Despite his dislike of the man, the professor was curious about the case – it was obvious in the tilt of his head and the gleam in his eye. The fact that he'd let Lazko finish his sales pitch was the biggest tell of all. Fennimore would make a crap poker player.

'I can't believe you're taking him seriously,' Josh said. 'He's a scummy journo who did everything in his power to make you look guilty of abducting and murdering your own *wife*.'

Once again, he felt the journalist's intense, dark gaze on him.

'Do I know you?' Lazko said.

'I don't think so,' Josh said, but his mouth went dry and he avoided eye contact.

'I think I do. I think I've seen you somewhere before.' The reporter took a step towards him.

'No, mate.' Josh backed away. 'You got me mixed me up with someone else.' He turned abruptly and plunged into the fog.

9

Abduction, Day 2

There's hope, Julia thinks.

Over the hours, the close, suffocating darkness, alive with furtive scurryings and high squeaks, turned from black to a dirty sepia and she could just make out the grey square that Lauren had seen high above them the night before. A thin sliver of lighter grey marked the line of a skylight; one of thirty – she counted them all – they'd been boarded up, but the hardboard or metal plate covering this one must have slipped a fraction. It was the source of the constant ticking sound, and rainwater dripped from it almost continuously. But it did let in a little daylight, too, and they were grateful for it. In those hours, their place of captivity changed by subtle degrees from the stifling closeness of a tomb to the soaring emptiness of a vault. High rafters emerged from the smoky darkness.

The iron frame that holds Julia immobile and helpless has taken shape – faintly at first, but gradually gaining substance. Now she recognizes it. *A loom*, she thinks. *We're in an old mill.*

Julia takes careful stock. Above the loom, a rail as thick as her forearm runs for twenty feet; at the far end, a section has fallen, gouging a line in the concrete. On stormy nights the wind must rock the entire structure. Julia shivers, imagining the remaining stays working loose, the rail, the roof, the entire *building* crashing down on their heads. She shakes off her fear – the weakness of the building could help them to get out, to find a way home. She has made herself measure the length of it, estimating the span of one section of rail and, with the help of Lauren's sharper eyes, counting the total number of sections. The place must be at least thirty metres long and fifteen or twenty wide. Her eyes can't penetrate the gloom sufficiently to locate a door, but Lauren sees it, about two-thirds of the way along one wall.

'Mummy, I think I can see your bag.'

'My bag – where?' Julia strains to see. 'Where is it?'

'By where he left the shopping bag. I couldn't see it before. I'm sorry, Mummy.' Lauren sounds close to tears.

'It's all right, love – it's very dark in here – and *I* can't even see it now. Can you point to it?' She follows the line of her daughter's finger and sees a faint black hump in among other debris – discarded cloth and broken machinery. 'Can you reach it, Lauren?'

She hears her daughter grunt with the effort.

'I can't. It's too *far*.' Lauren begins to cry.

'Never mind. Have a little rest, I'll see what I can do.' Julia rubs the plastic around her wrist against the rusted iron of the loom until it's hot, but there are no sharp edges, and soon the skin of her wrist chafes and tears and she has to stop, choking back a sob.

'Lauren. Sweetie . . .' she says, raising her voice above her daughter's grizzling. 'You're going to have to try again.'

'I *told* you, I *can't*.'

'Hey, YP, come on, it's all right . . .'

'It isn't. Stop *calling* me that.' Lauren's voice has risen to a screech.

It was Julia's mother who gave Lauren the nickname YP – meaning 'Yellow Peril' – a reference to her particularly strong reaction to the food dye, Sunset Yellow. But it wasn't only food additives that set Lauren off: lack of sleep; sugary or salty foods; chocolate – they all had their effects, and Lauren has had little sleep and a *mountain* of junk food in the last two days. She's teetering on the edge of a full-blown episode. And Lauren's episodes can be frightening in their intensity.

They hear the sound of a key in a lock, and Lauren gives a yelp of fear. The click of a padlock hasp follows, the rattle of a chain. Finally, the solid sound of a door-bolt being drawn back.

Lauren sees him first, standing in the doorway. Her breathing comes fast and shallow. 'Mummy,' she whispers.

'Stay very still,' Julia says. 'Don't say a word.' Her own heart is beating so hard that she can hear it reverberating in her ears, in the tremor of her voice.

A second click and she is blinded.

The man shines a flashlight from Julia to Lauren, as if checking it's safe to enter. Satisfied, he strides towards them alarmingly fast; Julia braces herself, expecting violence. He plays the beam over Lauren and she shrinks back.

'Hey,' Julia says, but he ignores her.

He dumps a carrier bag on the floor, two blankets. In the reflected light of the torch beam Julia can see that he is masked, as before, and she feels almost weak with gratitude.

'What do you want?' she says, still trying to distract him from her daughter. But the beam remains on Lauren, and Julia takes the opportunity to search her child's face, her arms, her limbs for signs of injury. *Unharmed. Thank God, she looks unharmed.*

'We don't have much money,' she says, trying again. 'But—'

Abruptly, the man crouches, seizing Lauren's ankle. The child lashes out with her free foot, scratching, screaming, 'Get off! Get *off* me! You horrible— Get *off*! Mummy. *Mumm-eee!*'

'Get away from her,' Julia screams, trying to pull her arm free of the bindings, to catch him with her foot, but he's too far away.

Suddenly, the man falls flat on his rump and scuttles backwards to escape the clawing, spitting fury of her child.

'Get her under control.' His voice is high-pitched, panicky. *Is he afraid of her?*

'I *mean* it.'

'Cut me loose, I'll get her under control,' Julia says, sounding far braver than she feels. 'Let us go, she won't bother you ever again.'

'Can't do that.'

'Why? What do you *want*?'

'Respect.' He is disguising his voice and he avoids her gaze.

'You have our respect – and fear.' Julia glances at Lauren, sniffling a few feet away.

She feels his eyes on her and drags her gaze reluctantly from Lauren to him. Even behind the mask, she can tell he is contemptuous. This isn't about her or Lauren – he doesn't require the respect of women – the notion has never even occurred to him.

'All right,' she says. 'You have a point to make, and you're using me and my little girl to make it. But does that mean we have to die of thirst?'

He straightens up. 'I *gave* you water—'

'I can't open it,' she snaps back.

He places the flashlight on the floor, angling it towards her so the beam dazzles her, then he lifts the twenty-litre bottle with one hand – the bottle she wrenched her back trying to move. He wraps one long arm around the barrel and grips the plastic top with the other. Twists it open with a loud *crack*, like bones breaking. Julia flinches involuntarily. He looks down at her, then switches his attention to Lauren. His message is clear.

He dumps the bottle carelessly on the floor and a whale-spout of water shoots out, wetting Julia's jeans.

'Satisfied?' he says.

He's offended that I think he's cruel. 'Since you ask,' she says, 'I'd like my handbag. There are things I need.'

'What "things"?'

'I—'

'Your phone – is that what you want? 'Cos you know, that's *long* gone.' He must see the disappointment in her face, because he spits, 'D'you think I'm *stupid*? *Do* you – bitch?'

Julia knows men like this. Men with egos like glass; men who will always respond to an imagined insult with their fists. A sudden inspiration makes her say: '*Women's* things. "Time of the month" things.' She stares past the mask, into his eyes, and although he looks away, she does not. This is not the time to back down.

He stoops, snagging the handbag by the shoulder strap and flings it at her, catching her in the chest. Winded, she whoops in air.

He takes a step towards her and Julia flinches. Lauren sets up a wail.

'Easy . . .' He retrieves the torch, spotlights the water container, the bag of food, the handbag, the blankets. 'You got what you need,' he says, his voice a harsh rasp. 'Now I want something from you.'

10

Lying is a form of deception, but not all forms of deception are lies.

A UNIVERSAL TRUISM

Aberdeen, Thursday Night

Back in his apartment, Fennimore shucked off his jacket, damp after his walk through the fog, and hung it over a dining chair to dry. His mobile phone *thunked* against the chair leg and he fished for it in the pocket, came up with a business card. Lazko's.

'Crime reporter, *Essex Chronicle*,' it read. It seemed Lazko had moved on a step or two along the yellow brick road towards achieving his London ambitions: when he'd raked up muck on Fennimore and Simms five years ago, he was an all-rounder and general dogsbody on a free newspaper in Hampshire.

Fennimore's first impulse was to shred the damned thing. He slotted the card in the machine, but for reasons he could not explain, held off flicking the switch. Instead, he set up his netbook and started checking the journalist's story. Lazko had been campaigning for two years; the convicted man's family for much longer. He found a blog created by Mitchell's sister, an inevitable Facebook page entitled 'Justice for Graham Mitchell'. He scrolled back through the timeline to read the posts in sequence. It began with a diatribe against a criminal justice system that assumed guilt when it espoused the presumption of innocence. The outcry of an anguished family unable to acknowledge the terrible truth that their son or brother or father was a killer.

To all appearances, as a story, this was a lame duck. Mitchell was a loner who haunted the red light district of his home town and paid prostitutes for sex or company. He had even confessed to the murder. Lazko had set his sights on a staff position at one of the national newspapers – and this story wasn't a career-maker. So why had he invested so much in Mitchell – gambling his reputation, convincing his editor to revisit the case, to run appeals for information?

A two-tone notification warned Fennimore that someone was trying to reach him on Skype. He checked the caller ID: it was Kate Simms. He accepted the call and a moment later, Kate was onscreen. He saw a bay window behind her and darkness beyond it.

'Hey, you're back,' he said, smiling into the webcam.

She peered into her own laptop screen. 'I'm guessing you are, too. Unless you saw sense and stayed home.'

'No, I went.'

'Flying visit,' she said.

'Literally.'

'Find anything useful?'

'Not yet,' he replied honestly. He saw in her face that she suspected he was up to something. 'So how come you're up so late,' he asked, to change the subject. 'Jet lag?' It was almost midnight.

'It's the cocktail hour back in St Louis. It'll take a while to adjust,' she said. Then: 'Did you just avoid my question?'

'You look great,' he said, and meant it. Her dark hair gleamed under the lamplight.

Kate narrowed her eyes: she knew every diversionary tactic in his repertoire.

'All right . . . I acted on your advice,' he said.

'Hmm . . .' she said. 'That sounds a lot like evasion.'

Her eyes, normally a warm hazel, flashed amber, and he knew he was testing her patience.

He took a breath. 'All right. I've accepted that they might never chance to walk down that same street again, that I can't be there all the time and I can't watch the place twenty-four/seven.'

She sniffed the air, wrinkling her nose. 'There's a definite whiff of bullshit in the air.'

He shrugged. 'What can I say – you're not the only one who needs time to adjust.'

She nodded. 'Fair enough.'

'So,' he said, relieved, 'how was the homecoming?'

'Muted,' she said. 'Becky's exams have finished and she's away in London, visiting old school friends. Tim is punishing me with indifference and Mum disapproves of the fact that I "abandoned" my family in the first place.'

Fennimore was intrigued that she hadn't mentioned her husband. He couldn't help asking, 'And Kieran?'

She seemed to consider. 'He's okay – he popped home to see me after work, but couldn't stay – rehearsals, prize-giving – end-of-term stuff. Since he got this promotion to Head of English, he's rarely home before seven – it's expected in the private sector.' She stopped.

Fennimore wasn't the best at reading people, but he heard the defensiveness in her tone and, judging by the flush on her cheeks and her unwillingness to meet his eye, she was aware of it too. It had been five years since Kieran had learned about their hotel 'tryst' from Lazko's headline, and he also knew that she and Fennimore had worked closely since then on the I-44 killings in the US.

'Has the media interest died down?' she asked. Kate always had a knack for reading his mind. 'I haven't heard a thing from Carl Lazko.'

'He came to find me at the university this evening,' Fennimore said.

'He *what*?'

Fennimore related his strange encounter with the journalist. He also told her how Josh Brown had appeared out of the fog like an avenging ninja, but backed down after Lazko claimed to have recognized him.

'Suspicious, no?' she said, raising an eyebrow.

'You're a cop,' Fennimore said. 'Your default setting is suspicion.'

She rested her chin on one fist and smiled. 'You're a scientist – isn't your default setting supposed to be scepticism?'

He dipped his head. 'Fair comment.'

Simms watched him for a few moments longer. 'So – will you take Lazko's case?'

Fennimore glanced at his notes on the table. 'I haven't decided.'

'You should think about it,' she said, a hint of mischief still in her eyes. 'Might keep you out of trouble.'

★ ★ ★

He stared at the screen for a few minutes after she disconnected.

He hadn't been lying when he told Kate that he'd accepted he couldn't hang around Paris watching for his daughter. He had, however, done the next best thing, paying a visit to his favourite climbing shop before his flight and splurging on some serious gadget purchases.

He retrieved a Samsung tablet – another new purchase – from his shoulder bag, flipped the cover, converting it to a stand, and opened an app on the device. An image filled the screen: a dark street, lit on two levels. On one side a high grey wall, on the other a lower wall, lit by swan-necked lamps. The street was cobbled; it sloped down to what he now knew was a gravel walk running alongside the River Seine. He clicked through to the settings icon and made an adjustment. Instantly the screen divided into multiple images: the same stretch of road from below; from east and west; and three more showing views of a bridge.

11

Abduction, Day 2

'I think he's gone, Mummy,' Lauren whispers.

'I think you're right, love. I think you scared him away,' Julia says, hearing the wonder in her own voice.

'*Me?*'

'Well, perhaps YP, rather than you.' When the man said he wanted something from her in return for the handbag, Julia had steeled herself for something far worse than moistening the seal on an envelope. He hadn't touched them – wouldn't so much as *look* at Lauren after she lashed out at him. Bizarrely, he had even gone part-way to an apology: he was only checking her bindings, he'd said.

Lauren has fallen silent, and Julia knows she is thinking about her new-found power.

Julia drags her handbag closer with her right foot and reaches down with her left hand to rummage through it. Tissues, Lauren's sweets, some spilled at the bottom of the bag.

70

No phone, no scissors – not even a nail file. He must have turned it inside out to make sure there was nothing she could use to get them out of this terrible place.

Julia dumps the bag on the floor, blinking back tears.

'If he comes back, I'll hit him,' Lauren says. 'Why's he have to wear that horrible costume, anyway?'

'I think he's hiding behind it,' Julia says, without thinking. A memory itches at the back of her mind, just out of reach.

'Well, he looks like a big black spider.'

'Shh! Don't say that.'

'Why?'

What can she say? *We wouldn't want to hurt the kidnapper's feelings when he's been so nice to us?* Julia can't help herself; she giggles.

Lauren responds in kind: 'I'll pull his nasty spider-legs off and jump all over him and squish him and squash him.' She makes squelching sounds, one hand to her mouth to amplify the rude belches of noise. 'What're you *laughing* at, Mummy?'

Julia snorts and they both screech with laughter.

Lauren stops first, subsiding in hiccups and gulps, and finally silence.

Julia goes on, crying with laughter until her ribs ache.

'Mummy?'

You have to stop. Appalled, she finds she can't.

'Mummy, *stop*,' Lauren begs. 'Please – *stop*, you're scaring me. Mumm-ee-*ee*!'

Her little girl's fear penetrates Julia's hysteria and at last she gets herself under control.

'It's all right, poppet,' she says, hoping that the faint aura of light from above won't betray her; that Lauren's sharp eyes won't spy the snot and tears running down her cheeks. She sighs, wiping her face with her free arm.

'Sorry, sweetie. Something just tickled my funny-bone.'

Lauren giggles and that almost sets her off again. *Find a distraction.* Maybe if she wraps the tissues around her wrist it will dull the pain of grinding the plastic against the metalwork of the loom again.

She'd begged their captor to switch the bindings to her left wrist and right foot – her skin is raw – but he didn't even reply. Just stood with his hand stretched out, that damned envelope quivering in his fingers.

'Lick it.'

She had turned her head away, but one long arm flicked out, seizing her hair. She recalls the shock of it: his reach was freakish. His arms too long for his body.

Something clicks in her mind and Julia experiences a series of prickling shocks from the base of her skull to the crown of her head; chills run down her arms to her fingertips.

Oh, dear God, I know this man.

He might wear a mask and change his voice, but she knows him. She tries not to think. Won't even allow his name to come to mind in case it finds its way to her tongue. He has just sent a ransom note – why else would he go through that pantomime, making her seal the envelope? The mask; disguising his voice – *surely he means to let us go?*

He does, she thinks. *He will.*

If she doesn't fail. They are safe only for as long as he is convinced of his anonymity. If he suspects for one moment that she knows who he is, they are lost.

12

Any truth is better than indefinite doubt.

A. C. DOYLE, 'THE YELLOW FACE'

Aberdeen, Friday, Early Morning

With one eye on the street views captured by his e-tablet, Fennimore had returned to the Mitchell case. At 5 a.m. multiple tabs were open on his computer screen, and a mass of papers and doodles littered his sitting room floor. Kate could be right: working on a case might keep him out of trouble – holidays were always difficult for him. Too much time to brood. But before he made up his mind, he needed more data. He ducked his head to take a look under the table at the document shredder. One edge of Lazko's business card was just visible in the feeder. He plucked it from the machine and dialled the journalist.

'No promises,' he said. 'But you can send over the case summary.' This done, he got a few hours sleep.

Just before 9 a.m., Fennimore put a fresh pot of coffee on to brew and sleepwalked to the shower. He heard an electronic trill. He opened the cubicle door to listen: it was the intercom for the flat. No one ever visited him here. Puzzled, he grabbed a towel and checked the video monitor.

Lazko.

He snatched the receiver up. 'What the hell are you doing here?'

The journalist was at the gate to the rear of the property. He leaned out of the driver's window to speak into the intercom; the fish-eye lens distorted his round, shiny face until the camera finally came into focus on the narrow bridge of his nose and one large brown eye.

'You need to buzz me in,' he said.

'How the hell did you get hold of my address – did you follow me home last night?' Fennimore watched the journalist take a breath – a sure prelude to a lie. 'Forget it,' he said. 'I don't want to hear it.'

The enlarged eye blinked. 'D'you want to see this or not?'

Fennimore considered cutting the connection. Let the little Hobbit stew for a bit. But curiosity – at once his greatest asset and most wretched failing – made him press the entry button.

He was dressed by the time Lazko arrived at his door, panting and red in the face, carrying a large cardboard box in his arms.

'Could use some help,' Lazko wheezed.

'If it's CPR you're wanting – you can forget it,' Fennimore said. 'I'd rather give mouth-to-mouth to a basking shark.'

Lazko dumped the box so that one corner inched over the threshold, which was at least a variation on the foot in the door. Fennimore made no move to help and the reporter leaned against the door-frame for a moment, sweat trickling from his thinning hairline and gathering in his eyebrows. He gave

Fennimore a baleful look before turning to the stairs. The professor watched him go, but when he heard the journalist begin the return trip, he hooked his keys from the table and sauntered down the stairs. Four more boxes were stacked at the bottom of the stairwell.

'Two more in the car,' gasped Lazko, continuing past him up the stairs, the rasp of his shoe leather on the sandstone drowned out by the rasp of his breath.

'Wait a minute,' Fennimore said.

The smaller man stopped, easing his burden on to one of the wide steps.

'What is this?' Fennimore demanded.

Lazko armed sweat from his face with his shirt sleeve. 'Police interviews, witness statements, evidence logs, post-mortem reports, lab results, court transcripts . . .' He shrugged. 'Everything you need.'

Fennimore trotted up the stairs till he was at eye level with the journalist. 'I asked for a summary.'

Lazko jammed a knee against the box to prevent it from falling, plucked a slim folder from the top and pressed it into Fennimore's hand. 'The summary,' he said. 'I've had a word with Mitchell's family and his new defence team: you've got full access.'

'I'll say it again,' Fennimore said. 'I haven't decided to take the case.'

Lazko grinned. 'You will. And when you do, you'll want everything.'

Fennimore took the summary file and walked past Lazko to his apartment. He edged the first box outside his door with the toe of his shoe.

'I'll call you when I've read the summary,' he said.

The reporter's eyes bulged. 'What am I supposed to do with this lot?'

Fennimore smiled. 'I'm sure you'll find somewhere to stick it.'

He closed the door and set the intercom to mute before heading to the kitchen to get more coffee.

After two hours, he called the journalist on his mobile. 'I'll take the case.'

A few seconds later, he answered a knock at his door. Lazko stood outside; beside him, eight boxes neatly stacked in sets of two.

He had the good sense to hand the boxes of notes and reports to Fennimore without comment. Fennimore took them, stacking them against the wall just inside his front door. This done, he held on to the door-frame with one hand, the door with the other, and looked at Lazko.

'I will do this my way, at my own pace, without interference. I will discuss details when I'm ready, on my terms.'

The reporter nodded.

'I haven't finished yet. If the evidence says that Graham Mitchell is guilty, I will say so – and publicly.'

'Understood.' Lazko nodded amiably. 'Well, now we've got that cleared up' – he peered around the door into the apartment. 'Coffee smells good – aren't you going to invite me in?'

Fennimore relaxed into a smile and he saw hope and journalistic avarice bloom on the other man's face.

'Not a chance,' he said, and swung the door shut.

13

Evidence must wait for the appropriate question
before revealing any answer.

JON J. NORDBY, *DEAD RECKONING*

Aberdeen, Saturday

Fennimore had worked through the Mitchell case
documents for the rest of Friday, taking cat-naps on his sofa,
topping up his caffeine reserves from a pot of coffee he kept
simmering on the hotplate. The stack of notes next to his
laptop had grown taller and messier. Having read the case
files through once, he'd dragged a flipchart from the back of
his wardrobe and within hours multi-coloured mindmaps
and charts covered the walls and lay strewn across the sitting
room floor.

Mitchell had admitted to murdering Kelli Rees, a prostitute
whose services he had used on many occasions, but he quickly
retracted his confession. His solicitor claimed that his client
had been coerced; prosecution counsel contended that police
interviews showed no evidence of duress. Fennimore added a
note to request the taped recordings of Mitchell's testimony.
The circumstantial evidence was strong: Mitchell's DNA had

77

been identified in saliva on a love-bite on the victim's neck and from epithelial cells found under her fingernails – rough, but consensual sex, he claimed.

The court transcript showed that prosecution counsel cited 'semen stains' on Kelli Rees's skirt, linking it to Mitchell's DNA found on her body. Fennimore made another note, dumped his pad and pen on the sofa and stretched.

For the hundredth time, his eyes strayed to the CCTV recordings replaying on his new tablet. As he'd toiled through Friday into Saturday, the tableaux of Parisian streets had changed from dark to light, to dark and back again. People came and went, triggering the cameras, which were set to three-shot bursts; cars passed by; it rained for a time; a mist crept up the cobbled slope from the Seine and then receded in a milky, time-lapse wave. It was now mid-afternoon, the time stamp told him, and although this stretch of the river was off the main tourist track, the cameras had been set off many times by office workers and dog walkers, lovers taking a quiet stroll, families looking for a sunny spot to eat a picnic lunch.

A two-tone notification signalled that a new email had landed in his inbox. He called up the message: it was from the firm who managed his accounts, and he realized he hadn't replied to the earlier voicemail. They would like to 'review' his investments – a ploy, no doubt, to pitch him another 'opportunity'. He filed it, snagged his coffee cup and headed to the kitchen for a refill but stopped, hearing a knock at his door. He returned to the table, placed the e-tablet face-down to hide the Paris surveillance shots, and checked the confusion of lists and mindmaps scattered around the room. Those would have to stay.

He peered through the spy hole. Lazko – who else? He swung the door open. 'How'd you get in?'

The journalist shot him a pained look. 'You don't get stories by—'

'Respecting people's privacy?' Fennimore said. 'Newsflash, newshound – you won't get *this* story unless you *do*.'

'I am – I mean, I'm playing by your rules – *trying* to, anyway.' Lazko took a breath. 'Look, can I come in?'

Fennimore noticed with a rumble of foreboding that the reporter was pale and sweaty.

'What's happened? Why are you here?'

Lazko ran a hand over his thinning hair, and Fennimore saw a tremor in his fingers.

'Let me in,' the journo said. 'I'll explain.'

Fennimore didn't move. 'What have you done?'

'Nothing. Anyway, it's all straightened out.'

'If it was nothing,' Fennimore said with implacable logic, 'why would it need straightening out?'

Another intake of breath. Lazko let it go slowly. 'All right – but don't freak out, okay?' Another hesitation, then he spoke in a rush. 'Mitchell's sister posted on the "Justice for Graham Mitchell" page that you're reviewing the case.'

Fennimore turned on his heel, leaving the door to swing shut under its own weight; Lazko must have caught it, because a moment later he heard the journalist crunching flipchart paper underfoot.

'I spoke to her as soon as I knew about it. She's taken it down,' said Lazko, talking fast, staying out of reach.

'So it's fixed.'

'You might get a request on Suzie's Faceb—'

But Fennimore had his daughter's Facebook page onscreen

already. Someone named Geena had made a request to post on Suzie's wall. The posting included a photograph of Mitchell, a thug with facial tattoos and a mono-brow.

'Is this sister's name Geena?' Fennimore said.

'Um . . .' Lazko squinted past him to the screen. 'Like I said – misunderstanding. Ignore it, it'll go away.'

Fennimore jammed his hands in his pockets. 'It won't,' he said. 'It never does.'

'Look, I'm sorry – I really am.' Lazko sounded like he meant it. 'But you can't drop the case.'

'Give me one good reason.'

Lazko took in the notes stacked on the dining table, the sheets of doodles and mindmaps on the walls, the sofa, under his own two feet. 'Because . . .' he said, 'you think he's innocent.'

'I think he's a thug,' Fennimore corrected.

Lazko's eyebrows twitched and Fennimore realized he had seen the evasive remark for what it was. 'You really *do* think he's innocent.'

'I think he's a Neanderthal who *maybe* didn't do this *particular* bad thing,' Fennimore said.

The scrunched flesh of Lazko's forehead relaxed abruptly and he rubbed his hands briskly together. 'So what will it take to convince you?'

Fennimore thought about it. 'Evidence that Kelli Rees was alive and well when Mitchell left her flat.' He waited for the disappointment to show on Lazko's face before adding, 'But it's not me you're trying to convince. And neither you nor I, nor his legal representatives, need to prove Mitchell's innocence – only that his guilt is in doubt. What *you* need is evidence that his conviction was *unsafe*.'

Fennimore saw a gleam of excitement in the journalist's eyes. 'You found something.'

'I found a void,' Fennimore said, and Lazko's forehead wrinkled again – this time in question. 'The prosecution talked about semen stains—'

'Mitchell never denied he was with Kelli,' Lazko said, instantly on the defensive. 'They had sex, it got rough – but he didn't kill her.'

'I'm not talking about the DNA evidence,' Fennimore countered. 'The prosecution referred specifically to *semen* stains on the victim's skirt and underwear. But there's nothing in the lab reports about those items of clothing. Which means they didn't analyse the stains.'

'They had a confession,' Lazko said. 'They had his DNA on the body – they didn't need to—'

'Yes,' Fennimore said. 'They did. The prosecution brought the skirt and underclothing into evidence. Make a claim like that, you need to prove it. You can't just *assume* a greyish-white stain on a skirt is semen: it could be a milk spill or toothpaste, or a drip from a medicine bottle – or a dozen other things. The police had a match to Mitchell from the skin cells under the victim's fingernails and the love-bite – so they assumed it was his semen on her clothes. But Mitchell was one of Kelli Rees's regular customers – he would almost certainly have worn a condom, so he wouldn't have left semen stains on her clothing. Mitchell's defence should never have allowed that to go unchallenged.'

Lazko grinned. 'See – that's why I wanted you on the case – you've just given us a new suspect.'

Fennimore winced. 'You're jumping to the same conclusion the prosecution did. We don't know *what* those stains are. First, we need to find out. Then, *if* they are semen, and *if* the DNA isn't too degraded for testing, it *could* give you the DNA profile of another suspect, but if it's a match to Mitchell, it will only strengthen the prosecution's case.'

Lazko nodded, still frowning. 'You're saying it's a risk.'

Fennimore fixed him with a hard stare. 'Get this through your thick skull – I'm not out to prove Mitchell's innocence, I'm here to find the truth.'

After a moment's hesitation, Lazko gave another quick nod of agreement. 'All right. What next?'

'We need to request analysis of those stains. We'll need to arrange with Essex Police and their preferred crime lab to examine the evidence. At a minimum, they'll want their crime scene manager and the forensic scientist who advised them on the case to be present. It could take six weeks; any complications, you can double that.'

Lazko smirked. 'I think we can do better than that. Mitchell's lawyers have been working on this for months – they requested access to all the physical evidence five weeks back – all you need to do is agree a date.'

Fennimore raised an eyebrow. 'And you didn't think to mention this?'

Lazko shrugged. 'You said you wanted to do things your way.'

He was right – Fennimore wouldn't have taken the case if Lazko were constantly at his elbow feeding him snippets of information.

'Okay,' Fennimore said, forcing the tension out of his shoulders. 'I'll talk to Mitchell's legal team, make sure the police don't inadvertently leave the clothing off the inventory.'

'Great. I've got to head back home, but I'll be in touch.'

'Surely you're not leaving?' Fennimore said in mock sorrow.

The reporter grimaced. 'I just got word my flat's been broken into – they trashed the place.'

Fennimore didn't know how to respond. He couldn't bring himself to commiserate with the man, but after a second's hesitation, he said, 'I'll see you out.'

He waited until Lazko was out of sight, and was about to go back up to his flat when a Post Office van drew up.

The driver poked his head out of the window. 'Professor Fennimore?'

'That's me.'

'Special delivery.' The postman ducked back in the van and picked up an envelope and his hand-held scanner from the passenger seat.

Back in his flat, Fennimore slit the envelope open with a kitchen knife. There was no letter, only a newspaper clipping. He tipped the flimsy strip on to the counter. It curled as it fell, straightening as it slid across the marble surface.

The headline read: FEARS FOR MISSING MOTHER AND CHILD.

He felt a stab of horror, thinking, *Rachel, Suzie*.

With the tip of the knife, he turned over the slip of newsprint. On the reverse, a scrawled message:

'Do I have your attention?'

14

The true art of questioning is to discover what the
pupil does know or is capable of knowing.

ALBERT EINSTEIN

Aberdeen, Saturday

Crank, Fennimore thought. *Has to be*. It wouldn't be the
first time someone had faked a newspaper article to look
like news of Rachel and Suzie. Even so, his mouth went dry
and his heart thudded against his ribcage. Those others had
been photocopies rigged up to look like the real thing, but
this had the feel of genuine newsprint. He leaned closer and
sniffed, caught a faint whiff of printers' ink; everything about
this flimsy strip of paper seemed chillingly real. He carefully
flipped the cutting again and read the text: a woman named
Julia Myers and her daughter Lauren were missing. Police had
put out an appeal for information.

Fennimore went to his laptop, leaving the envelope and
its contents where they lay. The abductions filled three pages
in the *Manchester Evening News*: they had vanished on their
way home to Prestwich, just north of Manchester, after
watching a film at Salford Quays multiplex cinema – a treat

84

to celebrate Lauren's sixth birthday. He checked the date: three days ago.

Fennimore returned to the marble kitchen counter and stared hard at the small slip of paper and the envelope, trying to glean every possible detail as he speed-dialled Kate Simms.

In the second before Kate spoke, he heard music playing, a peal of childish laughter: her son, Timmy.

'Nick,' she said, a smile in her voice. 'Can this wait? I—'

'The Myers case,' he said, 'are you investigating?'

'Me personally?' She laughed. 'I've only been home a day and a half, Nick.'

'Kate, I think I've had a message from the abductor.'

'Internet?' she asked, all trace of humour gone.

'A press clipping.'

The sounds of family life became muted as she covered the mouthpiece and he found himself straining to hear the boy's voice. He heard Kate say, 'I need to take this, Mum.' Then a door closed and the background noise was abruptly silenced.

'What have you got?' she demanded.

'A fifteen-by-ten-centimetre white envelope. Postmark: Manchester; special delivery.' He read the tracking number from the label and waited for her to repeat it back to him. 'Handwriting on the envelope and the back of the cutting; it looks like biro.' He turned the envelope with the tip of the knife blade and scrutinized the seal. 'Gummed flap.' *Evidence*, he was thinking, *DNA*, knowing he didn't have to say it, because Simms's thoughts would mirror his own.

'The guy's an amateur,' Simms said, and in the long, interconnected corridors of Fennimore's memory, an echo reverberated. 'But what makes you so sure it's the abductor?' she asked.

'The message on the back of the cutting,' Fennimore said. 'It reads: "Do I have your attention?"'

He heard a slow release of breath at the other end of the line.

'I'll talk to the senior investigating officer, get back to you,' Simms said. 'Meanwhile, you know what to do.'

He should: Fennimore had helped write the protocols for evidence collection in the days when UK policing still had a government-funded Forensic Science Service. He needed equipment and that meant a trip to his office – ten minutes each way – another twenty to gather what he needed. But he was reluctant to leave the evidence unguarded; he felt an almost superstitious dread that he would return to find the envelope and slip of newsprint gone. The statistician in him disparaged this as a gut response to the way Lazko had dodged the building's security system, but the break-in at the journalist's flat was objective proof that nowhere could be entirely secure.

He dialled Josh's mobile number. The student sounded wary at first, perhaps waiting for Fennimore to name his new supervisor. Fennimore outlined the situation.

'Tell me what you need,' Josh said.

Josh arrived in under thirty minutes with a scene kit, camera and the extras Fennimore had requested, sealed inside a clear plastic bag. There was no need for scene suits: Fennimore's DNA was already on the evidence, but he opened a fresh pack of nitriles and gloved up. Josh closed the door and followed his example, but remained by the doorway while Fennimore returned to the kitchen counter and placed sample boxes, labels and sterile equipment to hand. This done, he took the scene kit camera out of the case Josh had brought. He had a photocopier but using it would destroy the evidence: the static charge on a photocopier glass could suck up fibres more effectively than any vacuum cleaner. So he photographed the envelope and the cutting, turning them with disposable forceps to get both sides.

Although Josh remained silent during the entire process, Fennimore was conscious of his intense scrutiny. As he reached for the first evidence box, Josh asked, 'Why boxes and not evidence bags?'

'You tell me,' Fennimore said.

'Uh – there could be indented writing on the evidence?'

'And you wouldn't want to mess that up,' Fennimore said, regretting that he'd spoken. He always found it hard to resist a teaching opportunity – but he didn't want to give Josh hope of a permanent reprieve: he'd needed assistance, and he knew the student was on campus when few others were, that was all.

He signed the CJA evidence label, thinking ruefully that Simms would chalk this up as another example of his using people, building their hopes, only to drop them when they had outlived their usefulness. He lifted the envelope carefully into the first box, sealing the lid along every edge with one continuous strip of Sellotape, signing it in two places along each edge, taking care to write half on the tape and half on the box. Even if someone peeled the tape off without tearing it, they would never match it perfectly to the signatures if they tried to reseal it. Finally, he added the exhibit label, taping just one edge, so that the chain of custody details could be completed on the reverse by the police. He signature-sealed that, too.

His mobile phone rang as he lifted the slip of newsprint into the second box.

'Probably DCI Simms,' Fennimore said. 'Put her on speaker, will you?'

Josh moved to the dining table and picked up Fennimore's phone.

'Kate, you're on speakerphone,' Fennimore said. 'Josh Brown is with me.'

Her momentary silence said everything he needed to know about her distrust of the young doctoral student; that distrust was reflected in Josh's eyes and magnified by an unease that Fennimore still hadn't fathomed.

'Two detectives are on their way to take custody of the evidence,' Simms said. 'Should be with you in about six hours.' She gave him their names and hung up.

'They're taking the evidence across the border?' Josh hadn't spoken a word while Kate was on the line.

'They'll probably drop them into the forensics lab in Chorley – it's the nearest to Manchester,' Fennimore said, stacking the second sealed box on top of the first.

'Quicker to process it here, surely?' Josh said.

'England and Scotland have different evidential protocols,' Fennimore said. 'English courts expect police to abide by English protocols.'

Josh nodded, non-committal.

Finally, Fennimore swabbed the area of the counter where the evidence had lain, using sterile medical swabs: one dry; one wet with sterile distilled water; and a third, unopened, as a control sample. He placed them in the same evidence bag. Fennimore rarely did crime scene processing, but he enjoyed the meticulous nature of evidence collection; the precision, the attention to detail, had a soothing effect on him. This kind of task required complete attention – like the rock climbing he would escape to when his regrets became too painful – only with less risk of broken bones.

When he had the last lot of labelling finished, Fennimore straightened up.

'All done,' he said.

'I'll shoot off, then,' Josh said, reaching for the door handle.

Fennimore knew he was anxious about the two police officers still hours away from Aberdeen.

'Josh?'

The student turned back.

'Thanks,' Fennimore said.

'No problem,' Josh said, but Fennimore could see that mentally he was already out of the building, merging with the crowds, safely anonymous.

15

Chief Inspector Kate Simms pulled into the car park of Greater Manchester Police's new glass-fronted headquarters. It was 8:10 p.m., and she had been called in to a meeting with Chief Constable Enderby. Simms had ten days' leave owing, and she'd promised her family she would take them, but Enderby had arranged the placement with St Louis PD after her first murder investigation the winter before. Brutally punishing, that investigation had made her a few enemies on the force and the St Louis assignment had given her breathing space she needed – a few hours out of her leave wasn't much to ask in return.

She rode the elevator to his office, prepared to chat about her American trip and congratulating herself on how it had changed her fortunes at work. A few months ago she'd been a mistrusted outsider – worse still, an officer from the Met – tainted by scandal after the disappearance of Fennimore's wife and child. But the success of the joint US/UK taskforce investigation had earned her the respect of others on the force, as well as the approval of the chief constable.

The first surprise was seeing Professor Varley sitting in one of the chief constable's easy chairs, his long, undertaker's face lugubrious and unsmiling. The second was seeing a tech seated at Enderby's desk, working on multiple screens, positioning and freezing frames, tapping, pinching or splaying his fingers on the glass to shrink or enlarge the images, repositioning them like an impresario conjuring up a light show.

'Kate!' Enderby came around the desk to shake her hand. Simms dragged her gaze from the swirl of colour and light on the monitors to give her boss her full attention.

'Congratulations on your American placement,' he said. 'Your triumph made national news on both sides of the pond – did you know?'

'It was a team effort, sir,' she said modestly, feeling Varley's flat-eyed stare on her. When they first met, the psychologist had been dismissive of her – as both a non-scientist and a woman – but he had advised on the American investigation and she had sensed a change in his attitude during that time, perhaps even the beginnings of a grudging respect.

'Professor Varley is advising on the Myers abduction,' Enderby said. 'You've been following the case?'

'Only what I've seen on the news,' she said. 'Is this about the letter Nick Fennimore got yesterday?'

'John is one of our IT specialists,' Enderby said, sidestepping her question.

John raised one hand in greeting, but kept his eyes on the array of screens. 'In a moment, he'll take us through the sequence of events immediately prior to the disappearance of Mrs Myers and her little girl.'

'Ready,' the tech said.

They stood in a loose arc around his chair.

'We had to extract footage from CCTV and traffic cams along the route,' he said, 'so the quality is variable. If you look in the bottom left of each screen, you will see a time stamp.'

The first short sequence showed mother and child in the leisure park, Julia Myers grim-looking and determined, half-dragging the child along a footpath. Suddenly, the child broke away, made a dash for the road, straight into the path of a car. Simms's heart contracted and she gasped. The men had clearly seen the footage before, because none of them reacted. The tech tapped the next still image and it sprung to life. Mrs Myers, with her little girl in her arms, lifted the boot-lid of her car a few inches and slammed it, still soothing a tearful Lauren. She disappeared for a second.

'She's buckling Lauren into the child seat in the back of the car, there,' the tech explained. The next clip jerked forward in a series of three-second bursts as they moved out of the range of one camera and into the next. Checking the time stamps, Simms calculated that it took the pair ten minutes to get from the parking bay to the car park exit.

'Everything seems fine until about a mile down the road,' the tech said, tapping a new section of the screen. 'This is a traffic cam at the intersection with the A56.'

The car veered erratically, bumped the kerb, swerved, narrowly missed a car, corrected and then almost ran into the back of a lorry at a traffic light. As they drove through the lights, Julia Myers was still at the wheel, but she looked terrified.

'That's the last anyone saw of the car,' Enderby said. 'Until it was found abandoned five hours later.'

'The abductor was inside the car,' Simms said, a cold

hollowness seeping into the pit of her stomach. 'He ambushed them.'

'It looks like it,' Enderby said, his face grim.

She thought back through the sequence. 'If he broke into the car and hid in the boot while it was parked at the leisure complex—'

'He should be on the security cameras,' Enderby finished for her.

'We checked frame-by-frame – got nothing,' the tech said. 'It's possible he used the cover of other vehicles.'

'We found the car burned out behind an abandoned furniture outlet about half a mile away,' Enderby said. 'The back seat is split-fold – half of it had been folded down – the abductor must have released the lock but held it upright. When he saw his chance, he crawled out of the boot into the car. And he must've had a second car waiting.'

'Tyre tracks?' Simms said.

Enderby nodded. 'The wheelbase and treads suggest an SUV – we hope to get a more precise identification soon.'

Simms said, 'I'm a bit vague on that part of the city, but I'm thinking small–scale factory units and retail?'

'A fair percentage empty or even derelict,' Enderby confirmed. 'Teams have searched every empty building in a two-mile radius and found no trace.'

Simms looked from Enderby to Varley. The senior investigating officer must have briefed the chief constable on the details; she couldn't help wondering why he wasn't present – and why Enderby had called her in at this late hour – and on a Sunday.

'Question, Kate?'

'I spoke with the SIO leading the case yesterday; I know

he already has a full complement of detectives and support staff assigned to it, so . . .'

'You're wondering why you're here?'

Kate answered Enderby with a nod.

He thanked the tech and asked him to give them a minute. Simms watched the tech leave with a qualm of unease.

'The letter Professor Fennimore received,' Enderby said.

'You've got the lab results?'

He nodded. 'No indentation, no fibres. But they recovered spores – fungus or mould – a mycologist is looking at them as we speak. And there were fingerprints – as you'd expect. A few were matched to Fennimore, but the rest gave no hits on AFIS.'

'It was special delivery,' Simms said. 'The tracking number—'

'It was posted at a small sub-post office,' Enderby said. 'Their CCTV was out of action. The postmistress remembered an adult man in a baseball cap. That's the best description she was able to provide.'

'What about the seal on the envelope?'

'Fennimore was right,' Enderby said, his face tense. 'It was a gummed seal and it *had* been moistened with saliva.'

Simms felt a little kick of excitement under her ribcage. 'They found DNA?'

Enderby nodded and the two men exchanged glances, like that was a bad thing.

'What?' Simms said.

The chief constable spoke, his face solemn: 'Kate – the DNA on the envelope is a match to Julia Myers.'

'The mother,' Kate said softly.

Enderby nodded.

'He forced Julia to lick the seal, then he sent it to Fennimore?'

'Which suggests the abductor has a psychological connection with Fennimore,' Professor Varley said.

Simms resisted the temptation to say, 'You *think*?' – Varley did not take sarcasm well. Instead, she spoke directly to the chief constable: 'Sir, why am I here?'

'I like Nick Fennimore,' Enderby said. 'He's done valuable, even brilliant work in the interests of justice. But he is liable to be—'

'Unpredictable,' Varley said.

'A bit of a loose cannon,' Enderby said, as if that sounded any better.

Simms didn't like where this was going.

'The abductor seems to want to engage with Fennimore,' Varley explained. 'If Fennimore decides he can do better than the police—'

'*Professor* Fennimore has passed on everything he's received,' Simms interrupted.

Varley flashed her a chilly smile. 'So far.'

Arrogant tosser. She focused her gaze on Enderby. 'Sir . . .'

'History has proved that the professor is not above withholding information,' Enderby said, his tone reasonable but firm. 'If he does, I want to know.'

So that was it; she was here because, like the abductor, she had a connection with Fennimore. 'You want me to spy on him.'

'I want you to keep me briefed, Chief Inspector,' Enderby countered, implacable.

16

I cannot think of any need in childhood as strong
as the need for a father's protection.

SIGMUND FREUD

Aberdeen, Sunday

Fennimore sat back and rubbed his eyes; the Paris surveillance
had become an obsession. He needed a distraction, but he
was still waiting for Essex Police to agree a date for him to
examine the victim's clothing in the Mitchell case. He could
get started on the process of emptying his office in Andrew
Street ready for the property developers to move in, but he
sagged at the thought of it. So instead, he turned to his other
obsession and checked Suzie's Facebook page. A new post
awaited his approval. Fennimore characterized himself as an
objective scientist and a hard-headed realist, but sometimes, on
the point of viewing one of these postings, even as his finger
hovered over the mouse button, he would fantasize a message:
'Daddy, please come and get me.' Suzie, assertive, coherent,
commanding him to act. She would supply an address, even a
photograph, so that he didn't have to imagine what damage
more than five years in a void had done to his little girl.

Of course, it wasn't from Suzie – they never were.

'There's two kinds of people doomed to repeat the same mistakes over and over,' the message read. 'Arrogant pricks who think they can never be wrong, and the incurably stupid. Seems you've got a bit of both in you, Fennimore.'

Another rant. He quelled the inevitable disappointment and tapped the mouse pad, seeking out the delete option onscreen. But a phrase further down the message caught his eye: 'What goes around comes around.' Where had he read that before? 'Just remember,' the message ended, 'everything – all of it – it's all on your head.'

His heart contracted, seemed to hold still for a beat, then kicked in again. He knew those words. He grabbed his jacket and keys and ran, crossing Union Terrace Gardens at a sprint, rounding the corner into St Andrew Street and entering the university building in under five minutes. He took the stairs to his office two at a time, his footsteps booming through the empty building, ID card ready in his hand. He waved it over the proximity reader. The LED flashed red. He tried again. Again, red. For one wild, paranoid moment he thought he was locked out, but he took a breath and tried one more time; the reader flashed green and he heard the door latch click open.

The phrasing of the Facebook message was almost identical to the hate mail he'd received after his lecture went live on YouTube. Buff envelope, special delivery: 'If you're such a genius, why can't you find your own daughter?' The accusation still burned. And the taunt – *or threat?*: 'What goes around comes around.'

He needed to find that note.

It wasn't on his desk. He recalled lobbing it at the bin. But the rubbish bin wasn't beside his desk. He cursed the efficiency of the cleaning staff, already thinking how he might access the inner courtyard where the building's rubbish silos were stored. Then he remembered Lazko's letter of apology: he had binned the journalist's self-serving bullshit and then hoofed the basket across the room. He peeked behind the door, and let his breath go in a whoosh. There it was, jammed in the corner, the wire mesh dented on one side, and yes – still brimming with junk mail. He snatched it up, ready to tip the lot out on the floor, but stopped just in time: in reality, the cleaning staff rarely made it all the way up to his eyrie – and never, to his knowledge, with a vacuum cleaner. He scouted the room for something clean to cover the scuzzy carpet and his eye lighted on a roll of black bin bags on his desk. A Post-it note in the office manager's handwriting read, 'You'll be needing these.'

'Joan,' he murmured, spreading two bags, overlapping, on the floor, 'you are a pearl among women.'

He emptied a jumble of torn paper and envelopes on to the plastic, but there was no sign of the letter. Cursing, he dragged out boxes and files from under his desk and away from the walls. Still nothing. Then he saw it – to the right of the door – a balled-up letter and crumpled buff envelope, wedged between a bookcase and one of his plastic storage boxes.

He snapped on a pair of nitriles and gently lifted the ball of paper from its hiding place. With index finger and thumb, he gingerly eased out a corner of the envelope. He remembered that he had slit it open with his paper knife, that it had been sent special delivery, just like the news cutting, and – just like the cutting – it had a gummed seal. He went to his office window and, holding the crinkled ball up to the setting rays of the sun, saw a tiny, brownish stain in the corner of the envelope flap. *Paper cut*, he thought. *Blood*.

He placed the ball of paper on a clean bin bag and speed-dialled Kate Simms. She sounded awkward.

'Are you okay?' he said. 'Can we talk?' He wondered for a moment if her husband was close by.

'I'm in Chief Constable Enderby's office,' she explained. 'Professor Varley's here, too. I'm putting you on speaker-phone.'

So Manchester Police were consulting with Alistair Varley. He seemed to be their go-to guy for psychological insights.

Fennimore explained about the Facebook message. 'It reminded me of a letter I received, earlier in the week. I have that letter in my hand now.'

'Surely, your recent . . . *debut* on YouTube has made you something of a target for social media trolls?' Varley's soupy drawl suggested he held publicity-seeking media trollops in as much contempt as the trolls that persecuted them.

Fennimore was not about to explain himself to Varley. He bit down on his irritation and said evenly, 'This is not just another troll.'

'What makes you so sure?'

'The evidence,' Fennimore said, knowing he was on firm ground. 'My lecture appeared on YouTube on Monday. I got this letter – buff envelope, special delivery – on Wednesday. Like you, I thought it was run-of-the-mill hate mail – I screwed it up and lobbed it at the waste basket. Saturday, I get the newspaper cutting, and today, this Facebook message.'

'Ye-es,' Varley said. 'But I don't see how they are linked.'

'The wording,' Fennimore said. 'The Facebook message is almost identical in phrasing to the letter I have here.'

'Didn't you say you'd balled the thing up?' Varley said. It was unthinkable that Fennimore would risk interfering with the evidence.

'He's working from memory,' Simms said, and Fennimore thought he heard a protective pride in her voice.

'How . . . impressive,' Varley said, no doubt with a theatrical roll of his eyes.

Fennimore refused to be rattled. 'He mentions Suzie – her abduction.' He had that by heart, too, but he wasn't about to repeat it. 'It finishes: "What goes around comes around. Everything – all of it – it's all on your head."'

Varley had worked with them on language pattern analysis in the United States. It had helped them to solve the case, so he would know they could not ignore the similarities between the two messages.

'Package the evidence up,' Enderby said. 'I'll ask the investigating officer to arrange collection.'

Fennimore told them about the fleck of reddish-brown staining, the gummed envelope flap; they all knew it could lead them to the killer.

Simms said, 'Sir?' and Fennimore had the sense that she was asking for permission to speak.

'Go ahead,' Enderby said.

'Nick, we got DNA from the envelope you were sent yesterday.' A slight hesitation. 'It's the mother's.'

'You know what this means?' Varley said. 'The abductor—'

'Is playing games,' Fennimore interrupted, not wanting to hear it from Varley.

'It's personal,' Varley said. 'He has singled you out – he probably planted the victim's blood on this envelope, too.'

'If there *is* DNA on this letter, you can be sure it won't

be Julia and Lauren's,' Fennimore said. 'I received this letter by special delivery on Wednesday – the day Julia and Lauren Myers were taken, which means he would have to've posted it on Tuesday – the day *before* the abduction.'

'All right,' Varley said. 'But he is forensically aware – I can't believe he would be so stupid as to deposit his *own* DNA on the first letter.'

'I'm not the psychologist,' Fennimore said, 'but I'm guessing he was angry when he wrote it. He must have known I'd have a lot of that junk to sort through after the YouTube farrago – maybe he was banking on it – I *did* nearly throw the damn thing out.'

'I'll have someone to you by mid-morning tomorrow.' Enderby, at least, sounded convinced.

Fennimore checked his watch. 'I've missed the last flight out of Aberdeen, but if I catch the first morning departure, *I* could have the evidence with you by eight-thirty,' he said.

'No.' Enderby seemed determined. 'Box it up and stay where you are. What *you* need to do is think who might be targeting you. The SIO will need a list of cases you've worked on – this could be someone you helped to put away.'

Fennimore debated. He didn't want to piss Enderby off and risk being barred all access. 'Okay – if someone can send me the investigating officer's contact details, I'll liaise with him.'

'DCI Simms will be your point of contact,' Enderby said. His tone brooked no argument.

Fennimore wasn't particularly good at reading people, but he wished he could see their faces now. Was Kate Simms to be the *cordon sanitaire* between him and the investigation?

'Nick?' Simms said; his silence had gone on too long.

'I'll put you in my favourites,' he said, and regretted it immediately. This wasn't Kate's doing. He knew damn well that she wouldn't ask to be his minder – she had stood between him and an investigation before, and that hadn't ended too well for her. In the months after Rachel and Suzie disappeared, he had manipulated and cajoled and coerced Simms into breaking just about every rule in the Murder Manual. It was Simms who had been battered by the media storm that followed, while he ran and buried himself in academe. Fennimore would hate to compromise her in that way again, but if this was linked to Suzie's disappearance – however obliquely – he couldn't guarantee to play by the rules. Not even for Kate.

17

Abduction, Day 6

'Mummy?'

Julia Myers fought to turn her head. What *was* that noise – a loose bolt? The exhaust housing? The constant jangle of metal on metal made the hairs rise on her arms; she wanted to turn and look behind her but she had to face forward, keep her eyes on the road; it was so *dark*. What had happened to the headlights? Why couldn't she see any streetlights?

'Mummy.'

Lauren. She sounded frightened.

'Mumm-ee!'

Something was in the car – she felt, rather than saw, a black shadow.

'Lauren?' Julia turns, wrenching her shoulder; she feels something tear around the socket. She wakes, struggling to make sense of her surroundings: the smell of damp, the cold; the ache in her right arm. The burning pain in her wrist. She remembers. The rattle in the car, the sudden void where the seat-back should be. The thing emerging from the shadows like something from a horror movie—

Lauren is calling her.

'Lauren – baby – Mummy's here. What's the matter?'

'You were crying.'

Julia wipes her eyes. 'All right, poppet. Just a bad dream, that's all.'

A ring of fire encircles her wrist. Even the slightest movement sends jolts of pain through her shoulder. She has tried everything, but she can't break free.

On the fourth day, they had heard a police helicopter overhead; it shone a knife-blade of silver light through the gap in the displaced boarding of the skylight, and for five heart-racing minutes they really thought they were going to be rescued. But it went away, spiralling up and up, the clatter and buzz of its rotor blades becoming fainter and more indistinct, until it was gone.

She leans across and starts gnawing at the plastic binding on her wrist. Her saliva sears the torn flesh. *Tissues. I need to protect the skin under it.* She reaches down for her handbag and screams as the muscles give in her shoulder.

Lauren wails.

'All right – *shhh*, now, it's all right,' she soothes, reaching inside the bag, feeling for the few remaining tissues. The bag tilts and she almost drops it. Something shifts, sliding from one end to the other. She tilts it back in the other direction, feels something hard move and slide again. Sweat breaks out on her upper lip. *There's something inside the lining.* She pokes about, finds a small hole, tears it wider. Her fingers close on cold metal. *Scissors.* Her nail scissors must have slipped inside the lining.

She goes to work on her wrist binding, and ten minutes later, with both arms free, Julia can reach across the
three-foot gap that separates them. Lauren has never been a
cuddly child; from infancy she was all bone and sinew and
savagely beating heart, but now she falls into her mother's
arms and they hold each other fiercely. Julia kisses the top
of her little girl's head, smelling the biscuity odour of sweat
mingled with damp plaster dust. 'We have to be quick,
sweetie,' she says.

She feels Lauren twist in her arms, peering frantically over
her shoulder in the direction of the door. 'Is he coming?'

'I don't know. But I want to get far away from here as soon
as possible. Okay?'

She feels Lauren's head bob in agreement, and she pinches
and pecks at the plastic tie around her daughter's ankle with
the tiny blades of the nail scissors. Her hands are still sore
from trying to break open the water bottle, but she grits her
teeth and carries on. After a minute or two, the blades twist
and the scissors buckle. The points scrape Lauren's ankle.

'Ow!' she shouts. 'You *hurt* me.'

'I'm sorry, darling. Sh-shhh,' Julia soothes. 'Nearly there.'

Lauren squirms, crying, trying to pull away, but Julia grips
her daughter's foot tightly, trying to hold it steady as she cuts
through the last of the binding. This done, she turns to the
plastic on her own ankle. Lauren moves to sit next to her,
drying her eyes and snuffling disconsolately.

'There's some tissues in my bag,' Julia says. A second later,
Lauren is blowing her nose.

For a few minutes, Julia scrapes and picks at the binding
with the blunted and now distinctly wobbly scissors, while
Lauren rummages in her handbag.

'*Mummy* . . .' Lauren gasps. 'You told a big fib.' She hears wonder and shock in her daughter's voice.

'Mmm?' Julia says, sweat stinging her eyes as she works on the stubborn loop of plastic around her ankle.

'*You* said you threw my sweeties away.'

Julia groans inwardly. *Those bloody sweets.*

'They're bad for you, darling.' She holds her hand out for the handbag. Her daughter scoots out of reach. 'Lauren, don't you dare . . .'

She hears a busy crunching as Lauren stuffs sweets into her mouth. 'Lauren – you *stop* that.' She works the scissors furiously. Suddenly, they buckle again and snap in two. Julia screams in agony as one of the blades drives deep into her flesh.

'Mummy!'

Julia breathes fast, hyperventilating to control the pain, then pulls the blade out by the handle, biting down on another scream.

'Mummy – I didn't mean it!'

'I know,' Julia says. A wave of nausea sweeps over her and she is suddenly cold. 'It's all right.' She clamps her hand over the wound and feels a warm trickle of blood through her fingers. 'Not your fault. Just pass me the handbag.'

She wads up a few tissues and binds them in place with the silk binding torn from her blanket using one blade of the nail scissors. Her hands sticky with blood, she rotates the ankle binding and with grim determination resumes scraping at the plastic. A minute later, she begins to feel weak.

'There's blood on the floor,' Lauren wails. 'Mummy, I'm sorry.'

'I know that, love.' She tears more silk from the blanket edging and tries again to staunch the wound. The dressing is soaked; she must have punctured a vein.

106

Oh, my poor little girl . . .

'Come here,' she says. 'Come and sit with me.' Lauren moves closer, and Julia feels the welcome weight of her daughter against her body. She hugs Lauren, stroking her hair, feeling grit and dirt sticking to the blood on her fingers.

She thinks about flinging the sweets into the far corner of the room, but a clear-eyed rationality stops her.

'Lauren, you know why Grandma calls you her Yellow Peril, don't you?'

Lauren bows her head. 'Because the yellow sweeties make me be horrible.' Even in the dark, Julia can make out the tormented look in daughter's eyes. 'I *try* to be good, Mummy – but it's like there's someone inside me *making* me be naughty.'

'Yes. That's because of the stuff they use to make the colours.'

'I won't be naughty, this time,' says Lauren.

'I know it sounds strange,' Julia answers. 'But just this once, I *want* you to be Grandma's Yellow Peril.'

Lauren gasps, twisting on her lap. 'Why?'

'To keep you safe.'

'But I nearly got squished by a car after the film. You said I could of been *killed*. You *always* say I do silly things when I eat E-numbers.'

'You also do brave things,' Julia says. She has never before described Lauren's hyperactive behaviour as anything but naughty and reckless and silly. But sometimes there *is* a kind of bravery in her daughter's wild disregard for her own safety.

'But it will make me do something bad.' Lauren begins to cry again. 'Tha— that's why the man came and got us and locked us up.'

107

'No!' Julia says. '*No*.' She takes her daughter's face in her hands. 'Lauren – this *isn't your fault*. He's just a bad man and we were unlucky he picked on us.'

Lauren's breathing hitches and she wipes her nose with the palm of her hand.

'Remember the princess in the film?' Julia says. 'She thought *she* was a bad girl because when she sang the high notes, all the mirrors and windows in the castle would shatter.'

She feels Lauren nod.

'She was naughty,' Lauren says. 'Because sometimes she did it just to upset the King and Queen, and everyone was very cross with her and she had to sit in a corner and BE QUIET.'

Julia can feel her gesturing sternly.

'But they changed their minds, didn't they, when the town got overrun by rats and the Piper-man held them all to ransom?' Another nod, more hesitant this time, and Julia can tell that Lauren is trying to follow her line of reasoning. 'What did they do, Lauren?'

Lauren squirms in her lap, leaning back into her like it's story-time, and Julia wraps her arms around her.

'The King and the Queen and the prince and the mayor and all the people of the town went to her and begged her *not* to be quiet,' Lauren says. 'So she sang very high and very, *very* loud and all the rats ran away.'

'That's right.'

'And all the dogs came from miles around – "From the fields and the forests, from the barns and the backyards, baying and barking and killing the rats as they fled, eager to do her bidding,"' Lauren quotes perfectly.

'She didn't know it, but her worst fault was also her secret *superpower*,' Lauren whispers. 'Like your ADHD.' Lauren's hair tickles Julia's skin as she turns again to study her and in the gloom, Julia thinks she sees puzzlement in her daughter's face. 'It *was* naughty of the princess to use her superpower to break windows,' she explains. 'But when she used it to chase away the rats . . .'

'Everyone loved her and she broke the Piper-man into a thousand pieces!' Lauren is quiet for a time, then her voice fills with wonder: 'Mummy, have I *really* got a superpower?'

'Well, the nasty man *is* scared of you . . . Remember when you screamed and kicked and he left you alone?'

'Mm . . .' Lauren plucks at her T-shirt. 'But he wears a mask like a super-villain. So maybe *he's* got superpowers, too.'

'Now you *know* superheroes are always stronger than super-villains,' Julia says.

Lauren sighs as if it's all too complicated.

'He *is* scared of you, Lauren, and that's a good thing,' Julia says, bringing her back to the point. 'He's most scared of all when you get hyper, so . . .'

'I've got to eat the sweeties and be bad?' Lauren still sounds unsure.

'Lauren, I want you to be the naughtiest little girl in the whole world.'

'But—'

The sound of a car engine outside the building makes her stop. They both listen; the engine is silenced. Julia strains to hear. He has always come on foot the other times. What does this mean?

'He's here,' Lauren whispers.

Their abductor unlocks the padlock and Julia hears the rattle of the chain as he unthreads it from the hasp. She seizes Lauren's bony shoulders, fighting a woozy sickness. 'Listen to me, Lauren. I want you to scare him like the princess scared the Piper-man. But you have to keep far away from him.'

'*How*, Mummy? We're locked *in*.'

'Yes, but there are places you can hide.' Julia casts about for inspiration. In the almost dark, she can make out the hulking shapes of the giant metal looms. 'You're a good climber – I want you to climb high up, out of reach,' she adds, thinking, *Please don't fall*. 'Okay?'

The door creaks open and Lauren pants, terrified.

'Quick,' Julia orders. 'Gather up as much food as you can find. Hide it. Then climb. Climb as high as you can.' She catches a gleam of fear in her daughter's eyes and gives her one hard shake. 'Do you hear me, Lauren Myers? If he finds you, run away. If he tries to grab you, spit and scream and kick. Are you *listening*? Be brave, like the princess, and don't believe anything the bad man says. Mummy and Daddy love you. And you're allowed to be naughty because *I say so*.'

18

No amount of experimentation can ever prove me
right; a single experiment can prove me wrong.

ATTRIBUTED TO ALBERT EINSTEIN

Cambridgeshire, Tuesday

They say it pays to advertise, but over the years UK forensic
labs and their employees have had anthrax in envelopes, letter-
bombs in jiffy bags. Added to that, ram-raids, fire-bombs and
cyber-hacks, while not always an immediate threat, were
certainly a background hum in their working lives. So, when
it came to advertising, forensics services tended to err on the
side of caution. Click on a website's 'Contact us' link, you'll
get a PO Box number; paste the post code into Google, the
closest you'll get to a physical location is a Royal Mail sorting
office. Which was why Fennimore was driving down a quiet
lane in Cambridgeshire, navigating the old-fashioned way, by
road signs and landmarks, a map open on the seat next to him.

He pulled the car off a two-lane A-road on to a business
park like any other in the south-east of England, except there
was just one building – an unassuming four-storey concrete-
and-steel structure. He had visited this lab a few times when

he worked for the National Crime Faculty, so he recognized it for what it was, but come upon it by chance, and you might mistake it for an office supplies business – except for the ram-proof steel bollards set three feet apart in front of the building.

Essex Police had arranged for him to take samples of the stains on the victim's skirt as part of his evidence review for the Mitchell case. Fennimore had taken an early flight from Aberdeen to London City airport – a ninety-minute trip. From London, it was another hour's drive by hire car to the lab.

The forensic scientist acting for Essex Police met him in the foyer. Doctor Jane Wilton was tall, her grey hair cropped close to her head; Fennimore had met her a couple of times at conferences. She offered and he declined refreshments and the use of the facilities, and within minutes they were in a dressing area outside the lab, getting kitted out in hairnets, long-cuffed gloves, overshoes and face masks; DNA-free disposable lab coats completed the look.

They exchanged small talk about his journey as they dressed: 'Did you ever think of moving somewhere more convenient?' Dr Wilton asked.

'Convenient for whom?' Fennimore said.

She smiled. He knew from that smile that she knew his history, and that he had once lived and worked at the heart of police forensic policy-making.

They accessed the lab through an ante-room, feeling the positive pressure within force air out into the corridor as the door opened, reducing the chances of stray contaminants entering the lab. Crossing a tacky mat designed to pick up stray particulates from their footwear, they moved on into the cool, filtered air of the lab.

The evidence was already laid out, the chain of custody tag on the evidence bag noting that the skirt had been subjected to testing just two days before Fennimore's visit.

He glanced across the table to Dr Wilton. 'You started the party without me.'

'Can't have it said that the appeal team got in before us,' she said.

'Appeal?' He broke the new seal and laid the skirt on a plastic sheet. The pink linen had been marked in crayon: three neat circles just above the hemline indicating the areas that had been tested. 'Does that mean they're having doubts about Mitchell's guilt?'

She shrugged. 'Jury's out. Though I did get a personal call from the chief constable, urging – how did he put it? – "promptitude".'

Fennimore placed a large sheet of forensic-grade filter paper over the skirt and marked its outline on the sheet. 'Promptitude,' he mused. 'Sounds like an attack of nerves.'

'Caution maybe,' Dr Wilton said. 'Making sure the mistakes of the past don't tarnish him.'

'Oh, yes,' Fennimore remembered. 'He's new to the post, isn't he?'

'Still got the shine on him,' she said.

Fennimore misted the filter paper with distilled, de-ionized water, then placed it damp-side down on the skirt and laid a second sheet of plastic over the top, firmly pressing the area of staining as he spoke. 'So behind closed doors they *are* talking about mistakes?'

'You wouldn't want me to spoil the surprise, would you?' she said, folding her hands neatly in front of her, smiling behind her mask.

Fennimore lifted the filter paper and hung it in the fume cupboard to the side of the room, before misting the entire sheet with acid phosphatase reagent.

'I'm going to apply the Teesside Protocol,' he said. 'Is that okay with you?'

'Knock yourself out,' she said.

The acid phosphatase test was introduced by Stuart Kind in 1957. A colour change from orange to purple indicated the presence of semen. No colour change after two minutes meant no semen. The method had remained unchallenged for half a century – until 2013, when two Teesside University scientists proved that over *three-quarters* of 'press test' samples gave a false negative in the two-minute cut-off period. Horrifying to think of all those men who had got away with rape because of an arbitrary choice made nearly sixty years earlier. But in Fennimore's eyes that was the beauty of science: it wasn't bound by doctrine or belief; all it took to change half a century of accepted practice was for someone to ask the right question. So they waited way past the two-minute cut-off, and at twelve minutes and thirty-one seconds, several purple blotches appeared on the filter paper.

The AP test was presumptive only – a few other bodily fluids could yield the same result – so he followed up with a microscopic examination. The staining was old, and most of the sperm had lost their tails – but they were there all right.

Next, he took samples directly from the linen: wet, dry and control swabs which he would take away for DNA testing. Dr Wilton stepped back to give him more room to work, and when he'd sealed and labelled the last of the samples, Fennimore began packing them into plastic bags for transport.

'I'm guessing you've already submitted your DNA samples for profiling?' he said.

'I have,' Dr Wilton said. Since the point of the exercise was to find out if the semen belonged to Mitchell, her lab would do a one-to-one comparison of the sample profile with Mitchell's DNA already on the national database, and those results would come through days before Fennimore's.

He cocked an eyebrow. He didn't like being behind in the game. 'I'll leave my contact details, in case you feel like sharing – in the interests of collegiality.'

Carl Lazko had agreed to drive over from Chelmsford for a lunchtime meeting. The venue was a country pub a few miles outside of Cambridge. It was sunny, and after the sterile atmosphere of the lab, Fennimore breathed deep of the unfiltered air. The place was busy with retirees and a few business types, but schools weren't out for the summer break just yet, and he managed to find a quiet spot in the beer garden. He had missed breakfast and ordered immediately, tearing quickly through a sandwich and half a pint of the local brew. Forty minutes later, and still no sign of Lazko, Fennimore's phone buzzed. He checked his text messages: 'In bar. U? – Lazko.'

'I'm outside,' Fennimore texted, properly spelling and punctuating his message. 'You're late.'

The reporter emerged from the pub a few minutes later, pale and blinking in the sunshine, carrying a laptop bag and a pint of bitter, already a third down. He moved to the table without comment and dropped on to the bench seat, lifting his right and then his left leg over the rough-hewn timber as though they were dead weights, before swivelling to face

Fennimore. He looked gaunt, as if he'd lost pounds in the few days since they last met.

'Are you all right?' Fennimore asked.

'My flat's a wreck,' Lazko said. 'And dealing with the insurance company is a bloody nightmare.'

'Would some good news cheer you up?'

Lazko leaned forward, gripping his glass with both hands. 'You found semen stains on the skirt?'

Fennimore patted his shoulder bag, stashed in the shade under the table. The journalist's eyes glowed as if he already saw himself installed in the London offices of one of the nationals.

'How long till we know?'

'Under a week,' Fennimore said.

'Can you stay till tomorrow?' Lazko asked. 'I could introduce you to Andrew Haverford, Mitchell's solicitor. He's done most of the donkey work on Mitchell's review.'

'Let's see what the DNA database comes up with first,' Fennimore said. He checked his watch. 'Anyway, I need to head north. It's a four-hour drive to the lab in Chorley and I want to get there before their offices close.'

In fact, he'd chosen to drop the samples into Cellmark in Chorley because he knew the lab was processing the letters from the Myers abductions. He was friendly with a couple of scientists there and might be able to wheedle some information out of them.

Lazko downed the last of his pint. 'I'd better get back myself – I've got the loss adjuster coming in a couple of hours. But before I go' – he lifted his laptop bag on to the table. 'That bloke, calls himself Josh – the one with the anger management issues?'

Fennimore eyed the reporter coolly. 'What about him?'

116

'Well, his name isn't Josh, for starters.'

Fennimore didn't react, and Lazko said, 'You already knew.'

Fennimore inclined his head.

'Well, there's a hell of a lot more I bet you don't know.' Lazko fished in his bag and drew out an A4 document wallet bulging with papers. 'Here – see for yourself.' He placed the folder on the table next to Fennimore's empty plate.

Fennimore slid it back to him. 'Josh's private life is none of my business.'

'You keep it, mate – I don't want it,' Lazko said, holding up his hands.

'Not a good enough story?'

Lazko snorted. 'Oh, it's dynamite. But I wouldn't want some of the faces in that folder to think I've been poking my nose into their affairs.'

The journalist's dark eyes found his and Fennimore saw a shadow of fear behind the bravado.

'Lazko – I didn't ask for this.'

'Well, you got it.' The journalist extricated himself, clumsily swinging his legs back over the seat. 'Just be careful how you use it.' He walked away without looking back.

Fennimore regarded the folder with distaste. He tapped his fingers on the stiff card, wondering if he should follow Lazko into the car park, chuck the damn thing in his face, but finally he scooped it up and jammed it into his shoulder bag.

19

The drive northward was easy under blue skies dotted with white summer cumulus, but turning westward, the clouds gathered, crowding the horizon and blurring the hilltops. As Fennimore skimmed Manchester's outer ring road it began to rain, and by the time he reached the A6 into Chorley a thunderstorm was raging overhead. The windscreen wipers couldn't cope with the sheer volume of water and he slowed to a crawl. Even so, he nearly missed the turn-off to the lab. Rain bounced six inches off the tarmac and he got drenched just rolling down the window to announce his presence at the security barrier.

He signed over the evidence to one of the scientists from the DNA lab at ten minutes to five. A fresh-faced kid who looked young enough to be one of his students.

'Is Bob Levert around?' Fennimore asked.

'Doctor Levert's out,' the youth said.

'Is he likely to be back soon?'

The youth shrugged.

Fennimore mentioned another contact, but apparently she had left two months earlier. It looked like he was out of luck. He wondered how Kate Simms would react if he rang and invited her out for a drink, but she was under orders to report his activities, and Kate always saw through his lies and manipulations. He was almost ready to give up, when the doors opened and a man in a leather hat and calf-length raincoat swept in out of the storm. Fennimore recognized Bob Levert instantly, but as the automatic doors slid shut, cutting off the hammering of the rain on the pavement outside, Levert bent forward, dripping water from the brim of his hat to join the growing pool at his feet. He cursed softly, flicking more from the arms of his raincoat, sending a rainstorm of his own on to the linoleum floor of the foyer.

'Well, look what the rain washed in,' Fennimore said.

Levert straightened up, grinning. 'You're looking a bit on the spongy side yourself, chum,' he said, extending a wet hand. 'What brings you south of the border?'

'Actually, I've been travelling north most of the afternoon. I was in Cambridgeshire, collecting evidence for a case review I'm working on.'

'And you just dropped by for a cuppa?' Levert's eyes twinkled.

'It breaks the journey,' Fennimore said. 'But the fact is I'm using your lab for the analysis.' He nodded in the direction of the youth who, still holding the bagged evidence, was eyeing the two men with open curiosity.

Levert seemed to notice him for the first time. 'Where's your manners, leaving Professor Fennimore standing in the foyer?'

A flush of colour chased across the youth's face and he began to stammer an excuse. Levert shook his head impatiently, sending a fresh spatter of droplets left to right, in an arc. 'Never mind.' Then, to Fennimore, 'Let's get that brew.'

In the kitchen, Levert hung his dripping coat and hat on a chair and ruffled his fingers through his hair. At sixty years of age, there was still plenty of it, though he had turned quite grey. Fennimore wondered how he had taken that: Levert had always been rather vain about his thick black thatch. The room was big enough for four tables and was equipped with a fridge, microwave, kettle and cafetière. With the thunder still growling overhead, Levert brewed fresh coffee and they caught each other up on teaching schedules and university politics – Levert was a visiting professor at Manchester University.

'I hear you've moved to a plush new campus,' Levert said.

Fennimore rolled his eyes.

Levert wrinkled his brow. 'New office, riverside setting – what's not to like?'

'*Smaller* office, *busier* setting,' Fennimore said.

'Sounds like you're having trouble adjusting.'

'I haven't even moved in yet.'

Levert laughed. 'There speaks a man in denial,' he said, handing Fennimore a mug.

'Good coffee,' Fennimore said, refusing to be drawn any further.

'One of the perks of privatization.' Levert watched him speculatively. 'Worth travelling fifty miles out of your way?' Coming to Chorley rather than dropping the samples off at LGC's lab in Wakefield had added at least an hour to Fennimore's journey time.

'We both know why I'm here, Bob,' Fennimore said.

'The Myers case.'

'The letters, yes.'

Levert seemed momentarily surprised, as if he had expected something else. 'You know we got Mrs Myers's DNA from the first one?'

Fennimore nodded. 'It's the second one I'm interested in. I actually received that first. He must have posted it the day *before* he abducted Julia and Lauren Myers. I was hoping he took less care over it.'

Levert shook his head. 'We got nothing, Nick.'

Fennimore felt his eyebrows twitch. 'The seal on the envelope?'

Levert pulled out a chair and sat opposite. 'Moistened with distilled water.'

'The brown stain on the flap?'

'Chicken blood,' Levert said.

Fennimore experienced a dull thud somewhere deep in his chest. Another taunt. Varley was right – the abductor planted the blood, just as he'd planted Julia Myers's DNA on the other envelope.

'We ran all the fingerprints – partials, the lot – through IDENT1,' Levert said. 'No matches. No indented writing on the envelope or paper. No fibres, no hairs, no mould spores.' He paused, giving Fennimore a moment to digest this.

'So the mould spores must be in the environment where the abductor is holding Julia Myers and her little girl.'

Levert inclined his head.

'What do we have on the spores?'

'A mixture of aspergillus and some kind of rust,' Levert said. 'We're culturing them so the mycologist can give us a better identification, but it all takes time.' He glanced out of the window after another rumble of thunder. 'And by then it could be too late for the little girl.'

Fennimore stared at the older man's profile. 'You mean the girl and her mother.'

Levert's eyes snapped to him and Fennimore felt a second thud. 'Julia Myers is dead?'

'You didn't know?' Levert said. 'I thought that was why you were here. Nick, they found her body two hours ago.'

'There was nothing on the radio news,' Fennimore said, his voice sounding hollow to his own ears.

'The police are keeping it quiet till we've gathered what evidence we can from the scene.' He jerked his chin towards the window. 'But this isn't helping.'

Fennimore stared glumly at the storm raging outside, and imagined fibres, fingerprints, biological trace floating in muddy rivulets away from the body.

He checked his phone. There were four messages from Kate Simms. He speed-dialled her number and launched straight in: 'I hear our man's been busy.'

'Did you pick up my messages?' she said.

The question seemed like an evasion and her voice sounded tight.

'I've been driving. I called you as soon as I heard.'

'Where are you now?' she asked.

'On my way back to Scotland – I've been down in the south-east today, gathering evidence for the Mitchell case review.'

'Are you driving?'

'No. Look, Kate – what was the message?'

'The mother – Julia . . .' she said, and again he had the

sense that she was hedging – delaying what she had to tell him.

'Just say it, Kate.'

She took a breath. 'Julia was found in a pool on marshland near Rivington Reservoir.'

Fennimore saw a flash of Rachel, his wife. A crime-scene photo – her body pale and bloated, draped in pond weed at the edge of a marsh pond. Five years ago – nearly six – but it still had the power to knock the wind out of him.

'Nick, are you all right?'

'Why wasn't I told?' His voice sounded thick to him.

She hesitated. 'You haven't heard from your FLO?'

The investigation into Rachel's murder and Suzie's disappearance was still open: Fennimore should have heard from his family liaison officer. Any discovery that bore even a passing resemblance to the case would qualify for an update.

He checked his notifications again; the only messages were from Kate. 'I haven't heard from *anyone* since I sent in the first letter,' he said, tasting bitterness at the back of his throat. 'Were they waiting for me to hear about it from some journo wanting a reaction quote?'

She didn't answer.

'Who's the pathologist?' he asked, damping down his temper.

'I don't know,' she said. 'And even if I did, I wouldn't say. This is *not* my case, Nick. There are protocols – you know I can't go poking about in a case I'm not assigned to.'

He knew it all right. Helping him to meddle in the investigation into Rachel and Suzie's disappearance had stalled Kate Simms's career for four years. But he needed that

123

information. So he forced himself to relax his shoulders, and caught Levert's eye. He even managed a smile.

'Great,' he said. 'Thanks, Kate, I appreciate it.'

'Nick, what are you up to?' Simms demanded. 'Is someone there with you?'

'Yeah,' he said. 'It's good to know she's in capable hands.'

'Nick, I'm telling you—'

He cut her off mid-warning and slid the phone into his suit pocket. 'So . . .' he said, turning his full attention to Levert.

'She told you Cooper's doing the post-mortem?' Levert said.

Fennimore tilted his head, not wanting to tell an outright lie.

'He's a good man,' Levert added. 'Thorough.'

'Yes,' Fennimore said. 'Yes, he is.'

20

Oldham, Near Manchester, Tuesday

Kate Simms pulled into the staff car park of the Royal Oldham
Hospital mortuary at five-thirty. She had visited the place
before, but even if she had been new to it, she would have
known the building's purpose from its generic design: mud-
coloured brick and high windows, the white concrete stack
of its incinerator chimney a grim indication of the work that
went on behind the discreet façade.

She backed into a parking space so she could keep an eye
on the roadway and turned on the radio to pass the time
while she waited. A drive-time show was playing listeners'
requests – oldies, mostly. REM's 'Losing My Religion' had
just segued into Billy Joel's 'River of Dreams' when a grey
Audi sport swung in off the road with Fennimore behind
the wheel. He drove nose-in to the chain-link fence and she
strolled over while he was gathering his belongings from the

passenger seat. As he reached to open his door, she slapped her police ID on the side window.

He was startled, but only for a second, then he smiled sheepishly and buzzed the window down. 'Are you going to arrest me?'

'I damn well ought to.'

'I'm just dropping in on an old friend,' he said.

'Don't lie to me, Nick.'

His eyebrows twitched. 'How about you? You said you didn't know who was performing the post-mortem.'

'I didn't need to,' Simms said. 'All forensic PMs in Greater Manchester are done here. All I had to do was drive over and wait.'

'Well, you got me,' he said. 'Can we go inside now?'

'Not a chance. The senior investigating officer actually charged with investigating the case is in there – you're not even supposed to *be* here,' she said, glancing towards the security doors thirty yards away. 'And neither am I.'

'So why are you?'

'Fair question,' she said. 'I could just leave you to it, wait for you to get yourself arrested. I'm doing what I always do – covering your backside.'

A flash of sunlight prismed off the rain-beaded entrance door and two men emerged, both in business suits, one of them carrying an A4 bound notebook.

'Oh, hell . . .' Simms opened the back passenger door and slid into the seat behind Fennimore.

'Is that the SIO?' Fennimore said. 'Why don't you introduce me?' He was watching her in the rear-view mirror, and he looked like he was having fun.

He reached for the door lever and she said, 'Don't make me hurt you, Nick.'

126

He laughed, holding both hands up in surrender. 'Okay, but can we go inside when they're gone?'

'*No.*' Hunched down in her seat, Simms kept a close eye on the two detectives.

'Come on . . . who would know?'

'*I* would. Look – I didn't ask for this,' she said, 'but I'm stuck with it. I've been given a job to do – if I let you in there, it makes *me* look bad.'

He shrugged. 'You could leave. You can't be held responsible for something you didn't even witness.'

She wasn't getting through to him.

'I'm *already* a witness. And this is *not your case*, Nick.'

'So you keep telling me.'

'I wouldn't have to if you'd *listen*.'

'Okay, you didn't ask for this – well, neither did I,' he said, serious at last. 'The man who took Julia and Lauren Myers made me a part of it. He wants me involved – he made it personal – so if you need to arrest me, go ahead, but I need answers and I'm not going to get them sitting out here.' He opened the door.

'Nick, wait.' Simms closed her eyes. *Why are you doing this? You should call Enderby and let Fennimore face the consequences.* But she wouldn't; she couldn't . . . 'All right,' she said. 'There is another way.'

An hour later, they were in a pub a mile down the road, supping cask ale and waiting for forensic pathologist Dr David Cooper. Simms had phoned him from the mortuary car park, offering to buy him coffee. She had worked with Cooper on her first murder case. He fancied her and she knew it – and she wasn't above using that to her advantage. So when he said he would gladly spend an hour with her if she made it a pint of real ale in a decent pub, she readily agreed.

Cooper was short, neat, bearded, and had the cocky strut of a nineties rock star. Heads turned when he walked through the door. He hadn't been expecting Fennimore, but he showed no surprise, merely nodded to both of them, maybe a glint of mischief in his eye.

He slid on to the bench seat next to Fennimore, raised his glass in thanks to Simms, took his first swallow of Lakeland Gold and sighed contentedly before he spoke a single word.

'So,' he said, 'what's the story, morning glory?'

'We were hoping you'd tell us,' Fennimore said.

'Leave me out of it,' Simms said. 'I'm just here as chaperone.'

Cooper looked from one to the other over the rim of his glass. 'I thought that was my job in this threesome.'

Simms shot him a warning glance and he grinned.

'Julia Myers,' Simms said.

Cooper had grown up on the streets of Salford, Manchester – Lowry country – mills and red-brick terraces: generations living cheek-by-jowl with poverty and desperation. Although he now swanked it up in the affluent suburbs of Knutsford with footballers and soap stars as neighbours, he remained proud of his urban roots and street smarts. He took another swallow of ale before responding.

'Well, you know me – I like a chinwag,' he said. 'But this is police business.' He sucked his teeth. 'And given you didn't want to meet at my office, I'm thinking you're not here in an official capacity?'

'I'm ... not ... directly involved in the investigation,' Simms said carefully.

Cooper smirked. 'You'll have to do better than that.'

She watched him watching her. He knew she was taking a risk – she could see it in his face – the question was, how much did she need to tell him?

'Come on, Kate.' He crooked one finger, beckoning. 'You know you've got to give to get.'

Cooper had done Simms a big favour when she was new to Manchester Police and very much the outsider. She knew him to be straight-talking, unbound by protocols, yet paradoxically capable of a discretion and sensitivity that belied his salty language and his hard-lad swagger.

'Nick has been getting letters from the abductor,' she said, with a quick glance at Fennimore.

Cooper switched his attention to the scientist. 'And you think it could be linked to your Rachel and Suzie?'

Fennimore flinched. 'I'm not leaping to any conclusions, Coop,' he said.

Simms glanced at him. *Can he really believe that?*

'Kate thinks I'm paranoid.' He smiled, and she saw a weary acceptance in his grey-blue eyes. 'But there are parallels.'

'There are,' she agreed. 'But the fact is, you're all over the Web, Nick. Hundreds of articles and blogs written on you and' – she hesitated – 'what happened to you. I agree that whoever abducted Mrs Myers and her daughter is pushing your buttons. I just don't think you should make assumptions about *why*.'

'Which is how we come to be on this fact-finding mission.' A ghost of a smile played across Fennimore's face.

Cooper took another sip of ale, set down his glass and looked at them both. 'Okay,' he said. 'Off the record.'

They nodded in agreement.

'Julia Myers disappeared a week ago, but she probably died

in the last forty-eight hours. Hadn't been in the water long before she was spotted.'

'Did he botch the disposal or did he mean for her to be found?' Fennimore asked.

'Beats me,' Cooper said. 'But I will say this – I'm surprised he wasn't seen – Rivington Pike is *very* popular with walkers.'

'So maybe he doesn't know the area,' Fennimore said, thinking out loud.

'She had bruises on her arms and face, ligature marks on both wrists and her left ankle.'

'What was the ligature?' Fennimore asked.

'Probably zip ties, judging by the striations on her ankle – her left wrist showed almost nothing, her right was too much of a mess to see any clear markings,' Cooper said.

'She was tethered to give her some freedom of movement,' Fennimore said. 'So she could care for Lauren?'

'Maybe – the SIO is going to have a word with your forensic psych about that. You ready to hear the rest?'

Simms saw a fractional hesitation before Fennimore nodded.

'She was malnourished and dirty. We got scrapings from under her fingernails; puncture marks on her arms and legs suggest that she was probably drugged a couple of times.'

'Tell me they're rushing the tox screen.'

Cooper shrugged. 'That's up to the SIO. Her last meal was a chocolate bar and blackcurrant juice. She wasn't sexually assaulted. The SIO asked me to send nasal swabs to a palynologist – said something about a possible match to mould spores.'

Fennimore nodded. 'They found spores in one of the letters I received,' he explained. 'Aspergillus and rust mould.'

130

Simms gazed at Fennimore. 'How do you know that?' She thought back to their earlier phone call. *Oh, you sneaky—* 'You went to the Cellmark lab in Chorley, didn't you? *That's* how you knew where to find Coop.'

Fennimore dipped his head ambiguously. 'I didn't want to compromise you, Kate.'

She gave an exasperated laugh. 'What do you call *this*?'

Fennimore looked hurt and Cooper put in: 'Just three old pals having a natter over a pint.' He tapped Simms's hand lightly. 'Give the man a break. The good news is, if the mycologist can narrow the spores down to a species, it could point you to a location.'

'But with over seven thousand species of rust mould alone, that could take a while,' Fennimore said.

Cooper cocked an eyebrow. 'Thank you, Mr Sunshine.'

'I'm just thinking about Suzie,' Fennimore said quietly. 'Out there in some damp basement, surviving on chocolate bars and fruit juice.'

'You mean *Lauren*,' Simms said.

He glanced up. 'That's what I said.'

Simms looked at Cooper, but he was staring into his half-empty glass, embarrassed.

'No, Nick, it isn't.'

The stricken look on his face made her want to comfort him, but he had to think this through rationally – for Lauren Myers's sake as well as his own – and she added quickly, 'Okay, so we know the similarities between the two sets of disappearances – what about the differences? Mrs Myers was only gone a week, but Rachel was gone for months.'

Cooper looked shocked by Simms's bluntness, but Fennimore nodded. She was getting through to him.

'Rachel was in good health before she was murdered,' he said, 'and there were no signs of abuse.'

'No ligature marks,' Simms added.

'And she was well-nourished,' Fennimore said. 'She'd eaten a meal of pork, rice, sweet peppers and spring onions shortly before her death. There was alcohol in her blood, but only in sufficient quantity to suggest she'd had wine with her meal.'

He seemed to take some comfort from this recitation of the evidence that Simms knew he had memorized and gone over thousands of times in the years since.

Simms turned to Cooper. 'How did Mrs Myers die?'

'Strangled with a ligature,' Cooper said. 'Zip tie again. She also had a small penetrating wound on her left ankle. A short, wedge-shaped blade – possibly nail scissors.'

'She tried to escape,' Fennimore said.

'Seems likely,' Cooper agreed. 'The wound almost bisected the small saphenous vein – she'd lost quite a bit of blood; if he hadn't strangled her, she probably would've bled out.'

Simms took the baton, ran with the evidence: 'There are plenty of differences, Nick: Rachel was manually strangled,' she said. 'For a while, it looked like Rachel had just walked out on you. She'd packed bags for herself and Suzie, cleaned out your joint accounts—'

'You're assuming that *Rachel* did all that.'

'Come on, Nick – she'd been pissed off with you for months before they disappeared – all that was missing was a "Dear John" note.' Cooper shifted uncomfortably in his seat, but Simms ignored him. 'Julia and Lauren Myers, on the other hand, were snatched from the family car on their way home from watching a film.'

Fennimore rubbed his chin. 'What do we know about the Myers' family situation?'

'Like I said – I'm not on the team,' Simms said, patient but firm. 'But from what I've seen on the news, they were like any young family struggling to pay a mortgage through a recession. My guess is, even if she'd wanted to clear out their bank accounts, they didn't have the spare cash to make it worth her while. And as far as I know, they're not looking at the husband for this.'

Simms paused, and she and Cooper waited for Fennimore to respond.

'All right,' he said, after a few moments. 'The differences are striking.' He seemed calmer, less haunted with this realization. He took a thoughtful sip of beer. 'Abduction from a car – that's got to be unusual, hasn't it?'

'I'm sure the SIO is looking into it,' Simms said.

'Worth making sure, though.'

She threw up her hands, exasperated. 'Why do you assume you're the only one who knows how to do things right?'

'I don't – I just like to be reassured that they *have*.'

She laughed despite herself.

'I know,' he said, a gleam in his eye. 'I'm an arrogant bastard. But it's too late to change, so . . .'

'I can't go blundering in, Nick,' she said. 'I'm supposed to be *preventing* you from interfering. This investigation is complicated enough without me coaching from the sidelines.'

He gazed at her steadily and she felt control shift from her grasp to his.

'No,' she said, hearing the pitch of her voice rise. 'The investigating officer won't want it – Chief Constable Enderby won't want it—'

'*Varley* is impartial,' Fennimore said, his tone wheedling.

'One of the *nicer* things Professor Varley says about you is you're "unpredictable",' she said.

'And that's a bad thing?'

Do not laugh — he'll take it as acquiescence. She took a breath. 'Here's what I will do: I'll talk to Enderby, find out what kind of analysis has been done. If he tells me it's none of my business, that's the end of it — okay?'

'Okay,' he said. 'But make sure they asked about the family situation of the victims, their occupations — and the zip tie's got to be worth a mention.'

'*Nick.*'

He shut up, but she could tell he was still compiling a list of search refinements in his head.

21

There is a higher court than the courts of justice,
and that is the court of conscience.

MAHATMA GANDHI

Fennimore sat back, exhilarated by the roar of the jet engines and the rush of tyres on asphalt beneath him. The instant when a jet lost contact with the runway always gave him an adrenaline rush. He thrilled to the tug of gravity as it climbed; sometimes it felt as if the earth, intent on maintaining the natural order, would drag the improbable weight of steel, fuel, baggage and human flesh back to solid ground. Not a particularly healthy way to think, he acknowledged. But how many roller-coaster crazies, screaming as they plunged from the top of a ride, could swear they had never experienced that same buzz of delighted horror?

As the pilot banked to turn southward, he glimpsed Manchester's urban sprawl. The top-heavy shard of Beetham Tower, a grey monolith, dominated the Victorian jumble of red-brick and black-slate architecture. In high winds the glass blade howled like a soul in torment.

As soon as the seatbelt warning went off, he retrieved his shoulder bag from the overhead locker. Reaching in to the padded section for his laptop, he discovered the document wallet that Lazko had handed him in the pub earlier that day. He shoved the sheaf of papers back inside and opened his laptop; Wi-Fi wasn't available on-board, but he had downloaded a list of emails in the airport lounge and he skimmed the names and subject lines for anything urgent. Most were queries from students, but there was one from his accountancy firm – he hadn't answered their earlier message and he made a note to call their offices when he returned home.

He closed the laptop and slid it back into his shoulder bag. A corner of Lazko's folder caught in the zip and he eased it free, placing it on the seat next to him, remembering the reporter's nervousness as he slid the folder across the pub bench, his parting comment: 'Be careful how you use it.' Fennimore still hadn't arranged for someone to take on Josh as a doctoral student – he regretted asking Josh for help with the abductor's letter – it would only make his reassignment more difficult. Fennimore picked up the folder.

Inside were at least a hundred sheets of paper: computer print-outs of online articles; downloads from national newspapers; photocopies from the archives of the *Essex Chronicle*, Lazko's own newspaper. The first article was dated six years earlier. Under the banner CONSPIRACY BROTHERS ACQUITTED, a group shot in front of Chelmsford Crown Court: three men, one of them not much older than a boy. The caption read, 'Collins family "jubilant"'. He scanned the text – the three had been accused of conspiracy to evade excise duty, but the case had collapsed after key witnesses disappeared. No mention of Josh, though.

The exonerated brothers were Greg (32), Liam (30) and Sean (17). Could Sean be Josh Brown?

The Collins family's notoriety carried far beyond the borders of Essex, and reading the journalist's catalogue of previous arrests and prosecutions, Fennimore was reminded that he himself had been involved tangentially as a forensic scientist at the National Crime Faculty, analysing evidence in a few of the cases.

He thumbed through the bundle of papers: smuggling offences, harassment, assault, threats against witnesses and money laundering. 'All but three prosecutions failed,' Lazko had written in the margin.

Three? Fennimore had only counted two.

He turned to the back of the folder and found four sheets paper-clipped together. On the top, a photocopied newspaper clipping, dated five years before. The headline: MURDER TRIAL BOMBSHELL – COLLINS BROTHERS ARRESTED. Fennimore skimmed the report. Ahmed Azan, a British national, had been on trial for the abduction, torture and murder of his business partner, Bangladeshi Deepak Hafiz. Torture implements had been discovered at Azan's house, together with the gun used to kill Mr Hafiz. The two had been involved in a smuggling operation, bringing shisha tobacco into the UK from Dubai. The tobacco was legal. Avoiding Customs and Excise, however, was not. The prosecution's case was that the two men had fallen out over percentage shares of the profits, Mr Hafiz had hidden the stash of goods and Mr Azan had tried to torture its whereabouts out of his former partner. But on the third day of the trial, Liam Collins and another brother, Steve, both known associates of Azan, were arrested in a dawn raid on the family home.

New evidence took the police to the hidden contraband – in a Southend-on-Sea lock-up owned by the Collins family. Audio evidence emerged of the two brothers giving details of the torture, murder and disposal of Mr Hafiz's body. But most damning of all, Sean Collins, eighteen-year-old brother of the two men, gave an eyewitness account, stating that they, and not Mr Azan, had carried out the abduction and murder of Hafiz.

Fennimore stared at the intense young man in the photograph. So Josh Brown was really Sean Collins.

He had always assumed that Josh was hiding a shady past; he hadn't reckoned with him being part of a gangland dynasty.

It explained why Josh refused to have his DNA on record. He remembered something Professor Varley had said: when Josh graduated in psychology with distinction, nobody had attended the ceremony. Small surprise, given what he now knew. Josh had been offered a bursary to continue his studies in Nottingham – he might have become a star in his chosen field – yet he had changed courses, chosen to train for a job that would place him under constant threat of exposure. And where he, in turn, could expose miscarriages of justice. Fennimore couldn't decide if that was perverse or foolish – or the definition of heroism.

He stacked the papers in order and stowed them carefully as the seatbelt lights came on and the pilot alerted passengers to their first views of Aberdeen. It was late evening, and the sun was still a pale shimmer of light, setting to their left. This put him in a dilemma: if he told Josh what he knew, he ran the risk of the student skipping town again. But at least if he hinted at Josh's circumstances to Kate Simms, it might relieve some of the tension between them, and didn't he owe it to Kate to be honest? He sighed, fastening his seatbelt; Josh had got out of that life – wasn't he entitled to keep his past where it belonged – in the past? Torn by two very different loyalties, Fennimore decided on one thing: the student had earned a second chance; he would remain under Fennimore's doctoral supervision.

22

Manchester, Tuesday Evening

Kate Simms arrived home at just after eight. Her mother poked her head around the kitchen door and Simms could read the evening's disputations in her face.

Make an effort, Kate. 'Hi, Mum,' she said, forcing a smile.

'You're late.'

'Work,' she said, shrugging out of her jacket. She hung it on the stair newel and started down the hall towards the kitchen, but her mother slipped out, pulling the kitchen door closed behind her, blocking the way.

'You were *supposed* to be taking some leave,' she said. 'Timmy pined for you, those weeks and months you were in America. He refused to go to bed, scared you'd disappeared off again—'

'I know it's late,' Simms interrupted, 'but I had some stuff to deal with and then I had to call in to speak to the chief constable.'

'You're not in trouble again, are you?'

'No! For heaven's sake, Mum – why would you assume—'
Simms took a breath and let it go. *I am not going to argue this evening.* 'The chief constable has asked me to do some work on the Myers investigation.' She felt a slow flush creep into her cheeks; *the chief constable – what is this need to impress?*

Her mother's face creased. 'That poor woman. Is there any news about the child?'

'Not yet.'

'Well, what *are* you doing?'

'You know I can't discuss an ongoing investigation, Mum,' Simms said. 'And anyway, I don't know the details – I'm not directly involved – I have more of a . . . monitoring role.'

'Monitoring? Monitoring *what* exactly? You don't even seem to know what's going on. How can you *monitor* anything?'

Simms regarded her mother. *It's like this, Mum: I've been appointed Fennimore's unofficial minder.* She blew air out through her nostrils. *Yeah, Kate, that'd go down well.* Her mother still hadn't forgiven her for the press speculation that spiralled around her after Rachel and Suzie's disappearance five years ago.

'Mum,' she said. 'It's past Timmy's bedtime – do you think we could call a truce – just until I've got him off to sleep?'

An appeal to her mother's sense of duty often succeeded when all else failed, and it worked this time, too. Her mother sniffed, but stood aside to let her pass.

As Simms reached the kitchen door, her mother took the jacket from the newel and hung it on the coat rail next to the hall dresser. Simms opened her mouth, shut it before she said something she would regret, and walked into the kitchen with a smile on her face.

Timmy was drawing at the table, tomato sauce smeared on his chin, a fat turquoise crayon in one fist.

'Wow, that's a lot of blue,' she said.

He looked up, but continued wearing the crayon down on the sheet of paper. 'It's a swimming pool,' he said. 'I been swimming.'

Her mother had followed Simms through, and Tim added as an afterthought: 'With Nanna.'

'Well, it's beautiful,' she said. 'But mind you don't colour over the swimmers – you wouldn't want them to drown.'

He took the crayon off the paper, a look of alarm on his face.

'What a thing to say!' her mother scolded. 'Mummy's only joking, Timmy.'

'I know,' he said, offended. 'It's only a pitcher.' He lifted it up for Simms to see. 'That one's me – at the front. I swum a breath and I beat *everyone*.'

'You swam a breadth?' Simms widened her eyes. 'My goodness, that *is* something.'

'I cooked dinner,' her mother said, walking past them to the stove. 'Well, I didn't know when you'd show up, so . . .'

'Thanks, Mum.' *Of course, Kieran could have cooked dinner.* She almost said it, but a worried look crossed Timmy's face, and she relaxed her shoulders deliberately and laughed. 'I can see you've already eaten, young Timothy.' She plucked a kitchen towel from the dispenser and ran it under the kitchen tap before wiping his chin.

He squirmed, dropping the drawing and wiping the wetness off his face with his forearm.

'I got a badge, Mummy,' he said, kneeling on his chair. He squinted down at his T-shirt, pulling it out of shape so

142

that he could see the badge and show it to her at the same time.

'Feet off the furniture, Timmy,' her mother said.

He wriggled to a sitting position again and snatched up the picture. 'I beat him and him and *him* and her and *him*.' He was practically shouting now, almost poking holes in the paper as he pointed to each of his competitors. This had become a pattern since Simms's trip: sensing the tension between his mummy and his nanna, he would get louder and ruder until he collapsed in tears or exploded into a full-blown tantrum.

Diversion worked best and Simms said, 'Gosh, that's – how many people, Timmy?'

He counted them three times, just to be sure.

'I saved something for you,' her mother said. 'It's in the pot – if you haven't already eaten.' She made it sound like an accusation.

'Thanks, Mum,' Simms said. *Keep the peace, Kate. Just smile and keep the peace.*

Her mother crossed the kitchen to the stove.

'It's all right, Mum – I'll sort it,' she said, more firmly this time.

'Suit yourself. It's only Bolognese.'

'It smells delicious,' Simms said. 'But you must be tired – why don't you sit down, relax? Is Kieran not home?' she added, realizing that there were only two dirty dishes stacked next to the kitchen sink.

'He's in the shower,' her mother said. 'Poor boy has to go back to work.'

No hint of disapproval there.

Simms lit the gas ring to reheat the pasta sauce and ran some water for the washing up, chatting all the time with

Timmy. He was still overcompensating, trying in his little boy way to make the bad atmosphere better, showing off his new badge again, telling her how many children he'd beaten again, glancing uncertainly up at his nanna, who hovered by his chair. Simms answered his boasts and excited descriptions of how fast he'd swum, how far, how big the other boys were, with gentle exclamations and soft murmurs. Finally her mother gave up and left the room. A minute later, Simms heard a mumble of voices interspersed with music: she was watching TV. Gradually, Timmy calmed down.

He clung to her neck when she picked him up to carry him to bed. He was warm and soft and at his cuddliest. 'Bath time,' she murmured, 'then I'll read you a story.'

'Don't need a baff,' he complained, rubbing the back of one hand across his eyes. 'I been *swimming*.'

'Timmy, you smell of chlorine.'

'No,' he whined. 'I'm already clean.' He began to squirm and she hushed him.

'Okay, but you have to brush your teeth.'

The bathroom was steamy and fragrant and she could hear Kieran getting ready in the bedroom next door, listening to music as he dressed. *Going-out music*, she thought, remembering with a pang the times when they would listen to upbeat tunes together as they duded themselves up ready for a night out.

They almost collided on the landing as she led Timmy to his room.

'Hello, you,' he said. He was wearing a suit and tie, and the duty free cologne she'd brought back from her American trip. He seemed happy to see her. 'Sorry I have to rush out. Prize-giving.'

'I thought it was the school play tonight?' she said.

'That was *last* night. We had the matinee today – which was a sensation,' he added, miming dusting off his lapels.

'Of course it was.'

He smiled.

'So no performance today?'

'*Prize*-giving today, final performance *tomorrow*,' he said, still smiling.

'It's awfully late,' she said.

'Which is why I have to dash,' he said. 'Actually, they've already given the prizes, but I've been asked back for wine and canapés with some of the governors and the board of trustees.'

'Wow!'

'It's a *very* big deal.'

'And all very different from state school teaching,' she said.

He laughed heartily, kissed her on the nose and Timmy on the crown on his head. 'You don't know the half of it,' he said.

When Timmy had got off to sleep, Simms peeked in on her mother and found her dozing in her chair. She went to the kitchen and poured the pasta sauce into a bowl and ate it with a chunk of bread, barely tasting it as she brooded over her meeting with Chief Constable Enderby.

Deciding how much to tell him had been the hardest part. It seemed that whenever Nick Fennimore was in the picture, she was always having to make these choices, wondering how much she could withhold before it became tantamount to a lie.

She'd had to tell her boss that Fennimore had dropped by the Chorley lab – and that he'd heard about the discovery of Mrs Myers's body from one of the forensic scientists there, rather than from his family liaison officer.

'Is he meddling, Kate?'

'He's interested, sir. It's only natural under the circumstances.'

Enderby frowned.

'The letters, the taunts – the way Julia Myers was found . . .' She paused. 'It's not unreasonable, is it?'

Enderby exhaled – a long-drawn-out breath, as though he had been holding it. 'No,' he said. 'No, it isn't.' His tone was conciliatory.

'He wondered if the Serious Crime Analysis Section had taken a look at the abductor's MO,' she went on, taking advantage of Enderby's sympathy. 'Lying in wait in the car like that – it must be unusual.'

'We looked into the car abduction,' Enderby said. 'There were no linked crimes on the books. We're keeping an open mind about the rest – and that includes any possible links to Fennimore himself. I'll ask the SIO to brief you if there's anything significant in the post-mortem report.'

'Thank you, sir.' Simms looked away so Enderby wouldn't see her relief that he didn't know about their trip to the mortuary. *Not lying*, she told herself, *only withholding*. 'I'm sure Nick will be grateful.'

Enderby surprised her with a laugh. 'I very much doubt that. Look, Kate, I understand your loyalty to Fennimore. You knew Rachel and Suzie, didn't you?'

'Becky – my daughter – was best friends with Suzie,' Simms said.

'I'm sensitive to that,' he said. 'And I've allowed you a fair amount of latitude.' He paused. 'But I do know what Fennimore is up to.'

'Sir?' Simms kept her hands still and her face blank.

'His communications with Paris police,' Enderby went on. 'I know about the photograph.'

Simms held her breath.

'I know,' Enderby went on, 'that he believes the girl in it is his daughter.'

'Sir, he's—'

'He's a grieving father grasping at straws,' Enderby interrupted. 'I know that, too,' he said, not unkindly. 'But I also know that you facilitated his communication with the French authorities.'

Oh, bugger . . .

'There's loyalty,' Enderby said. 'And then there's stupidity. I hope you know the difference.'

Simms's mother went to bed at ten, and soon after, Kieran texted that he would be home late. Her head still buzzing with the events of the day, Simms turned to her computer. There were photographs and video clips of Mr Myers, recorded during a press conference earlier in the day. He sat next to Julia Myers's father, looking grey and sedated. He remained calm for the first part of the appeal, but then he looked into the camera and said, 'My little girl can't harm you. Please, let her come home.' His voice cracked on the word *home*. 'Please, she's all I've got – let Lauren come home.' He broke down, sobbing, and Simms closed the tab, feeling like a voyeur.

She logged into her work email account, dealt with a few queries and, scrolling down the screen, found something from one of the investigators on the St Louis Major Case Squad. She replied, sending her good wishes to the rest of the team. She touched the screen, ready to shut down, just as the Skype alert sounded. She didn't share her Skype ID with many people; she squinted at the task bar, expecting it to be someone from St Louis, but it was Becky. Her daughter had accepted an invitation to visit Francine Chabert, a school friend, in London shortly after her exams finished.

Simms hit the 'Reply' icon and a second later Becky appeared onscreen. She had styled her hair differently – it was tied up in a loose chignon, revealing the slim contour of her neck. 'Becky, what are you doing up so late?'

Becky rolled her eyes. 'Mum, it's eleven o' clock and I'm sixteen years old.'

'Are you all right?' Simms scanned her daughter's face for signs of fatigue, but in truth Becky looked more relaxed and happy than she had for months. 'Nothing's wrong?' She peered past her daughter and caught a glimpse of a sofa and table lamp.

'*Chill*, Mum – I'm at Madame Chabert's – see?' She picked up her tablet; the image tilted alarmingly and Simms experienced a momentary sensation of vertigo. Becky panned left to right; Francine was sitting at the far end of the sofa, texting on her mobile phone. She looked up and waved.

'So,' Simms said. 'Having fun?'

'Great.' Becky reappeared in another tipsy blur of movement. 'We had a ride on the London Eye yesterday and went to watch the skateboarders on the South Bank afterwards – I wish I'd brought my board.'

Simms regretted that they had never made enough time for family excursions when they lived in London.

'My French has really improved.' Madame Chabert had been Becky's French teacher at her old school and Becky had chosen French, German and English for her A-level subjects. 'They speak it all the time here – isn't that right, Francine?'

148

Off-screen, Francine said, '*Pratiquement*', injecting a novel-length treatise of boredom and sarcasm into the word.

Becky poked her tongue out at her friend. 'Madame Chabert calls me her "*petite Parisienne*",' she added, pronouncing it in what Simms took to be an authentic French accent – Becky certainly hadn't inherited her linguistic talents from her.

Francine whispered something and Becky glanced side-ways and popped her eyes wide in a gesture that was usually accompanied by, '*What?*'

'Becky,' Simms said, 'what's going on?'

'Nothing, just Francine bugging me.'

Her friend whispered, '*Ask her.*'

'I *am*,' Becky said. She seemed flustered, but gathered herself, tucking a hank of hair behind her ear – a gesture of determination. 'The thing is,' she said, 'Madame Chabert said I could go with them to Paris on Thursday.'

'Oh, Becky, that's very kind of her, but—'

'Madame Chabert says she'll take us to dinner on a *bateau mouche*, and we'll go up the Eiffel Tower – Francine says the views are amazing. I'd get to practise my French loads, 'cos we'll mostly be going to museums and art galleries. It'd be *sooo*-ooh cool.'

'You mustn't overstay your welcome, Becky,' Simms said, thinking, *Since when had art galleries become 'cool'?*

Francine appeared in the Skype window. 'Oh, she'd be very welcome, Mrs Simms – I asked specially. Since living in England, I sort of lost touch with my friends in France and I want someone to hang out with.'

Simms's cop instinct kicked into high alert. 'Hang out?' Simms said. 'At these art galleries and museums?'

'Of course!' Francine widened her eyes a tad too much.

How many petit Parisien boys hung around these places of culture and enlightenment? Simms wondered.

'It's only for a few days, Mum,' Becky put in.

'Dad and I think we should spend some family time together over the school holidays.'

Becky huffed. 'Like *that's* going to happen.'

'Becky . . .'

Her daughter shrugged at the note of warning in her voice. 'What? He's never home.'

'He has to work,' Simms said, feeling an itch of disquiet.

Becky arched her eyebrow and it was like looking in a mirror. 'Yeah, right.'

'Becky, don't be rude.'

'Well, it's true – if you don't believe me, ask Nanna.'

The itch became a stab of alarm and Simms, intensely aware that Francine was listening, gave Becky a stern look and said, 'I'll talk to your dad about Paris.'

'Can't you ask him now?'

'He's not here just now.'

Becky treated her to another haughty twitch of the eyebrows.

'I'll call you tomorrow,' Simms said, 'but before we decide anything, I would have to make sure it's really okay with Mrs Chabert.'

Becky's face lit with sudden eagerness. 'Oh, you can do that now – she's just in the next room.' The image tilted, and Simms caught a glimpse of coving and a light fitting, then a blur of movement. She looked away from the screen and heard Becky speaking excitedly in French. Seconds later, a rather surprised-looking Mrs Chabert appeared on the screen.

'Good evening,' she said.

'I'm so sorry, Mrs Chabert.' Simms had met the woman a few times at parents' evenings and staff socials, but didn't know her well.

'Not at all,' Mrs Chabert said.

'I wanted to postpone this conversation until I'd spoken with Becky's father.'

'I understand.'

'I have no idea what Becky was saying, but I want you to know that while it's clear that she's had a lovely time with you, I wouldn't want her to impose on your hospitality.'

A hint of amusement played around Mrs Chabert's eyes. 'Allow me to translate: Becky begged me to confirm that I have not been coerced into inviting her to stay with us.'

Off-camera, Becky groaned in embarrassment.

'She implored me to assure you that she will be properly chaperoned throughout her visit, and will sample the cultural delights of Paris with the heart and mind of a philosopher.' Mrs Chabert laughed. 'I exaggerate a little.' She paused, looking into the webcam. 'And I can promise you that it would not be the slightest imposition; on the contrary, it would be a genuine pleasure to have Becky extend her stay with us.'

Simms hung up a few minutes later, having promised Becky again that she would discuss the holiday with Kieran. The green phone icon was lit next to one of her Skype contacts – Diane Jayston was online. Diane was an SCAS analyst Simms knew from her years in the National Crime Faculty, and they had been in communication long-distance on almost a daily basis during her American trip. It seemed perverse to pass up the opportunity to sound Diane out on the Myers investigation.

She hit the Call icon, but the chief constable's warning rang in her head: 'There's loyalty, and then there's stupidity.'

She hung up. But she couldn't seem to let go of the mouse. Instead, she cupped it in the palm of her hand, circling the Call icon with the mouse pointer, daring herself to redial. The Skype ringtone chimed out and her hand jerked violently. It was Diane. Simms gave her heart a second to recover, hesitated for another second, then clicked to answer.

Diane appeared onscreen, eyelids lined with Kohl pencil, hair dyed deep purple and cut straight across to her eyebrow line; the rest was coal-black and spiked. She was forty-three and had worked her way up from tech support to crime analyst over the past twenty-two years, surviving reorganizations and staff cuts and a moratorium on 'visible tattoos'. She treated each as though they didn't apply to her – until a verbal warning from her line manager about her tattoos. After that, she began wearing men's suits with a shirt and tie to cover up, dealing with any that showed above the collar line with sticking plasters. She would wait them out, she said – they would eventually get over themselves and lift the ban.

'Did you just hang up on me?' she demanded. Judging by the amount of ornamented flesh currently on display, Diane was at home.

'I disconnected before you picked up,' Simms said. 'There's a difference.'

'It still hurts.' Diane batted her eyelids, managing to look simultaneously combative and coquettish.

'It's late,' Simms said. 'I didn't want to disturb you.'

'You're talking to an insomniac who is currently working at her computer after a ten-hour stint of what?' She tilted her head. 'Oh, yeah – *working at her computer.* A call from a friend at this hour isn't a disturbance – it's a timely intervention.'

Kate smiled. 'I just got an email from the Major Case Squad in St Louis – they wanted to thank you guys for the work you did on the I-44 case.'

'I do get paid,' Diane said, but she looked quietly pleased. 'So what's keeping you up late?'

'Jet lag,' Simms said. 'And the Myers case. You heard about the mother?'

Diane nodded. 'I did the analysis on that one.'

Simms experienced a fizz of excitement, which was immediately followed by a cold thud of apprehension. *You shouldn't be doing this, Kate – it's none of your business.*

Even so, she said, 'Chief Constable Enderby says you got no similar abductions?'

Diane's eyebrows shot up. 'Woo! Did you say the Chief Con? You *do* move in exalted circles these days. So he brought you in on the team?'

Simms twitched her eyebrows and let Diane believe what she wanted to believe, while Enderby's words, *There's loyalty, and then there's stupidity* repeated in her head like the tick of a metronome.

Diane was talking: 'It depends what you mean by "similar" – car abductions are more common than you'd think. But mostly divorced mums and dads getting into a spat about child custody. I did find a few carjackings where the crap-heads who had their sights on a brand-new Beamer dragged Mum out of the driving seat and failed to notice Baby anchored in the back.' She grimaced. 'What happened to the Myerses is a whole 'nother level of creepy.'

'Did you look into the occupations of the victims?'

Diane shook her head. 'Wasn't on the list of search terms.'

She could leave it there – she had asked Fennimore's question. But curiosity made Simms ask, 'What *was* on the list?'

Diane squinted suspiciously at her. 'You don't know?'

'Enderby didn't specify.' *Not lying, only withholding.*

Diane leaned back in her office chair and ticked the criteria off on the fingers of one beringed hand. 'Mother-and-child combos; back seat folded down; abductions from car parks . . .'

'Use of a zip tie?' Simms asked.

Diane sat up so fast her seat-back twanged like a catapult. 'He used a zip tie? Was that in the PM report? Because nobody mentioned a zip tie. Why wouldn't they mention something distinctive like a *zip tie*, for crying out loud?'

Simms hesitated. *One step further and there will be no turning back.* 'Forget it,' she said. 'It was just a thought.'

'Like *hell*,' Diane said. 'If a zip tie turned up in the postmortem I should *absolutely* revisit the data. I'll check back with the SIO, get his okay—'

'Uh, Diane – I'd rather you didn't,' Simms said quietly.

Diane narrowed her eyes, the kohl outlining giving her the look of a Siamese cat. 'So when you say "forget it", what you *mean* is, "I'm not supposed to know this"?'

'Not officially,' Simms admitted. 'At least, not yet.'

'Oh.' Diane knew her history: the disciplinary action after she played too fast and loose with Crime Faculty resources when Fennimore's wife and child disappeared; the hard slog back up a career ladder that was rigged to throw women off without the benefit of a safety net.

'Is Fennimore mixed up in this?' Diane demanded.

'Yes.'

'Oh,' she said again.

'But not by choice. The abductor seems to want him involved.'

'Hm,' Diane said.

It was a relief to hear her say something different, but Simms couldn't read her mood. 'So you'll leave it alone?'

Diane snorted. 'Well, *that's* not going to happen.'

'Diane— '

'Look,' Diane said, 'some of the files are still boxed up in my office – on past performance they'll probably sit there for weeks before they get sent back. Who could blame me if I riffle through them once in a while?'

'Diane, no,' Simms said. 'It's one thing wheedling case details out of you and quite another asking you to reopen a file you've already reported on.'

'I didn't hear you ask,' Diane said. 'And they don't call me "Double-check Diane" for nothing. I got outed as obsessive my first year in the job. Everyone on the team has seen me crack open a box of files I've just sealed to have one last rummage.'

Simms shook her head, but Diane kept on talking:

'*Relax* – it'll be fine – I'll do it on my own time. No one will even raise an eyebrow.'

23

Abduction, Day 7

Lauren Myers stares up at the small square of grey until her neck aches and her eyes burn. The sun will come in through that square when it's morning time again; it tells her that there is still an *outside* where Daddy is, and Mummy, too – although she's scared something bad has happened to Mummy, because she hasn't come back. It's been ages and ages: one daytime and one bedtime. But she can't sleep properly without Mummy. She tries to be brave, like the princess in the story. Well, like the princess, but not like the princess – she doesn't want to rescue anyone – she wants Daddy to come and rescue *her*. But the man said Daddy would be cross because she was a very naughty girl. He told her, 'Come here RIGHT NOW!' – and Lauren almost did, because she *was* bad when he came to take Mummy away. But Mummy *told* her to be bad, she said she was *allowed* to be bad, so she was being *good* by being bad. But the man said nobody would come for her because she was

156

such a bad girl, and there wouldn't be no more sweeties. So maybe next time she'll do what he tells her to. But Mummy said no. Mummy said climb up high and fight and spit and scream. She *told* her to be naughty. She *told* her to eat the sweets. She *told* her to be Grandma's Yellow Peril – 'cos that was her superpower. Mummy said the man was bad – so she didn't have to do what he said.

Lauren sighs. It's so hard being brave – not like in a film. Her head feels hot with all the thinking, and her eyes won't stop crying. She covers her face and sobs.

24

Context is everything.

ANON

Aberdeen, Tuesday Night

Fennimore's apartment was fusty and stale. He flung open the windows, letting in cold damp air – a northerly weather front had blown in from the Atlantic and the temperature in Aberdeen had dropped to around ten Celsius.

He ducked into the shower and immediately his mobile began to ring. It was Dr Wilton in Essex.

'We have the DNA results from the Mitchell appeal semen samples,' she said.

'Wow, that was fast.' He wondered if she had known even when he was at the lab that morning.

'Essex Police put a rush on the analysis because they thought *you* would put a rush on *yours*.'

He had.

Fennimore trapped the phone between his shoulder and his ear while he tucked a towel around his waist. 'So is it our guy?'

'Now, why would I tell you that?'

'In the interests of collegiality,' he teased. 'And because the only other reason I can think you would call is to gloat – and you don't seem the gloating kind.'

'Did you just pay me a compliment?' she said.

'A bit back-handed, but . . .'

She chuckled. 'I'll take what I can get.'

'So . . .'

'The DNA on the skirt is not a match to Mitchell.'

'It's not our guy,' Fennimore murmured. 'That's . . . interesting.'

'Isn't it?'

'So the case has been reopened?'

'It has.'

'Your review team will have done a wider search of the database . . .' By now they might even have matched the unknown DNA to someone already in the system.

'If you're angling for a name, you'll have to go fish in Essex Police's pond.' He heard a smile in Dr Wilton's voice.

'Well, thanks for letting me know,' Fennimore said.

'My pleasure,' she said. 'Just as long as you remember that collegiality works both ways.' She would expect a return on the favour at some point. 'And, Nick?'

'Yes?' he said.

'You didn't hear this from me.'

'Hear what?'

She laughed.

He hung up, smiling, and rang Lazko's number to give him the good news.

'So,' Lazko said, 'we have enough new evidence to launch an appeal?'

'Essex Police have already started a review of the case.'

'*Fantastic* – the family will be chuffed.'

'No doubt. But you can't tell the family – not yet. This is unofficial and strictly off the record,' Fennimore said.

'Not a problem,' Lazko said. 'We just quote an anonymous source close to the investigation.'

'Lazko, you can't go public with this yet.'

'What are you talking about? This is the best news the Justice for Graham Mitchell campaign has had for years.'

'I have to protect my source – you should know all about that.' Lazko gave a grunt. 'And before you start celebrating, there are several ways to interpret this evidence.'

'The DNA isn't his – end of story.'

Fennimore laughed. 'It's only the prologue. Context is everything: Mitchell's DNA *was* found on the love-bite and his DNA *was* under the victim's fingernails – that has never been in dispute. It could be that Mitchell is telling the truth and he paid the victim and left her well and unharmed, but it may be that Mitchell had an accomplice. Or maybe Mitchell did kill her and the guy who left his DNA on Kelli Rees's skirt was a client she saw *before* Mitchell.' Fennimore paused to give Lazko time to assimilate the information. 'We do this right: we wait until our lab has cross-matched their profile with the sample Mitchell donated. And then we wait until they send us their report.'

'So what's the point in telling me now?' the journalist huffed. 'You said you wanted to work at your own pace, I agreed. Why give me something I can use, then tell me to sit on my hands?'

'Because,' Fennimore said, 'I think the DNA database gave Essex Police a name. I want to know what that is, but they won't be keen to share that little snippet with Mitchell's appeal team. Which means we'd be relying on overheard conversations, a memo left lying on a table in the canteen. Information like that has a short half-life – after a day or two the excitement dies down, the time to listen in on tea-room gossip has passed, the reports are typed and logged securely behind the police server's firewall. So we need to get it fast – while their guard is down.'

'You're asking if I have someone on the inside?' Lazko said. 'I am.'

'You know, things aren't so cosy between the police and the press since Leveson stuck his oar in.'

The Leveson inquiry into press and public standards had led to multiple sackings, criminal prosecutions and even the closure of a national newspaper. Fennimore gave the journalist time to sift through his mental database of police sources.

'I'd need a public interest justification,' Lazko said at last. 'Seriously?'

'You want the info, that's what it takes.'

'Okay,' Fennimore said. 'Okay . . . Try this: if the DNA on Kelli Rees's skirt is from a known offender, and that offender has committed further crimes since Mitchell was locked up – how would that look for Essex Police?'

'Bad,' Lazko said, sounding a lot more cheerful. '*Very* bad.'

'Enough public interest for you to work your contacts?'

'I'll talk to a police chum, ask him to keep his ear to the ground.'

Unable to sleep, Fennimore let himself into the St Andrew Street building at 8:15 a.m. on Wednesday. He didn't recognize the security guy and had to fish in his pocket for his ID before the man would let him pass. With labs and offices now largely standing empty, every footstep echoed eerily, and the scuffs and marks on the walls that had given the place a warm lived-in look, now conveyed neglect and decrepitude. He made his way to his office, pausing on the third-floor landing, wondering if Josh Brown might be in the staff kitchen. But that would keep; he continued up to the top corridor and unlocked his door.

The desk, phone and chair were gone. So were his bookcases, the books dumped in an untidy heap on the floor. The plastic crates he used to store papers, journals and articles had been moved away from the walls, presumably to get at the phone and Wi-Fi cables: both had been stripped out. The filing cabinet was still in place – this was where he stored his more sensitive case files and reports. He checked the lock; it was intact, and a quick look inside reassured him that its contents hadn't been tampered with. Well, Joan did warn him they wouldn't wait for ever.

Three hours and ten bin bags later, he had whittled the mass of papers and articles down by a third. Not nearly enough, but it was a start. He dumped the bags of paper on the landing for shredding and as he dusted his hands off his mobile began to ring in his office. He searched for it among the remaining jumble of boxes and bags, following the sound, lifting and dumping papers, finally locating it under a journal on the window ledge.

'Professor Fennimore?'

'Yes.' Fennimore didn't recognize the voice.

'Lazko said you wanted to know if we got a name on the DNA from the Mitchell case.'

'Yes,' he said again.

'David Hazle. That's H–A–Z–L–E.'

He snatched up a scrap of paper and a pen and used a plastic tote box as a desk.

'Anything else? Criminal record?'

'That's all you're getting. Tell Lazko he owes me one.'

'I will. Are you about to make an arrest?' Fennimore said.

'Not unless we dig him up.' The line went dead.

Fennimore checked the phone log, but the number had been withheld. He folded the slip of paper and tucked it in his shirt pocket, thinking Josh Brown would be the man to research Mr Hazle – the doctoral student had a facility for winkling out information on people. Ironic, given his own circumstances. Replacing the phone on the window-ledge, Fennimore turned around and saw Josh himself standing in the doorway.

'Spooky,' Fennimore said. 'I was just thinking about you.'

'I didn't see them shifting the furniture out,' Josh said, ignoring the pleasantry. 'But I made sure they didn't get their mitts on your papers.'

'Thanks,' Fennimore said. He looked around the room. 'So it's really happening – we're really relocating.'

'Yeah.'

'You don't look any happier at the prospect than I am. What's the problem – new campus too far from the city?'

'It's all right. A bit too open plan for my liking.'

I bet it is.

It occurred to Fennimore that his office was a bit out of the way for Josh just to happen to be passing, so the student must have made a special journey; he could guess why. Time to put him out of his misery. 'That call was about a possible miscarriage of justice,' he said, coming at the subject sideways.

163

'The Mitchell case,' Josh said.

Fennimore frowned. *Now how does he know that?* Of course – Mitchell's sister had briefly posted about his involvement. 'Got MOJ's on Google Alerts, Josh?' he asked.

The student allowed a faint smile. 'Something like that.'

Fennimore called Lazko, and Josh backed away from the door. 'Stay,' he said. 'I need to talk to you.' Josh remained in the doorway, his brow furrowed.

Lazko's number went straight to voicemail and he left a message: 'We've got a name and he has a criminal record. Get back to me as soon as you get this.'

He hung up and Josh regarded him quizzically.

'The physical evidence wasn't fully processed at the time of Mitchell's trial,' Fennimore explained. 'And now that it has been, Essex Police have identified another potential suspect. I've just had an off-the-record call to give me a name.' Josh watched him, revealing nothing. 'Fancy doing a bit of background research?'

A flash of eagerness lit the student's face. He quickly suppressed it. 'That depends,' he said.

'On what?'

'Does this mean you're not reassigning me?'

Fennimore smiled. 'Second chance,' he said. 'Don't screw it up.'

25

Manchester, Wednesday, Early Evening

Kieran arrived home from school at four-thirty. Barely forty minutes later, he was already getting ready to go out again: the final performance of the school play was scheduled that evening.

Simms left her mother supervising Timmy and followed her husband upstairs. She heard a thrum of water – he was in the shower. She closed the bedroom door and went through to the en-suite.

'Kieran, we need to talk about Becky's Paris trip.' They had discussed it, briefly, over breakfast, but the matter was still unresolved.

'Let her go,' he said, raising his voice above the drum of water.

'I'm worried about her,' she said. 'It's like she's distancing herself from the family.'

He laughed. 'She's sixteen – that's what sixteen-year-olds do.'

'What do you know about the Chaberts?' Kieran and Mrs

Chabert had worked at the same school when they'd lived in London.

'She's a good teacher,' he said. 'Inspirational.'

'I got that impression,' Kate said. 'What about him?'

'He's a translator,' Kieran said.

'I know that – what do you *think* of him?'

'I only met him a few times. He seems okay – why?'

'We're thinking of placing our daughter in his care,' she said. 'I'm astonished you need to ask that.'

Behind the shower screen, Kieran turned off the shower and smoothed his hands over his face and hair. 'She'll be with *Mrs* Chabert most of the time.' He stepped from behind the screen and she handed him a towel. Kieran had toned up in the weeks she'd been away and she felt a tug of longing for him.

'It'll be like she's going on a school trip,' he said, towelling himself dry. 'Stop worrying.'

'It's just Becky and one school friend – it'll be *nothing like* a school trip,' Simms said. 'And I'm not worrying, I'm assessing.'

'Assessing what?' He smiled, squeezing past her, naked. She reached out to touch him, but he caught her hand, kissed it and let it drop. Another laughing rejection.

He hadn't shown any interest in her since she got back; a quick hug, a kiss on the cheek – using tiredness or stress, or her mother's presence in the house as an excuse.

She closed her eyes, took a breath and stepped into the bedroom. Kieran was already halfway dressed.

'I was hoping we'd get some family time together, just the four of us,' she said.

'Aren't you working on that kidnapping?'

'I am, but I thought afterwards . . .'

166

'We both know how this works,' he said, with an irritating smirk.

'What does that mean?'

'There's always something else, Kate.'

'*You* can talk – I've been home a week and I'd be surprised if we've sat together for half an hour.'

He turned away, unhooking a pair of suit trousers from the wardrobe. 'End of term is always busy – you know that. And what about you? *You're* supposed to be on leave, after your little field trip to the States, and yet police business just keeps *drr-ragging* you away from home.' His tone was light, but she could see the tension in his shoulders as he stepped into his trousers and tucked in his shirt.

'Is *that* what this is about, Kieran?' she asked. 'Are you punishing me for going away?'

'I'm asking for some give and take,' he said. 'I made sacrifices.' He sat on the bed and pulled on his socks. 'We moved here because *you* messed up your opportunities at the Met. I went along with it' – he gave a harsh laugh. 'Literally. *You* wanted Becky to go to college, rather than following me to my new school. Guess what happened?'

'It's what *Becky* wanted, Kieran.'

He spread his hands wide. 'Well, *this* is what she wants – so let her go.'

'And you moved from your first job in Manchester to this new one at Cheadle Towers mid-year – which would have been more disruptive for Becky if you'd been teaching at the school where she was studying.'

'That's not the *point*, Kate.'

'I think it is. You're doing well since we moved up here, aren't you? You're happy at the Towers?'

167

'Yes, and yes,' he said. He seemed to make an effort, and after a moment, he went on in gentler vein: 'Look, I didn't want to bother with this, but the Head of Sixth Form is retiring at the end of next term. I've got a lot to prove, competing with staff who've been at the school practically since they graduated, but I think I'm in with a chance – *if* I play this right.'

She felt a surge of pride for him. 'Kieran, why didn't you tell me?' She crossed the room and hugged him.

He laughed, holding her at arm's length. 'It's a long shot, I'm just doing what I can to get noticed.'

'I'm coming with you,' she said, moving to her wardrobe to find something suitable.

'No, you can't – Timmy . . .'

'Mum will look after Timmy. What do you think – little black dress?' She reached for a cocktail dress from her wardrobe.

'One of us should be here—'

'Or this?' She switched the dress for a shimmery sequinned top she'd worn for their last anniversary.

He snatched the top from her. 'Kate, *no*.'

She stared at him, shocked, and he grinned sheepishly.

'Sorry – the strain's clearly getting to me. I meant to say it's *fine*.'

'It's *fine*, you want me to come,' she said, 'or it's *fine*, I should stay home?'

He shrugged. 'There's no *need* for you to come – I've got this all worked out,' he said.

'Marvellous,' she said. 'Maybe you can explain it to me, because I'm confused.'

He paused, a selection of ties in one hand, the suit jacket

he would be wearing in the other. She picked out a tie for him and he dumped the rest on the bed, along with the jacket.

'Independent school ethos – *loyal devoir*, all that. It's bollocks, of course, but you know how it is – you have to play politics to get on.'

She searched his face, thinking, *Yes, and I recognize bollocks when I hear it.*

He looked away and flicked his shirt collar up, looping his tie around his neck, turning to the mirror to work on the knot.

She stood watching his reflection in the glass for a moment, remembering what Becky had said about Kieran never being home, his avoidance of her, and felt compelled to add, 'But I don't understand how "school ethos" would mean I shouldn't come along. Kieran—' She broke off – once she'd asked this question she couldn't un-ask it. She took a breath, asked it anyway: 'Is there something you're not telling me?'

His eyes snapped to hers. 'You've got a nerve asking *me* that.'

'Jesus, Kieran – that was *five years* ago,' she flared back. 'When are you going to stop punishing me?'

He sighed, dropped his hands to his sides, giving up on his tie. 'I just want some normality in our lives, Kate. I want to know that you're here to take care of things, that the kids are looked after, that I can rely on you. That you're safe.'

'That's all very worthy,' she said, 'but I can't help noticing that my safety ranks bottom of your list of priorities.'

'Jesus – do you *have* to be such a *bitch*?' He dragged his tie off and rolled it around his fist, his face flushing angrily.

Her heart pounding, she stared him down until the angry glitter left his eyes. 'You don't want a wife, Kieran. You want a housekeeper for yourself and a nanny for your kids.'

'I can't talk to you when you're like this.' He scooped up his jacket, jammed his phone and keys in his pockets and barged past her. 'Don't wait up,' he said.

Simms waited for the front door to slam before she ventured out of the room. Her mother was standing at the foot of the stairs, looking up at her.

'What on earth did you say to him?'

'I don't know.'

'You don't know what you said?'

Simms started down the stairs. 'I know what I said. I just don't know what set him off.'

'He's working terribly hard, Kate.'

'So you keep telling me. But doing what, exactly?'

'This play . . .'

'They started rehearsing the play three weeks ago.' She stopped, three steps up. 'What was he doing the rest of the time?'

Her mother opened her mouth and shut it again. 'That's something you will have to ask him,' she said at last.

'I just did.'

Simms watched her mother struggle with her natural tendency to blame her. 'Kate, love—'

Simms's phone rang in her palm, the vibrations shooting up her arm like pulses of electricity. *Diane, from SCAS.* 'Work,' she said, holding the phone up like an ID card. Like a shield. 'I have to take this.'

She returned to the bedroom, feeling her mother's disapproving gaze at her back.

'Hey, Diane,' she said, trying to sound upbeat, 'got something for me?'

'Good news, bad, news,' Diane said. 'Bad news: I lost the paper files to some over-efficient bureaucrat. He practically stole the damn things from under my nose.'

'Oh,' Simms said, disappointed.

'*Good* news,' Diane went on. 'With the older files out of reach, I had no choice but to rummage through the more recent cases.'

Simms heard the excitement in her voice and her scalp tingled. 'You found something?'

'Oh, *yeah*.' Diane paused. 'The guy leading the investigation at your end said he was only interested in mother/child abductions, so that's all I looked for first time around.'

Diane liked to explain things her own way and if she'd found a lead in the case, she had earned the privilege. But it didn't make the waiting any easier. Her nerves jangling, Simms began to pace.

'Broadening the criteria,' Diane went on, 'I found *four* cases – same tactic – bogeyman in the boot, folds down the back seat to gain access to the victim. The difference is, these all happened around Greater London and the south-east; all single women, twenty-two to twenty-four years old, no kids.'

'Julia Myers was thirty-four,' Simms said. 'And she has a daughter. What makes you think there's a link?'

'Zip ties were involved in all four.'

Simms stopped dead. 'Four murders . . .' she breathed. 'We're looking at a serial killer.'

'Make that *three* murders,' Diane corrected.

'One of them got away?'

'The intended victim deliberately crashed her car, ran into a school for help. Police found the zip tie in her car when they searched it.'

171

Simms gripped the phone tightly. 'Tell me they got DNA.'

'Nothing usable,' Diane said. 'Plenty of fibres and other trace evidence – but nothing to match it to.'

'We need to speak to the survivor,' Simms said. 'D'you have any details?'

'Everything you need. But before I tell you – d'you know what freaked me out?'

Simms waited.

'She's from Lymm.'

It wasn't the grand revelation Simms had been expecting. 'Lymm,' she said, bewildered by the digression. 'That's in Cheshire, isn't it?'

'Technically,' Diane said. 'I looked it up and it's just a whisker outside the southern edge of Greater Manchester – it's practically on your home turf, Kate.'

Simms felt like the breath had been knocked out of her. 'But because Cheshire is a different constabulary, they wouldn't see the link to our case.'

'D'you know what else freaked me out?'

'Please, Diane, just say it,' Simms said. 'You're about to give me a heart attack.'

'Sorry,' Diane said, 'I'm just so fricking excited. This is *fresh*, Kate.'

'How fresh?'

'Three weeks ago fresh.'

'Three w—' Simms took a breath. 'Diane, we *really* need to speak to that woman.'

'Not a problem. It's officially on the books now – the SIO has asked for a search for abductions from cars where zip ties were involved – who'd've thought? I'm putting together my report as we speak, but I'm with you on this – the sooner they get to the survivor, the better. So I've just emailed her contact details to you. You might want to talk to your new best pal, Enderby.'

Simms didn't think she would be on such good terms with Enderby when he found out what she'd done. Interfering with an ongoing investigation was a serious infringement of police protocol – Enderby had already warned her off – but she couldn't think of any other way to get the Myers investigation team on to the abduction survivor, so she braced herself and dialled the chief constable.

Enderby listened in almost total silence, but Simms could feel his anger mounting as she admitted to each new infraction of the rules.

'Isn't this precisely why I asked you to keep an eye on Fennimore?' he said, when she had finished. 'To prevent this flagrant abuse of privilege?'

'Sir, I couldn't prevent him talking to an old friend – he and Cooper—'

'Don't insult my intelligence, Kate,' Enderby said. 'You should have put a stop to any discussion of the post-mortem. And where exactly did this friendly chat happen? No—' he interrupted himself, 'don't tell me. I don't want to know. Do you realize what you've done – bringing Cooper in on this . . . this *caper*? And now this analyst – what's her name?'

'Sir, she didn't have a clue – she thought I was on the investigation team.'

'You lied to her?'

'I . . .' Simms hesitated. 'I neglected to correct a misapprehension.'

Silence.

'The point is,' she pushed on, 'it's given us a head start. The analyst found a survivor we can interview.'

'That does not excuse your behaviour,' Enderby said. 'I've backed you, Kate – but there are limits. You could have a good career here in Manchester, but you keep crossing the line. The moment will come – and soon – when I won't be able to protect you.'

'A six-year-old girl is out there, sir,' she said. 'I don't think she would care too much about the rules.'

'Watch your tone, Chief Inspector,' he warned.

Simms took a breath, apologized.

'You will stay well away from this investigation from this point onward,' Enderby said. 'Enjoy the rest of your leave.'

She heard four tumbling notes as he hung up. For a few seconds she stared miserably at her phone, then the bedroom door burst open and Timmy came charging in.

'Nanna said you'll read me a story,' he said.

'After bathtime,' she said.

'Nooooo-oh!'

She scooped him on to her lap and tickled him. 'Yeeeeee-es, smelly boy!'

For once, Tim didn't seem inclined to put up a struggle, but giggled joyfully.

She stood, tucking him under her arm, and carried him, still chortling to the bathroom. Her mother came up the stairs and watched, an approving look on her face, and Simms couldn't help thinking that the way things were going, Kieran might get his wish – he might make a housewife of her yet.

26

Experience is the name everyone gives to their mistakes.

OSCAR WILDE

Aberdeen, Wednesday Evening

Fennimore had continued the tedious job of sorting his office, sending eight more sacks of rubbish for shredding. The papers, files and disks he wanted to keep were stacked in boxes, labelled and ready to be transported to his office on the new campus. The more important or sensitive files and folders, he had shifted temporarily to his flat, until he was satisfied that security in the new building would not take any risks with confidentiality. He kept his laptop nearby during the whole operation and checked the Paris surveillance cameras regularly.

As he dumped another rubbish bag outside the door, his academic email account burbled – he had a new message. Josh had completed his research into David Hazle, their new suspect in the Kelli Rees murder. It looked like the Mitchell appeal was finally beginning to motor.

Fennimore went looking and found the student in the

empty forensics lab. Most of the equipment was gone, but Josh stood at one of the benches, gloved, capped and booted, a lab coat over his student-issue jeans and T-shirt. The bench was covered with a sheet of white paper on which he had placed a hand-held magnifier, stereo microscope, a roll of fibre-evidence tape, backing cards and high-power torch. The room had a sharp, slightly astringent smell. Josh lifted a black pea coat out of an evidence bag, glancing up as Fennimore came through the door.

'I got your report,' Fennimore said.

'Cool,' Josh said. He placed the coat carefully on the paper and began examining it through the magnifier.

'So Hazle's been dead three years?' Fennimore said.

'Yeah.' Josh put the magnifier down and took a strip of adhesive tape, pressed it on the coat fabric and peeled it back, sticking it face-down on a piece of backing card and labelling the card to indicate where on the jacket the lift had been taken from. 'Doesn't look a likely suspect to me, though,' he said.

'Why?' Fennimore said, moving around the table to face him. 'Hazle was alive at the time of the murder.'

Josh frowned. 'Is this a test?'

'I'm asking for an opinion.'

'Okay . . .' Josh paused in the collection of evidence and gathered his thoughts. 'Hazle had form. He was prosecuted for possession of cannabis with intent to supply.'

'Which explains why he's in the DNA database,' Fennimore said, 'but not why you think he's innocent.'

'He claimed the weed was for "medicinal use",' Josh went on. 'No other criminal prosecutions. He left a widow; there was no recorded history of spousal abuse.'

No *recorded* history – Fennimore liked qualification – Josh's attention to detail put him head and shoulders above his peers.

'All right,' Fennimore said. 'But there has to be a first time for everything. Let's look at what we've got: the weed – medicinal use, he said – did you get anything more on that?'

Josh shook his head. 'He was given a suspended sentence, so the judge must've believed him. We could ask the appeal solicitor to request a copy of the court proceedings.'

'We'll do that, but it'll take time and Essex Police are already way ahead of us on this. So . . . common medicinal uses of *Cannabis sativa* would be treatment of glaucoma, epilepsy, migraines, insomnia . . .'

'And nausea associated with AIDS and chemotherapy,' Josh added.

'If I were on the police review team,' Fennimore said, 'I'd suggest they go to the hospital records, dig through old files. But I'm not, and while hospitals might share that kind of information with a murder investigation, we wouldn't stand a chance.'

'I could try and get into the hospital database.'

Josh had managed something similar on their first case, but that hadn't involved hacking; it was all achieved with guile and a measure of charm that Fennimore had not previously suspected of the student.

'We stay within the law,' he said.

Josh glanced down at the coat on the bench, then up at Fennimore. 'So you'll want to talk to the widow.'

Fennimore felt the corners of his mouth twitch; this was another of Josh's strengths – he was always thinking, always trying to get one step ahead. 'I don't suppose you have an address?'

He saw an answering flicker of amusement in the student's eyes. 'Home phone number, as well.'

'The police will be aiming to establish a timeline that rules Hazle in or out as a rapist, a killer, or the killer's accomplice,' Fennimore said. 'So you can bet they've already interviewed the wife. My guess is she won't be keen to take phone calls from strangers.'

'So where do we go from here?' Josh said.

'Essex, I think.' Fennimore watched closely for a reaction, but Josh avoided his gaze.

'You're going to doorstep her?' he said.

'I'm not good with that sort of thing,' Fennimore said, meaning the bereaved, those outside his professional sphere. 'I thought you might come along, smooth the way.'

'To Essex.'

'Assuming she still lives there.' Fennimore looked into his face. 'Is that a problem?'

Josh lifted his chin, acknowledging the challenge, but didn't answer.

'Josh?'

For a few seconds, Josh stared at the coat on the bench as if it were a corpse awaiting dissection. 'I did some . . . bad things,' he began, each word seemingly an effort, '. . . when I was a kid. I—'

'I know,' Fennimore interrupted – it seemed cruel to make him go on.

The student's brow furrowed. '*What* do you know?'

'What happened to you. That you had to change your identity to stay safe. That you did the right thing.'

Josh stared at Fennimore, his face grey. 'Who told you?'

'Lazko.'

'Oh, shit . . .' Josh wiped a gloved hand over his face, then stared at it, as though the stain of contamination were visible. He peeled off the glove and dumped it. 'When?' he said.

'Yesterday.'

'Well, that's it, then.' Josh stripped off the other glove. 'I got to call my handler.' He moved away from the bench.

'Lazko isn't going to tell anyone,' Fennimore said, holding up a hand to stop him.

'He's a journo – 'course he is.'

'He's also a coward. He seemed badly scared by what he found.'

'He should be.'

'Is it really that bad?'

'Worse.' Josh exhaled and Fennimore heard the breath stutter in his throat. 'There's a contract out on me. Has been ever since I broke with the firm.'

'Okay,' Fennimore said, 'you should stay here – forget I ever mentioned Essex.'

Josh bowed his head; he seemed in silent conversation with himself. When his head came up, Fennimore saw cold, hard determination in his face.

'I'll do it,' he said.

'No. Josh . . .'

Josh shot him a shrewd look. 'You want the widow's co-operation?'

'I won't get far without it,' Fennimore admitted.

Josh lifted one shoulder. 'Then you need me. Book a cheap tourist hotel away from the towns, hire a car with tinted windows. I'll stay low.'

It was a risk. But Fennimore thrived on risk – and he really needed Josh on this. 'All right,' he said. 'We'll take the earliest flight out tomorrow morning. I'll meet you at my apartment at five-thirty.'

Josh flung off the rest of his protective gear and swept the coat off the bench.

'You're going to *wear* the evidence?' Fennimore said.

'It's not evidence – it's my jacket,' Josh said. 'Practice,' he added, by way of explanation. 'So I'll know what to look for when things go wrong – the mistakes people make.'

Fennimore nodded, approving.

'So how's my technique?'

Fennimore appraised the bench. 'Your work space is organized; your "evidence" retrieval was methodical – but if you'd overlaid the coat with a grid, you could have mapped the exact position of any fibres you retrieved.' He paused, sniffed. 'There was an odour when I first came into the lab – I can't quite catch it now – tea tree oil, maybe?'

'Wet wipes,' Josh confirmed, taking the pack from his jacket pocket. 'I used 'em to clean the bench before I put the paper down.'

'Of course, you should've used sterile distilled water and swabs. You've got at least half a dozen ingredients in those wipes: oils, perfume, chelating agents, anti-microbials, alcohol – added to that, the tiniest imperfections in the bench can slough off fibres which might contaminate a sample.'

Josh nodded. 'Had to improvise,' he said. 'The lab techs took all the proper stuff.'

'Except the microscopes?'

'No, they're gone as well. This little beauty's mine,' Josh said, lifting it from the bench into a sports bag.

27

Manchester, Wednesday Evening

Simms was folding laundry when Fennimore called.

'Any news on the little girl?' he said.

'I'm not supposed to be talking to you,' she said.

'That sounds ominous. I'm guessing it's my fault.'

'Only partly. I called a mate in SCAS, she reviewed the case analysis with the zip tie factored in, found some related cases.' Simms paused, relishing this next detail, despite what it had cost her. 'And a survivor.'

'A *what*? Kate, that's *fantastic* – have they interviewed her yet? What did she say?'

'I don't know, Nick.'

'What d'you mean, you don't know?'

'It's a weekday and I'm standing in my kitchen, doing housework,' she said, with dry humour. 'Take a guess.'

'Enderby locked you out?' Fennimore sounded outraged, and she felt a surge of warmth towards him. 'The man's an idiot.'

She laughed. 'He speaks very highly of you. Look, I went behind his back, I broke protocols, I meddled in an investigation – I'm lucky he didn't suspend me.'

'Kate, I'm—'

'Forget it.' She didn't think she could cope with his sympathy just now; since her row with Kieran, she had yearned for Fennimore in a way that could only lead to trouble. 'So,' she said, brightly, 'what's going on with your MOJ?'

Fennimore gave her a brief summary, outlining the discovery of DNA on Kelli Rees's clothing, that it was not a match to Mitchell; he named the new suspect, who, it seemed, was with Kelli the night of her death. He elaborated on the defence barrister's ineptitude, the missed opportunities, his intention to interview Hazle's widow.

His ability to keep all the facts in his head and present them concisely was one of Fennimore's strengths – and why he was so popular as an expert witness in court.

'So you're off to Essex tomorrow,' she said.

'First flight.'

'You *will* bear in mind the widow isn't a hostile witness?' Simms said, only half-joking.

'Of course,' he said. 'But we *do* need to establish if her husband was involved in a rape-murder or he if simply paid for the victim's services that night.'

Simms winced. 'You must see that she won't find either option particularly comforting?'

He paused. 'Now you mention it.' He sounded chastened. 'Which is why I'm taking Josh with me.'

'Josh,' Simms said. 'I thought you'd dropped him?'

'I changed my mind.'

'I think that's a mistake.'

'That's because you're a cop, and he has a natural antipathy to cops – but I need someone who can smooth-talk the widow.'

'I've seen him in action – I know he can turn on the charm,' she said. 'But you skimmed over his "natural antipathy".'

'He's okay, Kate.' This was Fennimore the rock-climber, the risk-taker, the betting man who didn't mind losing as long as he came out even.

'You mean you *think* he's okay.'

'I *know* it,' he said. 'Lazko did some digging.'

That came as a surprise. 'What did he find?'

'It's not my story to tell.'

'Well, *that* can't be good,' she said, thinking, *Fennimore, you're going to get hurt.* 'Maybe I should do some digging of my own.'

'No—' He sounded alarmed. 'Kate, you can't do that.'

'Give me one good reason.'

'It could put his life in danger.'

She thought about it: the secrecy, Josh's discomfort around cops; his chosen career – and now this. 'So Josh is in witness protection?'

'I didn't ask. But, Kate – you can't go looking. He had a bad start in life; he turned it around. He deserves a chance, doesn't he?'

Simms had met a lot of drug addicts and prostitutes looking for a second chance in her fallow years of community/police partnerships at the Met before she landed her promotion with Manchester. She believed passionately in second chances; hadn't her own move to the north of England been her second – her final – chance? But she knew it wasn't only victims who went into witness protection. Manipulative, violent, evil men did, too. And Fennimore had been the target of too many of those since Suzie's disappearance.

'You know his real name?' she said. 'Give me that, I'll do a few discreet checks.'

'No. Please, Kate,' he said. 'Promise me you'll leave it alone.'

She began to weaken. 'What if he's just using you?'

'We *all* use each other. The more important question is do I trust him?'

'And *do* you?'

'Josh Brown has a first class honours in psychology, but he attends undergraduate courses in forensics because he wants a firm grounding in the basics. He comes in early and stays late to practise techniques he'll probably never need. He even blew a minimum of five hundred quid on a stereo microscope so he can have exclusive use of it.'

'That makes him a good student,' she said. 'It doesn't make him a good *man*.'

'He turned down a promising academic opportunity at Nottingham, relocated here and started all over again with forensic science, *because he cares about justice*. He's genuine. I trust him.'

'All right,' she said, against her better judgement. 'I'll leave my spade in the tool shed – for now. But please – be careful.'

28

Doubt everything but the facts.

N. FENNIMORE, PARAPHRASING A. LEOPOLD

Aberdeen, Thursday, 5:30 a.m.

Fennimore called Carl Lazko's number and left a message to let him know he was on his way; since he would be in Essex for a few days, now would be a good time to meet with Mitchell's solicitor. The door entry buzzer sounded: it was Josh.

'Taxi's here, an' all,' Josh said.

'Give me two minutes.' Fennimore picked up his carry-on bag, slid his laptop into his shoulder bag, set the alarm and, with a last swift glance around the room, was out the door. As it swung shut, he heard the landline ring.

Leave it? He should, but what if it was Lazko, returning his call? He pushed the door open with his fingertips, tapped in the alarm code and scooped up the telephone receiver in one smooth sequence.

'Professor Fennimore?' A male voice, vaguely familiar.

'Speaking,' he said.

'Oh, thank goodness. This is John Vincent, auditing

185

accountant at Laurent Wealth Management.' The company that dealt with Fennimore's accounts and investments. 'I'm sorry to ring so early, but I have left several messages. Are you free to talk?'

'*Early?* It's five-thirty in the morning, Mr Vincent,' he said. 'And I've a plane to catch.'

'Oh . . .' The accountant sounded disappointed. 'If we could schedule a chat – we really do need to review your investments.'

Fennimore stifled a groan. 'Can't you put together some suggestions and I'll take a look?'

'Of course, of course.' Vincent sounded a bit breathless. 'But it's not a simple matter of moving investments around. Diminishing returns from your publications are a complicating issue.'

Diminishing returns? What the hell is he talking about? Fennimore checked his watch. 'Look, I really have to go,' he said.

'Very well,' Vincent said. 'But please don't leave it too long; if you have a pen, I'll give you my direct line.'

Fennimore jotted the number down and hung up, frowning. The drop in sales was puzzling: he had recently done a book tour in the USA where there was a lot of interest in *Crapshoots and Bad Stats*. Hurrying down the staircase to Josh, and the waiting taxi, he resolved to deal with his finances when he got back.

By mid-morning, they had arrived at Mrs Hazle's home, a 1960s semi-detached on the edge of Basildon. Essex felt positively tropical compared with the dull, damp chill of Aberdeen. A ramp and handrail had been built up to the extra-wide front door. She opened it on the safety chain and peered out, a spare, dark-haired woman of about forty, her brown eyes hard with distrust.

'What are you — police?' Her gaze switched from Fennimore to Josh. 'Journalists?'

'We're neither, Mrs Hazle,' Fennimore said. 'We're forensic scientists.' He introduced himself and Josh, and handed her his business card.

'Aberdeen,' she said, reading the address on it. 'What's a scientist from Scotland got to do with my husband?'

A neighbour walked past pushing a pram. The young mother slowed and her head swivelled to watch the exchange on Mrs Hazle's doorstep.

'If we might step inside, Mrs Hazle?' Fennimore said. 'It would be more private.'

With a gasp of indignation, the widow unhooked the door chain.

They followed her through to the kitchen.

'All right,' she said, when they were seated. 'You better tell me what this is all about.'

'I'm helping with the review of the rape-murder—'

'We're not accusing your husband of anything, Mrs Hazle,' Josh interrupted, throwing Fennimore a warning look. 'Professor Fennimore is looking at some new evidence that came to light.'

'You're talking about my husband and a murder in the same breath — sounds a lot like an accusation to me,' she said. 'Well, I told the police and I'll tell you — my David was no killer.' Her eyes, already red and puffy, filled with fresh tears.

'Like we said,' Josh soothed. 'We're not police. We're scientists — we got no axe to grind.' Normally, Josh toned down his accent, but now he played up the Essex vowels. 'We just want to get at the truth.'

Mrs Hazle bit her lip, tears brimming over, and Josh stood and reached a box of tissues down from the kitchen counter. 'Why don't I make us a nice cup o' tea,' he said, his tone gentle, sympathetic. 'The professor will explain.'

'Our client is appealing against his conviction,' Fennimore said.

'And now the police want to pin it on my husband. Well, he's not here to defend himself – it's not *right*.'

'You're husband was ill before he d—' Josh bugged his eyes and Fennimore corrected himself: 'Before he passed away?'

She nodded, but didn't elaborate.

'He was a wheelchair user?' Fennimore asked, thinking that might rule Mr Hazle out before they got started.

'Sometimes,' she said. 'He had MS for ten years before he . . .'

Fennimore was ready to ask the next question, but Josh caught his eye and gave a barely discernible shake of his head.

'That must've been hard for you,' Josh said.

She bit her lip. 'Worse for him.'

Josh nodded solemnly, handing her a mug of tea, one to Fennimore.

Fennimore knew that his educated accent and smart business dress had got them over the doorstep, but it was Josh who had them sipping tea in the grieving widow's kitchen, so he followed the student's lead, giving Mrs Hazle space to think.

'They said they wanted to eliminate him from their enquiries,' she said. 'Like he was some kind of criminal.'

'He *did* have a criminal record.'

The widow threw Fennimore a hot look.

'That cannabis was *medicine* – he grew it for himself. But there was a big thing going on – an "initiative" they called it. Name and shame, all that. The police wouldn't listen. Now they say they've got evidence proving David was there when that poor girl died.'

'Evidence doesn't *prove* anything,' Fennimore said. 'It's context and interpretation that establishes conformity to one narrative or another.'

She looked to Josh, confused.

'The evidence doesn't tell the whole story,' Josh explained. 'Like Mr Hazle growing pot,' he went on. 'Stated as a stone cold fact, it looks bad. You need to know the whys and the wherefores before you can see how the facts fit together.'

'And sometimes they don't fit at all,' Fennimore said, grateful for Josh's nifty bit of interpretation. 'The police do have evidence, there's no denying that—'

'I *told* you—' Mrs Hazle began.

Fennimore raised a hand, placating: 'Mrs Hazle, I'm not making any accusations. I'm saying if they got it wrong once, they could do it again. Which is why we're here.'

She set her mug down carefully on the table. 'Oh, you should've said – you're here to protect my David's memory.' Contempt burned in her eyes. 'Well, that's very *nice* of you.'

Fennimore felt for her, but he needed information and he was sure she could give it to him. He would not fly back to Aberdeen empty-handed, so he returned her stare and put steel into his voice. 'The new evidence puts your husband in close sexual contact with the victim around the time she was murdered.'

Mrs Hazle sat back, a look of shocked dismay on her face.

It was an overstatement and Josh began to speak, but Fennimore dismissed his protest with a shake of his head.

'You're right on both counts,' he went on. 'I'm not a very "nice" person. I'm not here to protect your husband. If I'm honest, I don't really care if he's guilty or innocent.'

She gripped the table edge and shoved her chair back, the fire in her eyes again. 'So it's all about getting your client off.'

'No,' Fennimore said. 'You see, I don't care about *him* any more than I do your husband.'

She gasped.

'I'm a scientist, Mrs Hazle,' he went on. 'I doubt everything but the facts; choose statistical probability over feelings every time. But that's what makes me good at my job – because I *do* care about the evidence. I care about the truth. I care when science is mangled by incompetents to prove their own prejudices. So – no matter what the outcome – I can promise you that I will look at all of the evidence objectively.'

Mrs Hazle looked winded; she released her grip on the table and let her hands slide into her lap. 'Well,' she said, 'I suppose that's honest, at least. But I don't see what I can do.'

Fennimore relaxed. 'Right now the only new evidence is your husband's semen on the murder victim's dress.'

She flinched.

Josh shot an exasperated look at Fennimore. 'It sounds brutal, but—'

'I don't like your professor very much, Josh,' she interrupted. 'But it's like what you said: he wants more facts so he can see how they fit in the story.'

'Precisely.' Fennimore paused. 'My guess is the police are driving down a one-way street: they're thinking those stains got on to the victim's clothing because your husband raped her.' Josh shifted in his seat, but didn't intervene. 'But evidence without context is a two-way street: they should be looking at the evidence from both directions — asking what is the likelihood the stains got on to the victim for *some other* reason.'

'I can't tell you that — I don't know!' she exclaimed.

'There's no reason why you should,' Fennimore said. 'But if you're willing to talk about some painful things, answer some tough questions, maybe we can find out.'

She thought about it for a full minute, wiping her eyes and twisting the wet tissue till it came apart in her hands. At last she sighed and plucked two more tissues from the box.

'All right,' she said, 'ask your questions.'

'Mr Hazle had MS,' Fennimore said. 'And you say he sometimes used a wheelchair. If we could establish that he was wheelchair-bound at the time of the murder . . .'

'When did it happen?' she said. 'The murder, I mean.'

'Four years ago,' Fennimore said. 'April twenty-sixth.'

Her forehead creased with pain. 'David had just finished his first lot of chemo then,' she said.

Fennimore looked at her in question.

'It wasn't the MS that got him in the end. It was cancer. David died of prostate cancer.' She went eagerly to the Welsh dresser on the far side of the room and brought out a diary, thumbing through it. Her face fell. 'He wasn't at the hospital on the twenty-sixth of April.'

'But you have a record of hospital appointments, treatments and so on?'

She handed Fennimore the diary, and he leafed through dozens of dates and times, 'chemo' or 'radio' noted next to the treatment days, 'Dr Ghosh' on others.

'Dr Ghosh was his oncologist?' he asked.

She nodded. 'Lovely man.' She returned to the dresser and drew out a bundle of letters. She held on to them, as if reluctant to let go, but after a moment she handed the letters over. 'Read them,' she said.

It wouldn't sway his judgement either way, but for her sake, Fennimore glanced through the letters, seeing messages of hope: 'shrinkage of the tumour', 'positive signs', 'cause for cautious optimism'. Then requests to return for repeat scans, and a rapid decline into suggestions about palliative care, finishing with a contact for Macmillan nursing.

'He went through so much,' she said. 'He was weak and terribly sick right through the chemo – but the treatment didn't take. The cancer spread. *That's* why he was growing cannabis – it reduced his stress, helped with the pain. And those heartless bastards prosecuted him – made a criminal of a dying man!'

'Did you show any of this to the police?' Fennimore said.

She wiped tears from her face and drew herself to her full height. 'I didn't like their manner,' she said.

Fennimore smiled.

'I don't think I like yours any better,' she added sharply.

'What if I said that I believe I can prove your husband's innocence?'

'How? You've seen the diary. He wasn't in hospital on the twenty-sixth.'

'True,' Fennimore said. 'And we only have your word for it that your husband was too ill to be involved in the mur—' Josh's warning look made him revise what he was about to say: 'To be involved.'

'You want Dr Ghosh to tell the police how ill David was?'

'That'll help,' Fennimore said. 'But it's just possible he has evidence that proves your husband's innocence.'

She scoffed. 'Didn't you say evidence doesn't prove anything?'

'Without context, it doesn't. But Dr Ghosh can provide that, too.'

She stared at him, uncomprehending.

'We have physical evidence and part of the context – the whys and wherefores, as Josh so elegantly put it – but there are gaps,' Fennimore said. 'Dr Ghosh might be able to bridge those gaps, but he won't do it without your permission.'

'I'll call him,' she said. 'What do you want me to say?'

Dr Ghosh met Fennimore in his office after morning clinic.

He had David Hazle's file ready on his desk. He looked sad and tired, and Fennimore guessed he had spent more than one consultation that morning telling people the worst news possible.

'I appreciate your taking the time to see me,' Fennimore said.

'David was a brave man,' Ghosh said. 'Did Frances tell you he raised ten thousand pounds for the oncology unit while he was undergoing treatment?'

'She didn't.' They were on first-name terms, then – a good sign, given what Fennimore was about to ask.

'Frances said the police believe David was involved in the rape and murder of a young woman – it's preposterous, of course – he could barely lift his head off the pillow, after the chemo.'

'A lot of prostate cancer patients suffer from erectile dysfunction following treatment?' Fennimore asked.

Ghosh nodded. 'David was one of them. And your surmise is correct: he wasn't physically capable of rape.'

'Yet his sperm *was* found at the scene.'

'The police must have made an error on the DNA sample.'

'I took a sample from the same item of clothing and had it tested at an independent lab,' Fennimore said. 'There's no error.'

'Then, I don't . . .' Dr Ghosh frowned.

'He underwent both chemo- and radiotherapy?' Fennimore said.

Another tired nod. 'Two cycles. He was too weak to continue after that.'

'Mrs Hazle would have been in her mid–thirties when her husband was diagnosed?'

'Yes, but what has that to do with—?'

'I imagine Mr Hazle banked sperm prior to chemo in case it caused infertility?'

Dr Ghosh looked suddenly energized. 'It is usually advised in younger couples,' he agreed, flipping open the folder and riffling through the pages. 'Yes,' he said. 'David donated sperm on three occasions over the course of the second week in March. His first cycle of treatment began at the end of March. Do you think someone stole one of the samples?'

'I think it's worth checking,' Fennimore said. 'And the police should be told.' He paused. 'But before you call them, Doctor, I'd like to ask two small favours.'

29

Never go back.

ANON

Essex, Thursday Lunchtime

Fennimore brought Josh up to date in the car heading to their motel. He had chosen a small, family-run inn, just off the A13, eight miles south-west of Basildon, and twenty-five miles from Chelmsford, where his family was based, as the safer option for Josh. They had Mrs Hazle's diary documenting her husband's hospital visits, and the letters sent by Dr Ghosh to Mr Hazle in the months before his death. Dr Ghosh had given Fennimore a copy of the post-mortem report and had promised to arrange for him to collect a sample of Mr Hazle's semen before he returned to Scotland: he wanted independent verification that the sample from the victim's skirt was a genuine match to Hazle.

'Hazle didn't do it, did he?' Josh said.

'Dr Ghosh says he wasn't capable after the cancer treatment,' Fennimore said.

'So the evidence was planted.'

'It seems likely.'

'Which means Mitchell *is* guilty after all?'

'It's possible,' Fennimore said. 'Graham Mitchell could have murdered the victim and tried to implicate Mr Hazle.'

'Yeah, but if he *did* plant Hazle's DNA on her, why would he confess?'

Fennimore shrugged. 'Duress?'

'The police say there wasn't any, and he never claimed that in court – even after he changed his plea. Speaking of which, if he planted the evidence, wouldn't he get his defence to demand DNA tests on Kelli Rees's clothing?'

'You'd think so, wouldn't you?' Fennimore said, with a sly glance; he wanted to see how far Josh could reason this through.

'And Mitchell was a roofer,' Josh said. 'How would he get access to a hospital lab? He'd have to've had an accomplice.'

'That's possible, too,' Fennimore said. 'On the other hand, it could be that neither Mitchell *nor* Hazle is guilty. Maybe Mitchell told the truth about paying the victim for her services the night she was killed. The killer, unaware that Mitchell's DNA was already on the victim, planted Mr Hazle's semen on her to deflect attention from himself.'

Josh turned to Fennimore, his expression excited and intense. 'We need to know who had access to the banked sperm.'

'That would take a court order,' Fennimore said. 'Which we will ask for, but in the meantime, there's work of a more mundane nature to be done.'

'Okay, what?'

'You photographed the oncologist's letters?'

'And the diary. I emailed the jpegs to you,' Josh said.

'Good. Hazle's PM report is in my backpack – dig it out, will you, and do the same with that.'

196

Josh snagged the bag from the back seat and retrieved the folder.

'I'll want photocopies of everything, too,' Fennimore said. 'We'll file the originals with Mitchell's solicitor while we're here.' He fished in his pocket and handed Josh his mobile.

'Try Lazko, see if you can raise him.'

Fennimore turned on to a country lane, and as they passed a traditional weatherboard house, Josh twisted to get a better look. For a second Fennimore saw a glimpse of the intense boy of seventeen in the press photo outside the Crown Court.

'How does it feel, being back?' he asked.

'Like . . . nothing. Doesn't mean anything to me any more,' Josh said, facing straight ahead again, listening to the phone.

Is that how it would be for Suzie – if he ever found her? Fennimore wondered. Like home and family meant nothing to her?

'It's gone to voicemail,' Josh said, interrupting his thoughts. 'Want me to leave a message?'

'Don't bother, I must've left a dozen already.' Josh handed the mobile back and Fennimore pocketed it, slowing for the turn into the motel car park. 'I'll drop you at the hotel, then head into Chelmsford to see the appeal solicitor.'

Fennimore dumped his car keys and bags with Josh while he went to the reception desk to check in. As the clerk slid the keys across the counter and launched into his script about room locations and breakfast arrangements, the entrance doors opened and three men approached the desk.

'Professor Nicholas Fennimore?' the shortest of the three said.

Fennimore gave him a cursory glance. 'I prefer Nick. Who are you?'

'Detective Sergeant Benton, Essex Police.'

He was squat and solid, with the bull-neck of a weightlifter and the broad hands of a labourer. Fennimore checked his ID. Dr Ghosh would have told them of his visit to the hospital by now. He looked at the other two grim-faced men; it seemed that Essex Police were pissed off he'd beaten them to the oncologist, but three cops to deliver the message seemed a bit extreme. 'What can I do for you, Sergeant?'

'Come down to the station, answer some questions.'

'I'd prefer to answer them here – I'm starving – and I'm told the food here is good.'

'We'll sort you some tea and a sandwich at the station,' the sergeant said.

Well, if they wanted access to Mrs Hazle's diaries and letters, they could ask Mitchell's solicitor for them. Fennimore chanced a quick glance at Josh; the student was staring at his mobile phone screen, but Fennimore could tell by the tension in his shoulders that he was paying close attention. He let his gaze slide over the younger man towards the hotel entrance and the three policemen eased into a semi-circle, crowding him.

'Afraid I might make a run for it, Sergeant?' he said with mild surprise.

'Just keen to have that chat, sir,' Benton said smoothly.

Fennimore experienced a pang of concern. 'About what?'

'Better if we talk down the station, sir,' Benton said, relaxing his stance, even trying an experimental smile. 'We won't take any more of your time than we have to.'

'Which station?' Fennimore asked, for Josh's benefit.

'Does it matter?'

'It might – I have business in Chelmsford.'

Another unconvincing smile. 'Then it won't even be out of your way, sir.'

The two silent cops flanked Fennimore, while Sergeant Benton walked a few steps behind him. One of the men glanced over at Josh, as they moved away. Josh didn't look up, but he scratched his eyebrow with his free hand, effectively covering his face.

30

It is a capital mistake to theorize before you have all the evidence.

A. C. DOYLE, *A STUDY IN SCARLET*

The police station was next to the Crown Court, not far from the cathedral. Fennimore had testified as an expert witness several times during his time at the National Crime Faculty, and he had enjoyed lunchtimes, strolling through the cathedral gardens in the shade of its honeyed stone-and-flint walls. Today they went by a less picturesque route, along Parkway, taking Fennimore into the station by the back door.

He was shown into an interview room; it looked recently refurbished, done out in aquamarine, with light beech furniture and a large flip clock on the wall showing date, day and time. The sergeant said he would be back in a few minutes. After the first five, Fennimore suspected the intention was to intimidate him. He checked the door. It was locked. He shrugged, taking an interest in the recording equipment bolted to the table top. The drive was empty, but he opened it and peered inside, closed it and tinkered with the audio balance. A plastic strip ran around all four walls at waist height, but he traced the recorder's wiring down a conduit to a socket below the desk, so the strip must have another purpose. A video camera was positioned at ceiling height in a far corner of the room, pointing towards the table. At fifteen minutes, he hit the strip hard with his elbow.

He folded his arms and leaned against the wall, listening to the sound of raised voices and running in the corridor outside. Sergeant Benton burst through the door first.

'What the hell are you doing?' he demanded.

Fennimore looked around him. 'I appear to be waiting,' he said.

Two constables in uniform piled in after Benton.

'All right, Sarge?' one of them said.

'You need to lean off the rail, sir.' Benton stood three feet away from Fennimore, his bull-neck pulled tight into his collar and his big hands clenched into fists.

Fennimore glanced down at the plastic rail. 'This?' He twisted to get a better look. 'Oh, don't tell me – it's a panic alarm and I've just been and gone and set it off.' He stared dolefully at the two constables. 'Sorry about that.'

The two men looked to their sergeant for instructions.

'False alarm,' he said briskly. 'Shut it off.'

'Now you're here,' Fennimore said, leaning off the rail, 'I'm ready for that chat.'

Benton's jaw tightened, but he managed a tight smile and dragged out a chair from against the back wall. Fennimore knew the suspect was always seated furthest from the door, so he ignored the offer, taking a chair on the other side of the table, his back to the camera.

'You got that wrong, Professor,' Benton said.

'Not if we're just having a chat,' Fennimore said, with a smile.

Benton took the seat opposite Fennimore with bad grace and flushed darkly.

A moment later one of the silent cops from the hotel came in and said, 'Uh, Sarge?'

'Just . . . stay by the door, okay?' Benton said.

The detective shrugged and moved to stand behind Fennimore.

'Do you know Carl Lazko?' Benton said.

'Ye-es.' That was not a question Fennimore had anticipated.

'How do you know him?'

'He's a journalist – I'm—'

'I asked how.'

Fennimore said, 'He's famous in these parts, isn't he?'

Benton clearly didn't find that a satisfactory answer. 'When was the last time you were in contact with Mr Lazko?'

'Yesterday. Why?'

'You didn't contact him this morning?'

'I tried to – he's not answering his phone.'

'You left a message?'

'Not this time.'

'So there were other calls.'

'Several,' Fennimore said, irritated. 'Look—'

'In fact, Professor Fennimore, you've made more than twenty calls to Lazko's mobile over the past week, eight of them today.'

'You're monitoring my calls?'

'What were those calls about?'

'You mean you don't know?'

'Answer the question,' Benton said.

'It's none of your damn business,' Fennimore said evenly.

Benton watched him coldly for a few moments. 'You and Lazko go way back,' he said. 'All that shit he stirred up about you and that cop from the Met after your wife disappeared.'

'Go to hell.'

Benton spread his hands. 'Don't get me wrong – if it was me, I'd want to rip his tongue out.'

Fennimore leaned back in his chair and stared at the sergeant. Why was Benton dragging up Rachel's murder? It made no sense.

'What I don't get is, why now?' Benton said. 'I mean, it's been, what – five years? Of course, we know Lazko called you multiple times when you got yourself in the news after that MOJ lecture. I can understand you'd be pissed off – he's been a thorn in your side for years, hasn't he?'

Fennimore continued to stare at the cop. 'Oh, I see,' he said. 'You aren't monitoring *my* calls, you're monitoring *Lazko's*.' It had to be about the Mitchell case. But they couldn't know that Fennimore was working on the review – Benton would have mentioned that, if he'd known. So what the hell was going on?

Benton was still talking and Fennimore caught the last few words:

'—decide to give a taste of his own medicine, did you?'

'Wait – you think I was badgering Lazko?'

Benton raised his eyebrows. 'Twenty calls in the last week, Professor. Speaks for itself.'

'I think you have it arse-about,' Fennimore said, smiling.

'You think this is funny?'

'I do.'

'Do you deny that you have made repeated calls to Mr Lazko?'

'No. But I don't confirm it either. Now get to the point or I'm leaving.'

'All right. I put it to you, Professor Fennimore, that you've been stalking Mr Lazko.'

Fennimore laughed.

Benton didn't. 'You deny that you broke into Mr Lazko's flat?'

'What, from Aberdeen? The break-in happened, what, five – no, six days ago? In fact, I was talking to Lazko in my apartment when he got the call.'

Benton looked over Fennimore's shoulder towards the silent detective and Fennimore heard the door open and close softly behind him.

'Mr Lazko's flat was broken into this morning,' Benton said.

'Again? Poor bastard.'

The sergeant's expression did not change and Fennimore experienced a thud of disquiet.

'Has something happened to him?' he said. 'Is he all right?'

Benton smirked. 'Your fake concern is very touching.'

'Okay – that's it.' Fennimore stood.

'Sit down,' Benton said.

Fennimore strode to the door.

'Professor *Fennimore*—'

Fennimore was through the door and into the corridor. People came running from both directions; Benton must have deployed the alarm. A uniform cop grabbed him by the arm as the sergeant emerged from the interview room.

Fennimore shook himself free.

'Behave yourself or I will arrest you.'

'On what charge?'

'On suspicion of the murder of Carl Lazko,' Benton said.

Fennimore stared at the cop. 'Lazko's dead?'

'Nice,' Benton said. 'Did you rehearse that in the mirror?'

Fennimore allowed himself to be escorted back to the interview room. This time Benton seated him firmly in the interviewee's chair, facing the camera. The sergeant's silent colleague sat next to Benton, on the other side of the table.

'Where were you between seven-thirty and eight-thirty this morning?' Benton asked.

'You're making an idiot of yourself,' Fennimore said. 'I didn't kill Lazko – I was working with him.'

'Bullshit,' Benton said.

'Language, Sergeant.' Fennimore checked the recorder ostentatiously. 'Or are we still *not* recording this?'

'Come on, Prof – you must hate Lazko's guts.'

'Must have,' Fennimore repeated, and Benton frowned.

'*Must have* hated,' Fennimore said. 'Past tense.'

The detective's face darkened and Fennimore watched with impartial interest as he balled up his great hairy fists. But before Benton could act, the interview room door opened and an affable-looking gent poked his head around the door.

'Ah, Professor,' he said, beaming happily at Fennimore, completely ignoring Benton. He wore a pale grey suit over a shirt so white it seemed to shine, and a lemon pocket handkerchief that was a perfect match to his tie. He crossed the room swiftly, trailing the aroma of expensive cologne.

'And you are?' Benton said.

He offered Fennimore his hand. 'Andrew Haverford.'

Fennimore recognized the name and so it seemed did Benton – Fennimore thought he saw a shiver of anxiety in the sergeant's eyes.

It seemed only polite to stand, so Fennimore pushed his seat back and shook Haverford's hand; it was smooth and dry.

'Such a pleasure to meet you, Professor,' Haverford said. 'I've admired your work from afar for many years.'

Haverford half-turned and raised a quizzical eyebrow at Benton, as though the detective had popped up from under the table. 'And who have we here?'

'Let me introduce you to Detective Sergeant Benton,' Fennimore said, unable to resist an approximation of Haverford's urbane good manners. 'Sergeant Benton, Mr Haverford is the lead solicitor working on the Graham Mitchell appeal.'

By now Benton's high colouring had toned down a few shades.

'And Professor Fennimore is our forensic consultant,' Haverford said. 'He's here at Mr Lazko's behest.' He waited and Benton's brow furrowed in perplexity. 'It's a terrible business,' Haverford added, and for a fleeting moment he looked genuinely upset. 'I understand you're investigating Mr Lazko's death?'

Benton sucked his teeth. 'Trying to,' he said.

'Oh, dear.' Mr Haverford gazed at Fennimore and Benton as though mortified. 'I'm so sorry — forgive the intrusion — I had no idea you were consulting on this, Professor.'

'Mr Fennimore is assisting us with our enquiries.'

Haverford frowned. 'Surely you don't suspect the *professor* of Mr Lazko's murder?' He studied Benton's face as though peering in through a fogged window. 'Oh.' He looked shocked. 'I see.'

'So, if you wouldn't mind, sir . . .' Benton glanced towards the door.

'Oh, no, no, no,' Haverford said. 'I think I shall stay — this should be fascinating — if you don't mind my advising you, Professor?'

Fennimore felt it would be rude to refuse.

Haverford brightened. 'Splendid.' He swept the free chair out from the table and sat, folding his hands neatly in his lap and watching the detective sergeant with rapt attention.

Benton glanced sideways at his colleague, cleared his throat and began: 'A few minutes ago, I asked you where you were between seven-thirty and eight-thirty today.'

Haverford raised a finger. 'Forgive me. Has Professor Fennimore been cautioned?'

'We're just having a chat,' Benton said, through gritted teeth.

'I see.'

'So—'

'Sergeant Benton may well have covered this already – if so, I apologize,' Haverford interrupted again, turning to Fennimore. 'You are free to leave at any time – and you are not obliged to answer any questions.'

'He's a forensic scientist,' Benton said. 'He knows the drill.'

'Always best to be clear, I find. Adherence to protocols protects everyone concerned,' Haverford added with a flinty edge to his voice. 'Now where were we?'

'My whereabouts between seven-thirty to eight-thirty this morning,' Fennimore said.

'Do you recall?' Haverford said with an encouraging smile.

'As it happens, I do.'

'And?' Benton said.

'I was on the seven-oh-five flight from Aberdeen to London.'

The detective sergeant looked sick.

'I hired a car at the airport and drove out to see a potential witness for the Mitchell appeal. After that I visited a consultant oncologist at Basildon Hospital.'

Mr Haverford looked from Fennimore to Benton, an

amused expression on his face. 'I hope you don't think me officious, Sergeant, but you might check those details.' He fluttered his hands. 'They should be easily verifiable.'

Benton stared hard at Fennimore for a few seconds, then he stood abruptly, sending his chair skittering across the floor. 'Watch him,' he told the silent detective.

'I think we can spare five minutes,' Haverford said, checking his own gold watch in preference to the ugly flip clock on the wall.

The detective sergeant continued to the door. 'If he tries to leave, arrest him,' he said, without looking back. 'If he tries to hit the panic rail, arrest him. If he starts poking about with the recorder – *arrest him.*'

Benton returned a few minutes later and slid into the chair opposite Fennimore. 'Tell me about Graham Mitchell,' he said.

Fennimore stared through him.

Haverford leaned forward, placing both hands palm down on the table. 'You have two choices, Sergeant Benton.' This time there was no lightness in his tone. 'You can charge Professor Fennimore or you can release him.'

The pulse throbbing in the detective's temple said he preferred the first option.

'But if you *do* charge him, I will advise my client to sue for false imprisonment, malicious prosecution, misfeasance and . . .' He gazed at the ceiling. 'Oh, I'm sure something else will come to me.'

Benton broke eye contact and shook his head.

Haverford brightened and said, 'Well, now that's cleared up, we'll leave you to your investigations, Mr Benton.'

31

Haverford didn't speak a word until they were safely inside his car.

'Your assistant, Josh Brown, contacted me,' he said, his tone subdued, all trace of amusement gone from his face. 'I knew immediately why they had taken you in – I'd already heard of Mr Lazko's . . .' He took a breath.

'What happened?' Fennimore said. 'How did he . . .?'

'I don't know. He missed a morning meeting at my offices. I couldn't raise him by phone, so I sent one of my paralegals to his home. She discovered the body.' He checked over his shoulder, as though afraid they might be overheard. 'Her description suggests that he was tortured.'

'What? *Why?* Was he working on any leads he hadn't shared with me?'

'No – at least I don't think so. We were in daily contact and – as far as I know – since his return to Chelmsford he'd been trying to get his flat in order.' Haverford drove out of the car park. 'Where do you want to go?'

'Lazko's flat,' Fennimore said.

But they couldn't get within fifty feet of it. Uniform cops stood duty at the two stretches of police tape; a plain white crime scene unit van was parked inside the cordon. Onlookers and journalists crowded the tape and TV cameras pointed towards the house, filming the comings and goings of white-suited CSIs.

'It's more than they did after the break-in,' Haverford said. 'The police told Carl that no one was available to process the scene. He was advised to lock the place up and leave it untouched – they would "try and get someone to it".'

'So he cleaned up before the CSIs were sent in?'

'He had no choice – the place wasn't secure.' The solicitor tapped the steering wheel. 'Where to now?'

'My hotel.' Fennimore gave him the post code and Haverford turned the car southward, out of town.

'Is this linked to the first break-in?' Fennimore asked, still trying to make sense of what he'd just heard. 'Did Lazko tell you what was stolen?'

'Nothing. That was the most disturbing aspect of it. They broke in, turned every drawer and cupboard inside out, and then broke or tore up everything – every mirror, every piece of electrical equipment, the soft furnishings, ornaments – the lot.'

'That sounds like a lot of rage.'

'I suppose it might have been frustration at not finding the case files – Carl had taken those up to you in Aberdeen. He had quite a lot stored on his laptop, of course, but he had that with him.'

'Are there any other copies of the files?'

'In the strong room at my offices.'

'How's your security?'

'Good,' Haverford said, without elaboration.

'The police will have the originals, too.' Fennimore stared out of the window, watching flat green fields flash by. 'So it wouldn't do him any good, even if he had got Lazko's case files. Unless the first break-in was a threat: "Back off or else."'

Haverford glanced at him. 'Carl had received a number of threats.'

'Since when?'

'Since he started looking into the Mitchell case.'

'He didn't mention it.'

'He didn't want you to know,' Haverford said dryly.

'Did Lazko keep these threats?'

'He gave them to me for safe-keeping,' Haverford said. 'Carl had an eye on a publishing contract if we succeeded in proving Mitchell's innocence.'

'Sounds like Lazko,' Fennimore said with grudging admiration.

'He recorded some of the calls, too.'

'The police will need access. But I'd like to take copies before they get their hands on anything.'

Haverford nodded. 'I'll make arrangements.'

'Good. I'll do the work myself, reduce any chances of damaging the evidence.'

'Do you think whoever was threatening Carl came back for the letters – tortured him to find out where they were?' Haverford asked.

'It's possible,' Fennimore said. 'Or maybe he just decided to carry out his threats.'

They were silent for some minutes.

'So,' Haverford said at last, 'your assistant tells me you spoke to the new suspect's wife. Is that good news for Mr Mitchell?'

Fennimore smiled. 'Jury's out on that.' He talked Haverford through the visit to Hazle's widow and the oncologist.

Twenty-five miles down the road, they swept off the A13, driving along country lanes to the inn where Fennimore and Josh were staying.

'Josh has the widow's diaries and letters,' Fennimore said. 'I want you to keep hold of the originals.'

Haverford glanced across at him. 'So you intend to continue with the case review?'

'Of course.'

'It could be dangerous. I would understand if you wanted to reconsider.'

Fennimore turned to the solicitor. 'I can't drop it now – it just got interesting.'

Haverford relaxed. 'I was hoping you would say that.' He paused. 'You know, you and Carl are – were – rather alike.'

'Lazko said something along those lines in a letter he sent me last week,' Fennimore said. 'I don't see it, myself.'

Haverford pursed his lips. 'Your methods differ, to be sure,' he conceded. 'But your appetite for the truth, your – forgive me, Professor – your ruthlessness in seeking it out . . .' He nodded to himself. 'Yes . . . yes, I do see a similarity.'

This sobering thought kept Fennimore silent as they parked and went into the hotel.

Josh wasn't in his room and there was no sign of Fennimore's luggage. The hire car wasn't in the car park either. Fennimore remembered the cop glancing at Josh in the hotel foyer. Then he flashed to Lazko, handing him the file on Josh's family, the fear in his eyes when he said, 'I wouldn't want some of the faces in that folder to think I've been poking my nose into their affairs.'

Fennimore returned to the foyer. Haverford was waiting in one of the easy chairs, talking to his office on the phone. He caught Fennimore's eye and glanced towards the restaurant area just off the reception area. Fennimore went to the desk and asked if Josh had left a message.

'No, sir,' the receptionist said. 'He just phoned from the motorway services to say he'd been called away unexpectedly.'

Fennimore turned away from the desk as two hard-looking men came out of the restaurant. They kept their eyes on him as they walked to the exit and out into the sunshine. He was on his way over to Haverford when the phone rang on the reception desk and the receptionist called him back. 'It's a Mr Haverford for you, Mr Fennimore.'

Haverford had pocketed his phone and was still seated in the easy chair, reading a newspaper he'd picked up from the coffee table. Fennimore took the receiver and held it cautiously to his ear.

'This is Nick Fennimore,' he said.

'Nick, it's Josh.'

'Okay,' he said, aware of the receptionist a few feet away.

'I'm at the library in St Martin's Square, Chelmsford. I'll meet you inside. I took the car — but don't use a cab — and make sure you aren't followed. There's a couple of blokes watching the hotel.'

'I think I know who you mean,' Fennimore said.

'Nick, you should turn off your mobile phone; they could be tracking it.'

'Right,' Fennimore said, keeping his tone polite, but formal.

213

'Thanks for letting me know.' He hung up and crossed the foyer to sit opposite Haverford.

'The two men who came out of the restaurant are members of the Collins gang,' Haverford murmured, smiling pleasantly, as though talking about a dinner invitation. 'Nasty bunch.'

Fennimore returned the smile. 'I thought as much. Can you turn off your phone and bring your car around to the fire escape at the back of the building in five minutes?'

'Certainly.' Haverford stood and shook his hand, a businessman bringing a meeting to a cordial conclusion. 'It's been a pleasure.'

Fennimore watched him leave, then slipped his room key from his pocket, jangled it from his finger for the benefit of anyone who might be watching and headed towards his room.

32

At twelve-thirty, Kate Simms was drinking coffee and watching Timmy eat an egg mayonnaise sandwich. BBC Radio Manchester played in the background and she listened with half an ear, waiting for news of Lauren Myers. There was nothing new – just a rehash of the discovery of Julia Myers's body and Mr Myers's breakdown as he begged the killer to let his little girl go. The bulletin ended with an appeal to anyone who might have seen something suspicious to phone the hotline set up by Manchester Police. She had no idea what was happening on the case: had the woman who survived the attack given them anything useful? Did they have a description of the attacker? Had the mould spores Cooper found on Mrs Myers given them any inkling about her daughter's whereabouts?

'Ugh!' she exclaimed, tipping the rest of the coffee into the sink.

215

This was torture. Her life was a shambles: she was barred from working on the search for little Lauren and she had alienated a powerful ally in Enderby. Her mother was chafing to return to her own life in London; Becky would be in Paris by the end of the day: unable to delay any longer, she'd given permission for her to make the trip. Kieran had come home at just after 2 a.m. He had slept on the couch in the sitting room and was still there now. Timmy was about the only member of the household who had warmed to her since her return.

Tim's voice penetrated her thoughts. 'Why are you sad, Mummy?'

Startled and feeling a little guilty, she exclaimed, 'I'm not sad, darling – just thinking, that's all.'

'Why do you look sad when you're thinking?'

'I didn't know I did. Let's see . . .' She tried a few expressions, naming each one: 'This is thoughtful . . . This is puzzled . . . And this is sad . . .'

'Sad,' he said, nodding to himself. 'Definitely.'

Definitely was his new word.

He took another bite of his sandwich.

'How about this?' Simms began with a clown sad-face and ended by crossing her eyes, just to make him laugh.

He chortled. 'Silly Mummy.' He chewed and swallowed. 'Why is Daddy asleep on the couch?'

Uh-oh . . . 'He had a late night.'

'Yes, but why isn't he in *bed*?' Tim spread the fingers of his free hand to emphasize his astonishment.

'I'm not sure. Finish your lunch and have a piece of fruit and then we'll go and ask him, shall we?'

'Mm-mm,' he hummed, to avoid speaking with his mouth

full. He took a swig of juice to wash down his food and wiped his mouth with the back of his hand. 'Definitely.'

Her mobile started buzzing on the kitchen counter and Simms snatched it up.

'Diane.'

'I heard you were carpeted.'

'Oh, where did you hear that?'

'Well, actually, I didn't *hear* it, I made a careful analysis of the data. Was I right?'

Simms trapped the phone between her shoulder and her ear and picked up an apple to slice for Tim. 'I'm at home, cutting up an apple for my five-year-old. Analyse that.'

'Thanks for keeping my name out of it,' Diane said.

Simms said nothing.

'Want the latest?'

'You probably shouldn't even be speaking to me,' Simms said.

'It'll be all over the six o'clock news anyway.'

'Is that something you heard or another prediction?'

'Turn on the telly at six, see if I'm right.'

Simms smiled. Diane was irrepressible.

'So your abduction survivor described her attacker as lanky – long arms and legs – out of proportion with his body. Weird body-shape, she said, freakishly narrow at the shoulders. When he came out of the back of the car, she thought it was an animal.'

Simms gave an involuntary shudder, thinking of Julia Myers and her little girl.

'Weird, huh?'

'Mm,' Simms said, handing Tim a slice of apple. 'Anything else?'

'He was dressed in black and wore a mask – like a ski-mask.'

'That won't help,' Simms said.

'No.'

'Are they of a type, the other women?'

'Mostly,' Diane said. 'They were all small – under five-three tall, pale-skinned, blue-eyed.'

'So not really comparable with the – um . . . latest,' she said, not wanting Tim to hear the word *victim*.

'Nothing like. Mrs Myers was five-seven, brown hair, grey eyes.'

Like Rachel, Simms thought. *Like Fennimore's murdered wife*.

'Nothing helpful on the occupations either,' the analyst went on. 'A nurse, a care worker, one temped as a clerical assistant. The survivor is a rep for a marketing company.'

'So no similarities there either.'

Simms sighed.

'There must be *something* they have in common,' she said.

'You would think,' Diane agreed.

She couldn't ask Diane to send pictures of the victims – that would leave a paper trail – but there was nothing to stop her looking them up online. 'Those, um, women,' she said. 'Can you give me their names?'

She jotted them down.

'Thanks, Diane, I really appreciate this.'

'So,' Diane said. 'What's up?'

'Up? Nothing.'

'O-kay . . . So why do you sound down?'

'I don't,' Simms said. 'I mean, I'm not – it's just this . . . investigation.'

Timmy crunched a piece of apple, gazing up at her, and she stroked his head, forcing a smile.

The letterbox rattled and Tim scrambled down from his chair. 'Postman!' he yelled, charging down the hall to pick up the post.

'Kate, this is Auntie Diane — you can't keep secrets from me.'

'It's nothing—' But it wasn't and she knew it, and suddenly she didn't want to go on keeping her worries to herself, acting like everything was all right. She lowered her voice. 'I think Kieran is having an affair.'

'What? *Why?*'

'He's been pissed off with me ever since I got kicked out of the National Crime Faculty.'

'I meant what makes you think he's having an affair?'

It was a fair question. Kieran had been sweet — if a little chaste — since she got back from the States. Until last night. The unprovoked flare of rage was unlike him.

Was it unprovoked? she thought. Cranking back through the timeline, examining incidents and actions was one of her strengths as a cop. He had flown into a temper when she asked if there was something he needed to tell her. Why had he assumed she was accusing him of having an affair? A voice whispered in the no-trespassing, don't-go-there backwoods of her mind: *Because he is*, it said.

'Mission Control to Simms,' Diane said. 'Do you read me?'

'Yes. Sorry, Diane. Forget it — I'm just being paranoid.' Tim hadn't returned and she peered down the hall and saw the sitting room door open. 'Uh-oh,' she said. 'I've got to go.'

'All right,' Diane said. 'But call me.'

She made the promise and hung up, cursing herself for having been so indiscreet.

What was she thinking? She hadn't seen Diane in over

five years. Why confide? Perhaps the time factor was part of it – it gave an implied distance, a false anonymity. But she had to admit she felt better having told someone and she knew Diane could be trusted to keep a confidence.

She headed down the hallway, fast-dialling Fennimore, but he wasn't picking up. She left a message and took a breath before stepping into the fuggy half-darkness of the sitting room. Tim was standing by the sofa, a bundle of letters in one hand, shaking his daddy's shoulder.

'Wake *up*, Daddy. It's daytime. I brought you a – apple for *lunch*.' He dug into his trouser pocket and brought out a segment of the apple Simms had cut up for him.

Kieran groaned and turned.

'Gimme a break,' he moaned.

'The *post*man's been. Look,' Tim said, dropping the crumpled envelopes on to his lap.

Simms leaned against the doorframe, watching them, smiling, and sudden tears sprang to her eyes.

Kieran cleared his throat. 'What time is it?'

Timmy picked up his daddy's watch from the coffee table. 'The little hand says it's twelve o'clock and the big hand says . . . I don't know what the big hand says.' He shoved the dial towards Kieran's face so he could get a closer look. Kieran winced, taking the watch and squinting at the time.

'Oh, God . . .' He glanced up and saw her for the first time. 'It's nearly one o'clock,' he said, unnecessarily. 'I should be at work!'

Simms blinked away her tears and leaned off the doorframe. 'Good party?' she said with a smile.

Tim clambered up and sat astride his daddy and Kieran gave another groan.

'Looks like Daddy needs coffee,' she said.

She sent Timmy out to play in the back garden and returned a few minutes later with two mugs of coffee. Kieran was sitting up when she came through the door and he ruffled his hair and rubbed his face vigorously with both hands before accepting the cup.

She waited until he had taken a few sips before asking, 'Do we need to talk?'

'*No.*' He glanced up sharply and winced against what she imagined was a cracking headache. After a pause, he said, more softly, 'No, Kate.'

He looked hungover and contrite. After a couple more sips of coffee, he flashed her a crooked smile. 'Term's almost over,' he said. 'I'll be more human after a few days' holiday, I promise. Look – why don't you call Becky, tell her to come home, we'll go off somewhere nice for a few days?'

'Ah . . .' Simms said. 'That might be a problem.'

33

The best way to find out if you can trust somebody
is to trust them.

ERNEST HEMINGWAY (ATTR.)

Essex, Thursday Afternoon

Haverford dropped Fennimore on the third level of a multi-storey car park, three minutes' walk from the library. He drove up to the fourth level, parked, went into the theatre nearby and bought tickets, then went straight back to his car. Fennimore was waiting in the stairwell at level three.

'I think you're in the clear,' Haverford said.

'No one following – you're sure?'

'No one – but give me five minutes to drive out, just in case they're waiting on one of the lower levels.'

'Okay, I'll see you at your offices as soon as I've finished here.'

'Your young assistant looked familiar,' Haverford said.

Fennimore kept his expression bland. 'Mistaken identity – he gets that a lot.'

Haverford's smile was tinged with sadness. 'That could be fatal in this part of the world.'

Fennimore nodded. 'I'm sending him home,' he said.

They passed on the stairs and a few seconds later, Fennimore heard the fire escape door close with a hollow thud. A minute after that, Haverford's Mercedes swept past. He waited and listened for another five minutes, before heading down the stairs.

On the short walk to the library he remained alert, but avoided glancing over his shoulder, despite the fact that it felt like a spiteful sprite was tugging at the short hairs on his neck. At the last moment, he ducked into the theatre and lingered there, reading the notices, picking up brochures, checking everyone who came through the door. At last he ventured into the library, walked slowly past the desk and through the main collection, pausing at shelves to give Josh plenty of opportunity to see him, then he found a table in a quiet corner and picked up a newspaper. He glanced up a minute later to see Josh standing in front of him.

'Your phone?' Josh said. He looked tense and pale, the laptop bag worn across his body somehow making him seem younger and more vulnerable than Fennimore had ever imagined him.

'Turned off.'

Josh led the way to a bay where they could talk without being observed. 'The cop at the hotel recognized me.' He hesitated. 'Who I used to be.'

'I gathered as much.'

Josh held Fennimore's gaze. 'Did you tell Lazko where we were staying?' His voice sounded tight. 'In your phone messages – did you tell him which hotel? Is that what got him killed?'

'Josh,' Fennimore said, 'I didn't even say I was travelling

223

down with you. What happened to Lazko isn't your fault. It was just unlucky that detective recognized you.'

Josh exhaled shakily.

'The two thugs at the hotel?' Fennimore said.

'They work for my family. The cop is in their pocket as well.'

Rapid footsteps. They both looked up.

A figure turned the corner into their bay and Josh tensed. But it was only a youth, sixteen years old maybe. He stood chewing gum, watching them, his hands in his pockets. Josh gave him a hard stare.

'Want something?' he said.

The youth jerked his chin. 'Book,' he said. 'Jim Butcher. Behind your head, mate.'

Josh plucked the book from the shelf and jammed it into his hand. 'Now piss off,' he said, thrusting his face inches from the boy's. The youth jerked back, then turned on his heel and hurried away, his trainers squeak-squeaking on the floor tiles.

'Where's the car?' Fennimore asked.

'In the multi-storey.'

Josh, why did you come here, of all places – you should have got out, found a quiet place out in the sticks where we could meet.'

'You needed those copies doing.' Josh snuffed air through his nose. 'Besides, library's about the safest place in town,' he said. 'My lot aren't big readers.'

'Josh,' Fennimore said, 'I'm sorry – I shouldn't have brought you here.'

'It isn't like you put a gun to my head,' Josh said.

Fennimore winced.

'Here's the stuff you asked for,' Josh said, reaching into his bag and handing over a bundle of papers, along with Mrs Hazle's diary. 'Originals are on top.'

'Thanks, I'll lodge them with the solicitor. And thanks for getting the message to him – I'd probably still be in Chelmsford nick if it weren't for Haverford.'

'No worries. So what now?'

'You need to get out of Dodge,' Fennimore said.

Josh frowned, began to argue.

'Haverford recognized you,' Fennimore said. 'That cop recognized you. Which means others will. Josh, you *have* to leave.'

The student nodded, though he still seemed reluctant.

'And . . . it's probably best you don't go back to Aberdeen,' Fennimore added. Experience had taught him that giving bad news in small bites sometimes made it more manageable.

Josh shook his head.

'Let your handler know – have him arrange a place of safety.'

'My thesis,' Josh said. 'I can't just ditch it.'

'You can work on that anywhere.'

'That's not how witness protection works,' Josh said. 'They'll drag me out, give me a new identity. Everything I've worked for will be finished, wiped out.'

Years of work. Fennimore couldn't imagine how it must feel to abandon all of that.

The younger man gripped the strap of his messenger bag as though the weight of it had suddenly become unbearable.

'Okay, tell me what you want to do,' Fennimore said.

'My notes and reference texts are back home,' Josh said. 'If I can pick them up – find somewhere to carry on working . . .'

'That could be risky.'

'I'll make it fast.'

'All right,' Fennimore said. 'Check for the earliest flight from London or Southend – I'll drive you to the airport. They're probably still looking for you here, so you'll have a good few hours on them.'

He stood and turned towards the glass-fronted entrance, but Josh jogged his elbow and headed towards a set of doors leading to the staircase. He opened a door with a push-button security lock and ducked through.

'You know the security code?' Fennimore asked.

'You learn a few skills growing up in a criminal family.' Josh led the way through a maze of stacked boxes and bookcases jammed with old books, and out the back door. He pulled up the hood of his jacket and walked fast, keeping his head down, but Fennimore got the impression he was hyper-alert as he made his way to the car park.

'So what's the news on Lazko?' Josh asked.

Fennimore told him all he knew, including Haverford's suspicion that the journalist had been tortured. 'It's likely that whoever killed him was also responsible for the first break-in at his place – statistically, it's highly unlikely a house would be targeted twice in the same week.'

'What do we think – the killer didn't find what he was looking for, so he came back when he knew Lazko would be there?'

'It seems to point that way,' Fennimore said, relieved that Josh seemed to have acccpted that Lazko wasn't tortured for information on his whereabouts.

'Did we miss something in the files?' Josh asked.

'I don't know.'

'Where've you stashed them?' Josh said. 'Are they still

in your office? 'Cos anyone could walk in there now the developers are in.'

'I moved everything sensitive to my apartment.'

Josh grunted. 'How's your security?'

Fennimore took a breath. He had thought it was reasonably strong, but Lazko had breezed through it easily enough. 'You're thinking I should move the files.'

'Your call,' Josh said. 'But if the first break-in *was* linked to the Mitchell appeal, he was probably after the files Lazko schlepped up to Aberdeen.'

By now they had reached the car. Josh opened up and handed Fennimore the key before sliding into the back seat.

Fennimore looked at him in question.

'If my lot've got their tame cops watching traffic cams, best I'm not in the front seat,' Josh explained.

Fennimore nodded, climbing into the driver's seat.

They were both thinking that Lazko's killer could be on his way to Fennimore's place right now. But Fennimore needed to return to Chelmsford to see the appeal solicitor. He glanced in the rear-view and saw Josh watching him.

'Look,' Josh said. 'I'm heading that way anyhow. If you want, I could move the case files somewhere safe, drop you an email to let you know where.'

Fennimore hesitated. 'I don't want to slow you down.'

'Like I said – I'll make it fast.'

Fennimore unclipped his door keys from his key ring and handed them, together with the key card for the residents' car park, to Josh.

'Call me as soon as you're safely away from Aberdeen.'

Josh shook his head. 'They could be monitoring your calls.'

'Then borrow a phone and text me. Or email me – and

check your emails. In a few weeks, we'll arrange to meet,' he said.

Josh's eyes blazed for a second, then Fennimore saw resignation and despair in the student's face.

'We'll find a way to make this work, Josh,' Fennimore said, leaning forward, looking him in the eye. 'You have my word.'

34

Manchester, Thursday Afternoon

Still trying to make amends for the previous evening, Kieran had called in sick, and offered to take Timmy swimming. Simms's mother accepted a lift into Manchester to do some shopping, and Simms took the opportunity to go for a run. An hour later, she sat at the kitchen table with a sandwich and a coffee, her hair still damp from the shower. Her laptop and the names of the three victims and the survivor beside her, she trawled newspaper webpages, social media websites and blogs for any reference to the women. She found plenty: memorial websites; Facebook pages; 'Justice for . . .' pages asking for information to help solve the murders. Warm air wafted in from the garden, and by three-thirty it stirred four neat stacks of pages she had printed out from the Web.

On top of each stack, a photograph of the victim; four fair-haired, blue-eyed twenty-somethings. And then there was dark-haired, thirty-four-year-old Mrs Myers. Simms wasn't a profiler, but she knew that serial killers didn't suddenly change their choice of victim. The letters, the way Mrs Myers's body had been left, seemed calculated to taunt Fennimore, but why had he been targeted in the first place?

She began scrolling down the Facebook page of Hayley Todd, the second victim – a care worker. The page was being maintained by her friends and family, and it was heartbreaking to read. Moving down to the months before the murder, Simms found an album. There were photographs of three groups of friends: her co-workers at the care agency, all dressed in pale green uniforms; a gang of women members of a glee-club she sang with; and a group of four women in pink uniform dresses. From pale green to pink; had Hayley changed jobs in the months before she died?

Simms clicked on the image and read the text; the women were auxiliary nursing staff at Colchester General Hospital. She knew that care staff were on the minimum wage, and some worked two jobs to pay the bills; could Hayley have been moonlighting as a nurse auxiliary? Julia Myers was a specialist diabetes nurse at Manchester Royal Infirmary. Frowning, she made a note and looked again at the other victims. Was it possible the clerical assistant had done agency work at a hospital, too? She called Diane.

'Interesting theory,' Diane said. 'I'll do some digging.' She hung up and Simms got back to her trawling.

Kim Restel was the woman who had survived the abduction attempt; she had crashed her car and fled to the safety of a school. Ms Restel worked for a national advertising company, and Simms couldn't think of a job much more removed from a vocational profession. The Myers investigation team would have interviewed her by now, but Simms had no access to their records and it seemed that Ms Restel didn't have a social media presence under her own name: no Facebook, Instagram or Pinterest, and no Twitter account Simms could find. She found the marketing company's website. According to Ms Restel's profile, after graduating from Manchester University, she had started out in marketing at a car manufacturing company. Within a couple of years, she set up as a freelancer, taking small retail commissions, before being head-hunted by her present firm. How did her new firm get to know about her? She must have done something big to attract their attention. Could the killer have discovered Restel in the same way her new employers had?

Ms Restel had only been with the national firm for two months, so the attempted abduction had happened after she started working for them. Since joining the company she had been involved in a supermarket-sponsored Sports for Schools campaign and a reading initiative. Nothing about hospitals.

Simms scrolled down and found a LinkedIn button; every ambitious professional used the site as a shop window and online CV to show off their talents – ex-cops included. She clicked the link and struck gold: a list of the retail commissions Restel had worked on as a freelancer. Her final project before moving up the career ladder had been for a hospice providing end-of-life care. Excitement sent a shiver through Simms from the crown of her head to her fingertips: nursing, hospitals, care facilities – there *was* a connection. She picked up her phone, ready to call Diane, just as her Skype alert sounded.

It was Nick Fennimore. She opened the link, feeling the old excitement at the prospect of sharing a new lead with him.

'Nick, I was hoping you'd call—' She broke off and peered more closely at the screen. 'Are you okay? You look terrible.'

He wiped one hand over his face. 'I've been better.'

Simms listened as he relayed the events of the day: his meeting with Mr Hazle's widow, his consultation with Hazle's oncologist, his tussle with Essex Police and the shocking news of Lazko's murder.

'Have you any clue who might have wanted him dead?'

'I was high on the suspect list, until I provided an alibi,' he said with a dry humour she recognized as a cover-up for the emotion he truly felt. 'If we rule out a random, sadistically motivated attack, there are three possible reasons I can see why Lazko was tortured: for revenge; as a warning; or to extract information.'

'Information about what – a feature he was working on?'

'The Mitchell case review,' Fennimore said. 'Josh thinks we might have missed something in the files – that the killer tortured Lazko to find out where he'd hidden them.'

'Didn't he have the files with him?'

Fennimore shook his head. 'I have copies and so does Mitchell's appeal solicitor.'

'So they *are* allowing an appeal?'

He raised one shoulder. 'We haven't had the paperwork yet, but it's a given.'

'You've read the files – what was he after?'

'I wish I knew, Kate.'

'The killer must know there are other copies – if Josh is right, all he's done is draw attention to them.'

'Maybe he thought the police would be less . . . rigorous than Mitchell's team.'

'Makes sense they wouldn't go all out to prove they convicted an innocent man,' she said. 'Which is why we have the Criminal Cases Review Commission.'

Fennimore's mouth quirked at the sarcasm. 'I don't think our man cares if Mitchell is found innocent, only that *he* isn't put in the frame.'

'Which makes both you and the solicitor a target,' Simms said.

'The solicitor tells me he has good security.'

'What about you – where are you now?' She peered past him, trying to find a clue from the room behind him.

'It's all right,' he said. 'I switched hotels. Josh is taking care of the files in Aberdeen.'

'*Josh?*'

He didn't seem to pick up on her shock, simply nodding. 'I needed to stay, process the letters.'

'You sent Josh to secure files that you believe Lazko was *murdered* for?'

Fennimore's brow furrowed. 'I sent him back to Aberdeen to get him out of harm's way.'

'I'm missing something,' she said. 'What? What are you not telling me?'

'Essex isn't a safe place for Josh,' Fennimore said quietly.

Josh rarely spoke in her presence, and then only a few words, but Simms had identified the salt tang of the Essex marshes in his accent. She gazed at Fennimore, thinking through their last conversation about the student.

'You took him home,' she said, feeling tension rise in her chest. 'You *put* him in harm's way.'

Fennimore began to speak, then stopped. For once, he seemed at a loss for words. He took a breath and started again.

'I made a stupid mistake,' he said. 'But he's out of it now – I put him on a plane to Aberdeen.'

'Nick – you just implied Lazko may have been *tortured* over the whereabouts of those case files.'

'He wanted to gather his research notes. But he'll be gone from there before nightfall.'

'You should have spoken to Police Scotland.'

'Josh's family have police on their payroll,' Fennimore said. 'I couldn't take that risk.'

'Then you could have spoken to *me*. I could at least have asked them to check your flat was secure before you let him blunder in there.'

'Josh isn't the blundering type,' Fennimore said.

'For God's sake, Nick – you put him in jeopardy. You can't keep allowing yourself to be manipulated.'

'What do you mean?' She saw that her words had stung.

'The Myers abductions,' she said. 'You're so sure Mrs Myers's murder is all wrapped up in what happened to Rachel and Suzie, you're not thinking straight.'

Fennimore leaned closer to the camera. 'Mrs Myers's body was staged to look like Rachel's – she even *looks* like Rachel.'

'Yes, she does,' Simms said, glancing down at the printouts of the victims on her kitchen table. 'I'm looking at photographs of the abduction-murder victims, and you're right – there is a striking similarity between them. They're all small, fair, pale-skinned, blue-eyed.'

'The physical *opposites* of Rachel,' Fennimore murmured.

She watched Fennimore's growing consternation. 'That changes the victimology entirely,' he said.

'You *think*?' she shot back. 'And all of the other victims

were single women. *All* of them. And not *one* of them had a child with her.'

Fennimore sat back, looking physically winded. 'What the hell is he doing, Kate?'

'I don't know,' she said. 'But he seems to want your involvement, and you're being *re*active to the situation, rather than *pro*active. It's not helping.'

'No,' he said, sounding dazed. 'You're right. It isn't.'

Simms's mobile rang.

'Hold on,' she said, 'it's my SCAS contact.' She slid the bar to 'Answer'. 'Diane, I have Professor Fennimore on Skype.'

'Oh, d'you want me to call back?'

'No, go ahead, we've just been discussing the victimology,' she said. 'I'm putting you on speaker.'

'Um, hello, Nick,' Diane said.

They knew each other from the National Crime Faculty and Fennimore greeted her politely, but the tightness in his voice betrayed his tension.

'Kate had a theory about the victims' occupations,' Diane said.

'Their social media profiles seemed to be pointing towards a hospital connection,' Simms explained. 'So what've you got, Diane?'

'Your care assistant did some agency fill-ins as an auxiliary nurse at a hospital in Harlow,' Diane said. 'The clerical assistant did some temping at hospital clinics around London and the south-east.'

Simms felt her pulse rate rising.

'We already know that Julia Myers was a nurse specialist,' Diane went on.

'And the woman who survived the abduction attempt

worked as a freelancer on a fundraising campaign for a hospice,' Simms said. 'They *all* have hospital connections.'

For a stunned moment, they were silent.

'Can you get dates for when they worked in each of the hospitals?' Fennimore said. 'It would narrow down the list of possible suspects—'

Simms stopped him with a look.

'Oh,' Fennimore said. 'This is off the books . . .'

She gave him a tight smile. If she went back to the chief constable, she could be facing suspension. *But Lauren is out there somewhere. A six-year-old girl—*

'I'll do it,' Diane said. 'I'll tell my supervisor I widened the search on the victims' occupations.'

'Diane . . .' Simms said.

'Kate, it's okay. Just send me the links for the survivor, I'll put it in a report update.'

They hung up a minute later and Simms stared at Fennimore on her computer screen. He was looking down, an expression of intense concentration on his face, and he seemed to be making notes – or doodling. He often doodled and mind-mapped when he was working through a problem.

He broke off for a second, glancing up with a frown on his face, saw her watching. 'You're right,' he said.

'I usually am.' She smiled, and his expression softened, too. 'So what am I right about this time?'

He took a breath. 'This isn't about Rachel and Suzie.'

'Okay . . .' She waited for him to explain.

He stared at his notes for a few seconds. 'The first letter I got taunted me with my failure to find Rachel's killer.' This was Fennimore in full analytical session; no hint of self-pity, no emotion as he talked about his wife's murder. 'The letter said, "What goes around comes around. Everything – all of it – it's all on your head." I thought he was talking about Rachel and Suzie.' His brow creased. 'But he was talking about Lauren and Julia Myers.'

'If it isn't about what happened to you, why did he take Lauren and Julia?' Simms asked.

'Precisely because he knew how it would affect me,' Fennimore said. 'He created a false connection to Rachel and Suzie, and arrogant tool that I am, I fell for it.'

The scientist in Fennimore forced him to examine even the most unpalatable truths, and when he admitted to personal failings, he was his own harshest critic.

'All of this – Julia and Lauren's abduction, his taunts about Rachel and Suzie – they all prevented me from thinking straight. He made Julia Myers lick that envelope to put me off-balance; he staged her murder and the discovery of her body to look like Rachel's murder.'

'But off-balance from what?' Simms asked.

'Mitchell,' Fennimore said. 'Has to be – it's the only thing I'm working on just now. The first break-in at Lazko's place came after I had agreed to review the case – Mitchell's family posted the news on Facebook. I think he went to Lazko's house hoping to get to the files before I did. I believe the same man returned to Lazko's house and murdered him.'

'That's a lot of supposition,' Simms said, doubtful.

'Look at it, Kate: Lazko's day job was reporting on petty crime and the occasional drugs bust for the *Chronicle* – what else could it be?'

Simms tried to think up a scenario and failed.

'There *must* be something in those files,' Fennimore went

237

on. 'He made a mistake – or revealed himself in some way during the commission of Kelli Rees's murder.'

'All right, let's say he did make a mistake,' she said, not convinced yet, but indulging him for the moment. 'How? What *could* he have done that would identify him?'

'The only thing that was overlooked in the original investigation was the semen stains on the victim's clothing – which anyway was planted evidence.' Fennimore shook his head. 'And that belonged to a man who died three and a half years ago – by definition it *can't* directly incriminate the killer.'

'So,' Simms said, 'it must implicate him *in*directly.'

The look on Fennimore's face was pure admiration. 'That's what I love about you, Kate,' he said. 'You cut right through the crap.'

Simms felt her cheeks flush at the word *love*, but she tried to keep her expression bland. 'I . . . do my best,' she said.

'It's about *access*, Kate. The man who planted David Hazle's banked semen on Kelli Rees's clothing would have to've worked in the hospital – and only a limited number of people would have access to the storage units. That was his mistake. Maybe he knew he'd fouled up from the start. It didn't matter then, because the police didn't find it, and anyway, they'd already decided Mitchell was guilty.'

'But you came and stirred things up, and he knew the trail would lead back to him eventually.'

Fennimore grinned. 'Find out who had access to those semen samples, we identify the killer.' The weariness dropped away from his face. 'Identify him and he has no reason to harm Lauren – you could bring her home to her family.'

Simms looked at the hope in his eyes and felt a sharp pain below her breast bone.

238

Focus, she told herself. 'We need to look at specialist nurses, lab techs, pathology techs, even porters,' she said.

'Which means getting the co-operation of the hospitals' HR departments,' Fennimore added.

'And your tame consultant can't help with that,' Simms said. 'I'll talk to Enderby.'

'It would help if we had a physical description – was the survivor any help there?'

Simms dipped her head. 'He wore a mask, but she said there was something odd about him.' She related the victim's description of the man with disproportionately long arms, who had crawled out of the boot of her car. 'Someone like that would stand out – other staff might remember him.'

Fennimore nodded, frowning.

'What?' she said.

'That description – it sounds familiar . . .'

'Call me when it comes to you,' Simms said. Fennimore carried a library's worth of obscure knowledge around in his head. If it meant something to him, she knew he would eventually match it to the relevant label in his mental database.

She was about to end the call when he spoke again.

'If he'd left a clean scene, no trace, the police would have put it down to forensic awareness. But he *deliberately* contaminated the scene – he went to the trouble and risk of stealing semen to plant *someone else's* DNA on Kelli Rees's clothing. That's *odd*, isn't it?'

'The CSI effect,' she said. 'They always think it's about the DNA. It's why your guy Mitchell was found guilty before he even got to trial – all those press photographs of Mitchell, big, physically intimidating. Bad DNA, XYY-guy, all that guff.'

Fennimore half-stood, gripping the table edges. 'That's *it*.' Despite the barriers of computer technology and a physical separation of hundreds of miles, the space between them seemed to pulse with energy. 'Every one of those bogus stories said something about Mitchell's chromosomal abnormality – it *is* about the *DNA*.'

Simms frowned. 'Take a breath, Nick. You're not making sense.'

He shoved his chair back and stepped over to the coffee table. Simms watched him cascade papers to the floor. He uncovered his e-tablet and returned to the desk, his image blurring because of the digital time-lag. He typed something on the tablet as he spoke.

'The description your survivor gave of the man who attacked her – long arms and legs – out of proportion to the body—'

'Ye-es?' Simms said.

'What if it's a genetic abnormality?'

'Such as?'

He turned the tablet around for her to see.

'Klinefelter syndrome?' Simms read from the screen.

'A genetic condition,' Fennimore said. 'Males born with an extra X chromosome. XXY?'

'XXY,' he repeated. 'Unlike Mitchell, who had XYY, sufferers of Klinefelter's have an extra female, rather than an extra male chromosome. Klinefelter's often goes undiagnosed: sufferers are average intelligence, unremarkable in many ways.'

'But I'm guessing it affects their physical appearance?'

'It varies, but it does include elongation of the limbs and fat deposition in the torso.'

'Like Mitchell,' she said.

'Not quite. XYY males tend to be taller, but well-proportioned. In Klinefelter's, there's an imbalance – short body, long limbs; narrow shoulders, wide hips. Think pear-shaped.'

Adrenaline surged through Simms's veins. 'Like the survivor described,' she said.

'And a lot of sufferers develop breasts, so the body shape can look very odd. Yet many only find out they have the condition when they can't start a family,' Fennimore said. 'Because one of the primary features is a low sperm count – even azoospermia.'

Kate sat upright, exhaling in a rush. 'No sperm? *That's* why he stole samples from the sperm bank?'

'He was covering for something the police would never even have considered,' Fennimore said. 'Classic overcompensation.'

35

Simms picked up her mobile phone from the table and stared at her own reflection in the blank screen for a full half-minute. She needed to pitch this right to the chief constable and she would only get one crack at it. The room seemed to have become hotter in the last ten minutes, and she got up and splashed her face with water at the kitchen sink. After another fifteen seconds, she took a deep breath, blew it out and fast-dialled her boss.

It went to voicemail.

Damn it! She chewed her lower lip. *You can't chicken out now.* 'Okay,' she murmured, 'here goes . . .'

She texted: 'I have vital information about the Myers case—' She shook her head, irritated with herself, deleted the message and started again.

'Fennimore arrested,' she began. 'Journalist on MOJ murdered. Need to speak urgently.'

A second later, her mobile rang.

'Fennimore — arrested for *murder*?' Enderby sounded incredulous.

'He believes the miscarriage of justice he's working on is connected to the Myers abductions. He thinks the journalist was murdered to protect the killer's identity.'

'Kate—'

Simms heard the warning in Enderby's voice. 'You asked me to keep you informed, sir — that's all I'm doing. Fennimore thinks he's found a link between his miscarriage of justice and the Myers case.'

He sighed. 'All right, let's have it.'

She summarized their conversation, the discovery of semen stains on the victim's clothing, the probability that it was stolen from sperm samples banked on behalf of an oncology patient, and planted on Kelli Rees's clothing. She went on to the links between the victims and hospitals, ending with Fennimore's theory that Kelli Rees's killer had Klinefelter's syndrome.

'The convicted man in Fennimore's MOJ — what's his name?'

'Mitchell.'

'Mitchell could just as easily have planted the evidence himself.'

'It's possible,' she agreed, 'but if he did, why didn't he demand to have the clothing tested? And anyway, Mitchell didn't have access to the hospital's sperm bank.' Simms winced; she had shown her hand and maybe too soon. She gripped the phone tightly.

Enderby was silent for so long her hand began to cramp.

'Is this why you called me,' he said, enunciating precisely, 'to smooth the way for Professor Fennimore's enquiries?'

'No, sir. He already has access to everything he needs to build his defence,' she said, stretching the truth a little. 'If Fennimore is right – if it *is* the same man – it could help us to find Lauren Myers.'

'Yes, thank you,' Enderby said. 'I can join the dots to make this ugly picture. But the connection seems tenuous at best.'

With Lauren Myers still missing, Simms knew he couldn't ignore the lead, tenuous as it was. So she waited and held her tongue.

'Here's what I'm prepared to do,' Enderby said. 'I will ring my counterpart in Essex and give him a breakdown of the situation. I will request an exchange of information with Manchester Royal Infirmary and the hospice our survivor was campaigning for. I'll need names and dates.'

'You'll have it in ten minutes,' Simms said.

'But any further enquiries or investigation will be delegated to others in the respective forces.'

He was telling her that she was still locked out. But Simms didn't care who took the credit if they brought Lauren home safely.

'Understood. I'll let you know if Fennimore turns up anything else,' she added, wanting to keep that line of communication open.

She hung up before he could say no, but she could swear the chief constable gave a short laugh as she disconnected.

Simms hurriedly collated her notes, put them in a short document and emailed them. This done, she put in a call to a detective sergeant she knew at Police Scotland. The sergeant had been very helpful on the I-44 murders she had just concluded with St Louis PD in the United States. He agreed to talk to colleagues in Aberdeen City Police and ask someone to swing by Fennimore's apartment building.

36

Aberdeen, Thursday Afternoon

Josh Brown went straight to Fennimore's flat from the airport, to pick up the Mitchell case files and move them to safety. Thirty minutes later, he stopped by the new university campus at Garthdee and sought out the office manager, Joan. He needed to borrow her mobile phone.

She sat at the centre of a thirty-metre-long open-plan office and she didn't look happy. He told her a story about drowning his own phone in a cup of coffee. That made her laugh and confirmed her sense of superiority over hopeless males. Invoking Fennimore's name as the recipient of the call completed the charm. He sent Fennimore a coded text to say where he'd hidden the files, then quietly deleted his message from Joan's sent messages folder before he handed the phone back to her.

She eyed him quizzically. 'I thought you were south of the border for a few days.'

'I was,' he said. 'Nick asked me to check on some files in his flat.'

'Oh, *that's* where he's shifted them to, is it?'

Of course, Joan would have checked Fennimore's old office and found it empty.

'Well, I hope he's binned some of it, because he won't fit much into the wee office he's been designated.'

'You're not keen on the new place, then?'

Joan looked around her as if the new building with its bright painted walls, clean, carpeted floors and low-level shelving had paid her a personal insult. 'All this *colour*, you'd think we were running a primary school.'

'I know,' he commiserated.

'And am I supposed to keep track of things in all this hullaballoo?' she demanded.

Josh glanced around, thinking there were advantages and disadvantages to open plan. The biggest advantage was line of sight, but only if you positioned yourself right. Here, Joan's desk was central to the space, but she would have her back to half her colleagues; added to that, a large support pillar practically blinded her to the elevator and a further quarter of the room, and Joan did like to keep an eye on things.

'If it was me,' he said, 'I'd take that spot over there.' He nodded towards an empty desk near the wide expanse of glass overlooking the river.

She looked sceptical. 'Stuck at the back of the room? I think *not*.'

'Come and have a look.'

She pressed her lips together and fluttered her hand at the paperwork awaiting her attention.

'Come on,' he said. 'It'll only take a sec.'

She stood reluctantly, and followed him, passing five workstations on the way. At the window desk, he angled his body, first towards the elevator, then the water cooler, then he crouched next to the desk and did a slow scan of the room. 'Yup,' he said. 'This is the one.'

She frowned, looking a little petulant, but he rolled out the office chair and invited her to try it. With a sigh, she sat down, and immediately perked up.

'Oh, I see,' she said, positively beaming.

'View out the window's nice an' all,' Josh said. She wheeled her chair around, and from her look of satisfaction he guessed she was more pleased by her vantage point over the footpath below the window than by her river view.

His next stop was to pick up some reference texts. Josh had taught some of Fennimore's summer school classes while the professor was away in the United States, and had been allocated shared office space with a sessional lecturer and another Ph.D. student. He preferred the tiny common room he'd used as his unofficial office in the old building, but Josh had learned to be comfortable in most places, and he'd set up quite a library in his corner of the room. He stuffed as many texts as he could into his rucksack, but he'd have to go back to his flat, then drive the car round to pick up the rest.

He stacked the remaining books on his desk and paused, remembering that he'd saved some notes to his P drive – the secure compartment of the university's system set aside for him. He would need those notes and he couldn't access them from anywhere but the university. How long would it take to set up a new email address, forward everything to that – a few minutes? *Time.* It all took time, and he needed to be gone.

Was there any point, anyway? Fennimore said they would make it work, but you couldn't *partially* disappear – all that did was put everyone you cared about in danger.

To hell with it – he wasn't ready to give up yet. He shoved the books to one side, sat at the computer and opened his university email account. There was a message from Fennimore: it looked like they were closing in on the killer. He read on, shocked that there might be a link between the Manchester case and Mitchell's miscarriage of justice. Maybe he should work out a way to stay and help. But Fennimore quashed that notion in the next sentence:

'You can't stay, Josh,' he wrote. 'You aren't safe there – the killer doesn't know what we have on him – and if we're to have even the slimmest chance to save the child, he *can't* know. But he might have followed you. He might even be there already. Your family knows your connection to me – *they* could be looking for you as well. Aberdeen isn't a big city – you'll be easy to find. Get out and stay out.'

On the next line: 'I'm sorry I got you into this. Watch your back.'

Josh stared at the words on the screen. He couldn't remember anyone caring enough to say those words to him since he was fifteen years old.

His throat tight with emotion, he copied his files and forwarded them to a new account via an anonymous remailer, then he digitally shredded the files on his drive.

Josh rented a one-bedroom flat in Rosebank Terrace, twenty minutes' walk from the old campus, but a good forty minutes away from Garthdee; he would have to take a bus. He headed out, towards the riverside path, intending to double back to the bus stop when he was sure he wasn't being followed. He heard a rattle from above, but ignored it; a moment later Joan's voice fluted from one of the windows on the first floor.

'*Woo-hoo!* Halloa there, Josh!'

He looked up.

'Wait,' she called. 'I'll come down to you.'

He met her at the entrance.

'It completely went out of my head,' she said. 'Someone was asking after you earlier.'

'He leave a name?' Josh said, his stomach muscles clenching.

'No. He said he would catch you later.'

'What did he look like?'

'Thirtyish. Tall. English. As a matter of fact, he sounded a bit like you.'

Josh felt a weakness in his limbs. *Family.*

He kept his tone level. 'Did you give him my address?'

'What a question!' She glared at Josh, outraged. 'I told him you were unavailable. He declined to leave a message.'

'Sorry, Joan,' he said, attempting a smile. 'It's been a hell of a day.'

She didn't smile, but he saw a softening of her features, perhaps even a hint of concern. 'If he comes back, what will I say to him?'

'Tell him I'm taking a leave of absence. I'll be away for a while.'

'And will you be coming back?' she said, watching him closely.

Joan's fussy persona might fool the majority, but she had a sharp mind and even sharper eyes.

'Probably not,' he said truthfully.

He found a bench and sat in the cold, watching people

come and go. Mostly foreign students and conference visitors, this time of year. He didn't recognize anyone and nobody seemed to be paying him any special attention. He couldn't complete his thesis without the notes he had at home. It was a calculated risk, but he intended to go and pick them up. He'd stayed under the radar, paying his rent in cash every month: it would take his family a while to get an address for him – even with their police connections.

And he needed his car – a nondescript grey Toyota Corolla, bought for cash in Leeds, no questions asked. It was still registered to the previous owner – an extra few hundred over the asking price had persuaded the guy to hand over the registration documents instead of sending his portion to the DVLA. Normally Josh kept it in a lock-up, under wraps, further down the street, but he'd parked it near home after dropping off the files for Nick Fennimore.

He caught the next bus into the city centre, staying on for a couple of extra stops, then swinging off in Union Street, by Gilcomston South Church. A banner outside the door read, 'TRY PRAYING'. He hoped it wasn't prophetic.

He pulled up the hood of his jacket, hoisted his bag on to his shoulder and strode out, taking the long route home, pausing and doubling back a couple of times. When he was sure he was in the clear, he jinked through to Rosebank. The Toyota was where he'd left it, and he saw nothing out of the ordinary in the street.

He dug his house keys out of his pocket and crossed the road, just as a black BMW turned the corner. He didn't break stride, but pocketed the latch key and took out his car keys, heading straight to the Toyota instead. He slid behind the wheel, turning his face away as the Beamer passed, then reached to adjust his rear-view mirror. His hand shook, jerking the angle too far, but he got a glimpse of the car's number plate. The first two letters were EA – an Essex registration. Two men in the front – maybe a third in the back. They'd come mob-handed. The road was closed at the far end; they would have to come back this way, but it would take them a minute or so to complete the manoeuvre.

His heart thudding, he fired up the ignition and pulled the car away from the kerb, heading towards Crown Street and the A93. He heard a squeal of brakes and in his rear-view he saw the BMW's brake lights flash, then the car was reversing back the way it had come, fishtailing madly. He jammed his foot on the pedal .

The Beamer kept coming. The driver did a handbrake turn at the corner, taking the front bumper off a Mini coming the other way. Josh swung left into Crown Street, screamed past a white van, into the path of an oncoming lorry.

Too close – *too close*. He braced for impact and veered left, just squeezing in front of the van. Horns blared on both sides. He skidded left again, on to the main road, heading west, away from the city centre, swerving in and out of slower-moving traffic. The BMW kept pace.

'Should've bought a better car, Josh,' he muttered. He ran a red light and dragged the wheel right, across the stream of traffic. Completing a couple more quick turns, he slowed to check his mirror. He'd lost them.

He took a few deep breaths, wiped his hands on his trouser legs, got a fresh grip of the wheel and pootled gently to the next junction.

A sharp crack behind him, then the rear seat-back tipped forward.

Something came out of the void, was on him before he could react. A flash of white looped over his head and he felt hard plastic dig into his throat. He hit the brakes and slammed his hand on the horn.

'Lay off.' A man's voice, no more than a harsh whisper. He was masked, all in black.

Jesus. I left it too late, took too long.

Josh brought one hand up, tried to work his fingers between the plastic and his throat, but the loop was too tight. His fingertips tingled and darkness crept in from the edges of his vision.

'Lay off or I'll squeeze the life out of you. I'll cut your fucking head off.'

The loop tightened still further; Josh felt it break the skin. He did as he was told, and the pressure eased.

A second later he saw the BMW in his rear-view mirror and felt a confused mixture of relief and blank terror.

37

Abduction, Day 9

Lauren Myers woke with a shout. She was tucked in the deep recess of a window ledge. twelve feet off the ground. There was a big steel thing on the other side, so she couldn't get out. Her breath came in short gasps as she peeped over the edge to see if the bad man had come back. She couldn't see him, but the shuffles and squeaks below told her the rats were stealing what was left of her food.

The man had stamped all over everything the last time he came. He screamed and shouted and pushed over the water bottle and she heard the water glug out on the floor. But he didn't climb up after her. He shouted and shouted till his voice went funny, and she screamed back because she ate the yellow sweeties like Mummy said.

'Come here, you little bitch!' he'd yelled.

'I *won't*. Go a–*way*, you horrible monster!' she'd screamed.

He couldn't make her come, because Mummy said she *had*

to be naughty, and you've got to do what Mummy says more than anyone in the whole wide world because Mummy grew you in her own tummy, and Mummy Always Knows What's Best. Lauren watched the man trying to jump up and grab her as she climbed high up the metal frame, but she was too fast. Then he tripped over something and she laughed – what Mummy called her nasty laugh – 'HahahahahaHA-HA!' like that, with her mouth wide open and her hands up by her head in bear's claws. Like when she was hyper on the E-numbers that one time and hit Jody Scott so she fell down in the playground and she didn't even feel sorry, just laughed and called Jody bad names. Jody looked scared. Lauren felt sorry about that now. The man looked scared, too – but she didn't feel bad about the man. He didn't bring her mummy back. And he told a big lie. He said Mummy had gone home without her because she was such a naughty girl. She called him a big fat liar and said he would go to HELL and the devil would stick a big fork in his horrible fat tummy and break off his horrible skinny legs and stick him in a big fire and he would sizzle like a fat horrible SAUSAGE.

She felt her face grow hot, thinking of all the things she had said, but she wasn't ashamed – just angry. The metal thing on the window wouldn't let her out, but it couldn't stop a tiny bit of light getting in, and Lauren stared at it for a while because it made her feel a bit stronger and less scared. Then, slowly, she peeped over the edge again. The light outside had blinded her, but in the dim light that trickled in from the roof she saw something move.

A rat. It was by the big metal thing where the man had tied her and Mummy up. She had a packet of biscuits and some sweeties on the ledge, but no drinks. Mummy was always going on about drinking plenty of fresh water and how you could get sick if you didn't drink enough. Lauren's head felt hot, like it did before when Mummy couldn't get the bottle open. She could hear Mummy in her head as if she was really there: 'You *have* to drink something, sweetie.'

But she would have to get down from the window and she was frightened the man would come back. Or maybe he creeped in while she was asleep and he was hiding, waiting for her to come out.

She listened very hard, but all she could hear was the rats. She looked up one way and down the other way, but she couldn't see anything hiding in the shadows. She peeped over the edge again, and the room started to spin like when she played whirligigs, going round and round in the garden till she fell down on the grass. Maybe she should wait a bit longer.

'Lauren – *please*.'

She flinched. 'Mummy?' She searched the space below her again, tears springing to her eyes. 'Mummy, did you come back?'

But there was nothing.

She bent her head to her knees and sobbed.

Something tugged at her leg and she shrieked, squishing herself into the corner of the window ledge. It happened again a minute later and the tugging turned into a pain that felt like someone squeezing her leg very hard, but she couldn't see anything.

She slapped at her leg and screamed, kicking out at the invisible hand and gradually the pain went away.

'Silly Lauren,' she murmured, trying to make her voice sound like Mummy's. 'It's just a cramp.'

A minute after that, she heard a humming sound and began to sing the words in her head: 'Hush, little baby, don't say a word, Poppa's gonna buy you a mock-in bird . . .' It sounded *just like* Mummy. Then the words changed:

'Hush, little Lauren, gotta climb down, Momma's gonna buy you a princess gown. Climb down here and get a little drink, and I will dress you all in pink . . .'

She stretched her legs out, testing them, before swinging them over the ledge. Then she grasped the edge of the steel thing that covered the window and eased herself around so she was facing the window, lowering herself as far as she could before dropping to the floor. But she lost her grip and fell too fast; she jarred her ankle and fell sideways, banging her hip. For a few moments she lay scrunched up and crying, her twisted ankle grasped tight in both hands.

A picture of Mummy, her ankle bleeding, flashed into her head and she opened her eyes wide to make it go away. Across the dusty floor, she saw the big water bottle as a humped shadow; shiny and blue, like a whale. She tried to stand up, but a pain shot from her foot to her hip and her ankle gave way. She fell with a shout and gazed for a few tearful moments at the shape.

Then she swung her injured leg out straight and sat, using her good leg to inch along the floor on her bottom.

'That's my girl!' Mummy said.

Lauren looked around to see where she was. But Mummy was only inside her head. She wiped snot and tears off her face with her forearms and set off again, boosting herself with both hands as well as her good foot until she could almost reach out and touch the bottle.

A big rat left off nibbling at the crunched-up biscuits and darted over to the bottle, as if it wanted to stop her, but it only wanted a drink. It put its whole head inside the wide mouth of the bottle and began to lap greedily. She could see its tongue flicking at the water like a small pink flame.

'Go a-*way*!' she shouted, her voice high with fear.

The rat ignored her. She scooted closer and shouted again, lashing out with her good foot. The bottle rocked and gave a sudden *Bloop!*

The rat squeaked, squirming as it backed out of the mouth of the bottle. Then it ran, dashing right, left, jumping over broken bits of stone and metal as if it thought she might chase it. She watched it, scared it might come back and bite her, but at last it disappeared into the gloom.

The water was nearly gone. The bottle was too big to pick up, so she lay flat on her belly and stuck her tongue in. But she couldn't get her head inside like the rat. She sat up again; her head hurt and it felt as if her whole body was rocking. Mummy's handbag was close by, and she got hold of it and pushed that under the back of the bottle so it tipped up. Water began to spill out and she gave a little squeal of dismay, swinging on to her tummy again, sucking at the water dripping out of the opening in jerky glugs.

It was spilling too much!

She reached for the handbag and tugged it away, but more water came out, making a small pool on the dusty grey floor. It stopped at the edge of one of the blankets, and this gave Lauren an idea.

She jammed a corner of the blanket into the mouth of the bottle and, when it had soaked up some of the water inside, she began to suck. It smelled funny and tasted like the stuff off the floor, but she sucked on it anyway, and after a while she began to feel a bit better.

Something clanked against the outside of the building and she sat up with a gasp. The man?

She listened hard and the sound came again: a soft *clank-clank* – the wind swinging something against the metal door. She breathed easier. She needed to climb back up to her window ledge, so the bad man couldn't get her. But her ankle throbbed worse than her head now, and it felt hot when she touched it. If she could take the blanket with her, she would have food and water until Daddy came to rescue her.

She swung herself into a sitting position and eased one foot under her, then used both hands to boost herself up. But her sore ankle hurt too much. She took hold of the blanket, gently easing the corner out of the bottle, and tried hopping. But she fell down. She stared at the window, at the thin grey thread of light at its edges, and wondered how she ever got up there, knowing she would never be able to get back. Without her magic Yellow Peril sweeties her superpower was gone. She curled up on the floor and wept.

38

Absence of evidence is not evidence of absence.

SIR MARTIN REES, ASTROPHYSICIST (ATTR.)

An Essex Hotel, Thursday, Early Evening

Fennimore's hotel room looked like a stationers after a hurri-
cane: papers spread out on the bed, the sofa, the desk-dresser
and even on the floor – copies of Lazko's hate mail the solicitor, Haverford, had kept in safekeeping. The journalist had
received fifty-one of them, warning him off the Mitchell
case. Ten of these were stacked on one corner of the bed
– discounted as threats from 'concerned citizens' convinced
of Mitchell's guilt and determined to force Lazko into making the 'right' decision. Seven more lay side by side on the
bed. Fennimore had labelled these with orange Post-it notes,
selecting them for similar phrasing, or use of threats that suggested a knowledge of the torture Lazko had been subjected
to. He would send copies of these to a language pattern
analyst. Fennimore had copies of the letters he himself had
received from the killer, and he crossed the room to the desk-
dresser to root them out on his laptop.

He couldn't resist switching screens to look again at the

surveillance recordings from Paris. For ten minutes he stood watching the movement-sensitive cameras deliver bursts of footage, *willing* the girl in the orange sundress to appear.

A Skype alert finally dragged him out of his almost trance-like state.

Kate Simms. Of all possible interruptions, hers was the most welcome.

He leaned forward and clicked 'Answer' and her face popped on to the screen.

He dragged out the chair from under the dresser, dumped his laptop bag on the floor and took a seat. 'What's up?' he said.

'We got a name.'

For a second, it felt like all the air had been sucked out of the room. When it came rushing back, he took a grateful breath and steadied himself.

'That was fast.'

'The survivor's description helped,' Simms said. 'His name is Vic Tremain. Divorced. A loner — and you're right — he has Klinefelter's. Seems he sought treatment for infertility early in his marriage. It was one of the reasons for the break-up, according to the ex-wife. Tremain has worked as a porter at hospitals all over London and the south-east; moved to Manchester six months ago.'

He leaned forward. 'You have an address?'

She nodded. 'The Tactical Firearms Unit was deployed.'

He felt the intensity of her gaze on him and realized she had used the past tense. '*Was* deployed?' he said.

'He wasn't at home and hasn't been at work for over a week. CSIs are working the scene now, but there's no sign of Lauren, no indication she was ever in his house.'

'Oh, hell . . .' He passed a hand over his eyes, suppressing a tremor.

'The palynologist has finished her evaluation of the fungal spores and pollen they found on the letters Tremain sent to you.' Simms shrugged. 'Maybe she'll have something that will give us a better idea of where he's been keeping them.'

'The investigators are talking to neighbours, work colleagues?'

'I imagine they are. I'm still out of the loop, Nick.'

'After all you've done?'

'It's not my investigation,' she said firmly, shutting him down before he could rev up his outrage to full throttle. 'But I can't seem to leave it alone . . .' Her tone was dry and she half-smiled, but he sensed a nervousness – perhaps even an excitement.

'So . . .?'

'I've been looking at the victimology again.'

'You found something else?'

'I don't know,' she said. 'Probably not – but your MOJ—'

'Mitchell?'

'No, the one before.' She looked away and he heard a rustle of paper; she was referring to notes. 'Gail Hammond – the nurse who disappeared from Ingatestone railway station. I've been looking at the lecture you gave – the one that ended up on YouTube.'

'What about it?'

'You said that you believed Gail was abducted from her car?'

'Yes, but what's that got to do with—?' Every hair stood up on Fennimore's head. 'You think Vic Tremain was involved in *Gail Hammond's* murder?'

261

'I don't know,' she said. 'But Gail *was* from Chelmsford, wasn't she?'

He leaned forward; adrenaline surging through him seemed to light the room like a spot lamp. 'And a nurse, yes. She worked at Broomfield Hospital, just outside the city.'

She paused, and his heart pulsed thickly in his throat. 'Kate, what have you got?'

'Where was her car found?' she asked.

'Outside her flat.'

Simms stared out of the screen at him; she seemed to be holding every muscle rigid. 'Where – *exactly* – was that?'

He gave the street name and house number from memory, and the rims of her irises sparked amber.

'Nick,' she said. 'Vic Tremain lived in that street. I have a map in front of me.' She glanced down. 'The house Tremain lived in was—' she broke off, checking the details. 'Yes – it was *directly opposite* Gail's house. He was probably interviewed by police during the house-to-house canvassing. And get this: he'd done some agency work at Broomfield Hospital.'

'When?' he said.

She checked her notes again. 'Early spring, the year Gail was murdered.'

Fennimore sat back in his seat, stunned.

'*That's* why he sent those threats to you,' Simms said. 'You'd already cleared Killbride of Gail Hammond's murder *and* you put forward the theory that she was abducted from her car. Tremain knew it was only a question of time before you made the connection between Gail and Kelli Rees's murder.'

'I showed photos of the road where Gail lived,' Fennimore said. 'Tremain recognized it.' The truth hit him like a punch in the head: if he hadn't given that lecture, Julia Myers would still be alive.

'Nick, this isn't your fault,' Simms said, reading his mind as she so often did.

'He murdered Julia Myers to distract me, Kate. Her little girl is out there somewhere, alone, because of me.'

Simms's expression didn't change exactly, it was more that it solidified into something unnaturally neutral, and Fennimore realized something he had been avoiding for the past day: Kate Simms believed that Lauren Myers was already dead.

39

Manchester Police HQ, Thursday, Early Evening

Thirty minutes later, Kate Simms was standing in Chief Constable Enderby's office with DCI John Ingrams, the man in charge of the Myers investigation. They listened to a précis of her conversation with Nick Fennimore, Enderby sombre and heavy-browed, Ingrams with a growing look of amused surprise on his face.

'You're saying the Myers abductions were a decoy?' DCI Ingrams was tall and lean, maybe fifty years old, grey-suited, the kind of man who shaved his head rather than be accused of trying to hide his baldness. 'A ... what ... A *distraction* crime to stop Fennimore investigating Mitchell's miscarriage of justice?'

'A ploy,' Simms said. 'To keep Professor Fennimore from reviewing the evidence.'

Ingrams shook his head. 'It doesn't make sense – all he did was draw attention to himself.'

'Tremain knew he could get away with Julia Myers's murder, but Kelli Rees was one of his earlier victims,' Simms said. 'He made a mistake – left a bread trail back to his real identity. He was safe while Mitchell's conviction held, because the evidence he planted stayed buried. But as soon as Fennimore talked about Gail Hammond in his lecture, Tremain knew he was in danger. And when Fennimore agreed to review the Mitchell MOJ . . .' She shrugged. 'Let's just say Tremain couldn't afford to let Fennimore do that.'

Ingrams slipped a hand into his trouser pocket and laughed softly. 'Well, Kate. You seem to think Fennimore is some kind of deductive genius.'

'He has his faults,' she said lightly. 'But it doesn't matter what I think – the evidence speaks for itself.'

Ingrams began to argue, but Enderby intervened. 'Yes,' he said, 'it does.'

He might not like it, but Ingrams was a political animal; he knew when to back down. He frowned, gave a tentative nod. 'All right. But I don't see how it helps us to find Tremain or Lauren.'

He was right. They had an identity but nothing to point them towards a location.

'What about the palynologist – did she find anything useful?' Simms asked.

Ingrams glanced at Enderby for approval before he replied: 'Concrete dust and cotton plant pollen under Mrs Myers's fingernails and in her nasal passages, together with two kinds of mould spores which suggest that she was being held in an old mill or warehouse.'

'Oh,' Simms said, disappointed.

'Yes,' Ingrams said, with equal lack of enthusiasm.

265

In the mid-nineteenth century, Manchester was 'Cottonopolis' – the commercial and manufacturing hub for the British cotton trade. At its peak, there were over a hundred cotton mills spread out across the city. After the Second World War, most had fallen derelict and although some had been redeveloped, searching the remaining ruins would be a monumental task.

'How many are we looking at?' she asked.

'Thirty plus,' Ingrams said. 'But that's just the mills – if you take into account the warehouses that served them . . .' He shrugged.

'You've spoken to Professor Varley about a geographic profile?'

Ingrams seemed offended by the question, but after another silent exchange between the two men, he said: 'Varley recommended starting from Tremain's current address and working outward in a spiral. As Tremain is new to Manchester, the professor thinks he will be working within a small area he's familiar with.'

'Any suggestions welcome, Kate,' Enderby said.

Ingrams's eyes widened. 'Sir—'

'DCI Simms gave us the link between the victims,' Enderby cut in. 'Her intervention identified a survivor. That survivor provided us with a description that helped us to identify Tremain. And now it looks like she's just given us a link back to Fennimore's case.'

'Actually, sir, I had some help,' Simms said, thinking now was the time to give Diane credit for her work.

'It's all right,' Enderby said. 'I know your tattooed friend had a hand in it.'

Simms caught a twinkle in his eye and the ghost of a smile played around his mouth.

'So,' he said. 'Ideas . . .?'

'Work with what we have,' she said. 'Tremain's identity. If he rented space—'

'*If* he did,' Ingram interrupted. 'We're checking his credit cards, of course, but the chances are he just broke in to wherever he held them.'

'But if he *did* rent a building, he's not the kind of man you would forget easily,' Simms said. 'And now we've got photos of him . . .'

'If it makes you happy, I'll send teams out to commercial property agents,' Ingrams said with a sigh.

'We should go to TV and social media, too.'

Ingrams scoffed. 'And drive him down a rabbit-hole?'

'Tremain doesn't know we're looking for him. He murdered Lazko to try to get the Mitchell case files because he thinks we don't know who he is, and he wants to keep it that way. If Lauren *is* still alive, we should use the photos.' She recalled the look of desperate hope on Fennimore's face as she echoed his words: 'He has no reason to kill Lauren if he knows we're searching for him.'

After a moment's thought, Enderby said, 'I agree. Where are the Mitchell case files now – do we need to look at protecting Professor Fennimore?'

She hesitated.

'Kate?'

'Not Fennimore,' she said. 'His Ph.D. student – Nick sent Josh Brown ahead to Aberdeen to move the files from his apartment to somewhere safe.'

'Can you contact him?' Enderby asked.

She tried Josh's number. 'No reply.'

'You think Tremain would go after the files?'

'I'd bet a month's salary on it.'

Enderby turned to Ingrams. 'Then the sooner we get TV and media announcements out, the better.'

Ingrams dialled through to his team manager, while Simms put in a call to Fennimore.

'I can't get through to Josh,' she said, without preamble.

'He ditched his phone,' Fennimore replied. 'Is there a problem?'

'I'll let you know.' She disconnected and scrolled through her contacts list to find Donal McLeish, the detective sergeant at Police Scotland she'd asked to check Fennimore's apartment.

He answered on the second ring. 'Kate – I was about to call you. Fennimore's flat is a wreck.'

'Any signs of struggle?' she asked.

'No – but you said Fennimore was in Essex, so . . .'

She took a breath and let it go. 'Josh Brown was supposed to call in and pick up some files for Professor Fennimore. He's not answering his mobile,' she added, not entirely truthfully, but she couldn't risk Josh's protected witness status getting out to the wrong people.

'Got an address?' McLeish asked. 'I could send out a couple of uniforms.'

She called Fennimore and got straight back to McLeish.

'Oh, wait a minute,' he said. 'A call came in a short time ago – there was a hit and run RTC on that street.'

Road Traffic Collision. 'Anyone hurt?' she said, hearing the tension in her voice.

'It was a fender-bender,' he said. 'The driver who remained at the scene was shaken up – it wasn't Josh, I'm afraid. Two other cars drove off at speed. We're on the lookout.'

He hung up, having promised to get back to her when they had checked Josh's flat.

Simms stared at her phone. When she looked up, Enderby was watching her.

'Kate, if you're holding something back,' he said, 'you need to think again.'

How much to tell, how much to withhold?

'I'm not withholding,' she said. 'I just need to talk to Fennimore first.'

Ingrams spread his hands, appealing to Enderby. 'What the hell does she thinks she's playing at?'

Simms ignored Ingrams, focusing instead on the chief constable. 'All I need is five minutes, sir.'

Enderby looked grave, but after a long half-minute, he said, 'All right. Five minutes, no more.'

She stepped outside the office, closed the door, fast-dialled Fennimore's number and laid out the situation for him. He listened in silence, but she could imagine what he felt.

'What can I do?' he said.

'Tell me everything you know about Josh.'

40

Lauren Myers dipped the corner of her blanket into the small puddle of water remaining in the bottle and sucked it. She was hot and cold at the same time and she had a pain in her back and legs. A while ago – she couldn't remember how long – she'd eaten some of the mashed-up biscuits the rats had left, but she sicked everything back up and now her tummy hurt, too. Her mummy's handbag lay on the floor nearby and she crawled to it, groaning at the shivery pains it sent down her legs and up into her head. The bag smelled of Mummy's perfume and it made her feel better, like Mummy was near.

She hugged the leather to her, comforted by the scent, and tried to sing 'Hush, Little Baby' again, but her voice came out as a croak. It made her think of the princess in the film who could scream so high all the rats in the kingdom ran away. She heard a high squeak, but couldn't see past the fog in her eyes and the mud-coloured dark around her. She wished the sun would come inside. It was horrible being in a place that was always night, but never bedtime. It made her feel tired and sleepy. Her eyes began to close.

A scratchy sound close by made her start up. Two points of light flickered a foot away from her face. A rat by the water bottle. She tried to shoo it way, but it just sat up taller and watched her. She wanted to scream like the princess, but was too tired. The rat covered its mouth to hide a snigger.

'Don't laugh. *Naught—y*,' she said, but her voice had no strength and her head seemed to beat so it felt like her heart had jumped up into her brain. The darkness turned red, curling in from the sides.

'*Naughty* r—' The red turned black and everything stopped.

41

Aberdeen, Thursday, Early Evening

'You're really screwed, you know that?' Josh said.

'*You're* the one in trouble, *dickhead.*' The man's accent, like his own, was pure Essex. Josh checked the rear-view mirror; the man's face was masked, but the crazed look in his eyes said it would be suicide to argue.

'Drive,' the man said.

'Where d'you want to go?'

'You know what I want.'

The case files. 'Just tell me where the girl is, I'll give you everything you need.'

The man tightened his grip.

Josh brought both hands to his throat, gouging his own flesh in his scramble to ease the pressure. Abruptly, the man released the noose, just enough for Josh to take a gulp of air. He coughed and retched.

The man dragged him back against the headrest by his hair. 'You don't get to call the shots,' he said.

Josh whooped, gulping down more air.

'Are we clear?'

Josh nodded.

'I can't hear you.'

'Okay,' Josh choked. 'But ease off. It's not gonna do either of us any good if I pass out, is it?'

The car had stalled and Josh leaned forward to turn the ignition key. He glanced again in the rear-view, past his attacker. The BMW hadn't moved; it idled on the street, thirty feet behind them. There were definitely three people in the car; he recognized his eldest brother, Greg, in the driver's seat, his cousin Mikey next to him. The third person remained hidden.

They were in a built-up area and Josh reasoned that Greg wouldn't move in while there were so many witnesses.

He had stashed the files at a self-storage facility in Muggiemoss, about fifteen minutes' drive from the city. He headed that way with no real plan in mind – except to stay alive until he saw an opportunity to act. Josh could see the BMW's day-beams glowing like a hunting animal's some way behind them, but he slowed his breathing and tried not to think too hard about the choice that lay ahead – between the noose and the gun.

Crossing the Great Northern Road, the urban sprawl of modern tenement buildings and commercial units dropped away at a stroke and from the railway bridge, wooded hills and farmland filled the landscape across the River Don.

Behind him, the BMW swung wide and Josh tightened his grip on the wheel, ready for impact. The road curved sharp left and he accelerated. They kept pace – into the path of an oncoming lorry. Horns blared and the Beamer tucked in fast.

'What the f—?' the man muttered.

Josh kept going. To their left, he saw an industrial estate of low-rise buildings: car sales and furniture repairs; pipe components and sub-sea technology businesses – local needs and oil industry requisites living side by side in what had long been the oil capital of Europe. A left at the next roundabout would take him to Muggiemoss industrial estate and the storage unit, but his family would be on them as soon as he stopped, and they would be armed. He would die, his freak-show attacker would die and Lauren Myers would never be found.

He indicated left, positioning himself to take the turn, but at the last second, swung hard right, accelerating, squeezing past a van taking the next exit, heading across the River Don towards Peterhead and Fraserburgh. The man lurched sideways and Josh heard a satisfying crack as his head hit the side window. The van driver swerved, sounding the horn; the vehicle tipped on to two wheels for a fraction of a second, then slewed sideways into the oncoming lane. Josh reached up and flung the zip tie away, but the man was on him in a second, his long, sinewy forearm locking around Josh's throat. Josh hit the brakes and the man's head made contact with the headrest, whipping back hard as Josh accelerated again. He fell backward, cursing, arms and legs flailing like an upturned spider.

Cars coming in the other direction slowed, giving Josh fifty yards of clear roadway. He blasted into it, overtaking a line of seven vehicles, leaving a cacophony of squealing tyres and angry horn blasts in his wake, but the Beamer kept coming, headlights blazing, horn blaring.

The abductor came at him again and Josh held him off with one hand.

'Listen to me!' he yelled. 'The men in the BMW are my family. They're here to kill me and they will kill *anyone* who gets in their way. So if you want to live – sit the fuck back.'

The man threw a terrified glance over his shoulder as the black BMW filled the rear-view mirror. The A90 curved eastward at this point, heading back towards Aberdeen and a cluster of housing estates where Josh might lose the BMW. His best chance was to loop back to the city, run his car into a police patrol car, if he had to.

He aimed for the next roundabout at sixty miles an hour, side by side with the BMW, Mikey grinning at him from the passenger seat.

He almost made it. Then the Beamer clipped the wing of his car, sending it off to the left, into the exit lane of the first turning. It slid anticlockwise, the rear wing connecting with a lamp post, then Josh hit the accelerator again, fishtailing down a country lane, past stone cottages and patches of woodland. A mile or so on, the trees thinned either side of the road and the vista opened up to hayfields and a slope down to the river. The BMW screamed alongside and Josh felt a sickening shove, heard the groan of metal on metal, as the car veered towards the wire fence.

His abductor screamed.

Josh jerked the wheel, forcing the BMW right. It braked sharply, dropping back as a tractor came at them. Across the next junction, trees crowded the left side of the road again. This was not good – he had to find a way back to the city. The trees vanished, replaced by scrubby grazing and low stone walls on either side. They flew over undulations in the

275

road, grounding at the dips. Up ahead a left turn with an in-out track and a flat patch of grass. It looked like a private road, but if he could use it to turn—

He wrenched the wheel left then hard right, using the grass skid to enhance the turn, feeling the wheels spin under him. The BMW kept coming. He accelerated out of the turn, hit a mound in the grass triangle and felt the front of the car lift. His passenger screamed again. Josh saw blue sky, white tree bark – then nothing.

He came to with his ears booming. The car was on its side and all he could see through his window was a muddy bank, clumps of grass and fragments of grey stone. He leaned off the steering wheel and the booming sound in his ears stopped abruptly.

He groaned at the pain in his ribs and reached for the door handle; couldn't work out why it wouldn't open, then realized he was stupidly trying to force the door open against a solid bank of mud and turf. He blinked, couldn't see straight, but he knew he had to get out of there, fast. He eased his left leg over the gear stick and squirmed sideways against gravity to manoeuvre himself into the passenger seat. Behind him, his abductor moaned and one large hand flopped through the gap between the seats. Josh tried to locate the handle through a fog of blurred vision. It opened as he reached for it, and he fell forward.

A cheery voice that was not his brother's said, 'Wakey-wakey, boys. Time to die.'

Two strong pairs of hands grasped him by the shoulders and heaved him out on to the roadside. They forced him to his knees and Josh felt a wave of dizziness. His head lolled back and he was squinting into the face of his eldest brother.

'Hello, Sean,' Greg said.

He blinked and finally his brother came into focus. The years hadn't treated him kindly; at thirty-eight, Greg's face was deep-lined and as grey as the stone that lay smashed on the roadway around them.

A second later, the black-clad form landed face-down on the tarmac next to him.

'Who's the gimp?' the second voice asked. Cousin Mikey – had to be – Mikey had always considered himself the joker of the family.

'We haven't been introduced,' Josh said, clamping his jaw tight to stop his teeth chattering.

Greg leaned forward and ripped off the mask, and the man whimpered.

'Wouldn't've thought he was your type, Sean,' Greg said.

'He's a sadistic killer,' Josh said.

Mikey clapped his hands, laughing. 'You *have* changed, Sean.'

Josh tried to turn his head to get a look at the third member of the team, but Mikey slapped the back of his head, sending a new shockwave through his skull.

He leaned forward and threw up on the ground at his brother's feet.

'Oi!' Mikey yelled and Josh heard him step forward.

'Mikey.' Greg spoke quietly, but the menace in that one word was enough to make Mikey back off.

The black-clad man was gibbering, begging to be let go.

'Who is he?' Greg said, disgust written all over his face.

'I told you,' Josh said. 'A killer. He kidnapped a mother and her little girl in Manchester. The mother's dead – a journalist as well.'

'Can't be *all* bad then, eh?' Mikey again.

This time a look from Greg was enough to silence him.

Josh still hadn't seen the third occupant of the BMW, and he began to turn again to look. Greg punched him, hard, in the left temple. His head whipped right. The fog descended once more and Josh began to shake; he slumped forward, saving himself with this hands, feeling grit and dirt scrape his palms.

Then Greg's hand snaked forward and gripped a handful of his hair; his head snapped back and he was looking into his brother's eyes. Josh had forgotten how fast his brother could move; age hadn't changed that in him.

'He do this to you?' Greg asked, tracing the line of the plastic garrotte around his throat, and not too gently.

Josh winced, despite himself. 'Yeah,' he managed on an out-breath.

Something flickered in Greg's eyes; Mikey moved in and aimed a kick at his attacker's side. Josh heard a crunch, a grunt of pain, then the gimp was begging:

'*Pleasepleasepleasedon't*', as Mikey brought his foot back for a second swing.

'Don't,' Josh said, his voice sounding dull and far away.

'You really *have* got a thing for him, haven't you, Sean?' Mikey said, finishing the kick almost as an afterthought.

'The girl is still missing,' Josh said, his voice hoarse. 'He knows where she is.'

'What's that to me?'

'She's six, Greg.'

Greg had raised three daughters of his own. He let go of Josh's hair and Josh swayed uncertainly for a moment before finding his balance again.

'Where's the girl?' Greg said, addressing the man cowering on the ground.

'Fuck off,' the man said, but there was no force behind the words.

Greg's lips curled in a snarl of disgust. Out of nowhere, he had a gun in his hand. He screwed a suppressor to the muzzle, taking his time, then raised the pistol, pointing it at the grovelling man's head.

'Greg, no, *please.*'

His brother's eyes slid slowly from the wiry man spitting blood on to the tarmac, to Josh. 'I never thought I'd hear you beg, Sean.' He sounded disappointed.

'The little girl – her name is Lauren, lives in Manchester. Her mother took her out for a birthday treat and this piece of shit took them. He killed the mother, but there's a chance Lauren is still alive. She's been gone over a week; we know it's an old building, because they found mould under her fingernails. But we got nothing else—'

'*We?* You know how much it *offends* me, you working with the cops?' Greg said.

'I'm just trying to find a little girl, Greg. Remember when Kim was six and she was scared of the dark?' Josh remembered a time – he was no more than eight – staying at his big brother's house after a family party, sleeping on a camp bed in Kim's room, Kim waking up screaming. Greg scooped her up in his strong arms and scared the demons away, banishing them from troubling her ever again.

The muzzle of the pistol lowered a fraction, but his brother's eyes remained hard. 'Not my concern,' he said. The muzzle came up again and the man who had remained hidden stepped sharply in front of Josh's abductor.

'She's just a kid, Greg.'

Josh felt a killing pain grip his heart. *Damon?* During this entire ordeal, he had been afraid and angry and desperate. Until now, he had not experienced despair.

'What d'you have to bring Damon for?' he said, choked with emotion.

'This is family,' Greg said. 'Family cleans up its own messes.'

'He's *sixteen*, Greg.'

His little brother spoke up: 'You got no say in this,' he said. 'You relinquished all rights when you grassed up your own brothers.'

There was hate in his brother's eyes and in the twist of his mouth, but Josh knew that half of it was bravado. He'd done it himself often enough – covering fear with rage. He latched on to that word, and in spite of everything going on around him, he felt a swell of pride. From the age of seven, Damon had used words like *relinquished*. All of them ragged him about it, called him the kid who swallowed a dictionary, but Damon said just because he was a gangster didn't mean he had to be ignorant. *Gangster*. Damon was the only one in the family could get away with using that word in front of their mother.

Damon held his gaze a second longer, but when Josh's eyes began to tear up, he looked away with a disgusted shake of the head.

'C'mon, Greg,' Damon said. 'Save a kid's life.'

'We can't stay here all night,' Greg said. 'It may be the arse-hole of nowhere, but someone's bound to come through soon.'

'It's the work of a minute,' Damon said. 'And think how virtuous you'll feel after.'

There was a warning in Greg's eyes, but Josh saw amusement

and affection, too. 'How're we supposed to get the message out?' Greg said. ''Cos I am *not* calling the cops.'

'Professor Fennimore,' Josh said. 'I got his number.'

'You ditched your phone in Essex,' Greg said.

'It's in here.' Josh tapped the side of his head, wished he hadn't.

'Yeah,' Greg said, and a look of regret crossed his face. 'You was always good with numbers.'

The killer's babbling had become background noise, but now Greg seemed to notice it again. 'Step aside,' he told Damon.

The youngest brother hesitated.

'Don't make me tell you twice.'

Damon moved, and Greg raised his pistol and fired. It sounded like a sneeze, but the effect on the abductor was devastating.

He howled. Clamping both hands to his shattered knee, he twitched on the ground, his functioning leg scraping at the tarmac, sending him in a small arc.

Josh held down a wave of nausea.

'Where's the kid?' Greg said.

'No-*oooooooh*,' the man howled. '*Fu*—uck you!'

Greg raised the pistol again and aimed.

The man screamed: '*Okayokay*. I tell you, just don't—'

Greg fired the second bullet into the flesh of the man's thigh.

'I haven't got time to piss about,' he said. 'Talk.'

The man gave them an address in Salford, just north of Manchester.

Greg nodded to Damon. 'Text it,' he said. 'Sign it from "Josh". Use a burner. Wipe it, ditch it.'

Josh gave him Fennimore's mobile number and Damon produced a cheap mobile phone from his jacket pocket.

'Done.' He switched off the phone, and removed the battery and sim card.

Greg looked at the man on the ground, whimpering and wheezing as he bled to death. 'Anything else you got to tell me?'

The man shook his head, tears mingling with the snot running down his face. 'I told you everything. Tell them I never touched her. I never did nothing to that g—'

Another sneeze of sound from Greg's pistol. Josh felt wet warmth on his face, a burst of blood spatter like hard rain on his jacket, and the man was silenced for good. A pool of blood fanned out on the tarmac beneath his head.

'Your turn,' Greg said.

In the scramble of thoughts that went through Josh's mind in that instant, he realized that he never did discover the abductor's name. In that moment of clarity, he knew it didn't matter. The man was nothing; a nobody who tried to be somebody by taking lives he had no right to. *Anyway*, Josh thought, *names don't mean a thing. It's how you carry the name that matters.* A name was just a label for people to remember you by.

42

Manchester, Thursday Evening

The Myers investigation team crammed into the Major Incident Room for a briefing at 7:05 p.m.

This time, at the chief constable's request, Kate Simms was invited. She relayed the message Fennimore had received.

'Do we know it's genuine?' someone asked.

DCI Ingrams looked to Simms.

'Josh Brown is missing and the number he used is not his usual mobile phone number,' she said. 'But Professor Fennimore confirms that Josh disabled his phone earlier today for . . .' she hesitated, not wanting to give away any more than she had to, '. . . unrelated reasons.'

'The message was sent from a burner phone,' DCI Ingrams said. 'This could be a trap set by the abductor – or just a crank, wanting their fifteen minutes of fame.'

'That being the case, it's unlikely they would use *Josh's* name,' Simms countered. 'Early afternoon, Josh was in

Aberdeen. He was seen by a member of staff at Robert Gordon University. She said a man had enquired after Josh earlier in the day – she identified that man as our suspect, Vic Tremain.'

Simms herself had spoken to Joan, the departmental office manager, and heard the woman's anxiety as she described the 'funny-looking fellow' who had come looking for Josh.

Kate glanced around the room. A good number of them seemed persuaded by her argument.

'What did the text say?'

A short, stocky police sergeant in full body armour asked the question. Like Simms, he wore a service pistol, holstered at his hip: the Tactical Firearms Unit had been deployed.

'That Josh had been attacked by the Myerses' abductor – and there *are* reasons why he would be a target,' she said, letting her gaze travel from one end of the room to the other. 'The attacker was described as male, masked, dressed in black.'

The sergeant gazed at her thoughtfully, as though listening to something far off, an echo maybe, or a distant conversation.

'It stated that Lauren could be found in a cotton mill near the Manchester, Bolton and Bury Canal, two miles from where Julie Myers's car was last seen,' she went on. 'It said that the abductor is now dead.'

This provoked a murmur of consternation: if the location was fake and Tremain really was dead, their chances of finding Lauren alive just dropped to zero.

'There is an old mill complex that fits the description and matches the location,' she said.

A few people started gathering up pens and pocketing notebooks. She saw one of the firearms officers adjust her body armour and touch the back strap of her Glock 17. If Ingrams remained sceptical, he was on his own – the rest of the team were collectively holding their breath, waiting for the order to act.

'Sergeant Unwin,' Ingrams said.

The short firearms officer walked to the front of the room and Simms stood to the side while he took them through the plan of action.

Five minutes later, the room emptied. Simms gathered her Kevlar vest and strapped it on while she waited for the exit to clear.

Sergeant Unwin hung back until Ingrams was out the door.

'Who sent the text?' he asked, keeping his voice low.

'I told you.'

'No. You didn't.' He looked into her face and his grey eyes held that same thoughtfulness; the sense that there was something he hadn't quite heard right. 'You said, "The attacker *was described*".'

Simms's heart beat slow and hard in her chest, and the straps of her vest seemed suddenly overcomplicated and difficult to manipulate. 'I don't know what you're getting at,' she said.

'You know who says things like that? A truthful person who doesn't want to tell a direct lie.'

She held his gaze. 'I believe the text is genuine.'

'But you don't believe Josh sent it.'

'We're wasting time,' she said. 'Let's go and find Lauren.' She made a move, but he placed a hand on her arm. Simms glanced down at it, then into his face. 'Take your hand off me, Sergeant,' she said quietly.

He waited a fraction of a second before complying. 'I won't send my crew in to a situation blind,' he said.

'Tremain is dead,' Simms said. 'There is no risk.'

'And you know this because . . .?'

He stood six inches shorter than Simms, but the sergeant carried an authority that she could not deny and she respected him for having voiced his suspicions in private.

She took a breath, still undecided if she should come clean – she hadn't even told Fennimore any of this. 'All right,' she said at last. 'If Josh had been able, he would have telephoned. He didn't. Someone else sent the text.'

'Tremain maybe?'

She gave a curt shake of her head. 'I considered it, but I don't think Tremain has either the conscience or the compassion.'

Unwin listened with his face turned up to hers, head slightly on one side, still striving for the truth behind her words. She lowered her eyes, finding his steady scrutiny unsettling.

'If not Tremain – who?' he said.

'I can't say—'

He began to object, but she spoke over him: 'It means trouble for Josh, but it has *no* bearing on the Myers case.'

One of the firearms unit poked his head around the door. 'Sarge? We're ready to roll.'

Simms was right behind him. They took the stairs down to the walled compound where a gunmetal grey Land Rover Defender stood on the tarmac. The officer who had come to find Sergeant Unwin clambered through the rear doors and Simms took a step towards the vehicle.

Unwin blocked her. 'No,' he said, gesturing for the officer to close the door. 'Sorry, ma'am – if you can't trust me, why should I trust you?'

'I'm an Authorized Firearms Officer,' Simms said. 'I've been practising for the past month on a police firing range with St Louis PD homicide detectives.'

His eyebrow twitched. 'Well, I can't argue with your credentials, but that still doesn't give me a reason to trust you.' He waited, but Simms remained silent. 'Find your own transport.' He turned on his heel, making for the passenger door.

Simms could pull rank, but she wouldn't. She shrugged and headed to a marked car.

43

Outskirts of Manchester, Thursday, 8 p.m.

The police convoy made an orderly approach to their target, passing recently built light-industrial units, on to 1970s concrete prefabs at the low-cost end of the market, heading fast down the commercial property scale past recycling businesses – black hills of used tyres, protected behind spiked aluminium fencing and crushed cars stacked as high as houses. This was the city's hinterland, good only for scrap metal dealers and fly-tippers.

They drove with no lights or sirens, along roads that got progressively narrower and increasingly potholed. They bumped over ragged cobblestones and pitted tarmac, finally turning left at a T-junction into what was unimaginatively named Mill Road. Per instructions, two marked units blocked the junction, while the rest drove on, pulling up outside the mill.

The building must have been imposing in its day, looming

288

large – literally and metaphorically – over the landscape and the lives of its hundreds of workers. Now it was little more than a shell. A fire had damaged a large part of the roof and burned rafters were visible in patches where slate tiles had fallen or been blown away. The windows accounted for more of the structure than the walls; scores of them, mullioned and high. The clouds that had hung low over the city for much of the day had finally burned off and the lowering sun glinted dully off the few remaining windows, but most were rotted or burned, their glass blackened or gone.

The firearms officers went in first, piling out of the Land Rover swiftly and quietly, four of them making straight for the front door of the building, two more pairs peeling off to stand guard over two possible exits. One officer carried an Enforcer – a battering ram of tubular steel capable of exerting three tonnes of force in a single swing. They stayed low, moving fast over the ruined terrain. Unwin relented, pointing at Simms and sending her with another officer to the furthest wing of the building which stood at a right angle to the rest. They crouched either side of a rotten doorway, about seventy yards down one long stretch of the outer wall.

She heard a dull boom: the Enforcer breaching the entrance door. Shouts of 'Armed Police!' and the thud of heavy boots followed as six armed officers stormed inside the building. Simms's partner carried an H&K G36 assault rifle with optical sight. He checked around the corner of the building while she scanned the weedy ground and scouted out the windows, alert to any movement.

The roar of traffic on the A6 was just audible to the west and, intermittently, the clatter of trains traversing the two rail lines they had crossed on their journey. It was punishingly hot under her layers of clothing; her Kevlar vest and helmet, both black, seemed intent on absorbing every photon of light, and Simms wiped sweat from her brow with the knuckle of one thumb.

'All right, ma'am?' her partner asked.

'Fine – but I'm developing a strong empathy with my favourite seafood,' she said.

'What's that?'

'Boiled lobster.'

He snorted, but didn't speak again.

The nervous excitement that had jittered in her chest on the drive over stilled as she waited. It didn't feel right. Tremain was no genius, but he had managed to stay below the police radar for nearly a decade – why would he choose somewhere so risky? The place was open to the elements. The fire must have burned fiercely, because the brickwork around many of the upper windows was soot-blackened. She imagined the internal floor covered in charred debris, yet there had been no mention of soot in the swabs taken at Julia Myers's post-mortem.

Sergeant Unwin re-emerged after ten minutes and gave the order to stand down. Simms joined him as he approached DCI Ingrams.

'The place is empty,' he said, perching his safety goggles above the rim of his helmet. 'Completely derelict, no locks, nothing.'

Simms's shoulders sagged.

'Is there a basement?' Ingrams angled his body towards the firearms team commander, cutting Simms out of the discussion.

'If there is, it's not accessible. We checked the entire floor area.'

'Do you want us to widen the search?' Unwin asked.

Ingrams shook his head. 'Waste of time, Sergeant,' he said, at last turning to look at Simms, cold, hard anger on his face. 'It was just bad intel.'

'Tremain was probably injured or under duress,' Simms said, refusing to respond to his hostility. 'It could be he just got some of the details wrong.'

'So, what – you want us to stick a pin in the map and try somewhere else?'

'I didn't say that,' she said.

'Do you know how much this operation cost?' Ingrams said. 'Do you have any inkling?'

'No doubt you have it down to the pounds and pennies,' she snapped back. 'Why don't you tell me the *cost* of a child's life, Ingrams?'

'Hey – this isn't your case,' he said. 'And it isn't your chance to make good on the mess you and Fennimore made five years ago.'

She moved forward. 'You bastard.'

Unwin stepped between them, facing her, his intense grey eyes full of warning. She stripped off her helmet and walked away.

The cool air on her neck was a welcome respite and she quickly got a grip on her temper, but she walked on, putting distance between herself and Ingrams.

Their local intel said that parts of the canal were in the process of being reclaimed by a group of local enthusiasts, yet this stretch remained untouched, weed-choked and even drained in places where the banks had been stripped of their retaining bricks. The ground beneath her feet became soggy and she stopped, clenching and unclenching her fists for a few moments. She took some deep breaths, her nostrils filling with the mingled smells of damp brick dust, mould and the pond-water reek of the canal a couple of hundred yards behind the mill.

Ahead the ground rose slightly, and here and there scrubby bushes grew out of the brick dust and clay. Ingrams was right – they should cut their losses and go home – there was nothing here but rubble and two hundred years of city grime.

She lowered her head, preparing for the ordeal of admitting to him that she had got it wrong. As her head cleared, she focused on a pattern of ridges and troughs in the wet clay. At first she didn't know what she was looking at, but her heart rate kicked up a notch a microsecond ahead of her thought processes. She dropped to a crouch and looked more closely. Tyre tracks.

Bikers, she rationalized, *mini-scooters – the scourge of inner cities.* But this place was so far removed from any housing development it seemed unlikely. She got lower and viewed the tread marks from an acute angle. Too wide for a pedal cycle or a scooter. She scanned right and found another faint impression, stood to get a feel for the distance between the two tracks. *Too for wide a quad bike. An SUV would be more like it – and hadn't they found SUV tyre tracks near Julia Myers's burned-out car?*

She stood to the side of them; they seemed to be heading up over the slight incline.

Walking a couple of feet to the left of the tracks, she followed them over the rise and then down into a dip, heading in the direction of the canal. The area was overgrown with bushes and whippy saplings, but the vehicle had flattened a pathway. She kept to the edge and, fifty yards on, entered a clearing of sorts.

It was a large concreted area, overlaid with moss and creeping grasses, and at its centre, a red-brick building, three storeys high – small in comparison with the mill they had searched, but still substantial. She remained at the edge of the clearing, taking in the steel shutters on the windows and skylights, a few slipped tiles on the roof. Most of the roof lead was gone, as were the guttering and downpipes. Ferns, buddleia and even a few small rowan trees grew out of cracks in the walls. But these were the only signs of life.

She carried on towards what must once have been a clock-tower, stepping over broken glass and spalled bricks, softened by damp and penetrating frosts. The clock-tower was blind, the faces long since taken down or looted for scrap. A wrought-iron canopy over the main entrance sagged, its glass in shards on the ground. She stepped back and found a date embossed in the brickwork: 1820. Faded painted lettering above the canopy read: 'CHAMPION COTTON'. The once grand front doors were covered in steel plates, secured by rusted bolts and padlocks.

The tyre tracks had vanished at the edge of the concrete, but as she walked around the perimeter, she noticed some flattened willowherb: a vehicle must have been parked parallel to the wall. A short distance on, she found a large sliding door. The rollers were ancient, but it looked like new grease had been applied top and bottom, and three brand-new hasps had been fitted, each with a bright brass padlock.

The rat came back. Lauren kicked the water bottle and it skittered away, but it came back again. She put her hand inside Mummy's bag to find something to throw. Her hand closed around a lipstick but it was too light and her hand felt floppy, so it just bounced and rolled, far away from the rat. She tried again, wanting something heavier to throw at the nasty old thing, and found Mummy's purse. That missed as well, but it did make a loud *thunk* on the water bottle, and the rat ran away, squealing. Lauren dipped her fingers inside the bottle and sucked the dampness from them.

Simms heard a faint sound, something being dropped maybe? She felt for her mobile phone and called Ingrams. 'I think I have something,' she said.

'For God's *sake*, Simms—'

'Listen,' she said. 'Three hundred yards north-west of your location, there's another mill. It's smaller, secured, locked and bolted from the outside – and I think I can hear someone inside the building.'

'All right,' he said, sounding resigned. 'Wait for back-up.'

'Just follow the line of the canal,' she said, closing the phone.

The rat was coming back.

Lauren's tears felt hot on her skin. *No. Go away.*

She felt inside the bag again, and her fingers closed around something small and round. She pulled her hand out and looked at the shiny prize, hardly able to believe her luck. A yellow one. She put it in her mouth and chewed greedily, while she ransacked Mummy's handbag for more. She found three and popped them in her mouth, even though they did taste a bit of Mummy's perfume. For half a minute, she felt her old strength. But when she tried to get up, she couldn't.

Even the special sweeties couldn't give her superpowers back to her. She slumped to the floor, sobbing.

Simms pressed an ear to the door and listened. *Is that a child crying?* Was she imagining it – conjuring up the sound because that was what she wanted to hear?

'Lauren,' she called softly. 'Lauren Myers? It's the police. Can you answer me, Lauren?'

Silence.

Mummy was calling her: 'Lauren Myers,' she said, like when she was in trouble and Mummy got cross. But Mummy was just in her head, and anyway her throat was too sore to speak out loud, so she answered inside her head. 'I didn't do anything, Mummy. I been good.'

Mummy called again: 'Lauren, are you there?'

'Yes. Yes – I'm here!' Lauren shouted back, but only in her head.

Simms felt a hand on her shoulder and wheeled to face her attacker, shoving his chest hard with her left hand, her right hand already on her Glock.

It was Unwin.

'Woah,' he said, raising both hands in a gesture of surrender.

Simms exhaled in a rush.

'You're strong for a skinny lass,' he said.

'And you're quiet for a chunky guy,' she said. 'You're lucky you didn't get your head blown off.'

She saw a gleam of amusement in his eyes and coughed a shaky laugh.

Tension defused, she turned to the door.

'There's someone in there,' she said.

'I've got two lads on the way over with bolt-cutters,' he said. 'We just need to hang tight a couple more minutes.'

From inside the building, a child's voice began singing: '*Hush, little baby, don't say a word. Poppa's gonna buy you a mock-in bird . . .*'

Simms shushed him. 'You hear that?'

'What?' he said.

'There's a *child* in there, Sergeant.' She pulled frantically at the door, but two burly cops appeared and eased her aside, their bolt-cutters slicing through the padlock hasps as if they were liquorice. Two more armed officers arrived and they paused, waiting for the go signal. Two of them gripped the sliding doors while Unwin counted them down. The metal screamed over the rollers like a beast in pain and Simms's heart seemed to grind with it like rocks over gravel. Finally, it yielded, flooding light into the dark interior.

Unwin's men went in, their scope lights penetrating the furthest recesses of the old mill, scattering rats right and left. Simms followed, weapon drawn. The place was empty. The men looked to Unwin for guidance, weapons lowered.

Simms continued scanning. She hadn't imagined that voice. She turned one-eighty and caught a slight movement to her left. She nodded to a humped blanket next to a rotting loom. Signalling the men to be quiet, she began singing softly, her voice trembling: 'If that mockingbird don't sing, Poppa's gonna buy you a diamond ring . . .'

A tousled head appeared from under the blanket. Lauren was filthy and flushed with fever, and she looked half-starved.

Simms holstered her weapon and moved in slowly. 'If that diamond ring is brass . . .'

'Poppa's gonna buy you a look-in glass . . .' The little girl tilted her head and she seemed to be staring at something over Simms's left shoulder. 'Are we going home now, Mummy?' she said.

Simms smiled down at her. 'Yes, sweetie,' she said, 'we're going home.'

44

Kate Simms rode in the ambulance with Lauren to the hospital. She stayed, keeping out of the medics' way, as they performed a gentle preliminary examination of the little girl. A nurse drew every blind and switched off the lights to protect Lauren's eyes from the sudden shock of daylight. When Simms had tried to leave, the girl became hysterical, screaming for her mummy.

Lauren's father arrived just as they were finishing up. By now Lauren was on a saline drip and they had cleaned her up a bit. He stepped into the room tentatively: the family liaison officer would have briefed him to remain calm and to gauge Lauren's reaction instead of rushing in. The doctor stepped back, with a smile.

'Look who's here, Lauren,' she said.

The child stretched out her arms. 'Daddy!'

Mr Myers rushed to his daughter's side, tears brimming,

but making an effort to control his emotions. 'Hey . . .' He crouched at the side of the bed. 'How's my brave girl?'

'I ate the sweeties to make the Yellow Peril scare off the Bad Man when he took Mummy away and I shouted Bad Things at him and climbed up high but he whispered horrible things and Mummy didn't come back, so I had to get down and I hurt my leg and couldn't get up again and the rats was stealing everything but then Mummy did come and she rescued me.'

Mr Myers choked back a sob, turning to the doctor for an explanation.

'She's slightly delirious – it's possible she picked up Weil's disease from drinking contaminated water,' she said. 'Does Lauren have any allergies to antibiotics?'

He shook his head and the doctor gave instructions to the nurse.

Simms sidled towards the door, and Lauren began to breathe fast and shallow. 'No, Mummy, don't go.' She held out her arms. 'Stay, Mummy, stay, Mummy, *pleeeeease.*'

Mr Myers turned, a look of horror, mingled with heart-wrenching hope on his face. Seeing Simms, his face contorted for a brief moment, the hope dislodged by pain. Simms could see the physical effort it took to hold himself together.

'You're the one who—?'

'Detective Chief Inspector Simms,' she said, holding out her hand, gripping his tightly and willing some of her strength into him. 'She's just confused, sir,' she added quietly. 'She'll be better soon.'

When Lauren was medicated and calm, Simms slipped outside to take a call from her contact at Police Scotland.

'Bad news,' he said.

A smiling DCI Ingrams was heading towards her, his hand outstretched. Simms raised a finger, asking for a moment, and the smile froze on his face.

'There's been a double shooting on a country road six miles north-west of Aberdeen,' the sergeant went on.

'Josh?' she said.

'Aye. We found him in a ditch a mile up the road from a crashed Toyota Corolla. There was a body in the boot of the car – answers the description of your carjack killer.'

45

If you have the bad luck to get murdered, try not to
survive as far as the hospital.

A TRADITIONAL SAYING OF
PATHOLOGISTS AND CSIS

Aberdeen Royal Infirmary, Thursday Night

Fennimore stared down at Josh's still form. When Simms
phoned to say they had found the girl safe, it felt like a rock
had been lifted off his chest. Now an entire mountain had
crashed down on him.

Detective Chief Inspector Gordon, the SIO in charge of
the case, stood by Fennimore's side in a treatment bay at the
hospital. Fennimore gazed at the carnage of blood-soaked
pads and other detritus scattered on the floor.

'Why is he still here?' he asked. He had taken the first
flight back and grabbed a taxi straight from the airport, but
even so, it had taken three hours in all to reach the hospital.

'They worked on him for an hour at the roadside before
they could risk moving him,' Gordon said.

Fennimore took in the tube, draining fluid from Josh's side,
a catheter delivering straw-coloured liquid into a bag below

the trolley, a line carrying blood into a vein on the back of his hand. He couldn't bear to watch the steady drip of blood in the IV delivery chamber, and switched his attention instead to the multi-coloured traces on the electronic monitor that confirmed – despite all appearances – that Josh had survived the shooting.

'What's the damage?' he asked.

'Two bullet wounds – one to the back of the head, one to the chest.'

'Professional hit,' Fennimore said.

Gordon tilted his head. 'Maybe not. They botched it. The first bullet nicked his heart and damaged his left lung, but just missed the aorta.'

'The head wound?' Fennimore said.

'The bullet's still in there, lodged behind the left brow-bone. There's a chance they can get to it, but they want to wait until he's more stable. Josh's heart stopped just as they wheeled him in here; they got it going again, but couldn't get his BP up – he was bleeding internally – it took them a while to find the source.'

A doctor stood a few feet distant, talking rapidly into a phone, and with some force, but too quietly for Fennimore to get the gist.

'They're trying to find an ICU bed,' the cop said.

Fennimore resisted the urge to wrest the phone from the doctor's hand and threaten physical harm on the bureaucrat at the other end of the line. 'You know Josh's family has a contract out on him?' he said.

The chief inspector glanced sharply at Fennimore. 'I'm surprised *you* do.'

'Lazko recognized him.'

'The journalist who was just murdered?'

Fennimore nodded. 'He handed me a file on Josh – and his family.'

'So Lazko exposed Josh?'

Fennimore chose not to answer that one.

'Did you catch the shooter?' he asked.

DCI Gordon seemed to be debating whether to answer, and Fennimore said, 'Come on, Chief Inspector – you know me.'

Gordon ran his tongue around his front teeth. 'Aye, all right,' he said at last. 'We sent out a nationwide alert for a BMW involved in an RTC near Josh's place,' he went on, coming at the answer crab-wise. 'Pretty soon we were getting calls about near-misses from the west of Aberdeen city.'

'The upshot?' Fennimore said, unable to curb his impatience.

'We arrested three men trying to board a plane at Aberdeen airport an hour ago,' the cop said. 'Josh's two brothers and a cousin. They'd dumped their car down a farm road on the east side of the river and hoofed it from there.'

'Tremain was found in the boot of a Toyota – so that was Josh's car?'

A slight dip of the head. 'It's registered to a low-level criminal in Leeds – he *claims* it was stolen.'

'Josh covering his tracks,' Fennimore said. 'It means the brothers dumped Tremain and moved Josh in their car . . .'

'Obviously.'

Fennimore scrutinized Josh's hands and wrists, thinking of that first night Lazko had come to him about the case, looming out of the fog like a half-pint troll. Josh, fast and ruthless in neutralizing the threat, as he saw it.

'What?' Gordon said.

'No sign of ligature marks on his wrists,' Fennimore said. 'And his hands . . . Look at them – they're clean, no bruising, no scrapes. I can't believe he didn't put up a fight.'

'Hard to argue with a gun,' Gordon countered. 'And he'd already taken a blow to the head – probably in the crash.' He frowned. 'That said . . . the younger brother *has* got a cut to the bridge of his nose and both eyes are blackened . . .'

Good, Fennimore thought. 'The gun?'

'They must have tossed it – but the two brothers *did* test positive for gunshot residue. They're claiming they lost Josh after the collision with the Mini Cooper near his apartment; they were just heading for home when the police stopped them. It's bollocks of course – Josh was found barely a mile and a half from where they dumped the Beamer. And the BMW is badly damaged – we're confident that paint transfer will confirm it was the vehicle that collided with both the Mini *and* the Toyota.'

'You need to examine the BMW very carefully.'

The cop gave him a solid look. '*Really?*' he said.

Fennimore passed a hand over his eyes. 'Yeah,' he said. 'I'm sorry – you know that. It's just—'

'You two are close.'

Surprised to find that it was true, Fennimore nodded, unable to speak.

'We've got Tremain's blood type spattered on Josh's clothing – we're waiting on DNA analysis to confirm it's his,' the cop said. 'There was mud on Josh's shoes and soil particles in the weave of his jacket, as though he had fallen during a struggle. We'll gather every shred of evidence we can to link the brothers to both scenes.'

Josh's doctor hung up the phone. 'We've got the okay,'

he said. 'You gentlemen need to step back.' The staff swiftly moved the trolley out of the treatment bay.

Fennimore watched as it passed. 'His hands do look *remarkably* clean,' he said, cold scientific clarity elbowing his emotions to the sidelines.

DCI Gordon looked shocked – even offended.

'It could be significant,' Fennimore insisted, keeping pace with the trolley. 'Did you clean him up?' he said, addressing the doctor.

The medic refused to acknowledge the question.

'*Doctor*,' Gordon said.

The medic glared at Fennimore across the trolley. 'No, we didn't. It's taken us all this time to get him stable.'

One of the nurses had hurried on ahead to call the bed-lift, and the doors opened as they arrived. They wheeled the trolley inside and Fennimore squeezed in with them. One of the nurses exclaimed in alarm and the doctor pressed the button to hold the doors.

'Sir, you shouldn't be in here,' he said.

Fennimore lifted one of Josh's hands. It was *really* clean – even though his nails were black with – something. *Grime?* He sniffed the hand and the doctor reached across, seizing his wrist.

'Let go of him.'

Fennimore complied.

'Now get out.'

Fennimore didn't budge and the doctor spread his hands, appealing to the chief inspector.

'The evidence puts Josh's brothers at the scene – but it doesn't make them guilty,' Fennimore said, talking fast. 'They could argue they were trying to rescue Josh – hence the scrapes

305

on the car. They lost the Toyota for a bit on the country lanes. Found Josh shot at the roadside, hunted Tremain down, shot him. They're heroes. The media will love them – they avenged their brother and wiped a murdering child-abductor off the face of the earth in one stroke.'

Gordon stepped inside the lift alongside Fennimore.

'Your patient should have a police escort,' he told the doctor. 'For your own safety, as well as his.'

The medic gave a grunt of disgust and pressed the button to take them up to the ICU.

'What are you thinking?' Gordon asked Fennimore.

'Tea tree oil,' Fennimore said, recalling the last time he had seen Josh practising lab techniques in the old university building in St Andrew Street, cleaning down the lab bench with wipes before taping his own jacket to practise taking fibre-lifts.

'Hand-wipes,' he said, remembering that fresh, slightly astringent smell. 'Josh's hands have been wiped clean.' He leaned closer and sniffed the skin of Josh's forehead. 'His face, too.'

'A mark of respect?' the DCI suggested. 'Or regret?'

Fennimore leaned against the metal side of the lift as he considered. 'Forensic awareness,' he said, feeling a powerful hatred for Josh's brothers.

The lift doors opened and the trolley was manoeuvred on to the polished vinyl flooring of the ICU foyer.

Then they were moving fast towards the double doors of the unit. Fennimore continued by the side of the trolley, but at the doors the doctor held up his hand and spoke directly to the chief inspector. 'This is a sterile area,' he said. 'You both need to wait outside.'

'Okay,' Fennimore said. 'But don't clean his hands.'

The doctor threw him a hostile look.

'Bag them or glove them – I don't care which – but you need to preserve the evidence,' Fennimore said, holding his gaze.

'He's a *patient*, not a damned crime scene,' the doctor said, his voice roughened by anger.

'That's *exactly* what he is,' Fennimore flared back. He turned to face the chief inspector. 'I think Josh made sure of that. He would do everything in his power to provide forensic evidence against the men who did this to him.'

Gordon nodded. 'He's right. I'll do all I can to accommodate your health and safety protocols, Doctor, but I need you to protect Josh's hands. I'll send someone here to collect samples.'

The medic remained by the door while the rest of the staff moved the trolley into a newly cleared bay.

'All right,' he said. 'But I want *him* out of here.' He nodded towards Fennimore.

Fennimore held up his hands, backing away. The door swung to and Gordon let out a whoosh of breath. 'Professor, you've got to ease up,' he said.

'I'll ease up when his brothers are behind bars,' Fennimore said. 'You need to have CSIs vacuum out and tape-lift every inch of the car.'

'I know my job,' Gordon said, but his tone was forgiving, compassionate.

'You'll need soil experts – talk to the Hutton Institute – they can type a sample to a patch two metres square.'

'Professor—'

'A palynologist, too. I'll pay for the tests myself if there's any quibble over the budget.'

'Professor *Fennimore*!'

'What?'

'You have to let us get on with this, now.'

'You can't let them get away with it. You don't know what Josh—' Fennimore's throat closed and he swallowed hard. 'What he had to do to . . .'

'I've spoken to Josh's Witness Protection handler,' Gordon said. 'I've been briefed – I know what he sacrificed.'

Fennimore began to speak, but Gordon talked over him.

'The night Josh witnessed the murder of Hafiz, his mother had sent him to the warehouse where his brothers Liam and Steve were torturing the poor bastard,' Gordon said. 'They'd been working on Hafiz for five hours. Liam Collins tried to make Josh finish the job; it was to be his initiation. But he refused.'

Fennimore stared at Gordon, shocked. These details were not in the press reports Lazko had given him.

'Josh was in disgrace with the family, but he kept quiet; family's family, after all,' Gordon went on. 'Then Ahmed Azan's murder trial started. Azan's wife saw Josh in court – asked him if the brothers could do anything to help – she trusted the family implicitly. Before he even took it to the police, Josh recorded his brothers talking about the details of torture and the shooting. Barely eighteen years old and he gathered the evidence we needed to convict them. He gave up everything – family, wealth, status – for a life as a hunted man, *because it was the right thing to do*.' He paused. 'I know you care about Josh,' he said. 'So do I.'

Fennimore looked into Gordon's face and saw that he was in earnest.

'I won't let him down,' the chief inspector said. 'And I won't allow the system to either.'

Fennimore nodded, feeling a little punch-drunk. 'I believe you,' he said.

He turned on his heel and went to the fire escape stairs. Halfway down the fire door boomed shut behind him. For some reason this started a shaking he couldn't control. His legs gave way under him and he collapsed on the floor. Leaning backwards, he spread his arms wide against the wall's brickwork for support; it felt like the ground could drop away at any moment and send him plummeting downward.

46

Manchester, Thursday Night

The house was quiet when Kate Simms got home. She hung her jacket on the stair newel and peeped in through the sitting room door. It was empty. From upstairs she heard her mother's voice, soft and rhythmic. Was she talking on the phone? She kicked off her shoes and headed up, following the sound to Timmy's bedroom. He was sitting up in bed, Nanna beside him, reading from a *Despicable Me* book.

'Had a nightmare,' her mother said.

'Oh, sweetie, it was just a nasty old dream . . .' Simms said, and he gazed at her, his face anxious.

She perched on the other side of the bed and put her arm around his shoulder. Timmy turned to look up at her and a moment later, he clambered into her lap for a rare cuddle; he didn't even flinch when she kissed the top of his head.

Simms's mother slid her a sly look. 'See what you've been missing?'

Simms laughed, too tired to argue.

'How is Lauren?' her mother asked.

'She's . . .' Simms ruffled her son's hair and smiled. 'She'll be okay – her dad's with her now.'

'Who's Lauren?' Timmy said, turning to a page in the book in which a bald man with an improbably pointed nose was addressing an assortment of small pill-shaped creatures, some with two eyes and some, like mini-Cyclopses, with only one.

'What are those jelly-bean creatures?' she asked, as a distraction.

'They're not jelly beans, they're Minions,' he said. 'Who's Lauren?'

'A little girl,' Simms said. 'Why are the Minions wearing goggles?'

He turned to look at her, his eyes large and solemn. 'No one knows.' Then: 'Is the little girl sick?'

'Yes, but she's going to get better.'

'Why wasn't her daddy with her before?' Timmy asked. 'Is that why she got sick? Did he go far away?'

Simms winced.

Her mother murmured, 'Out of the mouths of babes . . .'

'Lauren got lost,' she said, refusing to meet her mother's eye.

'And Mummy found her,' her mother said.

'*My* mummy?' Timmy asked, twisting to look up at Simms again, astonishment on his face.

'Your mummy was very clever, and she found Lauren and brought her home to her daddy.'

Simms glanced at her mother, surprised.

'Well,' her mother said, 'it's true.'

Timmy was still staring at her, a frown on his face. 'Where is Lauren's *mummy*?' he asked.

For a second, Simms's heart stopped. 'In heaven,' she said.

'With God, and Baby Jesus, and all the angels?'

'Yes.'

This seemed to satisfy him and he turned his attention to the book.

She and her mother exchanged a look of relief, then her mother slipped away, and for a few minutes Simms read from the story, while Timmy drowsed.

Kieran popped his head around the door. 'He okay?' he said.

'Come and join us,' Kate said, patting the bed.

'Wish I could.'

He opened the door wider and she saw that he was duded up for a party. 'Staff end-of-term bash,' he said.

'Didn't you call in sick earlier?'

'Migraine,' he said, with a grin. 'All better now. I'd have asked you to come but you were so busy with . . .' He glanced at Timmy, implying that he didn't want to say more.

Simms felt herself withdraw slightly.

'You okay?' he asked.

'I'm fine,' she said, making an effort to smile. It really wasn't Kieran's fault. 'It's been a hard day.'

'Yeah. Congratulations, by the way.' It sounded forced, over-formal, and he jingled the keys in his hand. 'Well, you relax,' he said. 'You've earned a rest.'

A moment later he was gone, and as she read on, Becky's words – *He's never home* – chimed over and over in Simms's head.

Later, with Timmy safely asleep, she decided on an early night, but she couldn't sleep. An hour after that, still wide awake and feeling sad and dissatisfied, she picked up her laptop, tiptoed past her mother's room and headed downstairs.

Fennimore was online. She hit the Skype call icon and he answered in seconds.

'Hey.' He looked genuinely pleased to see her.

'You look terrible,' she said.

He raised one shoulder and let it drop.

'How is Josh?'

'No change.' After an uncomfortable silence, he asked about Lauren.

'She's dehydrated, undernourished and has a leptospirosis infection – rats contaminated the supplies Tremain left. She hurt her ankle in a fall and she's traumatized, but the doctors think she'll make a full recovery.'

'Was she—'

'He didn't touch her,' Simms said quickly. 'She seems to think he was afraid of her.'

'And the body in the car *was* Tremain?'

'It's him all right – he's been identified by his brother.'

'Well, let's hope there's a special kind of hell where people like him are tormented by baby-faced demons.'

She raised an eyebrow. 'You don't believe in hell.'

'I don't believe in *God*,' he said, 'but there are a thousand kinds of hell.'

Simms didn't doubt that her friend had lived in one of them ever since Rachel and Suzie vanished. Being honest with herself, she realized that she had lived part of it with him. Even when he disappeared from her life, the pain and guilt didn't go away, and since they had started working together again, she had read it in the lines on his face and the sorrow and regret in his eyes.

313

'Have you managed to sort out your apartment?' she said, to change the subject.

'The locksmith's been in and the alarm's repaired,' he said. 'As for the rest . . .' He slid out of the way, allowing his laptop camera to present a panorama of the room. 'As you see, it's a work in progress.'

She saw kitchen cupboards emptied out; papers, some stacked, some littered on the floor; a flash of a laptop screen showing some kind of street scene; then Fennimore was front and centre again.

'How're you doing?' he asked.

'Okay.' *He's never home* – the words that had clanged in her head for the past two hours – seemed quieter, less strident, when she was talking to Fennimore. She said, 'I'm okay' again, to test how she felt, and realized that she meant it.

'You did a wonderful thing today,' he said.

'Yeah,' she said, smiling. 'It was pretty amazing.'

'Keep telling yourself that, no matter what,' he said, and she felt the intensity of his stare despite the barriers of distance and low-resolution imaging.

What had he seen in her face? It was rare for Fennimore to have any kind of empathic insight and when he did it was unsettling.

'Well,' she said, suddenly anxious to finish the call, 'I'm going to try and get some sleep. Let me know if Josh's condition improves or—' She stopped; no need to add the other way things might go – they both knew that Josh's prognosis wasn't good. 'Call me if you need me,' she added firmly.

47

Every contact leaves a trace.

LOCARD'S EXCHANGE PRINCIPLE

Aberdeen Royal Infirmary, Friday Morning

'Do you not sleep at all?'

Fennimore looked up from an academic paper he was reading; DCI Gordon was standing over him. It was 9 a.m., and he had been at Josh Brown's bedside in the ICU for two hours.

'I was going crazy at home,' Fennimore admitted.

'How did you even get in?'

'The constable on duty recognized me from yesterday. I told the nursing staff I was family.'

Gordon rolled his eyes. 'Seems I'll have to brief them about the wisdom of allowing Josh's family in here,' he said. He drew up a chair. 'How's he doing?'

'Stable, but still critical,' Fennimore said. He had watched Josh's fluctuating BP and heart rate on the monitor until he found his own pulse began to follow the wild stutters and spurts of speed; now he rationed himself to checking at five-minute intervals. 'I notice he's been processed.' He glanced down at the student's hands; each nail had been clipped and scraped clean.

'Analysis is ongoing,' Gordon said. 'But we've matched fibres from under his fingernails to seat fabrics and carpeting in the BMW his brothers were driving. It's a hire car, but we got enough transfer from *their* clothing to put them inside the vehicle.'

Fennimore exhaled slowly. 'D'you hear that, Josh?' he said. 'You did it.' Josh's heart rate spiked. Fennimore remembered the clean, astringent smell on the student's hands in the accident and emergency department the previous day. 'What about the tea tree oil?' he asked, and saw the ghost of a smile on Gordon's face.

'That's part of the ongoing analysis, but the CSIs found wipes in Josh's pocket that will make it so much easier to compare it with trace they found in the BMW – they've already matched fibres from them to trace they found in the car. They also identified a paint fleck from the damaged bodywork of the BMW on Josh's jacket.'

'You *were* listening in the lectures, then,' Fennimore said, tapping Josh's foot.

Another responding stutter – three quick beats in succession and a corresponding increase in Josh's BP.

'That isn't all,' Gordon said. 'There's blood aerosol on Josh's jacket and T-shirt.'

'His younger brother's nosebleed,' Fennimore said, his own heart rate picking up pace.

'We're waiting on the DNA results, but my guess is, yes.'

Fennimore looked at the young student with fierce pride.

The voices seemed far away – somewhere he could not easily reach – but Josh did recognize Fennimore's, and that alone reassured him he was safe.

While Damon and Mikey had bundled the dead man

into the boot of Josh's car, Greg had instructed Josh to wipe 'evidence' off his hands and face. Of course, he'd complied – he didn't have much choice. Big brother Greg had grinned when he found the hand-wipes in his pocket. 'You always were a clean freak, bruv,' he said.

Then they heard a car approach. It crested one of the hills a mile down the road and the next second Josh was in the back of the Beamer, face down on the floor.

This is it, then, he thought. He felt more bitter than afraid. The fear he'd lived with day after day since he went into hiding had dulled his emotions, he supposed. But he did feel regret, and sadness. He'd always hoped that Damon would be spared this life.

Well, fuck 'em. Fuck the lot of 'em. He got busy, creating transfer, collecting evidence under his fingernails, on his jacket – he even snorted some of the fibres in case Greg made him wipe down again. They cruised for about twenty minutes, but he felt sure they had doubled back at one point.

When they dragged him out of the car, the landscape was subtly different and they were on a gravel road – an entrance to a farm maybe. Mikey hauled him to his feet while Greg held the gun on him. As he'd anticipated, Greg got him to wipe down again. Damon collected the wipes and pocketed them.

'We'll dump those a few miles up the road. The jacket an' all.'

'I just bought it,' Damon complained.

'I'll get you a new one.' Greg looked at Josh and smiled. 'I'm not stupid, bruv.'

Josh feigned disappointment. *Nah, just ignorant.*

Greg flipped the gun so the grip faced Damon. ''S all yours, son.'

317

The sixteen-year-old stared at the gun, his arms tight by his sides. 'Nah, you're all right, mate.'

'Take it,' Greg said.

Damon's eyes widened. 'No. I . . . I can't.'

'You asked to be here – now take it.' Josh heard the familiar warning in his brother's voice.

'Greg,' Josh said. 'You can't do this to him. Don't make him a killer.'

'We already had one brother turn Queen's evidence on the family,' Greg said. 'Not gonna happen twice.'

Damon stared at the gun as if it were alive. Greg's free hand snaked out, striking him, fast and hard, on the side of the head. Damon staggered and cried out, putting one hand to his face.

'Take it.'

'No, I don't want to, Greg – please.'

'You don't have to do this, Damon,' Josh said.

'I *do*,' Damon sobbed. 'You know I do.' He was a mess, crying, snot hanging in strings from his nose.

Josh took his younger brother by the shoulders, hugged him close.

'Whatever happens,' he whispered, 'remember, I love you.'

He grasped Damon by the hair and his brother began to struggle. Josh pulled away, launched a vicious headbutt and felt the cartilage of his brother's nose crunch.

Mikey stepped in, dealing a stinging blow to Josh's ear; he stumbled, grabbing hold of Damon as he went, dragging his brother down with him. Damon prised his fingers apart, blood bubbling from his nose – creating an aerosol so fine the brothers wouldn't see it on Josh's dark jacket. Josh held on for as long as he could, then let go without warning and Damon fell backwards.

A second later, the younger brother was on his feet, screaming. 'Bastard – you broke my nose, you—' He lunged, but Mikey caught him by the waist.

'Calm down, tiger.'

Damon swung wildly with his elbows and Mikey left off, laughing.

'Gimme it,' Damon screamed. He snatched the gun from Greg.

Josh raised an arm. In the distance the drone of farm machinery. Then a light flashed and—

48

In the field of observation, chance favours the prepared mind.

LOUIS PASTEUR

Fennimore's Apartment, Aberdeen, Friday, Mid-morning

Fennimore was watching the CCTV from Paris on his laptop and an e-tablet. One was live-streaming while the other replayed recorded footage of the street and the bridge from which the photograph had been taken. His flat was almost back to austere normality after the break-in, and he put together a sandwich in his kitchen, keeping one eye on the monitors.

The doorbell rang and, licking butter from his thumb, he went to his front door and checked the intercom screen. It was APC, courier delivery. A box; about thirty-five centimetres tall, fifteen deep. He signed for it and started back upstairs. He sat looking at it for a few minutes, then found a box of vinyls and gloved up. If this was Tremain's parting shot from beyond the grave, he didn't want to mess up any evidence. He opened the outer packaging with a scalpel, slicing across the top and then down one edge of the box before peeling back the brown paper. The wooden box inside was labelled Veuve Clicquot; Fennimore was no wine buff, but he recognized expensive champagne when he saw it. A discreet gift card attached was signed by his US editor. It read, 'Congrats – *Crapshoots* just made it into the *NY Times* top ten science books. You kicked Malcolm Gladwell's ass.'

He minimized the live-stream and looked up the *New York Times*. *Crapshoots* was there all right. Which was puzzling, considering the doomy call he'd had from his financial adviser just before he left for Essex. He'd scribbled the guy's name and number down as he headed out to the airport. He rummaged in the pockets of his jacket and sifted through receipts until finally he found the scrap of paper and smoothed it out on the kitchen counter. John Vincent. He began tapping the phone number into his mobile, but something on the second computer monitor caught his eye: the bridge over the Seine was filled with high-end cars, parked nose-to-tail.

He accessed the time stamp: the footage was taken at 3:15 p.m., two days earlier. Groups of men in uniform stood about, smoking, chatting. Chauffeurs. Fennimore stared at the frame. The photo of the man with the girl in the orange sundress had been taken from that bridge. Looking at the neat line of gleaming cars, he had the feeling this was a regular occurrence – he wondered if they dropped off their VIP clients at a nearby venue. A quick check online revealed that the Paris Chamber of Commerce met once a month, not far from the bridge; a fashion house gave occasional shows a short step away; two private art galleries were situated half a block down the road from the line of cars. He called up the image of the girl and the man, both well dressed – expensively dressed; the type who would not seem out of place stepping from a chauffeur-driven limo. He flicked back to the CCTV recording, watching the drivers disappear from one spot and appear further along the row, as the camera jumped between burst-shots. In one three-frame burst he saw the men stub out their cigarettes and straighten their uniforms: their clients were returning. A procession of chic, sleek Parisians slid gracefully into the waiting cars. He thought he recognized a British actress among them. As she approached the line, one of the chauffeurs took a mobile phone from his pocket and, folding his arms to partly obscure the device, he aimed it at the woman. Is that how the photo Fennimore had received was taken? Was it possible that this anonymous emailer was one of these chauffeurs?

49

Simms was in a debrief meeting with the carjack killer investigative team. She was still officially on leave, but didn't want to miss the opportunity. In generous mood, the DCI in charge invited her to the front of the room and even gave her credit for having discovered Lauren.

CSIs had previously found a minute trace of blood inside the car of Kim Restel, the Manchester marketing rep who got away: four tiny droplets, smaller than a pinhead, but they'd had nothing on the DNA database to match it to. Now, they had, and they were a match to Tremain. He was now linked to the earlier murders, as well as the murders of Carl Lazko and Julia Myers. They were still waiting on trace evidence from Fennimore's Tom Killbride appeal, but they were confident that would close the Gail Hammond murder investigation.

'Six murders, one attempted abduction – and Lauren

323

Myers returned to her family,' the DCI said. 'Brilliant work, everyone.'

A cheer went up, along with the sound of fifty-plus pairs of hands drumming on tables.

Simms grinned with the rest of them, elated and relieved, ready to punch the air with the sheer joy of it. Her phone buzzed in her pocket; she checked the screen – it was DS Donal McLeish, her contact at Police Scotland. She excused herself and stepped out into the corridor.

'Donal, how are y—'

'Kate, I don't know how to tell you this,' he cut in.

The smile faded from her face. 'Josh?' she said.

'The surgeons tried to remove the bullet from his brain. He died on the operating table forty minutes ago.'

She couldn't answer at first. 'Fennimore – does he know?' she choked out.

'DCI Gordon is calling him as we speak.'

'Thanks – f-for letting me know,' she stammered. She ended the call and stared numbly at the screen.

Her phone buzzed in her hand; it was Fennimore.

'Kate,' he said, 'I'm looking at a line of high-end cars with their chauffeurs, parked on a bridge in Paris – *the* bridge,' he said. 'I think the man who took the photo of Suzie with the older man was one of these drivers.'

He doesn't know. For a moment, she felt sorry for him, but then she thought, *And here he is, calling me, asking for another favour.*

She was suddenly blindingly angry – with him, with Josh, with herself. *And how the hell did he have pictures of a bridge in Paris?*

'How did you come by this information?' she asked stonily.

324

'Does it matter?'

'Are you employing a private detective – is that it?' Her voice was controlled, but even she could hear the tightness in it.

He hesitated.

Do not lie to me, Fennimore.

'No,' he said.

'So you've been using covert surveillance?'

She heard him take a breath, hold it for a second. 'Yes,' he said on the out-breath.

'Are you in*sane*?' she said.

'Kate, listen—'

'Nick,' she said, 'you set up covert surveillance in a foreign country – that's not only illegal, it's stupid.'

'Hear me out,' he said. 'I did some web trawling, sent a few enquiries to limo companies in Paris – but they won't talk to me. I've emailed the details to you – can you get CEOP's International Child Protection Network to take a look at him?'

'You're not listening, Nick.'

'I hear you,' he said. 'I broke international law – and I'll face the consequences. But if you could just—'

'What about the consequences to everyone around you?'

'What do you mean?'

'You'll do anything, use any means – any*one* – to get what you want.'

'Wouldn't *you*?' he said. 'If it was Becky – or Timmy – wouldn't *you* use any means necessary to get them back?'

For a second, she didn't have the breath to speak. When she found her voice she said, 'I'd like to think I wouldn't screw up a friend's life just to set mine straight.'

'Kate—'

He sounded apologetic, but Simms was way past conciliation.

'You spend half your professional life trying to show the police up as incompetent or vindictive, because it explains why they haven't caught Rachel's killer – why Suzie is still missing. That way you don't have to blame yourself.'

'Kate!'

'*You* screwed up, Nick. You – and me. No one else. We should have been at home that weekend. But we lied to our partners, and we interfered in a police inquiry we had no business meddling in. You've always blamed Lazko for diverting police attention from the investigation – have you ever thought how *our* actions affected it – how we might have held up the search for Rachel and Suzie?' Her voice was hoarse, but she spoke through the emotion that threatened to choke her.

'Has something happened?' he asked. 'Are you all right?'

'You *never* face the consequences, other people do – it was me, when Rachel and Suzie were abducted. I guess now it's Josh's turn.'

'What are you saying?' His voice sounded weak.

'He's dead, Nick,' she said. 'Josh is dead.'

50

Simms went home shortly after her debrief meeting broke up; like everyone else on the team, she had a report to write. She sat in her back garden with a mug of coffee, her laptop open on the patio table. Kieran's school holidays had officially started and he was playing kick-about with a half-size football on the lawn with Timmy. She listened to her son's squeals of delight, but couldn't stop brooding. Her thoughts went to Becky and that terrible case last winter — the breathless chase through the icy wastelands of Manchester, the suffocating terror that she might never see her daughter again. What if she had lost Becky as Fennimore had lost Suzie? What extremes would she go to in order to keep her safe? Every time she tried to put herself in Fennimore's position, her brain shut down — it simply wouldn't let her think in those terms. But watching her husband and son play in the sunshine, hearing Timmy's laughter, Suzie's absence still nagged at her. It was a dull ache that refused to go away.

She sighed, impatient with herself and resentful of Fennimore's question. Hadn't she already jeopardized her career, gone way over the line to help him find Suzie? And what about Josh? He had taken Josh's chance of a new life and squandered it – there was no excusing that.

She shook her head. *Enough.* Returning her attention to her report, she typed a few lines, but an image intruded: Mr Myers in the hospital, crouching beside his little girl, tears of joy and relief in his eyes. How many times had Fennimore fantasized a similar rescue for Suzie?

She groaned. *You need to write up this report, Kate,* she told herself, but two minutes later her thoughts had circled round to Suzie again. She gave up and called Becky.

'Mum, is everything okay?'

'Hey, that's my line,' Simms said.

Becky laughed, and the knot of tension just below her heart eased a little.

'*C'est Maman*,' she said, as an aside.

'Sorry, Becks,' Simms said, 'is this a bad moment?'

'*Pas du tout*,' Becky said. 'We're on our way to the Champs-Élysées, to take the tour of L'Arc de Triomphe. You can go right to the top and take pictures.' Her French pronunciation seemed authentic and unselfconscious, and Simms experienced a tingle of pride.

'So you're having fun?'

'I'm *loving* it. Is Timmy there? Can I say hi?'

Simms called Timmy and handed him the phone. 'Your sister wants to say hello.'

She handed him the phone and he said, 'Hello', answered, 'Fine' to two questions, then nodded mutely.

'You have to speak, Timmy,' Simms said. 'She can't see you.'

'Yes,' he said. '*I'm* playing football with Daddy.'

A pause, then he said, 'A beeyan-toe,' and handed the phone back to her. 'Becky says that means "see you soon" in French. Is she telling fibs, Mummy?'

'I don't think so, sweetie.' She asked Becky and was rewarded with another laugh.

'Oh, we're here!' Becky exclaimed. 'Love you, Mum, give Dad my love. Tell him I miss him.'

'He misses you, Becky. We all do.'

Then Becky was gone and tears came unbidden to Simms's eyes.

'You okay?' Kieran asked.

'Fine.' She smiled, blinking away the tears. 'Just this case, you know.'

'I know,' he said. 'It's been a tough one.' He swung her laptop around to take a cheeky peek at the screen and she slapped his hand.

He grinned. 'You don't seem to be getting very far with your report.'

She closed the laptop, disgusted with herself. 'I can't concentrate.'

'Oops,' he said. 'Sorry about that.'

'No, I didn't mean—'

'I know,' he said again. 'Look, why don't I take Timmy to the adventure playground – give you an hour or two to finish it?'

She hesitated. 'Are you sure you don't mind?'

'I want to go on the climbing frame!' Timmy yelled,

already tugging at his daddy's hand, and Kieran gave her a droll look.

'The decision is made,' he said, allowing Timmy to drag him inside the house.

She completed the report and emailed it in forty-five minutes. After that she washed up, changed the bed-sheets and put a wash on, but she could not shake the idea that she should be doing something – *anything* – to help Fennimore.

What if he was right and Suzie *was* somewhere in Paris? She might even be a few miles from where Becky stood now. Those two had been inseparable as ten- and eleven-year-olds, and now, listening to Becky, seeing how much she had grown and matured as a person, how much she had to look forward to in life, it seemed even more cruel that Suzie might never have those same opportunities.

Could she deny Fennimore a chance – however slight – to give Suzie her life back?

She found herself scrolling through her mental Rolodex of contacts; she wouldn't risk her job for him, not again. She'd had to resign from London Metropolitan Police and move her family two hundred miles north to escape the tedium of committee work and community initiatives she had been consigned to last time. Four years of inter-agency 'partnerships', and focus groups, political wrangling and target-setting. She would have quit after the first six months if it weren't for a few inspirational people she met along the way. She had to admit that during that time she had made some great contacts both in the job and in other agencies.

Her run-through of names and agencies snagged at Interpol. Its central function was to facilitate communication between law enforcement agencies around the world; surely it would be the best channel of communication in this instance? Simms knew that each of its 190 member countries had its own national bureau – she herself had worked closely with an Interpol officer in London on the disappearance of a prostitute that had later exposed an international trafficking ring. Yes, she thought, he was the man to call, and she sighed, resigning herself to the notion that she and Fennimore weren't finished yet.

51

You know my method. It is founded on the observation of trifles.

A. C. DOYLE, 'THE BOSCOMBE VALLEY MYSTERY'

Paris, Friday Afternoon

Fennimore sat drinking coffee outside a café on the bank of the River Seine. It was just over four hours since he'd learned of Josh's death, and in that time he had made a frantic call to DCI Gordon and had turned up at the hospital mortuary. Josh was on the table; Fennimore opened the door to the post-mortem room, but a detective blocked his way. Fennimore could see the pathologist, gloved and gowned, ready to make a start. DCI Gordon himself was witnessing the PM. He took Fennimore by the elbow and helped the detective to edge him out of the door.

'You shouldn't be here,' Gordon said. He looked exhausted.

'I saw him a few hours ago,' Fennimore said. 'He was stable – he was doing okay.' He heard himself apply the he-can't-be-dead,-he-wasn't-dead-when-I-last-saw-him logic of the grieving, but couldn't stop. 'What the hell happened?'

'He was shot in the *head*, Nick.' Gordon's voice was hoarse with emotion. 'It doesn't take a brain surgeon to work out his chances of survival.'

Fennimore looked past him, through the window to Josh, breathing tube still in place, per protocol for deaths in hospital care; the chest drain in place, covered with a dressing stained with blood and plasma seepage.

'Go home, Nick,' Gordon said. 'There's nothing more you can do.'

Fennimore couldn't help thinking that he had done too much – that if he had done less, Josh would still be alive.

He couldn't stay in Aberdeen. Couldn't even sit still – so he had made hurried arrangements to return to Paris. In the years since Rachel's death and Suzie's disappearance, Fennimore had become adept at compartmentalizing: he could shut off the part of his brain where worries and guilt and self-recrimination lurked, as long as he kept busy. But now he was here, he didn't have enough busy-work to keep his mind from Kate, and Josh, and the part he'd played in Josh's death.

His mobile rang on the table and his hand jerked, spilling coffee on to the screen. It was Kate. He hastily wiped the phone and thumbed the slider to accept the call.

'Where are you?' she said. 'Are you in Paris again?'

'What makes you think I'm—?' Fennimore said.

'The ring-tone.'

'Ah.' Hearing her voice, he swerved from regret to shame, and back again to sadness.

'The Préfecture of Police in Paris monitors alien residents,' she said, sounding all business.

He knew he should try to soothe her hurt feelings, but the notion that she might have something he could use to find

Suzie overrode his worthier sentiments, so he kept his mouth shut, gripped the phone tight and willed her to go on.

'A month ago they investigated the disappearance of a British national – a chauffeur by the name of Pete Slawson.'

A month ago? So Slawson had disappeared just after Fennimore received the anonymous email and the photo of the girl.

'The limo firm he worked for said that Slawson was one of their regular drivers – he moved from the UK to France last winter.'

'I was advising you on your drugs deaths in Manchester last winter,' Fennimore said.

When the press found out that he and Simms were working together on that case, Fennimore and his missing daughter had become news again.

'Yes,' she said, and he knew she was thinking the same thing, reliving the pain she had gone through when Becky had been placed in danger.

'I also launched Suzie's Facebook page at that time – and the aged-up image of her went viral on the Web,' he added.

'Which is why I'm telling you this,' she said evenly. 'The Préfecture looked into Slawson's disappearance: there's been no activity on his credit card, but it was maxed out even before he vanished, so that's hardly surprising. They checked out his flat – he wasn't there – and there was nothing to say where he'd gone. There wasn't much else they could do.'

'What's his address?' Fennimore dipped in his jacket pocket for a notebook and pen.

'No, Nick.'

'I just want to cast a forensic eye over it.'

'No,' she said again.

'You won't tell me his address?'

'I didn't ask for it.'

'Kate, I need more—'

'I don't want to hear it,' she said firmly. 'You have his name; what you do with it is up to you.'

Simms disconnected and he stared at the phone for a minute, wondering if he should call her back. He had already asked too much of her – he knew that. But he couldn't help himself – he still wanted more from her.

He tried her number. It went straight to voicemail; this time he was on his own. He sat back to think. He was within sight of the bridge where his CCTV cameras had recorded the chauffeurs and their limousines. He didn't expect to see another procession of them line up there, but it had seemed like a good place to come and think. Dimly aware of the conversations going on around him, and lulled by the static noise of traffic in the streets nearby, he watched a tourist boat approaching, the distant buzz of its engine deepening to a throaty rumble as it passed. Its backwash sloshed against the walls of the quayside and spilled on to the steps up to the bridge. Across the river, a dog barked.

He ordered more coffee and called all of the limo services again, asked to speak to Pete Slawson. When he got to the sixth on the list, the telephonist said, '*Monsieur* Slawson is no longer with the firm.'

'Do you know where he went?'

'Who is this?' Her voice was heavily accented, but he could still hear the suspicion in it.

'A mate,' he said. 'Pete said I should look him up if I was in Paris.'

'*Votre nom, monsieur?*' she said, reverting to French, her tone clipped. 'You didn't tell to me your *name*.'

'Nick,' Fennimore said.

'Well, *Neek*, I am not permitted to give out private information about employees.'

'Thing is,' he improvised, 'Pete said there were good driving jobs for English speakers in Paris. I was thinking—'

'He was mistaken.'

'I've got a clean licence, proof of no insurance claims, full UK passport—'

'*Désolée, monsieur,*' she said, sounding anything but. Then she hung up.

Even so, two hours later Fennimore was standing inside Slawson's apartment. He'd hopped on the Métro and hung around the limo firm's door, then followed one of the drivers to a bar. Where charm had failed, a few beers and a wad of euros had produced the goods.

Slawson's apartment was tiny, in a rundown block of flats in a seedy area of the city. The *propriétaire* was a tall man, unshaven, and thin as a pipe-cleaner. He had the drooping shoulders of someone who had been badly let down early in life and had shaped his future existence from that first disappointment. He agreed to let Fennimore check out the apartment – as he was a friend of *Monsieur* Slawson – for 'a consideration'. He insisted on being present, but Fennimore made him stand by the door so that he didn't contaminate any evidence.

Fennimore himself was gloved and wore disposable slip-ons over his own shoes. He moved through the place, checking drawers and cupboards. There was no sign that a girl had ever been there. The sitting room was furnished with an armchair, a small TV and DVD player, a drop-leaf table with two ladder-back chairs, and a side table with lamp. None of them looked new; so how had Slawson maxed out his credit card?

'You didn't re-let the room?' Fennimore said, scanning the dusty surfaces.

The landlord spread his hands. 'He paid his rent on time – but only until the end of this month – after that . . .' He shrugged.

Fennimore bent to get a better perspective on the table top; it was painted white, but from this angle he could see a void – a faint oblong where the dust did not lie as thickly. He took out a penlight and played the beam across the surface. Yes – something had lain here and been removed. He changed position and saw something caught between the dropped leaf of the table and the wall. He shone the light down the gap, before carefully tilting the table to retrieve the item: a slip case for a small laptop.

'Do you know what happened to this?' he asked.

The landlord spread his hands in a caricature of Gallic surprise. '*Non.*'

He was lying.

'I want the computer,' Fennimore said.

'I don't know where it is.'

Fennimore was no genius when it came to reading people, but he could spot a lie at fifty paces. He smiled. 'This is what will happen next: I will go to the police and tell them that my friend *Monsieur* Slawson is missing and some of his property has been stolen from his apartment. I suspect the *propriétaire*. They will search your place, see what else you have squirrelled away.'

'No-no-no. *Non* – it's not like that,' the man protested. 'I didn't steal anything.'

'So where's the computer?'

'Some fellow came for it.'

'What "fellow"?'

'He said he was a friend.' The *propriétaire* paused. 'Like you.'

'And you just *gave* this complete stranger your tenant's property?' Fennimore said. 'Or was this for a "consideration", too?'

The man ran his tongue over his teeth. 'This fellow, he paid two months' rent, cash – he said *Monsieur* Slawson sent it.'

'You told the police this?'

The man looked at his feet.

Fennimore watched him closely. 'You planned to take the cash *and* sell Slawson's property for non-payment of the rent.'

The man glanced up in alarm. 'No, I—'

'What did this "friend" look like?'

'He dressed well – *propre* – and he was well-spoken.'

'English?'

The man gave him a scornful look. '*Parisien.*'

Fennimore took out his phone and showed him the photograph of the man and the girl taken from the bridge.

'*Oui! Bien sûr,*' the landlord said. 'That's him.'

Fennimore held the man's gaze, hoping that *Monsieur le propriétaire* wouldn't notice the tremor in his hand as he pocketed the phone.

The landlord's gaze slid away from his, and sweat popped on his brow. 'Here,' he said, holding out the handful of euros he had just accepted in return for granting Fennimore access to Slawson's apartment. 'Take it. I don't want it.'

'Keep it,' Fennimore said. 'I'll make you a deal.'

The man held the notes out for a second longer, then snatched them back and they disappeared into his grubby shirt pocket. He tilted his head, listening with an avid, untrustworthy expression on his face. '*Votre plaisir, m'sieur?*'

'You will go to your apartment and bring me any items belonging to Mr Slawson – phones, cameras, thumb drives, recorders, SD cards, notebooks – *anything* that can store data.'

He looked doubtful.

'I *know* you removed property from here,' Fennimore said.

'Perhaps a *few* things,' the man said. 'To keep them safe – this is a bad neighbourhood, *monsieur*. But the police—'

'If I am convinced that you haven't held anything back, I will pay for everything I take,' Fennimore said. 'And I'll keep the police out of it.'

'Certainly,' the man said, brightening. 'I will bring them to you.'

While the landlord went to retrieve the stolen goods, Fennimore resumed his search. The kitchen contained a sink, a cooker and a narrow dresser, which Slawson used for storing food and cookware. Tinned food, mostly; a few packets of pot noodles; a jar of instant coffee, almost empty; British teabags; sugar in an earthenware jar. He stirred the sugar with his finger – such places were favourite hiding places for anything from cash to keys, to drugs. But not for Slawson, it seemed. Then, at the back of one of the lower cupboards, behind a box of cornflakes, he found an old tea box containing leaf tea. Slawson didn't seem a leaf tea kind of man. He dug to the bottom of the box and, with the tang of Darjeeling dust in his nostrils, withdrew a plain key fob with two keys attached. The smaller one looked like it might work a door latch, but the larger of the two looked like a spare car key, though it had no distinctive markings. He pocketed the fob as the landlord returned, carrying a shoulder bag.

52

The important thing is not to stop questioning.
Curiosity has its own reason for existing.

ALBERT EINSTEIN

Paris, Friday Evening

Fennimore had booked a room near the bridge so he could be on the spot if anything interesting came up on the surveillance cameras. He ordered room service and worked methodically through the items Slawson's landlord had handed over: a camera, two thumb drives and an SD card. The thumb drives contained hundreds of files – all music.

Setting these aside, he picked up the digital camera, retrieved its SD card and slotted it into his laptop. The first image was labelled 'Lola',

Oh, hell . . .

He took a breath, braced himself and clicked on the image.

It was a red Mercedes convertible.

Fennimore exhaled, laughing.

He clicked through the images – dozens of them – some of the car alone, but most with a man standing next to it or seated in the driving seat, a Paris landmark in the background.

340

Was this Slawson?

He struck gold with the SD card the landlord had given him: Slawson had taken photographs or scans of his bank statements, receipts, invoices and bills going back two years. There were images of his car documents, insurance certificates, driver's licence and passport. Fennimore compared the two photo IDs with the man in the sports car. It was Slawson all right.

Pete Slawson, it seemed, had a serious shopping addiction: a new TV, just three months ago; an iPod, DVD recorder and Xbox, all bought on the same day; a sofa and a new bed . . . none of which matched the sparsely furnished apartment Fennimore had seen a couple of hours earlier. It seemed the landlord had taken more than a camera and a few thumb drives. Had he stolen the car, too? Fennimore doubted it – items like electronics equipment were easily accounted for – or disposed of – but a car . . . well, that was more tricky. The bank statements showed a monthly payment of €547 to a loan company. Maybe this was for the car.

He scrolled through the images and found a jpeg of the purchase agreement – the amount matched, and the most recent payment was just a couple of weeks before. Slawson was still paying for the car. If future payments weren't met, the company would come looking to make good their losses, and *M. le propriétaire* did not seem the type to risk that kind of attention. So where *was* the car? It must be around, unless Slawson had taken it and fled the city and his debts.

Fennimore shook his head. A bright red Mercedes was too conspicuous for a moonlight flit. He scrolled through Slawson's bank statements; going back two years, his account had been in constant overdraft. Had he hoped to tap Fennimore for cash? Had he tried to blackmail the man in the photo?

That same man had bought Slawson's computer from the landlord – possibly to destroy all of the remaining copies of the photograph of him with the girl. So why hadn't he taken the camera Fennimore now had in his possession? Because the landlord had already stolen it? That was the likely explanation.

But if the evidence boiled down to a single photograph, surely he would have come after me, Fennimore thought. Which meant that Slawson must have had something more incriminating.

Emails. He exhaled. If Slawson *had* emailed him the picture, and if he had emailed the *Parisien* as well, Fennimore might be able to put a name to the *Parisien* – that's if he could find those emails, trace them. But Fennimore had clicked and scrolled through every image and file on Slawson's thumb drives and SD cards – there *were* no emails. No photographs of the mystery man with the girl in the orange sundress either. So where were they?

The simple answer was, there *had* to be another cache of images.

He searched the shoulder bag the *propriétaire* had given him, checking its pockets and linings, turning it inside out to make sure he hadn't missed anything. He hadn't.

He dumped the empty bag on the bed. The mystery man – the *Parisien* – had taken it, he must have. Unless . . . Fennimore's head began to swim and he had to sit down to think the next one through.

Slawson backed up his data in a way Fennimore had never seen before, taking screenshots or photographs of every invoice and document and then filing them. A man like that wouldn't risk keeping everything in one place – and he wouldn't leave the job half done — so . . . the emails and photographs relating to the girl must be stored elsewhere. Another thumb drive or SD card.

'Either the *Parisien* has them,' Fennimore murmured, 'or . . .' He stared at the photograph of Slawson's gleaming red sports car.

Slawson lived in a dodgy part of town; he was hardly likely to park the car outside his apartment block, which meant he must have rented garage space. Was the missing data hidden inside his precious car? What could be safer — or harder to find — in a city of five million households?

Fennimore snatched up his laptop and went back through Slawson's bank statements, looking for regular payments, cross-matching them to invoices received. He found one biannual payment that matched a remittance note made out by R. F. Doucet from what looked like a private address in Chesnay, to the west of the city, near Versailles.

He searched on Google Maps and switched to StreetView. The address was a house with a garage attached; if this *was* the place, Slawson was paying more for the garage than he was for the car itself.

With Slawson's key fob safely tucked in his jacket pocket, Fennimore packed his forensics kit and a laptop computer into his shoulder bag and set off to find a taxi. Thirty-five minutes later, he asked the driver to drop him a block away and he walked the rest. It was well after 9 p.m., and getting dark. The house was well-maintained, but all of the shutters were closed. He trotted up the steps to get a better view of the street, and pretended to ring the doorbell. There was no one around. He went straight down to the garage and tried the key in the lock; it worked. Heart pounding, he swung the door open. Slawson's car gleamed dully in the gathering gloom.

He slipped inside and shut the door, located the light switch, and a second later, two striplights above the chauffer's car flickered into life.

Fennimore kitted and gloved up, examining the exterior of the vehicle carefully before trying the other key in the car door. He checked the boot and the interior using a portable UV black light and filters. There was nothing of use and no signs of foul play. In fact, he didn't find so much as a latent print – Slawson must have polished the car inside and out before he disappeared, and worn gloves when he parked it up.

Or the *Parisien* did, a voice whispered.

Either way, he wasn't getting anything from the car. He was about to withdraw when he noticed the fascia of the car stereo bore an SD symbol. It seemed Slawson had kitted his classic car with a state-of-the-art sound system. Fennimore scrutinized the fascia. Odd – there was no SD card slot.

He looked for a catch release, but couldn't find one; he felt under the dashboard for a switch of some kind – there was none. But when he pressed the front of the fascia at the centre, it sprung free. Startled, he almost dropped the thing, but caught it and placed it carefully on top of the dash. The card slot was behind the fascia, and there was something in there.

He should let the police know, but they had ignored Slawson's disappearance for weeks. He couldn't risk them screwing things up again. So he took the card and slotted it into his own laptop: he could replace it as soon as he knew what was on it – call the police when he had what he needed.

The DCIM file contained three folders; he hovered the

mouse pointer over each and checked 'Date modified'. He clicked on the one dated last month, which was when he had received the email with the photograph attached. There was no preview. The pulse thumping in his throat, he clicked on the first photograph: the girl in the orange sundress and the man he now called the *Parisien*. There were others of the girl – some with the man, some not. Candid portraits, taken through the window of a restaurant, through glass doors – a hotel maybe? He scrutinized the photos, trying to make out a small diamond-shaped scar on the girl's left temple. At the age of ten, Suzie had injured herself in a skateboarding accident. But the way the girl styled her hair, and reflections from the glass, made it impossible to see clearly.

He clicked on the next image. The girl was walking head-on towards the camera; the wind had lifted the hair from her face and the scar was clear against the pallor of her brow.

Suzie. Tears sprang to Fennimore's eyes. It was Suzie.

He touched the image onscreen and, as if he had flicked a switch, the garage was flooded with alternating flashes of vivid blue and red light. Police.

He cast about for an another way out, but he was trapped.

53

Offices of the Police Judiciaire, Paris, Saturday Morning

Fennimore was seated in an interview room, looking about as helpless and lost as Simms had ever seen him. He had his hands in his lap, his head bowed to his chest. He had a greyish pallor, despite his tan and he looked like he hadn't slept.

When he'd called her just before midnight, he sounded half mad with grief and worry. Even as she listened to the things he'd done, the outrageous risks he'd taken, Simms was preparing herself for a difficult conversation with Kieran and her mother.

Fennimore didn't even look up when she opened the door. Her instinct was to go to his side, to embrace him. But she hardened her heart – she had to make him understand that he needed to start playing by the rules. So she placed both hands, palms down, on the table and leaned over him.

'You're an idiot,' she said.

His head jerked up and he gasped. The desperation and gratitude in his eyes was so pitiful she had to look away.

'Kate.' He reached for her, but she withdrew her hand.

She pulled out a chair and sat opposite him. 'I should let them lock you up and leave the consulate to sort out the mess you've made.'

'I know,' he said. 'But, Kate – it's Suzie. I *swear*, it's Suzie.'

She began to shake her head and he leaned across the table.

'I saw the *scar*, Kate.' He touched his left temple and his fingers shook. 'We need to process those images – there are geographic markers – they could give us a location.'

She blinked, lifted her chin and spoke to a point on the wall behind him, because she couldn't bear the torment in his eyes.

'That may be. But this is a French investigation. It's their call – they will decide if there's evidence to follow up. And if they do, they will liaise with the investigative team in the UK, and you will be kept informed only as a family member.'

He ran a hand across his face and his palm rasped over his unshaved skin. 'Kate, I can't—'

'You have to – if you want to walk out of here today, you *have* to let the police do their job.'

He clasped a hand over his mouth and again she steeled herself against her natural impulse to comfort him. 'Do you understand?'

He nodded miserably.

'A police officer is about to come in and ask you some questions,' she said. 'If you want to avoid going to prison, you need to answer honestly – and be civil.' She paused. 'Are we clear?'

He gave a juddering sigh that almost shattered her resolve. 'We're clear,' he said.

She exhaled, letting go of some of the tension that had

built up over the past nine hours, and slid a business card across the table.

He frowned. 'What's this? A lawyer?' He looked horrified. 'Do I need a *lawyer*, Kate?'

'This is the private investigator you hired to track down Pete Slawson,' she said, raising her eyebrows and adding with heavy emphasis: 'Should the question arise.'

'Kate, I—'

A shadow at the door window warned her the police inspector had arrived. 'Put it away,' she said softly.

Fennimore pocketed the card. 'Thank you,' he said, his voice hoarse with emotion.

The officer was in plain clothes, mid-thirties, with jet-black hair and a weather-lined face that aged him by five years. He carried a document wallet and a buff envelope.

He nodded to Simms and she gave up her seat, moving to the other side of the table to sit next to Fennimore.

The officer remained standing, his eyes fixed on Fennimore as he tipped the contents of the envelope on to the table.

Two thumb drives, two SD cards, a car key and a smaller latch key on a fob. The items Fennimore had taken from Slawson's apartment, she guessed. 'Is this everything?' the detective demanded; his English was accented but clear and precise.

Fennimore frowned. 'No,' he said. 'The SD card I found in the car radio isn't there.'

'The SD card you *stole* from *Monsieur* Slawson's car?'

'I was about to call you when—'

The cop held up a hand to stop him.

'You may tell it to the *juge d'instruction*,' he said.

Fennimore shot her an alarmed look and Simms said, 'The

examining judge – the French judicial system is inquisitorial – a judge directs investigations into serious crimes.'

'You have – how does one say, *"faites vos devoirs"*?' the detective said.

'Done my homework?'

'You speak French, madame?' Instantly, he seemed to warm to her.

'My daughter does,' Simms said with a smile. 'And she's had lots of French *devoirs* over the years.'

He straightened up and offered his hand. '*Inspecteur* Guerin,' he said. 'And you must be Chief Inspector Simms. It is my pleasure to meet you.'

Fennimore stirred restlessly by her side and Simms subdued an impulse to dig him in the ribs: he never was any good at the social niceties.

'Inspector,' he began, 'my daughter is in the hands of an abductor. I understand you're angry – I know I messed up your chain of evidence – but I was careful, I followed forensic protocols. Please, tell me you're working on that SD card.'

Inspector Guerin's right eyebrow twitched, but he didn't answer. Simms could see the Frenchman making a mental calculation, deciding how much he would reveal.

'We retrieved a fingerprint from the card,' he said at last, addressing Simms, cop to cop. 'It matched Pete Slawson's employee record. So he probably did take the photo of the girl. Unhappily, we cannot confirm that he emailed it to Professor Fennimore, because *Monsieur* Slawson's computer is still missing.'

He paused, and Fennimore took a breath and let it go slowly, folding his hands in front of him on the table top. Simms could see he was close to cracking, that he was doing all in his power to hold himself together.

'I *told* you, the landlord sold Slawson's laptop computer to the man in the photo,' Fennimore said.

'This man?' Guerin placed a copy of the photo of the man with the girl in the orange sundress on the table and Fennimore touched the figure of the girl tentatively.

'Yes.' He looked into the inspector's face. '*Yes.* You should be out looking for him.'

'Nick,' Simms warned.

'I'm sorry.' He clasped his hands together and stared at the knuckles for a few moments; the tension in him seemed to crackle like an electric charge.

'Slawson took that picture,' he said. 'You *know* that. Maybe he even chauffeured the man in this photograph.' He jabbed the image of the businessman with his forefinger. 'Ask the limo company who Slawson chauffeured in the two months leading up to his death and you *will* find this man.'

'Perhaps.' Guerin's calm brown eyes revealed nothing.

Fennimore ran his fingers through his hair, making it stand up in wild tufts. 'Have you even looked at the images on the card yet?'

The inspector ignored Fennimore, again addressing Simms. 'You knew Suzie Fennimore, I understand?'

She nodded. 'Before she disappeared, Suzie and my daughter were inseparable.'

The inspector opened the folder in front of him and handed her a photograph. Fennimore reached for it, but the cop gave a curt '*M'sieur!*' and he subsided.

Kate stared at the photo and tried to catch her breath.

'Chief Inspector?' Guerin said.

'It looks—' Her voice had no strength and Simms cleared her throat, tried again. 'It's so like her. And the scar

– it's exactly like one Suzie had—' She shot Fennimore an apologetic look. 'Like Suzie *has*.'

She passed the photo to Fennimore and he began speaking in a flat, quiet tone: 'You've seen the other photographs. I think Slawson was convinced the girl is Suzie – I *know* I am. And I've seen Slawson's bank statements – he was under a ton of debt.'

'You think he intended to *sell* to you information about this girl?' Inspector Guerin said.

'I think it's possible.'

'But he didn't contact you again after the first email . . .' Guerin shrugged.

'No,' Fennimore said tiredly.

Guerin frowned. 'You think that Monsieur Slawson is dead?'

'I do.' Fennimore swallowed. 'I know I overstepped the mark, Inspector. I should have come to you earlier. But I didn't think you would listen – even Kate stopped listening for a while.'

Simms winced, placing the flat of her hand on her stomach where a pain, half physical, half emotional, was centred, and Fennimore went on:

'This is your investigation, Inspector. I accept that – but you *have* to—' He broke off, his jaw working. 'I'm . . . *asking* you.' He took a breath. '*Please* help me.' He didn't take his eyes off the image once in his entire speech.

Simms looked for Guerin's reaction. He was a cop, with a cop's ability to hide his feelings, but the Frenchman's swift glance at her revealed he was not without compassion.

'Very well,' Guerin said, and Fennimore's head jerked up to meet his gaze. 'I will speak to the *juge d'instruction*. I will relate to him everything you and Chief Inspector Simms have told to me. We will conduct a search of the city morgues.' He took a slip of paper from the document wallet and slid it across the table to Fennimore. 'You will see the judge at four o'clock this afternoon at this address. It would be unwise to be late. For now, you must return to your hotel. This is a police investigation, Professor. Chief Inspector Simms's *médiation* and your own professional reputation have kept you from criminal charges on this occasion. But I will tolerate no further interference.'

Simms waited outside the police station while Fennimore had his confiscated belongings returned to him. The offices of the Police Judiciaire were housed in a wedge of stained concrete and shit-brown tile. Wider at the top than at the base, it seemed to crowd the more traditional shops and apartment buildings on either side. Her friend emerged on to the narrow street looking dazed. He seemed to cast about for a moment, uncertain which way to turn. She called his name and relief flooded his features.

'Thanks for coming,' he said. 'I – I mean, for everything.' She hadn't seen him so unsure of himself since Suzie and Rachel first disappeared.

'Okay,' she said. 'But keep in mind that my "*médiation*" won't count for anything if you pull any more stunts like this.' He had a distant look in his eye as if already deciding his next move. 'Nick, are you listening? They're looking into Slawson. It won't do you or Suzie any good if you get yourself arrested again.'

'No,' he said. 'I can see that.'

She almost believed him.

'Drink?' he asked.

'I can't. I told Kieran and my mother a blatant lie about coming here – I said I needed to see Becky.'

'Becky's *here*?'

'Has been since Thursday. I need to arrange to meet up with her – undo the lie, at least a little.' She checked her smartphone for the nearest Métro station, but hesitated to leave him looking so shell-shocked. 'Will you be all right?'

'I'll be fine,' he said.

She placed a hand on his arm and felt a shudder run through him. 'Look, if you want, I could—'

He took her hand and kissed the palm, tears glistening in his eyes. 'You should go and see Becky,' he said. 'I'm going to walk back to my hotel along the river. Get some air.'

She watched him go. At the corner of Rue Lagrange, he seemed to stagger, and she almost went after him, but then he was off, walking with purpose and, with some misgivings, she turned in the opposite direction.

54

I am an omnivorous reader with a strangely retentive
memory for trifles.

A. C. DOYLE, 'THE ADVENTURE OF THE LION'S MANE'

Back at his hotel, Fennimore showered and changed. With a
few hours to kill before his interview with the instructing
judge, he lay on his bed and tried to rest. Twice, as he began
to drift off, he heard the steady blip of a heart monitor and
saw Josh's face swim in front of him, bruised at the temple,
the brow-bone distorted as if the bullet in his brain were
about to burst through the skin. Twice, the blip–blip–blip of
the monitor stuttered and stopped, and he jerked awake,
sweating and breathless.

He gave up on resting, and began pacing the room. He
opened his laptop and started working through his email – it
was mostly academic admin – end-of-term round-ups, staff
awards, admissions news, research funding and requests for
new book orders. He skimmed through, but doubled back
to a subject line that didn't fit the list. It was a request for
a meeting from Laurent Wealth Management. His shoulders

slumped: he still hadn't got back to Mr Vincent. He dialled the number and announced himself, apologizing for the weekend call.

'Not at all, Professor Fennimore.' Vincent sounded in a bit of a fluster at hearing his voice. 'I'm pleased you found the time. Just let me pull up your file, I'll be right with you.'

Fennimore heard a flurry of activity at the other end of the line.

'Here it is, sir. Ah, yes – the unhappy fact is that your income is down by forty per cent on last year.'

'Forgive me, Mr Vincent,' Fennimore said, 'but that's bullshit. A matter of days ago I had a magnum of champagne from my US publisher because I made the *New York Times* bestseller list.'

'I'm looking at your *actual* income here, Professor,' the man said. 'Sales are all very well, but publisher discounting can have a marked – and detrimental – effect on the bottom line.'

Fennimore hadn't considered that; he supposed it was just possible his publishers had drawn a veil over their discount strategy: sales figures sounded so much more impressive.

'If you like, we could look at some aspects of your spending you might, um – rein in,' the accountant suggested.

'*What* spending?' Fennimore asked. 'I drive a four-year-old car; I have a one-bedroom flat in Aberdeen and a two-bedroom cottage in Cumbria, both of which I own outright. I do spend money on cameras and computer gadgets from time to time, but not a huge amount.'

'Sir, your outgoings in the last month alone were £6200.'

'Look,' Fennimore said, 'I was working in the USA for at least three weeks over the past month. My publisher paid for internal flights; I stayed mostly at a cheap roadside motel in Oklahoma; St Louis PD paid my hotel bills while I was there and my publisher paid for accommodation in Chicago. I don't have a lavish lifestyle, Mr Vincent.' Something Vincent had said a moment ago struck Fennimore as odd.

'How do *you* know how much I spent in the last month?' he asked. The way it worked was, he forwarded receipts, invoices and remittance notes, and they compiled a set of accounts that made sense, worked out his tax return and advised on investments.

'Your tax accounts.' Vincent's voice was faint.

'Really – are you guys clairvoyant?' Fennimore said. 'Because I haven't even gathered together my invoices yet – I *might* get around to it by autumn.' The silence at the other end of the line was like the pause before a violent thunderclap. 'Mr Vincent?' he said.

'I'm sure there's a rational explanation,' Vincent said, delivering the words staccato. 'I'll get back to you as soon as possible, Professor Fennimore.'

The line went dead.

Who was this Vincent anyway? Fennimore hadn't even heard the name until this month. He dredged up the first phone conversation they'd had – 'auditing accountant,' the man had said – which he took to mean an internal audit – and the likely target was Fennimore's financial adviser. *Whose name is . . .*

It didn't come.

After the runaway success of his first popular science book, *Truth, Lies and Forensic Alibis*, Rachel had been all for 'diversifying their portfolio'– whatever that meant. He'd agreed to meet with a financial adviser. She arranged a meeting, but Fennimore was called away on a case at the last minute. After he cancelled a second time, Rachel went ahead and met— *What the hell was the guy's name?*

It drove Rachel crazy that he could remember details of cases going back fifteen years, but forgot important stuff like birthdays and anniversaries. He had to admit, the financial adviser had done a good job – as Rachel kept reminding him over the year that followed. He'd even asked her once if she had crush on the guy. The way Rachel looked at him at that moment, he'd thought she would confront him outright about Kate Simms. But she didn't – instead, she said he hadn't a clue about investments, and without—

Dammit, he almost had the name that time.

Without *whoeverhisnamewas*, she'd said, their money would be sitting in a building society, devaluing month by month. It was true – Fennimore had never really been interested in money, nor adept at managing it.

After Rachel and Suzie disappeared, he fell apart, and the firm had organized him discreetly and without being patronizing. When the company merged with an international concern, he hardly noticed any changes – not even the name – just a grander logo and better paper quality on statements and letters. He simply glanced over what they sent and signed on the line helpfully Post-it-marked by Adèle Arnaud, the adviser's secretary.

Why the hell could he remember the secretary's name and not his adviser's? Rachel was right – he should have paid more attention. He remembered her presenting him with a glossy brochure. That was back when Laurent was a small company – just five team members.

In a flash of almost eidetic recall, he saw 'The Team'

photographed on the centre pages, standing in a V, suited and air-brushed, like reality TV stars. And he remembered their tagline: 'Your wealth is our business.' Which didn't sound as reassuring now as it did back then.

So where was that brochure? When he'd moved from south-east England up to Aberdeen, he had shipped a load of paperwork to his office at the university – and from there to the new campus at Garthdee.

As he so often did in times of organizational chaos, he turned to Joan, the faculty office manager, but her direct line went straight to voicemail, and he remembered again that it was Saturday. He called her mobile number.

'Professor, how *are* you?' she said, her voice full of concern.

'I'm fine,' he said. 'You heard about Josh.'

She sighed.

Of course she had – this was Joan, after all.

'Poor lad,' she said.

Fennimore didn't know what to say, so he shoved his emotion over Josh's death into one of the neat compartments in his brain and said, 'Look, Joan . . .'

'Och – I know *that* tone,' she said, sounding peevish, but he guessed that, like him, Joan was glad to have something to keep her busy.

'I moved some boxes over to my new office,' he said. 'If I direct you, could you find something for me?' The brochure would be in among his statements and letters, he explained.

She called him back fifty minutes later from his Garthdee office and grumbled about the mess he'd left the place in. She switched the phone to speaker so that she could set it down and he heard her muttering and tutting as she shifted boxes and rooted through the files.

358

Suddenly, she stopped.

'Joan?' he said.

'I think I have it,' she said.

'Can you turn to the middle page – there should be a group photo. Can you read out the names?'

'I can do better than *that*.' A few moments later, she said, 'Check your email.'

He put the phone down to look at his laptop. She had sent the middle-page photo image as an attachment.

With a sick thud of understanding, he recognized one of the faces. He scrambled for the image of Suzie with the man on the Paris street and resized it to fit alongside the brochure photo. A few years older, a little meatier around the jowls, but it was the same man. The man walking by Suzie's side on a sunny street near the Seine and the man in the brochure were one and the same. He was the financial adviser Rachel had praised so highly. The caption gave his name: Charles Branly.

Fennimore dialled Laurent Wealth Management again, half-expecting to hear a recorded message, but the switchboard was manned. He announced himself and asked to speak to Mr Vincent. 'He's not answering his mobile,' he said.

'Oh, Mr Trimble instructed that I should put you straight through to him if you called,' the telephonist said. 'He's one of the senior partners.'

Fennimore listened while Trimble talked emolliently about the business and the market, and how his investments were in safe hands.

'And yet you're in your office on a Saturday, when any self-respecting CEO should be on the golf course,' Fennimore said.

'Mr Fennimore, I assure you, we have everything in hand,' Trimble said smoothly. 'As soon as Mr Vincent has anything to tell you he'll—'

'That's *Professor* Fennimore – and I don't think I want to hear this from Vincent. I want to hear it from you.'

'Forgive me – Professor,' the man said. 'What is it you would like to know?'

Fennimore's real fear was that Branly had already disappeared, so he asked, 'Why didn't Charles Branly make the call to warn me about this . . . "anomaly" in my earnings? He's my adviser.'

'I'm sure he would *intend* to—'

Fennimore gripped the phone tighter. 'You mean you haven't spoken to him?'

'It's not quite that simple—'

'What could be simpler than picking up the phone?'

'You misunderstand me, Professor – I fully intend to—'

'*He* intends, *you* intend – well, you know what they say about the pathway to hell, Mr Trimble.'

After a few moments of silence, the partner began again. 'I can see that this may seem . . . alarming,' he said. 'But we *are* regulated by the Financial Conduct Authority – I want to assure you that your investments are safe.'

'You're citing the FCA?' Fennimore said. 'Just how bad is this?'

'We would want to complete our audit before commenting on the situation.'

'What "situation"?'

'I'm afraid I can't be more specific until the audit is complete.'

Fennimore sucked his teeth. 'When I spoke with

Mr Vincent an hour ago, *he* was convinced I was just splurging on too many luxuries – I'll take a potted summary for now.'

Another silence. 'I'm afraid that's not possible.'

'You don't have a clue what Branly has been up to, do you?' Fennimore said, forcing rationality and a semblance of cold control into his voice. 'He's been ripping clients off right under your nose and you were oblivious.'

'Mr Branly is working from one of our satellite offices. He—'

'Where?'

'I'm sorry?'

'Is it in Paris?' Trimble's silence told him he was right. 'I want the address,' Fennimore said.

'I'm sorry, I can't do that,' Trimble said. 'I can give you the number for the Paris office, of course, but they will only tell you what I've already said. It is vital that this is handled carefully, Professor. We *are* investigating and it would be unwise to do anything that might . . . fluster Mr Branly.'

'If Branly has been doing what I think he has,' Fennimore said, 'your audit will already have spooked him.'

Trimble began to reassure Fennimore again about his investments.

'I don't give a *crap* about the money – you know who I am, Mr Trimble. You *know* my history.'

Trimble muttered some platitude. 'But I don't see how that impacts upon—'

'I have evidence that your man in Paris has my daughter, Suzie.' His voice broke on her name and he coughed to clear his throat. 'So either you give me Branly's address or I take this to the police.'

'Then I believe I'll wait for the police request,' Trimble said stiffly.

'Your choice,' Fennimore said. 'But if any harm comes to my daughter as a result of the delay, I *will* sue.'

'Professor Fennimore, be reasonable—'

'I'll tell the press that you conspired with Branly.'

'But that's not true!'

'It doesn't matter,' Fennimore said, as cold and hard as stone. 'Doesn't matter if you countersue for libel either – Suzie Fennimore is international news – the damage to your reputation would finish the firm.'

Kate Simms's phone buzzed in her pocket as she was finishing lunch at the Chaberts'. She had warned them she might have to take a call, and apologized, leaving the table and stepping out on to the elegant balcony of their art deco apartment in the 7th arrondissement.

'Kate, listen,' he said, 'I think I've found her.'

Simms's stomach flipped.

'The photograph,' he said. 'I had it the whole time. I should have recognized him, Kate.'

'Who are you talking about? What photo – the one of the girl in Paris?' Simms heard traffic noise down the line, the agitated sound of car horns. *Is he driving?*

'The brochure – Joan found it – I have it in front of me. It's a match.'

'Nick, what brochure – a match to what?'

'You're not *listening*,' he said.

'I'm trying,' she said, 'but you're not making *sense*.'

She heard a juddering exhalation, then: 'The man in the Paris photo.' He took a breath. 'I knew he was familiar – I just

362

couldn't place him. He's a financial adviser – his photo was in an old brochure I had in my files.'

The blood roared in Simms's ears and she had to grip the balcony rail to stay upright. 'You have a name?'

'Charles Branly.'

'You think this Branly *abducted* Rachel and Suzie?'

'I don't know.' Fennimore took a breath. 'But, Kate – he's got Suzie.'

'Nick, it's all right,' she said, 'we have a name – we'll get him. We will. I'll call my boss, ask him to alert London Met. We'll—'

'Branly's not *in* the UK – he's here in Paris,' Fennimore said. 'And his firm has begun auditing his accounts – it looks like he's been embezzling clients' funds. If Branly knows they're on to him—' He broke off.

Sweat broke out on Simms's brow. 'I'll call Inspector Guerin,' she said.

'I've already done that,' Fennimore said. 'But he could make a break for it at any moment. Kate – we have to get Suzie out, *now*.'

She heard more car horns and a squeal of brakes. *Oh, God*. 'You're on your way to his apartment, aren't you?' She glanced over her shoulder at her daughter and her friends, chatting over coffee. 'What's the address?'

He gave her a street name in the 8th arrondissement. 'It's between the Champs-Élysées and the Trocadero,' he said.

'That's only minutes from where I am. I'll meet you there,' she said. 'We'll find her, Nick. Just – *please* wait for the police.'

The traffic on the street below her seemed to still to a shush and Simms felt the damp grip of a cold sweat on her neck. She leaned on the balcony and took a couple of deep breaths before stepping back into the dining room.

Becky stood, clattering her coffee cup into the saucer. 'Mum, are you okay? Has something happened?'

'I'm – I'm fine,' Simms said. She turned to Mrs Chabert. 'But I have to go. I'm so sorry. It's – an emergency.'

'Can I drive you?' Mrs Chabert asked. 'You are quite pale, *madame*.'

'No, it's fine. Really. That was—' She couldn't say it was Fennimore and she couldn't think of a reasonable lie.

'Mum, you're scaring me,' Becky said. 'Has Daddy had an accident? Is Timmy—'

'No, darling – it's nothing like that. I promise you, Dad and Timmy are fine.'

'So why are you *crying*?'

'Am I?' Simms dashed a tear from her cheek and held her daughter's face in her two hands. 'I can't say, poppet – not yet. But I promise I'll explain everything soon.'

Seconds later she was on the street, hailing a taxi.

55

Paris, 8th Arrondissement, Saturday Afternoon

Simms's taxi arrived outside Branly's apartment building moments after Fennimore. He had parked his hire car at an angle to the kerb and was halfway to the entrance when she got out of the cab. She managed to catch him and steer him out of sight of the concierge's desk.

'I have to get in there, Kate,' he said.

'No,' she said. 'You have to wait. You saw the concierge; they probably have security staff, too. And Branly knows you. If he really has got Suzie, you'll just place her in greater danger.'

'Where are the police?' Fennimore said. 'What's taking so long?'

'My guess is they'll be pulling together a team of specialists in kidnapping and hostage situations.'

His eyes widened. 'No – we can't let it get to a stand-off.' He tried to shake free, but Simms held him.

'It probably won't come to that, but they have to be ready, Nick,' she said. 'It's good strategy.'

His blue eyes searched her face. 'You're talking about strategy? This is *Suzie*, Kate.'

'Even so.' They had reached his car and she opened the passenger door. 'Take a breath,' she said. 'Think this through.'

Early afternoon sunshine bathed the limestone frontages of the buildings along the street. Simms risked a quick glance up at the balconied windows of Branly's place, but all of them on the upper level were closed, blindly reflecting the sunlight. When she fixed her gaze on Fennimore again, she saw that he had been watching her; perhaps he saw her in a different light at that moment, surveilling the building like a cop, because after another second's hesitation, he got in the car.

From where they sat they had a clear view of the steps and the grand front doors of the building, as the entrance was kept free for drop-offs and pick-ups. The stone sets of the roadway before it gleamed like slate.

'We can see everyone entering or leaving from here,' she said. 'The best thing we can do is wait for Guerin to arrive.'

A Daimler pulled out of a concealed exit twenty yards down the road and adrenaline flooded Simms's system.

'*Shit* – there's a car park. Hide your face,' she hissed, her pulse hammering in her throat.

Fennimore ducked his head and scratched his eyebrow as the car passed.

'It's not him,' she said, her heart steadying to a mild jitter.

'What if he's already gone?' Fennimore demanded. 'The company's auditor wasn't exactly subtle when he called me.'

He had a point. But the sensible thing to do would be to sit tight, wait for Guerin.

366

'What if we're sitting here,' he went on, his breathing irregular, 'what if we're waiting for the cops to get their arses in gear while he's already heading for the border with Suzie?'

Simms had a flash of Suzie tied up in the boot of a car and suddenly she couldn't take any more. 'Okay,' she said. 'I need a name.'

'What?' Fennimore seemed stunned.

'A name,' she said. 'Someone you dealt with at Branly's firm – a receptionist, an assistant, a PA.'

'Jeez, Kate – I couldn't even remember *Branly's* name till Joan looked it up for me. No, wait . . .' He made an effort to focus. 'There *is* a secretary. She signed letters on Branly's behalf.'

'The *name*, Nick.'

'Arnaud,' he said. 'Adèle Arnaud.'

Simms let down her hair and ruffled it, checked her look in the rear-view mirror, then reapplied her lipstick. She reached across him and pulled the car-hire documents out of the glove box.

'What are you going to do?'

'Find out if he's still in there.'

Sliding out of the driver's seat, she fastened her suit jacket and unbuttoned her blouse to show some cleavage. She rushed, breathless and smiling, to the reception desk and asked for permission to go up to *Monsieur* Branly's apartment. The concierge was dressed in a taupe grey uniform with gold buttons, the red Nehru collar of his jacket swallowed by the folds of his neck. He answered in French.

'*Monsieur Branly a demandé à ne pas être derangé.*'

She recognized *ne pas derangé* – 'do not disturb'.

'I know, but—' She waved the rental agreement. '*Très*

urgent,' she said, wishing she had made more effort in French classes. '*Oof*,' she said, with a giddy giggle. 'My French – sorry – um, *désolée*. I have urgent papers from Madame Arnaud. He *has* to sign them before he goes.'

The man was unmoved.

'It's *très important*,' she said, opening her eyes wide. 'Mr Branly will be *so* upset he forgot to do it.'

The concierge ran his tongue around the inside of his upper lip before saying, '*Monsieur* Branly has asked for a limousine fifteen minutes ago.'

The floor seemed to drop away from her and Simms took hold of the counter to steady herself. 'He's gone?'

'*Calmez-vous, madame*,' he said. Her stricken look must have melted the ice chip in his Parisian heart. 'He demanded the chauffeur should drive into the car park.' The concierge pointed downward with his index finger. 'It can take ten minutes for the limousine to arrive. If you hurry . . .' He raised one shoulder.

'What's the quickest way?' she said.

'*L'ascenseur*.' He jerked his chin to a brass–doored elevator to his right. The indicator showed it was on the fourth floor.

Too slow, *too slow*. 'Fire escape,' she yelled. 'Where is it?'

'Left,' he said. '*Au coin*.'

She darted left and found the door to the fire escape. She yanked it open, speed-dialling Fennimore as she ran down the steps.

'They're on their way out,' she said. 'Watch the exit.'

'*Oh, God* – I've been moved on by a traffic cop.' Fennimore sounded panicked. 'I'm doing a circuit of the block.'

'Well, put your foot down.'

As she swung the basement door open, a limo swept

by. Simms caught a glimpse of a girl through the window, solemn, anxious-looking. The girl saw her and turned as the car moved on, her eyes wide.

Simms mouthed, 'Suzie?'

Maddeningly, the girl's hair had fallen over her left temple.

Simms banged on the boot of the vehicle to attract the driver's attention. In response, the limo put on a spurt of speed, tyres squealing. She broke into a run, losing ground with every stride. It was already on the ramp; she sprinted up on to the street seconds after the driver turned right, merging with the traffic. Fennimore rounded the corner and Simms waved him to the kerb. She threw herself into the car and he pulled away.

'Black limo,' she said. 'Two ahead of the Renault.'

They set off in pursuit, zig-zagging through traffic.

Simms called Guerin and gave him their location, but as they twisted and turned through the capital's back streets, she was hampered by the unfamiliar geography.

'What the hell's he doing?' Fennimore yelled.

Back on one of the boulevards, the limo had swerved across two lanes.

Fennimore was blocked by traffic. He sounded his horn and edged over, but the limo made a sudden illegal right down a one-way street.

Fennimore braked, but missed the turn.

'Next right – twenty yards,' Simms yelled. He took the turn, blasting down the narrow street, clipping the wing mirror of a parked car. But by the time they made it to the junction, the limo had vanished. Simms gave Guerin the make and registration of the limo.

Fennimore turned into the traffic, still hunting it, screaming to Guerin to find out if the firm had GPS trackers on their cars.

At the next junction he glanced right and left. 'Which way, Kate? Which way?'

She scanned the road signs. 'Right,' she said. 'Follow the signs to the Périphérique – if he's trying to get out of the city, that would be the quickest route.'

Minutes later, Guerin called Simms.

'We have him in sight,' he said. 'Driving north-east on the Périphérique.'

'Jesus, Nick – we're heading the wrong way.'

'Hang on to something,' he said.

'No,' Simms said. 'Nick, don't do this—'

Fennimore cut across the yellow centre-line and u-turned the car to the sound of horns and the squeal of tyres as cars screeched to a halt around them. He blasted on, leaving irate drivers gesticulating furiously as they sped away.

The character of the city changed quickly to high-rise social housing and low-rise retail units, most defaced by graffiti. The roadway itself was scarred, pitted and patched, and as they drove through underpass after underpass, the mood changed to match the brutal architecture.

Five minutes on, they got word that Branly's limo had stopped – the police were closing in. Guerin hung up, but shortly after Simms's phone buzzed in her hand.

Fennimore was half crazy with grief and worry – if this was bad news, she didn't want to give it to him rolling at 60 mph. 'Pull over,' she said abruptly. When he was safely on the hard shoulder, Simms moved the slider to 'Answer' and switched to speaker.

'Is she safe?' she asked.

'We found the limo and driver, but Branly and the girl are gone,' the inspector said.

'On foot?'

'Branly had arranged a taxi to meet them.'

Fennimore gripped the steering wheel so hard she thought he might rip it from its housing.

'We are checking Paris taxi firms,' Guerin continued. 'But it could take hours – and anyway perhaps he changed taxis or he might even have a car – uh, *caché*?'

'Hidden,' Simms supplied.

'Yes, hidden,' Guerin said.

'The driver had no idea where they were headed?'

'No,' the Frenchman said. 'He was told only to head north-east.'

Simms hung up after extracting a promise that Guerin would keep them informed. She looked across at Fennimore. He had covered his eyes with one hand, and his shoulders shook.

She touched his arm. He muttered something, and she said, 'What?'

'I said, what's in the north-east?' He wiped his eyes and sat up straight. 'Pass me the e-tablet out of the glove compartment, will you?' He seemed unnaturally calm.

She handed over the device, thinking, *Don't give up, Nick. Not now – not when we're so close.*

Fennimore consulted the map, pinching and expanding images to enlarge it. 'See that?' he said. 'Le Bourget airport is just a few kilometres north-east of here.'

Simms rang Guerin and put him on speaker. 'It's a business aviation airport,' Guerin said. 'Exclusively private flights in and out of Paris. If Branly is there, he will go no further. Tell Professor Fennimore.'

371

'He hears you,' she said. She closed the phone and stared hard at Fennimore. 'Now we switch places,' she said.

'We need to get there fast.'

'We need to get there alive,' she corrected. 'You can navigate.'

She drove as fast as she dared, Fennimore balancing his tablet on the dashboard so that she could read the route. They peeled off the Périphérique on to Autoroute du Nord, an eight-lane highway. On the outskirts of the city they plunged into a tunnel, blasting out into dazzling sunshine and a more open landscape of modern buildings and motels. Just after the Stade de France, the road curved right and they saw the sign for Le Bourget, and half a mile ahead of them, a string of blue flashing lights. The police in convoy. They took the off-ramp, guided to the airport's main entrance by the emergency lights.

Simms tucked the car in behind the last of the convoy and they ran to the entrance. Guerin was already inside, directing operations. He looked grim.

Fennimore walked purposefully towards him, calling his name, and two officers stepped in his path. He forged on and they grabbed his arms. Guerin gave an order and they let him go.

'Where is she?' Fennimore said.

Guerin glanced at Simms.

'Tell the man,' she said.

'Branly chartered a helicopter – it took off minutes ago,' Guerin said.

'Well, tell the pilot to turn around,' Fennimore said.

'Flight control is trying to contact the pilot right now,' Guerin said. 'But . . .' Another nervous glance in Simms's direction. 'He is not responding.'

56

The game is afoot.

A. C. DOYLE,
'THE ADVENTURE OF ABBEY GRANGE'

'What are the possibilities?' Fennimore said. 'Where could he be headed? Does he have other properties in France?'

'We have officers checking Branly's apartment and we are making additional checks at international airports,' Guerin said. 'But a helicopter can land just about anywhere – it will be difficult to find him.'

'Is he holding the pilot hostage – forcing him to fly where he wants to go? Because that would be risky – especially with Suzie to control as well.'

'Suzie's been with him a long time, Nick,' Simms said softly. 'He might not need force to control her.'

Something flashed in Fennimore's eyes – fear? Anger? But the scientist in him would not allow him to deny the basic psychological fact that Suzie would almost certainly have formed a bond with her abductor, and the flare died, replaced by an agonized acceptance.

373

For the next few minutes, the police came and went; Guerin gave instructions, spoke to airport officials, communicated by radio and phone, marshalling his team, while Fennimore and Simms waited in breathless silence. Twenty minutes after they first entered the concourse, a French officer hurried over to Guerin and spoke in rapid, strongly accented French.

'What's he saying?' Fennimore asked.

'I don't know – I think he said "*à la terre*",' Simms said. '*Terre* is ground, isn't it? Inspector – have they landed?'

Guerin turned to face them: 'Air traffic control have made contact with the helicopter pilot. He has requested permission to land.' The inspector walked towards the back of the building and they made to follow. Guerin held up his hand. 'Better if you stay here, Professor.'

Fennimore shouldered forward and two officers moved either side of him.

'Hey,' Simms said. 'He found her, he's coming with you.'

Guerin looked from Fennimore to Simms. 'Okay,' he said. 'But *doucement*, yes?'

Fennimore looked far from gentle at that moment, but Guerin let him climb into an airport security vehicle with Simms, and they were waiting near the helipad when the chopper landed.

Only one man disembarked.

'Where are they?' Fennimore took a few steps towards the helicopter, but Guerin gave an order and two officers stepped forward, blocking him.

'You must stay here,' he said. 'I will talk to the pilot and I will tell you what he says – but you must not interfere.'

Fennimore looked like he might argue, but then he gave a brief nod and backed away. He watched as the inspector and his sergeant interrogated the pilot and it seemed to Simms that every nerve in her friend's body was humming with tension.

Guerin called over an officer and gave him instructions. The man ran to a Police Nationale vehicle and sped off in the direction of the terminal building. Guerin gave instructions over a radio before coming back to where the two uniformed officers had corralled Fennimore and Simms.

'The charter was a decoy,' Guerin said. 'Branly told him to go up, fly eastward for ten minutes, then return, maintaining radio silence before requesting to land at the airport. Branly was never on board. We will check the airport's security videos to discover the car Branly was driving. Every possible resource will be used to stop him, but . . .' He hesitated. 'You must prepare yourself, Professor . . .'

'Fuck's sake, stop torturing me and just say it,' Fennimore said, his voice hoarse with emotion.

'Branly has a pilot's licence,' Guerin said, with an apologetic shrug. 'He owns a Cessna 172 single–prop aeroplane.'

Fennimore seemed to have trouble breathing. He groped for Simms's hand and held it tight. 'Suzie is the only link between Branly and Rachel,' he said. 'The only person who can tie him to my wife's murder. If he gets airborne—' He stopped, his eyes red with unshed tears.

Simms squeezed his hand and said it for him: 'If he gets airborne with Suzie, there's no telling what he will do.'

Guerin nodded, his face solemn.

'Where is the Cessna?' Fennimore asked. 'Here at Le Bourget?'

'No. Light aircraft are not welcome at this facility. We are making enquiries as to where Branly keeps his plane, but the nearest is Toussus-le-Noble, south-west of Paris. I will head out there now, but I have given instructions to the local gendarmerie to detain him.'

An officer approached with a question and Guerin switched from English to rapid-fire French, walking off towards the terminal building as he conversed with the man in uniform.

Simms was ready to leave, but Fennimore kept hold of her hand.

'Wait,' he said.

'For what?'

He looked across the gleaming concrete of the airport apron and she followed his gaze. The helicopter pilot was still standing next to his machine on the helipad, looking anxious and perplexed.

Fennimore let go of her hand and headed towards the pilot.

The pilot estimated that once they were airborne, the twenty-one-mile journey would take seven minutes or less. Obtaining permission to take off took a painful ten minutes, but they had the Périphérique in view in under a minute, clearing the tower blocks of the outer rim of the city and flying in a straight line, south-west. A rust-red tangle of railway lines bulged like the sinews of an old man's arm, narrowing in the approach to a major station. Then the old city gleamed below them, lemon and cream in the afternoon. A flash of the white dome of the Sacré-Coeur to their left. The next instant they were high over the Arc de Triomphe, its inner and outer rings resembling the iris of an eye; the Eiffel Tower gleamed dully only a short distance away, truncated by their altitude, so that it might almost be a bronze tourist souvenir on the riverbank. They just clipped the southernmost corner of the Bois de Boulogne and seconds later crossed the grey-blue water of the Seine, flying fast over an island shaped like a canoe. The sky above was clear blue, but an iodine-brown haze blurred the horizon. They sped over a large forest, hemmed in on all sides by urban sprawl, though these were suburbs now, the tall buildings of the city giving way to two-storey houses with red-tiled roofs. A train swept along a railway line below them, silent and shining like a silverfish; woodland, carved and cultivated in lines, gave the odd impression of bacilli on a microscope slide. Then they slowed, passing over an industrial area of warehouses and steel cylinders, and the helicopter banked.

'*Nous sommes arrivés*,' the pilot said. Two grey slabs of runway and an expanse of flat, trimmed sward came into view as he spoke. The airport was a collection of small and medium-sized hangars of varying ages. The observation tower formed part of the art deco main building. A score or more single- and twin-prop aircraft were parked on the apron, and two were taxiing towards the runways. The pilot spoke to the control tower and soon they were manoeuvring on to a helipad just south of the second runway. As they made their slow descent, a car pulled up beside a small single-prop plane near one of the hangars, about two hundred metres away. Its propeller was already turning.

'That's him – it's got to be.' Fennimore turned to the pilot. 'Can you set down in front of the plane?'

'*Non*.'

'He's got my daughter,' Fennimore said. 'We have to stop him.'

377

'*Non, monsieur*,' the pilot repeated. 'Regulations state I must not put down less than one hundred and fifty metres from a hangar.'

'Shit,' Fennimore said. 'Shit!' He unclipped his seatbelt, ignoring the protests of the pilot, and was out of the chopper as soon as it touched the concrete. Simms followed after him, the humidity suffocating after the cool air-conditioning of the helicopter. They sprinted towards the plane as a man climbed from the cockpit and Branly stepped out of the car. The two men shook hands, cordial and apparently relaxed.

Simms and Fennimore both yelled to the pilot, but they couldn't make themselves heard over the noise of the helicopter and plane engines. The Cessna pilot opened the driver's door of the car and slid behind the wheel as Branly opened the rear passenger door and reached inside.

Suzie emerged, with Branly gripping both her elbows; she looked groggy. Branly slammed the door after her and waved the car away.

Suzie's legs buckled and Branly crushed her to him. Fennimore screamed his daughter's name and she tried to raise her arms, to push Branly away, but he held her tightly.

'Suzie! Suzie Fennimore!'

At the sound of her full name, she twisted fiercely in the man's grip and turned to her father. Branly dragged her towards the plane. She struggled weakly, but couldn't break free.

Too far, Simms thought. They were too far away.

Suzie continued to resist and Fennimore put on a heroic burst of speed, reaching the two as Branly got Suzie partway inside the cockpit of the Cessna. Branly held on to one wing strut, balancing with one foot in the doorway and one on the tarmac. Fennimore grabbed his back foot, tugging Branly to the ground. Branly landed hard on one knee and rolled, bringing his other knee up and flicking his foot out, catching Fennimore in the chest. Fennimore staggered, regained his balance and threw himself at the man.

As they fought, Simms saw Suzie try to back out of the plane. She powered towards the aircraft as Suzie slipped, tumbling backwards. Simms caught her, stumbling herself and skinning her elbows, but breaking the girl's fall.

'It's all right,' she said, 'I've got you.'

She heard the two-tone pulse of a police siren and saw a flash of blue light on the airport approach road. As she helped Suzie to her feet, two gendarmerie cars screamed around the curve of the access road, blue lights and head-lamps flashing.

Branly landed a punch to Fennimore's jaw and he fell. The abductor hurled himself into the cockpit and the plane's engine noise changed from a growl to a high-pitched drone. Fennimore tried to roll out of the way as the Cessna began careering crazily over the tarmac towards the airstrip, but his jacket caught in one of the wheels and he was dragged after the plane. He wrenched one arm out of its sleeve and held on to the wheel strut as he struggled to free the other. His body was flung violently sideways by the unsteady progress of the plane and he screamed in pain.

Suzie screamed in answer as her father hung by one arm from the plane's wheel, and Simms turned her head away.

Finally, the second sleeve tore and Fennimore was dumped on the tarmac. A plane had just begun its take off on the nearest runway and Branly veered left to avoid it, bouncing over the grass on to the second runway.

Fennimore struggled to his feet, his interest in Branly gone now that Suzie was safe. He limped towards them, his trousers torn and his left arm hanging uselessly. Suzie clung to her, but Simms said, 'It's okay. Daddy's okay – look.'

Fennimore touched his daughter lightly on the shoulder and she turned to him, flinging her arms around him. Despite his injuries, he didn't seem to feel a thing.

The police cars cut across the grass, churning up sods and spitting dirt from their back wheels. They forced Branly off the runway, but he kept going, the small plane bumping and tilting dangerously over every rut and dip in the field. Finally, with the throttle right out and the engine screaming, the Cessna left the ground, but its wing dipped suddenly, clipping the top of the perimeter fence. Simms watched in dull horror as the plane banked out of control, losing one wing as it sliced through the tops of the trees beyond the perimeter. For an instant it rose, then abruptly nosedived into a wheat field. A second later they heard the crump of impact. Smoke billowed from the shattered cockpit, followed by a flare of yellow flame.

Epilogue

A week later, Fennimore, Simms and Becky were making the forty-mile journey from Manchester to Garstang, Lancashire, where Suzie was staying with her grandparents. Child protection officers were in the slow, careful process of interviewing Suzie, with a child psychologist based in Lancaster providing therapeutic support.

Simms was driving. Fennimore, still strapped up after his fall from the plane, fidgeted constantly, adjusting his seatbelt, changing the radio stations, fiddling with the air conditioning. This was the first time since they had returned to England that he would see his daughter. He had been confined to a hospital bed for three days with a dislocated shoulder and concussion, and Suzie's psychologist had suggested that a week or two alone with her grandparents would give her the opportunity to acclimatize to her new situation. But two days out of the hospital, Fennimore had called the psychologist – he needed to see for himself that his daughter was all right.

She had agreed, reluctantly. It was Simms's idea to go with him and take Becky along, as Suzie's closest friend.

'So did you have to take any heat from Kieran for clearing off to Paris under false pretences?' Fennimore asked.

Simms darted a glance at Becky in the rear-view mirror: she was listening to music on her iPhone and texting simultaneously, oblivious to them.

'I told him that you called for help while I was there.'

'And he believed you?'

'It's true,' she said. *Just not all of it. And here I am again, withholding . . .* 'Anyway, I'm not sure he cares,' she added, before she could bite back the words.

'Are you two in trouble?' Fennimore's unwavering gaze was so intense it felt like his fingertips had grazed the side of her face.

Keep your guard up, Kate – now is not the time. 'I'll—' She took a breath. 'I'll let you know.'

'Is this about me?' he said.

'It doesn't always have to be about you, Nick,' she said, intentionally waspish. *Don't talk about it – just don't. Change the damn subject.*

'I hear that Josh's younger brother, Damon, has confessed to the shooting,' she said.

Fennimore nodded.

Simms glanced at him; his jaw was set, his brows drawn down. She could feel him physically withdraw. Fennimore hadn't talked about Josh since they'd heard of his death.

'The older brother and the cousin have been charged with murder under the joint enterprise law,' she added.

Fennimore turned to her in alarm – a recent high court ruling had put a number of such convictions in question.

'They *won't* get away with it, Nick,' she said. 'The older brother brought the gun – he put it in his sixteen-year-old brother's hand. When Josh fought, the cousin subdued him so that Damon could finish the job. Damon will testify to that.'

Fennimore faced the front again, easing himself back into the seat like a man in pain. 'Good,' he said.

For some minutes he was silent, and then he spoke, hesitantly at first:

'What happened to Josh is my fault,' he said.

'No – it's his family's fault.'

From the corner of her eye, she saw him shake his head.

'He was safe and I placed him in danger.'

'He was never safe,' Simms said. 'Not while his family were still out there. And he chose a career that would place him in danger sooner or later.'

Fennimore sighed. 'It should have been later.'

She couldn't think of an adequate response to that, so she said nothing, concentrating instead on the road ahead.

After a few minutes, he said, 'Thanks for doing this – and for bringing Becky. It'll be good for Suzie to see someone her own age.'

'How's she doing?' Simms asked, with another glance in the mirror at Becky.

He blew out some air. 'Hard to say. There's a lot she can't remember – or she's blocking out for now. She didn't know Rachel was murdered. Branly—' He stopped for a moment and stared at his hands. 'He showed Suzie her mother's body, Kate.'

'Oh, Jesus,' she breathed.

'Rachel was lying on her bed, fully clothed, a scarf around her neck.'

'To hide the bruises . . .'

'Seems likely,' he said.

Rachel had died of strangulation.

'There were pills by her body and an empty bottle of vodka. He told Suzie that—' Fennimore was struggling. 'That I didn't want them back.'

'*What?*'

'Branly said Rachel had rung me, begging me to take them back, but I refused. He told Suzie her mother had committed suicide because I told Rachel I didn't want her *or* Suzie.'

'Bastard,' Simms murmured. 'Does she say that Rachel went willingly?' Rachel and Suzie were missing for months before Rachel's body was found yet the pathologist judged that she had only been dead a matter of days.

He shook his head, at a loss.

'I know you and Rachel hadn't been getting on before they went missing, and she had every right to be angry with you, but I can't believe that she would deliberately torment you,' Simms said. 'If she could, she would at least have let you know where they were.'

'They're taking the interviews slowly, getting little snippets of information at each session, but the chronology is all messed up,' he said. 'Branly had been feeding her false memories and misinformation for years – it'll take a while to unscramble the real from the invented – if she ever gets that far. But she does remember Rachel packing bags, telling her they were going on holiday for a few days.'

'That makes sense.' Suitcases and clothing had been missing from Fennimore and Rachel's house when police searched.

'And she seems clear about being in an isolated cottage the weekend they disappeared.'

'So, Rachel and Branly were embarking on an affair, then something went wrong?'

'I don't know . . . maybe.'

'Does Suzie have any idea where this cottage was?'

'She says it was a long drive. There was a storm—'

'That should be easy to check,' Simms said.

He nodded. 'According to the Met Office, there *were* severe storms in the south-east that weekend. Suzie keeps telling them that a tree fell on Rachel's car – she says they got lost in the storm and Branly rescued them.' He shook his head and exhaled shakily. 'She keeps asking after him, Kate.'

'She's—'

'I know,' he said, 'she's Stockholming. But it's . . . hard to take.'

Simms ached to touch his arm, to offer him some comfort, but was afraid that Becky might misinterpret the action.

'She doesn't remember much about the weeks and months after her mother's death,' Fennimore said. 'The medics say it's likely he drugged her.'

Simms nodded, it made sense: Suzie had been heavily doped with phenobarbital during Branly's attempt to escape.

'Right up to the day we found her, he kept Suzie a virtual prisoner. He rarely let her set foot outside – and never alone. He home-schooled her; she had no friends, no company except his business associates and a succession of hired tutors. She wasn't allowed TV, a mobile phone or computer access.'

'So she never knew you were looking for her.'

He shook his head. 'He controlled every aspect of her life: how she dressed, the way she wore her hair, what she read, the music she listened to and played – he even made her speak exclusively in French.'

Simms checked again on Becky. Her head was nodding to the music on her phone, as she stared out of the window at the rolling fields and wooded hills off the motorway.

She lowered her voice. 'Why did he keep her? I mean, after . . .'

They both knew that the safest thing Branly could have done was to dispose of mother and daughter at the same time. The fact that he had kept a young girl, and isolated her from all contact with her peers, had obvious and terrible connotations.

Fennimore glanced across at her. 'That question has haunted me,' he said. 'He was controlling, psychologically manipulative and occasionally violent, but the medics say there are no signs of sexual abuse.'

'What does Suzie say?' she asked, dreading the answer, but feeling she had to know for sure.

'That Branly was only ever a father to her.' Fennimore rubbed his good hand over his chin. 'That should make me happy, I know,' he said. 'But you know what? I wish I could bring him back so I could kill him all over again.'

'You and me both,' she said. 'It doesn't make sense, though. Why keep her all these years – why risk it?'

'Branly has a long history of obsessive and controlling behaviour   and he didn't take rejection well. Two ex-partners took out restraining orders against him – one of them ended up in hospital.'

'He never meant to kill Rachel,' Simms said. 'He just couldn't stand to see her leave.'

Fennimore nodded. 'He had Suzie believing that he's always done what was best for her – looked after her when I rejected her, did right by Rachel. Respected her memory.'

'So this was some kind of guilt trip – making amends for murdering Rachel?'

'Who knows what kind of justification a twisted mentality like Branly's would come up with?' he said.

'But if he *was* intending a cosy weekend away with Rachel, why would he take Suzie along in the first place – and why would Rachel take Suzie with her?'

Fennimore sighed, rubbing his right temple with his thumb. 'You remember just after they vanished, the police discovered that Rachel had asked a friend to take Suzie for the weekend?'

Simms nodded grimly. 'But the friend fell ill with some kind of bug, so Rachel came to my house. Kieran told her I was presenting evidence in a court case.' Simms was, in fact sneaking off to meet Fennimore at a hotel that weekend. She hadn't gone through with it, but she hated herself for it, and now, knowing what it meant to Suzie – how it had affected her life – the burden of guilt was even heavier. 'You think Rachel decided to take Suzie, rather than cancel her weekend away with Branly?'

'I do,' Fennimore said. 'And something bad happened that weekend. Something that prevented Rachel from contacting me.'

By now they were on the A6, approaching Garstang, passing a mixture of red-brick and stone-built houses. Rachel's parents lived in a Victorian semi at the far end of the town. They drove the last few miles in silence, though the fingers of Fennimore's free hand, tapping his leg restlessly, spoke freely of his anxiety and nervous anticipation at the meeting.

Rachel's parents greeted him warmly and Simms thought

they seemed somewhat chastened. She knew they had accused Fennimore of tormenting them with his constant appeals. They'd wanted to be left alone to grieve the loss of their daughter and granddaughter, but every time Fennimore made the news they were dragged back into the media spotlight.

Rachel's grandfather showed them through to the garden, where Suzie was reading a book at a table, under the shade of a patio parasol. She wore heeled sandals and a fitted dress with a flared skirt in pink, yellow and shades of red. Her dark hair was beautifully swept up into a chignon. *Branly would no doubt approve*, Simms thought, but compared with her own daughter, relaxed in jeans and a soft-drape T-shirt, Suzie looked stiff and uncomfortable.

Suzie stood gracefully, however, moving around the patio table and embracing her father, then she turned and offered Simms her hand. It felt cool and a little clammy. *Poor kid's terrified*, Simms thought.

'How are you, Suzie?' she asked.

'Okay . . .' She tilted her head. 'Confused.' She spoke with a slight French accent.

She glanced past them both to Becky, who stood a little apart from Rachel's grandparents, near the French doors into the house, a sports bag slung over one shoulder.

'You remember Becky, don't you?' Fennimore said. He spoke softly, as though afraid of startling the girl.

Suzie nodded solemnly, eyeing Becky's clothes.

'*Ça va?*' Becky said, and Suzie brightened a little, and though she didn't speak, she raised one shoulder in an expressive shrug and the corners of her mouth turned up in the beginnings of a shy smile.

Becky said something in French that Simms didn't catch, but she heard the word *putain*, and Suzie's eyes widened as she glanced nervously from one adult to another.

'*English* please, Becky,' Simms said.

Becky gave her a mischievous look. 'You know your Facebook page has about twenty *kazillion* likes?'

'Facebook?' Suzie said.

'It's an Internet thing,' Simms explained. The social media phenomenon had been in its infancy when Suzie disappeared.

'Haven't you got a computer?' Becky said.

'No.'

'A tablet, then?'

'*Médicin?*' she said, looking to her father for help.

'Electronic tablet,' he said. 'It's a new thing.'

'I got my first one *three years* ago, Uncle Nick,' Becky said, laughing.

Suzie gave a single shake of her head, her brown eyes fixed on Becky.

'So you don't have a Twitter account?'

'No.'

'Instagram? Snapchat? Tumblr?' At every negative, Becky's eyes grew wider. 'Ohmigod, you are *so* lucky!'

'I am?'

'Well, *yeah* – 'cos *I'm* going to show you how it all works, so *you* don't get to make the stupid mistakes I did.'

'What mistakes?' Simms said, a hundred awful scenarios instantly crowding her brain.

Becky grinned. 'Chill, Mum – just teen stuff.'

Suzie didn't respond. Instead, she tucked one forearm tight across her waist and gripped her elbow.

Becky pretended not to notice, but Simms knew her

daughter well enough to see that it was a pretence. She strode to where Suzie was standing, swung the bag off her shoulder and dropped it at her feet. 'I brought you a few things,' she said.

Fennimore looked to Simms. 'I'm as much in the dark as you are,' she said.

Her daughter drew out a pair of elbow- and knee-pads, then dived back in and stacked them on top of a pair of trainers and jeans on the patio table next to Suzie.

Suzie looked at Becky as if she were slightly mad. 'What are these for?'

'Keys please, Mum.' Simms handed them to her.

'Becky, what on earth—?'

Becky yelled, 'Wait a sec!' as she darted past Suzie's grandparents into the house. She reappeared a moment later with two skateboards, one tucked under each arm.

'Pick your board,' she said, smiling at Suzie.

The perplexed expression on Suzie's face turned to recognition and she laughed, pointing to the board decorated with flames. She took the board and as Becky moved in for a hug, the two of them burst into tears. Becky said something in French, which set Suzie laughing again.

Simms looked over their heads to Fennimore; she read a tentative relief in his expression. He met her eye and gave a brief smile.

Simms decided at that moment that she would be there for Fennimore as Suzie worked through the pain of what had happened to her. It wouldn't be easy, but watching the two girls renew the bonds of friendship that had been so cruelly broken, she thought that there was a chance – slight, and shaky perhaps, but worth every possible effort – that Suzie would come out of it all right.

Acknowledgements

No book is ever truly a one-person effort. The lonely writer, wrangling words at his or her desk, can feel disconnected from the arcane machinations of their publishing house. But writing a novel is not the same as making a book: agents; editors, contracts and rights specialists; copy editors; proof-readers and cover designers; all play a role in the alchemy of book-making – and I am in awe of the energy and enthusiasm of the publicity and marketing team – not forgetting the reps, without whom booksellers would not even be aware that the books exist. So, a huge thank you to all at Curtis Brown, and Corsair Books for everything that you do.

I am deeply grateful for the editorial brilliance of my agent, Felicity Blunt, and publisher, James Gurbutt, whose painstaking reading, and attention to detail, help me to craft sleeker, more tense stories from the sometimes tortuous workings of my creative mind.

To Ann Cleeves, Mo Hayder and Jeffery Deaver: thanks for your inspiration and support. And, as always, my love and gratitude to Murf, my own superhero, and Ben, my little life-saver.